PRIESTLING

If You Want To Embark On The Ultimate
Adventure, You Have To Give Everything Away...
Including Your Baggage

WITHDRAWN

A Novel by Richard Mangan

Mangan, Richard

Priestling

ISBN: 9781076464330

Dedication

I would like to dedicate this book to the memory of my older brother David, without whose example I never would have been inspired to enter a religious order. I would also like to dedicate it to my dear wife Peggy, without whose companionship and encouragement I would never have completed it. And finally, I would like to dedicate it to the Jesuits, who are the finest group of men I have ever known.

January 5th, 2019

"It is only with the heart that one can see rightly; what is essential is invisible to the eye."

From The Little Prince, by Antoine de Saint-Exupery

Acknowledgement

I want to acknowledge the support of a number of people for helping me along the way with this work. First and foremost, Dr. Robert Pavlik, for his encouragement and assistance in bringing this book to completion. I am also grateful to Sr. Mary Lenore, S.S.N.D., Fr. John Eagan, S.J., Fr. Robert Purcell, S.J., Fr. Leonard A. Waters, S.J., and Fr. Robert McCown, S.J., for teaching me how to write, and to Rev. Fr. William Knoernschild, William Hargarten, Martha Bergland, Jerry Pierre, Tom Hooyman, Greg Kelsch, Rev. J. Denny Fischer, and David Gawlik for their helpful comments and suggestions.

I would also like to acknowledge my parents, David and Angela Mangan, and my siblings, David, James, Ellen and Gregory, for the life lessons I have learned from all of them. And of course my wife and best friend, Peggy, for her wonderful assistance. There are many other unnamed family members, friends and associates to whom I am forever grateful. God Bless You All.

I would also like to acknowledge the use of a few words from some popular songs, including "Surfin' USA" by the Beach Boys, "The Sounds of Silence," by Simon and Garfunkel, and "Where Have All The Flowers Gone," by Pete Seeger and Joe Hickerson.

Prologue

July, 1949

Two boys sit by the side of a stream on a warm summer day, listening to the gurgling of the miniature rapids flowing beneath them. One of them, Mike, stares downstream toward a little island in the middle of the current, where the waters separate and flow around it as they make their way toward Lake Michigan and, eventually, to the Atlantic Ocean. His older brother, Larry, seems to stare at the horizon.

"Mike?" Larry says to his brother.

"Yeah?"

"What do colors look like?"

"Well, I don't know. I mean, I know what they look like. But I don't know how to describe them. They're just...colors."

"Are they beautiful?"

"Beautiful. That's such a grownup word. But yeah, colors are beautiful, I guess. Watching a movie in color is really neat."

"And what about colors in the sky?"

"Yeah. The sky is blue, and sunsets are red and orange...yeah. They're beautiful."

"And rainbows?"

"Rainbows are the best of all. That one last summer at the lake was really bright. Remember? I told you about it when I saw it. All red and green and blue..."

The older boy continues to stare into space. "Why should I believe you?" he asks then.

"Why shouldn't you?"

"Because I haven't seen one. And I never will. At least not here, in this life. And why should I believe that you can see things that I can't? I mean, maybe you're as blind as I am."

"Larry, I wouldn't lie to you."

"I know," he laughs, "I was just kidding."

They sit by the stream a little longer, until Larry stands up.

"When I get to Heaven," he says, turning his head around, blinking, almost as if he is studying his surroundings, almost as if he can see everything, "I'm going to ask God to show me every color He ever invented."

"Me too," says Mike as he rises and takes his brother by the arm to guide him back along the path by the stream, down to where the rapids split at the little island. There the path makes an abrupt turn, and the boys follow it through the park toward their home.

Table of Contents

"For he who is least among you, he is the greatest."

Luke 9:48

CHAPTER ONE

Internment

Wednesday, August 14, 1963

"Crock," I say aloud as I contemplate the knot in my stomach. A gray haze over the afternoon sun is casting half-shadows over everything, and my gut is so tight I almost have to laugh. "Crock," I repeat as I grin, shake my head, and scan my surroundings. "What the f... okay, what the *crock* am I doing here?"

I am sitting on a curb at the edge of a parking lot in the middle of nowhere almost, thirty miles west of Minneapolis, feeling awkward as hell in a coat and tie as I grind my cigarette butt into the hot asphalt beneath my feet. I hum some bars of a Beach Boys tune I heard on the radio during the drive out from the Twin Cities, *"Everybody's gone surfin'... surfin' USA!"* It could be the last decent music I hear for an awfully long time, I figure as I check my watch. I wince at the stiffness of my ten-month-old forearm break and roll my eyes skyward. Despite the murky sunshine, I can tell by the ache in my wrist that it is going to rain soon. What's the weather like in Malibu, I wonder? There I go again with my fetish. Wherever I am, whatever I'm doing, if it's bad news I'll tell myself, *"Malibu would never be like this."* Or if I am, in fact, enjoying myself doing something really cool,

I'll say, "This isn't bad, but it's not Malibu." I've never told anybody about this except my older brother Darryl, oh yeah, and Sheila Murphy, and she's the one who called it a fetish. And now I'll never see her again, and Darryl's dead, and why do things always have to change so much?

I look up at the big oaken doors of "The House" and check my watch again. If I am lucky, I can squeeze in another smoke, maybe two, before I have to report to my angel. Some house. Over two hundred yards long, a hundred and fifty yards wide and three stories high. Shaped like a cross if you saw it from the air. Opened in 1960, just three years ago. Built to house two hundred young seminarians at a time, plus faculty, for the next century or more. And already operating at sixty percent capacity with a bunch of men who are doubtless as screwed-up as I am. Well, they're *here*, aren't they?

Half an hour ago I was inside the building, touring the uncloistered sections of the House (places where women are allowed) with my angel, Ken Matthews, and my Mom, Dad, and younger brother Scott. We were walking past the refectory, or dining room, when we ran into two guys I knew who entered last year from my high school. "*Crock*, it's good to see you," one of them said, and then I remembered that Darryl had always used that word "crock" as a substitute for nastier words, like a euphemism or an expletive or something like that.

My mind flashes on The Miracle now as I reach into my pocket for another Marlboro. Dumb. As if one more smoke would make a difference a year from now. If I'm even still here then. I light it up anyway, then spit some smokey saliva between my knees onto the pavement, almost drowning an ant. How could I be an atheist if I believe in miracles?

"You're not an atheist, you're just an agnostic," Sheila Murphy said during our last conversation. Anyway, I don't know if it even was a miracle. I used to think so, up until a couple of months ago, but now I have to think it through some more.

I put The Miracle to bed for the moment and recall the past hour. My Mom leaned up onto the toes of her high heels and kissed me goodbye, right on the lips. She had never done that before except once when I received a Boy Scout award years ago.

Lip-kisses are for lovers, I figure as I flinch from the memory. And now I think of Sheila Murphy again, and I cannot shut her out. Maybe I should have thought this whole thing over a lot more... I never kissed her, but that's because I was so damned shy. And besides, we were just sort of friends more than anything else, not really in*volved.*

And as far as my being in this place goes, I'm not really here because I want to be a priest or anything for the rest of my life, I'm just here to find out more about what it was like for Darryl. But I also have to admit, whenever I came here and visited him, I really liked the atmosphere of the place. And back then I be*lieved* more. For now I just have to sort things out a little, and I figure this is the best place to do it.

So back to my Mom. "Now Wally," she said after the kiss, "remember, you're always welcome back home, if you ever change your mind." *Sure Mom*, I thought then, *how about right now?* But I kept my mouth shut. She straightened my tie then, and I was embarrassed by all the attention, but I was also kind of glad in a way because I've heard that some poor bastards actually get ostracized from their families for entering novitiates. Either that, or they're *forced* to do it, because Grandma or somebody decides that Johnny should be the family priest.

"Thanks, Mom," I said without emotion.

And then the Dictator—my Dad—came walking up to me and looked me right in the eye like I was some kind of equal to him for the first time in my life, shook my hand, and said, "Write to your mother, now!" Talk about a weird feeling!

Then my younger brother, Scott, shook my hand and said that he was really going to miss me. Then they all got into the car, and I even felt a lump in my throat as they drove off, waving good-byes all the way down the tree-lined lane, out to the highway and out of my life. I didn't even think of crying though. Hey, I'm eighteen. The only thing I did was light up one last cigarette as the car shrunk to a speck and disappeared over a hill back toward the Twin Cities.

That was three cigarettes ago.

Now I glance up into the haze, take another drag off number four and wonder if it's hazy in Malibu. As I crush this latest butt into the manicured turf that spreads out for acres in every direction, I decide these folks can't be too weird if they cut the grass like regular suburbanites. I wonder what this Novice-Master priest is going to think when I tell him I'm an atheist? Okay, okay, *agnostic*.

"Wally," I hear from behind me, and I stand up. Approaching from the front door of the House is my angel, dark-skinned and blackrobed, yet somehow almost glowing and serene in the afternoon light. He is a nice-looking black man, sort of a cross between Sidney Poitier and Harry Belafonte, and I half expect him to break into a calypso song. "I've been looking for you," he smiles, and I feel guilty because I was really not supposed to be out here smoking up my last cigarettes. "*Ahem,*" he says, holding out his hand, and I sheepishly hand him the remainder of the pack.

Just then, I hear the faraway growl of an engine. I turn around to see, coming up the entrance drive in the distance, what looks like a small, red, convertible sports car with the top down, and two guys in it. It takes the last curve faster than it should and squeals a little bit, then pulls up to the front of the parking lot and screeches to a stop. The driver, clad in a very classy-looking suit like James Bond or somebody, gets out and opens the front trunk and takes out a bag.

"I know who that is," says Ken the angel, "he's the last one, name's Gallagher. Come on, let's you and I go inside and meet some people, and I'll send someone else out here for him."

I follow Ken through the oaken doors into the Porter's Lodge. Inside is a crowd of twenty-some sport-coated young men milling about, chatting with a half-dozen young blackrobed angels aboutwhatever. My eyes are drawn to a huge assortment of baggage lined up against one wall. I count among the suitcases at least three tennis racquets, four guitars, one or two fishing tackle boxes, and a scuba tank.

"Let's mingle," says Ken as we approach a blond guy with an Elvis haircut. I sigh under my breath, knowing that I cannot let my social introversions show up now. First impressions are everything, right? I extend my hand and say, "Hi, Wally Moriarty." I have to admit, he honestly does look a bit like a blond version of Elvis. He introduces himself as Clark somebody-or-other. I never remember names the first time, almost as if I can't hear them, or something.

"Where you from?" I ask.

"Iowa. And you?"

Milwaukee," I answer, looking around for Ken, who has suddenly disappeared.

"God-da..." he blurts out before cutting himself off, "I mean, gosh, I love that town, had a year of college there. More bars per capita than any other city in the US."

"Yeah," I say, "it's a nice town, all right."

I try to hide my surprise at his profane slip of the tongue by glancing around the room. All of a sudden I notice a guy named Pete Torre from my high school class. He got at least seven major letters in various sports, including football and track, but mostly swimming. And I heard he got so drunk at his high school graduation party that he had to go to the hospital. Hell, they let just about anyone enter this place, don't they? Drunks, cussers, atheists... okay, *agnostics*. I look around the room for someone else to meet, hoping I don't introduce myself to the same guy twice. Hey, I'll learn their names eventually, nobody's going anywhere, right? I start to wonder if any of them have ever been to Malibu, when I come across my angel, Ken Matthews, talking to some prissy-looking guy.

"Wally, meet Lou Ranier. We were just discussing apologetics. Or attempting to," Ken says with a grin.

"Oh," I grunt, shaking Ranier's hand and pretending to know what Ken is talking about. I notice that this Ranier guy is sort of pale and skinny as if he's been living in a tomb, or at least a library, for most of his life, and not been getting enough sunshine or exercise. Or food, for that matter.

6

But then, I should talk. I'm a little on the thin side myself, since The Accident.

"Well you know, according to Augustine..." continues Ranier. I quickly tune out as he and Matthews chatter on and I nod in phony agreement, hardly even listening to them as I scan the room every so often, craving another cigarette. This Ranier guy reminds me of a portrait I once saw of a writer named H.P. Lovecraft who specialized in horror stories.

"Why do you call yourself an angel?" I ask Ken during a lull in the conversation.

"Comes from the Greek word, angelos," he replies cheerfully, "for 'messenger,' or 'guide.'"

"You know some Greek, then?"

"Yes, a smattering," he says pleasantly. "We have to read..."

"Aristotle?" butts in this Lou Ranier guy then.

"No, I'm afraid not... just Homer."

"In the minor seminary," proclaims Ranier, "we finished Homer two years ago."

Swallowing hard, I turn and scan the crowd some more. I barely made it through two years of Latin before switching to the easier Spanish. I do not want to think about anything with a different alphabet right now. And what's this "minor seminary" crap? Maybe I should ask him to prove the existence of God...

And now I see another new guy leaning against the wall, away from the others, looking awkward as hell. His glasses are a little cockeyed, like they don't sit properly on his ears and nose. And he has some kind of a sad quality about him, like he honestly doesn't know how to mingle at all. I mean, we're all a bit ill-at-ease here, but he seems a couple of degrees further removed from the rest of us, like he's almost in a trance, or something. I go up to him and introduce myself.

"Leonard," he says, "Wentfogle. Ha hah!"

"Where you from?"

"Iowa. Ottumwa. Heh, heh!" He has a funny way of pronouncing words, kind of like an accent that I cannot place. And he seems to resist eye contact, and he laughs a lot.

"Those other guys were talking about apologetics," I say as I try to make small talk. "Do you know what those are?"

"Yeah, well, they're sort of like trying to justify doctrines. You know, like the existence of God? Heh heh!"

I stare at him for a second as I realize that was what Ranier and Ken were discussing, after all. Sometimes I have to admit, I'm a bit slow at knowing what's going on. Then all of a sudden we hear a commotion and I look up to see that it is centering on a guy across the room who just arrived. It takes me a second before I realize that he was the guy in the sports car. He is really impressive in that classy-looking suit, and now he is approaching us, grinning broadly as he swaggers right up to us and shakes Leonard's hand.

"Andy Gallagher, how you doin'?" Then he turns his blue-gray eyes on me and repeats, "Andy Gallagher," while squeezing my hand in a vice-like grip, almost like he's in charge of this whole gathering or something.

I introduce myself, half-consciously trying to imitate his almost-bankable smile. Who is this cocky bastard? Okay, maybe I should try to stop using words like that in this place. Who is this *self-assured crocker*, with his pricey threads, looking for all the world like he just stepped out from between the pages of some teen heartthrob magazine? How many female hearts has he broken by coming here, with his chiseled, movie-star looks? Was that *his* personal car?

"Great to be here, eh, Leonard? And Wally? It's great to meet you guys! Hah!" he continues, "Fantastic, fantastic!" He seems completely at ease, nodding as if he is in agreement to some heart-felt conclusion arrived at by all of us, and grinning out at the foyer full of young men. He seems to convey the distinct impression that *this* is where it's at, *this* is where things are happening, *this* is where everybody should be, here and now. All of a sudden, if only for a moment, I don't feel "out-of-it" any more. Then suddenly he is gone, dissolved into the chattering group of guys in order to "meet everyone before haustus."

"Haustus? Is that Latin for something?" I say to myself. Before I can ask anybody the meaning of the word, we are quickly herded into a dining room and are soon serving ourselves huge scoops of ice cream from large, khaki-colored institutional tubs. Although I have no appetite at first, I bring the spoon to my mouth and taste it and yes, it is very good for plain vanilla. My appetite starts to return as I continue to eat it. When was the last time I really enjoyed ice cream? It must have been before The Accident...

"You get haustus very often?" I ask the angel seated to my left.

9

"Every day," he happily replies as he heaps another helping into his bowl from the tub closest to him. "But," he adds, "it's usually not ice cream."

"Oh yeah? What is it, usually?"

"Bread and water."

"Oh," I say as I glance around the table, then scoop some more ice cream into my bowl as I try to recall whom I have met. The guy sitting to my right, the one with the foul mouth and Elvis haircut, is named Clark, I now recall, Clark Upton. I ask him again where he is from.

"Iowa... Waterloo," he allows before retreating back into his ice cream bowl.

Everybody here seems to be from Iowa, practically. And even with his cocky air, this Clark guy seems more scared than I am. I scan the room, looking for Andy Gallagher. Then I notice directly across the table from me another acquaintance from my high school class, a portly, red-haired guy, already on his third bowl of ice cream.

"Hi Wally, remember me?" he grins nervously. "Dubchek. Alex Dubchek."

I nod and smile and reach to shake his hand.

"...a Porsche Cabriolet," says another, quieter voice from behind me, and I lean back to hear more.

"He's from the Twin Cities," says an angel, "his brother drove it home..."

10

I figure out that they are talking about Andy Gallagher, and then I finally spot him, way down at the other end of the dining room, working his table like a politician.

"And he drives...uh, drove a Porsche?" says someone else, as if this Andy Gallagher is now deceased.

"I'll be Godda...uh, darned," says Clark.

I glance at the closest angel but detect little reaction to his profanity.

A Porsche Cabriolet. What is this Gallagher guy doing *here*?

***

The first night is a sleepless one. After collapsing onto my bed at 9:00 p.m., I toss and turn, recalling every memory I can from my eighteen-year-old life, almost as if I was at the brink of death where they say your whole life flashes before you. But it isn't a flash. It takes hours, actually. My memories parade through my brain like some great epic novel, enough to fill volumes if I would ever bother to write them all down.

Sandboxes, summer grass, winter sledding in stiff snowsuits. Kindergarten, finger painting, naps on floor mats. First grade, learning to read and spell and write. And draw. Arithmetic. Learning to ride a bike. Building forts. Watching birds. Summer trips in the car to see aunts and uncles and cousins. Flying kites. Baseball. Learning to swim and Boy Scouts and tents and camp and merit badges, with all the tasks they involved. Paper routes, high school, Algebra, Latin, Spanish, Chemistry, Physics, Trig. And thinking about girls. Football, basketball, track... and a girl named Sheila Murphy...

Thursday

We rise at 5:00 a.m., dress once again in our coats and ties, and head to a classroom to meditate for an hour on some religious "points" we heard last night. After Mass and breakfast, we have a little free time before we meet back in the classroom to listen to the Archangel read the rules of the Order to us.

"The manner of living shall be ordinary," he begins, and with that we initiate a week-long period called First Probation, which includes a series of meetings that will go on for four more days. During this time we learn as much as we can possibly absorb about this religious order we have opted to join, The *Collegium Domini*. These meetings and sessions are scheduled with periodic breaks when we go outside and play sports, get to know each other, and of course, pray. After these four days, we will have a three-day retreat, at the end of which we will get our cassocks, our black robes.

CHAPTER TWO

A Sort of Picnic

"Non in solo pane vivit homo."
(*Not in bread alone doth man live.*)
Deuteronomy 8:3; Matthew 4:4

I push open the shoe room, or locker room, door and step out into warm August sunshine. A glance at my watch tells me that it is 11:32 A.M. That's 9:32 in Malibu. A threesome is walking some distance ahead of me toward Villa, so I stand and wait for two more men to walk with. "*Always recreate in groups of two or three,*" echoes the voice of the archangel, "*and no particular friendships —whoever chances to come through the door just before or after you should be your recreation companion...*"

"*It's kind of like the army,*" I decide as I bend to pick a blade of grass and stick it between my teeth, "*but without furloughs, or girlfriends back home, or smokes, or just about anything else I might consider fun.*"

The Miracle has taken a back seat lately as the endless rules weigh heavily on my mind. The first two days of "First Probation" have already been filled with instructional meetings and nights of fitful sleep as I re-examine my motives for being here. I've also been getting nicotine-withdrawal headaches, and I'm trying to replace the nicotine with caffeine since they let us have coffee and tea. In spite of all this stress, or perhaps because of it, I am eating like a horse; cereal and french toast for breakfast this morning, and I am already hungry for lunch. If it wasn't Friday, they'd have served sausage or bacon with the french toast, but it's no big deal. I cannot get over how good the food is here, or at least how good it seems, maybe because I've gone so long without an appetite, and eating is one of the few normal things we are allowed to indulge in here, at the designated times.

Today is a "Villa day," so we get a picnic lunch, along with over three hours of "active recreation," instead of the usual one-hour daily rec period. Active rec includes not only the freedom to talk, but games of touch football, soccer, handball, basketball, tennis, or just a long walk through the countryside if you can find someone to do it with.

Now the door opens behind me, and who should emerge from the building but Alex Dubchek, my high school classmate whom I barely know at all. His presence here surprises me, since my most vivid memory of him in high school was that he received five demerits and five swats for emitting an incredible fart during Trig class. It honestly broke up the whole room for about five minutes. The teacher even laughed a little, before giving him the demerits. Dubchek was very apologetic at the time, but no one believed him, and Fr. Doyle actually gave him the swats for "insincere contrition." At least that's what somebody told me.

"Praise the Lord, Alex," I say with a nod. This is the phrase with which we greet each other when recreation is allowed.

"Amen," Dubchek answers with a grin. Just then the door opens again and out strides Andy Gallagher, clutching a football to his waist.

"Praise the Lord, guys," Andy says as he tosses the football in my direction, and I think just fast enough to make a respectable catch.

"Amen," I reply. "Is this our group then?" I ask as I turn southward, toward Villa. Just then the door opens again and Leonard Wentfogle sidles out.

He gives me a puzzled look—he always seems to have a puzzled look on his face when he's not laughing—and I try to smile as I say, "Praise the Lord, Leonard!"

"Praise the Lord," he answers. He is quite slender in a T-shirt and jeans, almost to the point that you might worry whether he gets enough to eat. And he has a funny gait, as if one of his legs is shorter than the other. Another person might have been able to compensate and disguise his walk so that you wouldn't notice, but Leonard doesn't try to do that.

"So what do you like to be called, Leonard?" I ask.

He looks puzzled again. "Just Leonard, I guess."

Then suddenly the doors burst open again and out rolls this old priest in a wheelchair, almost under-cutting Alex at the knees. He is dressed in a black robe and is wearing a biretta on his head.

"Quo vadis?" says the old father in an Italian accent, just as Brother Ritchie, the Infirmarian, pops out of the doors behind him and grabs the handles of his wheelchair.

"Hope he didn't scare you, fellas," says Brother Ritchie with a wry grin, "Come on Padre, time for lunch."

"He thinks I try to escape, heh, heh," says the old priest as he winks at me, before Brother Ritchie pulls him back through the doors into the building.

"Who was that?" I ask as we begin walking toward the Villa, which, according to Ken Matthews, is a sort of a rustic, glorified picnic shelter located halfway around the lake where we will have lunches twice a month, year-round.

"One of the Infirmary priests," says Andy, "Fr. Lugieri, I think."

"Someone ought to revoke his driver's license," laughs Dubchek.

"Hey guys," says Andy then, "There're four of us — maybe I should wait to join the next group."

Leonard hesitates and just looks at us. He was actually the last one out, so technically he should wait for the next group. The guy looks so lost.

"Hey," I say, "We may be the last ones out — maybe we should call it a foursome."

"Okay," says Andy, "I guess it's okay to have four guys once in awhile," and so we continue on toward Villa, Leonard in tow.

The paved road soon turns to gravel as we skirt the shore of the lake and head into the countryside. We ascend a hill and pass a barn and a farmhouse, and then a stand of woods, until we reach some planted fields.

"I heard you gave up a football ride to Stanford," I say to Andy as I toss the ball to him.

"Yeah, they wanted me to play quarterback. Did you play?"

"Right tackle," I mutter, "'til I broke my arm."

Andy scans me up and down. "Right Tackle? What did you weigh in at?"

"Oh, yeah," I say, "I was two-twenty-five, but I got sick and I lost a lot of weight since then, over the past months."

"Sorry to hear that. How about you, Alex? You play sports?"

"Nah...the only thing I played was pool. And music."

"Was that your electric guitar I saw the other day?" Asks Andy.

"I had to send it back with my parents," says Alex. "They don't like 'inordinate attachments' around here. Acoustic guitars are okay, though. And hey, there're a couple of pianos around."

Leonard keeps walking a little ways behind us. I trot out into the tall grass alongside the road and cup my hands down by my breadbasket, and Andy, with a little flick of his wrist, sends a really fast spiral to me, right on target.

"Hey Leonard," I say then, "catch!" I lob a very slow spiral to him that a baby could practically catch, but he completely flubs it. He lurches to pick it up and flips it back to me, end over end.

"So Leonard," I say all of a sudden, "did you have any... hobbies?"

"Well, let me think about that a minute, ha hah!"

"They don't seem too crazy around here about *any* kinds of possessions," I say then, just to keep the conversation moving, "no money, no radios...my fishing tackle is already up for common use. But I really didn't fish much, anyway."

"This place gives me the creeps," says Dubchek. "I'm willing to stick it out for a couple of months, but if anything happens at home, like if my kid brother so much as stubs his toe, I'm *otta* here. Hey, where *is* this villa, anyway?"

"Matthews says we'll adjust," says Andy as he catches a hike from me.

"That nig... oh, uh, black angel?" says Alex with a nasty smirk, just before a harsh bullet-pass from Andy finds his gut and sends him crouching to the ground. "Ow!" he complains, "just a slip of the tongue!"

"That's another thing," I say, "I haven't heard any good old foul language in days. Shit, damn, I've almost forgotten what it sounds like!"

"You talked to Clark yet?" Andy asks as he catches a lob from Dubchek.

"I was with him last night," says Dubchek. "Every other word was 'eff this' and 'geedee that.' Hell, I mean, crock, I never thought I'd hear that kind of stuff around here."

I almost say something but decide against it as I catch a throw from Andy, then turn and fake a pass in Leonard's direction. He is totally ignoring everyone, looking off at the horizon. "Leonard! Think fast!" I fake another hard pass, then lob an easy one to him. He bobbles it, but rallies and finally grasps and holds onto it, then hands it back to me.

"And something else that bugs me," says Dubchek, "My girlfriend promised to write every day, and I haven't gotten one letter yet. And this is the third day already!"

"*You* had a girlfriend?" I ask.

"*Yeah,* I have — uh, *had* a girlfriend."

"Haven't you been listening to the rules?" Andy asks as he trots out for a short one and I hike the ball to Dubchek. "They open your mail around here."

"So what?" Says Dubchek, catching my short hike and tossing a wobbly floater in Andy's direction.

"So if it's from a girl who's not your mother or your sister, it gets tossed in the circular file."

"You mean the wastebasket? Holy sh..., I mean crock," complains the red-faced Dubchek to the surrounding hills and fields, "Is this a prison, or what?"

"It's for your own good," Says Andy as he flips the ball back to Dubchek. "Priests can't have girlfriends."

"But it's so *sudden,*" Dubchek laments as he throws a desperate, wobbly pass in my direction.

I catch it and walk back to them, football in hand. "I could sure use a cigarette," I say to no one in particular.

"Hit me long," says Andy suddenly as he runs out across the ditch and into a field. He is really running fast, and even though my arm is warmed up, I have to throw as hard as I can to keep it ahead of him. Somehow the ball descends on target and Andy snags it over his shoulder for a perfect reception as he skirts the edge of a soybean patch.

"Nice toss," he yells as he trots back to us.

"Nice grab!" I tell him then. I feel a rush of pride, receiving a compliment like that from a guy who could've been Stanford's next quarterback. I turn toward Leonard and he is looking away again, acting like we're not even there, walking quietly with that funny limp of his.

"Leonard," I say then, "Where'd you go to high school?"

"Just my regular public school. Ottumwa high school."

"Who'd you talk to about entering?"

"Huh? Oh, ah, well, there was a priest from the Order who said Mass at our church on Sundays sometimes," he says without emotion. "Fr. Semler. He gave a really great talk about the Order and all the things they did. So I went and talked to him."

"Cool," I say. "Alex, who'd you talk to?"

"Doyle," he says without a smile.

"*Doyle*?" I say with a laugh. "The school disciplinarian? I thought the only thing he was good at was giving swats!"

"*Swats*?" says Andy, "you guys had *swats*?"

"Yeah, with a metal golf stick," says Alex. "As a matter of fact, it was right after he gave me some. That I talked to him about joining the Order, I mean."

I begin to laugh pretty hard, and so do Andy and Leonard. "Was it before or after your last suspension?" I blurt out after I catch my breath.

"After," he says, and everyone laughs some more. "Well, I knew him better than the other priests," he continues with a chuckle.

The laughter continues for another minute or so.

"Who'd *you* talk to?" Dubchek asks me then.

"Walsh." I want to ask him *why* he decided to enter in the first place, but I decide to hold off on that one because I don't know him well enough, yet...

"So *why'd* you enter?" He asks me.

"Oh, a couple of reasons — why'd *you* enter?"

"I wanted a free education," he says with a twinkly-eyed grin.

"How about you, Andy?"

Instead of answering, Andy runs out long for another pass, which I arc way over his head. But he sprints hard until he somehow catches up with it, dives and grabs it out of the air with one hand and falls and rolls in the tall grass by the side of the road.

Dubchek acknowledges the feat by extending his right arm out in front of his face, elephant trunk-like, and trumpeting by passing air between his tightened lips, "phhrehehehehhhhdddt!"

"Come on, Moriarty," he says to me then, "why'd you enter?"

"Because of a miracle," I say.

"Are you serious? What kind of miracle?"

A shrill, electric bell from the direction of the House cuts him short.

"Time for Examen," says Andy.

"Uh, huh," I say as I turn my eyes downward with an internal sigh of relief.

The four of us gradually drift apart as we continue our now silent walk through the countryside. Before us and behind us twenty-some odd new men and six angels do the same, each examining his conscience as we have to do twice a day, for fifteen minutes, at noon and again before bedtime.

***

After four days of First Probation, and listening to the archangel reading aloud the rules of the Order, and the reading of some Papal Bulls, which are so antiquated and boring that I have to fight to keep my eyes open, we begin a three-day retreat. This means lots of meditation and no rec. For everything other than rec, we have been required to wear our coats and ties, and I notice that my dress shirt is getting dirty. I did bring a second one, and so I put it on for the first morning of this retreat. Almost like a businessman, I figure as I straighten my tie in the mirror, but for a very different, less lucrative kind of business than those in the Fortune 500, to be sure.

***

"Man," begins Fr. McKittrick on the first morning of our three-day retreat, "has an *almost infinite* capacity for change." He repeats this, and I write it down in my notes.

"You and I are like a little three-year-old boy," he continues, "standing before God. And God is like a nice old Grandfather, and in one hand He holds a brand new, shiny toy fire engine, and in the other hand is a piece of paper with some writing on it. He says to us, 'Choose.'"

Then Fr. McKittrick says, "The piece of paper happens to be a check for a million dollars."

I have to admit to myself that I've always liked stories and parables like this, and I've always liked retreats and sitting around and thinking about God and other holy concepts.

"Yes," I tell myself as his words hit home, "yes, right now I can believe that God does love me." I sit up and listen, marveling at Fr. McKittrick's ability to elevate my mood with religious wisdom. For the moment, I am content that I can feel sort of good about being here.

"Out of the depths
I cry to you oh Lord,
Lord, hear my voice…"

Psalm 130:1

CHAPTER THREE

"De Profundis Clamo Ad Te Domine..."

Monday

"Why am I here?" I ask myself on the fifth morning as I again straighten my tie in front of my mirror. Yesterday I felt pretty good about things, but today I don't. My eyes drift down to the sink and the half-dozen or so hairs that fell out when I combed my head. Now I look up at the white ceiling of my room for a moment, as if it was a movie screen or something, and I try to picture a life-size image of Jesus up there, crucified. I used to be able to do that back in high school, when I was less depressed, and it seemed to give me some comfort. Comfort as in, 'if He did that for me, I can endure a little hardship for Him.' I do it now with limited success, before returning my gaze to the mirror. And now I stare into my own eyes, which is something that has never been comfortable for me to do, and I remember something Sheila Murphy once said, when we were sitting in the park..."*You remind me of Clark Kent. Mild-mannered, but with lots of strength under the surface, like Superman...*"

But I don't feel like Superman right now, I can guarantee you that. I look at my image in the mirror, and all I can see right now is one huge piece of low-grade ore, or raw rock, a sculpture that is hardly even started. A bell rings, and I shut off my light and head out the door and down the corridor to the stairwell and the basement classroom for an hour of meditation.

* * *

Soon I am kneeling in the classroom, trying to proceed with my meditation. Another day, another act. Isn't that what this is? I look at the other guys around me and I think, for a second, that we're all just a bunch of gullible bas... okay, *naive crockers*, buying into a bunch of nonsense. But then I stop myself, knowing that I have to climb up out of this cistern of negativity. I once heard that if I act as if I have faith, faith will be given to me. But now I am tempted to wonder, will I actually acquire faith, or will I only be brainwashing myself into *thinking* I have it?

"But you already have faith," a voice inside me whispers. And maybe I do, but it's hard to see, sometimes. I always used to presume that I had it, until the accident.

Lord? Are you there, Lord? Getting up at five A.M. is hard. Sacred Silence until breakfast is hard. Meditating for an hour before Mass — and breakfast — is hard. The Daily Order — *Ordo Regularis*, wherein every minute of the day is immersed in silent, recollected activity, save the precious hour of afternoon rec and the forty or so minutes of evening rec after dinner — is depressing...

* * *

It is now late morning, and I am standing in line in front of Fr. McKittrick's room, waiting to go to confession. The door opens, and Andy comes out. I'm next, and the knot in my stomach has returned as I enter the room. Fr. McKittrick, our friendly, curly-haired, forty-five-year-old Novice Master, is sitting in a chair facing the window, and there is a wooden kneeler on the floor at his left side. I slide the kneeler an inch or two further back behind him, just to make sure he can't glimpse me out of the corner of his eye, and then I kneel down.

"Bless me, Father, for I have sinned... it's been about a month since my last confession. Father, I... I don't exactly know how to say this, but I don't think I belong here, Father."

"Why not?" He says in an easy, quiet voice.

"Sometimes, Father, I don't know whether I believe in God or not."

"Then why did you enter?"

"To find out... to find out."

"Is this the way you felt when you first interviewed to enter the novitiate?"

"Ah... no. When I interviewed, I felt a lot different. I've... had a change of heart, sort of. After the interview, I mean. Due to some ah... extenuating circumstances, I guess." I don't go into detail any more than that because he'll figure out it's me.

"Understand, Wally," he says in a very kind voice, "that you are a child of God, and that He loves you beyond measure. You are here for a reason, and it may or may not be what you think. Give it some time...God has infinite patience, and we His children often come up short in that department. Keep praying, and give yourself some time..."

***

I am in the chapel, finishing my penance — an "Our Father" and a "Hail Mary" — and wondering how he figured out it was me, even though I was whispering, and he was staring straight ahead, out the window, the whole time. But then I figure that, since he didn't ask about my "extenuating circumstances" when I mentioned them, he already must have known it was me. I reflect for a moment about how much I prefer the translucent screens in the confessionals I've gone to in the past, where the priest has no way of seeing who you are when you strip your soul naked to him, so to speak.

But wait a minute... so what if Father McKittrick *did* figure out it was me? What's the worst that could happen to me? They'd kick me out, maybe. But no, they couldn't, because he would have to give a reason for kicking me out, and if it was something I told him in Confession he wouldn't be able to reveal it to anyone, and so he couldn't kick me out for it, could he? But even if they did kick me out I wouldn't mind one bit, except I'd probably lose my appetite again. *God, I must be insane! Like I want to get kicked out, even though I might be so stressed out if I was back Out-In-The-World that I'd stop eating again...*

And right now, after confession, I have to admit that, strange as it sounds, I actually feel relaxed, kind of, like everything's okay, at least for now.

And now I have to ask myself for the ten-thousandth time, what was my reason for choosing to enter in the first place? First off, it was The

Miracle. But after the accident that all changed, because my faith got a major kick in the ass, or the groin, if not worse. But then I started thinking about it, I mean *really* thinking about it, and I figured that if somebody has trouble, say, learning to read or something, what should he do? Should he become a bum, or should he force himself to read all day long until he gets better at it?

Or say, if someone wants to learn another language, like Spanish, doesn't it make sense to go somewhere where he is forced to listen to it all day long, and speak it all the time, until he masters it? The same must be true with faith, I figure. Go where you can learn more about it, and in the process maybe get some more of it. Which is why I'm here. So maybe I'm not so weird after all.

✳✳✳

Tonight, In the interim after lights out and before sleep sets in, I continue to think about why I am here. The more I think about it, this place is like a minimum-security prison, where everything's on the honor system. In fact, they don't even lock us in at all. If anyone wanted to, they could just up and walk out of this place. It doesn't happen too often, though. I mean, people leave, but they usually don't just sneak out, they first talk to Fr. McKittrick about it and everything. And the Order even pays for your ticket home.

I worked in a factory one summer, and that was like *maximum* security for eight hours a day. Everyone was always watching to make sure you didn't goof off, and of course there was a time clock you had to punch, and you'd better not cheat on the minutes.

So I ask myself, what would you rather have, Moriarty? Twenty-four hours of purgatory in this place, or eight hours of working-world hell every day?

***

The next night, just before bedtime, I write God a letter.

"Okay, Gramps," I begin, "can I call You Gramps? Fr. McKittrick says that You are like a nice old Grandpa, sort of, and You are offering my childish nature a choice between a toy fire engine and a piece of paper. And let's face it, it's much more than a fire engine, it's a life of freedom, and money and women and cars and big houses and food and drink and marriage and raising a family and 'The American Dream' and all the things that the world has to offer... versus a less exciting, quiet, alternative life in service to you. Like a plain piece of paper written in a language I don't understand, practically. I am just wise enough to see the choice I have made. But can I be faithful to it for the rest of my life? Please understand me, and be patient with me, because I still think that You really pulled one over on me, here. Please help me to think the right thoughts about all of this.

Yours, (I hope),

Wally M. Amen.

***

The next morning, and every morning, as soon as we rise after the bells, we novices have to kneel in the doorways to our rooms, in our pajamas, and recite the De Profundis, Psalm 130, in Latin, in unison with one another. I actually like this prayer, because when I translate it I can really connect with its meaning. I learn very quickly the Latin translation and I actually try to think in the Latin words when I say it.

Now I kneel in my doorway and begin to recite the prayer with my fellow novices:

"De Profundis Clamo ad Te Domine (*Out of the depths I cry to You oh Lord*), Domine, audi vocem meam (*Lord, hear my voice*).

"Fiant aures Tuae intente ad vocem obsecrationes meae (*Let Your ears be attentive to the voice of my supplication*)..."

As I recite the prayer, my gaze drifts to the other novices kneeling in their doorways up and down the corridor. My eyes stop at Leonard, whose room is across the corridor and one down. I notice that he is looking upward toward the ceiling as he prays, and he seems to be reciting the prayer with a surprising amount of feeling, considering what I know of his aloof personality. He almost appears as if he is actually looking at someone, or something, on the ceiling.

"...Speravit anima mea in Domino, majis quam custodes auroram...(*my soul waits for the Lord, more than watchmen wait for the dawn...*)"

I continue to watch Leonard as we end our prayer, and I cannot help but feel that there is much more to him than meets the eye.

"Vestis
virum facit."

"Clothes make the man…"

CHAPTER FOUR

Clothes Make the Man

*A*h, Malibu! I am lying flat on my back, feeling very warm and pleasant. I open my eyes and the bright sun makes me squint, even though I am wearing shades. I hear the sound of breaking surf, and I lean up on one elbow to see in the distance the deep blue ocean with huge, rolling waves. As I watch, a speck appears atop one of the waves, and as the speck gets closer it becomes a tanned guy in cutoffs hanging ten on his board as he rides the wave into shore.

Just down the beach some girls are playing volleyball. I lie here in my swimsuit, taking this all in, listening to the Beach Boys singing a surfing song on a portable radio that rests near my left ear. Now a volleyball rolls up and nudges me, and as I reach for it, one of the girls approaches me. I casually pick up the ball and toss it up to her.

"Thanks," she says with a smile.

"Don't mention it," I answer, flipping up my shades to get a better view, and yes, she is tanned and beautiful in her swimsuit. She turns away now, hesitates, then comes back and kneels down right next to me so that her knees are touching my ribs.

"You know, you're really cute," she says as she reaches out and caresses my hair. "I'd like to have you for my boyfriend. What's your name?"

I raise myself up on my elbows. "Wally. What's yours?"

Before she can answer, a second beauty, just as gorgeous, approaches. "Hey Marcia," she says, "let's have the ball."

Ignoring her, Marcia leans forward and kisses me right on my lips. This shocks the crock out of me, because she acts like it is no different than shaking hands, or something. Then she turns to her friend and says, "I want you to meet my new boyfriend!" She stands up, then reaches down and takes my hand and starts tugging and says, "Come on, take me for a piggy-back ride!"

I stand up, feeling very confused but also quite pleasant, wondering what Fr. McKittrick will say as this 'Marcia' promptly throws her arms around my neck and jumps on my back. "Grab my legs," she says. "Come on, I don't bite."

I do as she says, and now three more of them, all stunningly beautiful, are approaching from the volleyball net as Marcia leans forward and whispers into my ear, "On second thought," she giggles, "maybe I **do** bite," and she starts to softly nibble at my neck. I cannot figure out what's going on as I glance over toward the sea, and now the surfer is standing there at the water's edge, holding his board and waving to me. He's still far away and pretty much a silhouette, but he seems almost familiar...

"Hey, come on," says the second beauty, "I want a ride...it's my turn!" She tries to pull Marcia off my back, while a third one jumps in front of me, walks right up and takes my face in her hands and kisses me warmly.

34

"I love you I love you I love you," she says over and over again. At least five girls are now riding or pulling or tugging at me, and I am feeling this incredible mixture of guilt and pleasure all at once. Another girl is walking in front of me now, in the same direction I am going, and even though I can only see her from behind, I feel like I know her. She slowly turns around and smiles at me, and I realize that she is Sheila Murphy...

I leap awake, panting heavily, trying to get my bearings. The idyllic beach is gone, and I can hardly see anything in this dark room as conflicting rushes of pleasure and disappointment well up from the depths of my soul. Now I notice the dim form of the crucifix that hangs on the wall over my head. "Jesus," I whisper aloud, "Do I have to have *those* kinds of dreams?"

I recall the day back home when I interviewed to join this order. One of the priests asked, *"Can you go for a long time, like five or six months, without committing a mortal sin of masturbation?"*

"Yes..."

"It's not a sin, it's just a dream," I keep telling myself as my eyes begin to adjust to the dim forms of my room, and then I make out a foreboding shape looming in my doorway, a dark and ominous figure as tall as the door itself, almost. "Who...what?" I whisper. "Who's there?" I slip out of bed and move toward it warily, but wait, when I reach out and touch it, there is just empty, black cloth, a cassock hanging from the transom on a hanger, my new black robe.

✳✳✳

I am kneeling in the chapel at First Visit, just before Meditation, and

I turn to sneak a look at some of the new guys coming in. Alex Dubchek shuffles up the aisle like a fire-haired Friar Tuck in his new robe, with the cincture tied around his waist all wrong, in some kind of a square knot or something. And Clark, the blond guy with the foul mouth, whose Elvis haircut has now been reduced to a butch, trips on his hem as he genuflects and almost sprawls across the stone floor.

And Andy Gallagher? Well, if there was ever a catalogue entitled, "What the Well-Dressed Cleric Should Wear," it would have to include a photograph of Andy, the consummate jock, dream-maker/heart- breaker, potential boyfriend of every red-blooded young woman in America, standing in a bucolic meadow in his cassock, leaning against a fence or something, prayerbook in one hand and a rosary in the other, with that "all-is-well" grin of his. The caption could read, *"Come, follow me—I can take you to new realms of eternal joy and bliss."* In a spiritual, celibate way, of course...

I try to get back to what I am supposed to be doing, which is pray- ing, but of course I'm not very good at that, so I once again yield to the distracting sound of shuffling feet as another new novice enters the chapel. I turn as subtly as possible to witness Leonard ambulating down the center aisle, and I see that his limp is less noticeable when it is cam- ouflaged by his new black robe. And his detached demeanor doesn't seem to stand out so much, either. His normal aloofness now seems more natural; he appears to be recollected. Which of course is how we are all supposed to be anyway, during this time of Sacred Silence.

Cassock Day for us new men is also Vow Day for the new Juniors, who will today, after taking their vows, move to the other side of the house. And so, at 6:30 AM after our morning meditation in the classroom, we all head back up to the chapel for the sacred Votive Mass. It's pretty special, with lots of candles and incense and everything, and the sanctuary is crawling with clergy as priests are even filling the roles of the acolytes and servers on this special day.

"Reverend Fathers and brothers in Christ," Father McKittrick says as he begins the homily, "this year marks the four-hundred-twenty-second year of our order's existence. This morning, twelve of you men will pledge total commitment to our order by professing perpetual vows of Poverty, Chastity and Obedience to God our Heavenly Father. You will add your names to the company of over thirty-five thousand dedicated men of our order around the world..."

The words "total" and "perpetual" bug me a little, but what the crock, I've only been here a week, just visiting, really.

"Two short years ago," Fr. McKittrick continues, "you received your cassocks like these new men here..."

I turn and steal a look at some of the guys. Clark is squinting, and I can't tell if it's from concentration or displeasure. Alex Dubchek is sort of nonchalant, and Andy is relaxed and attentive. Leonard is unreadable; he could be a thousand miles away, or he could be listening intently to every word that Fr. McKittrick says. And me? I keep thinking about Darryl, and what brought him here.

"...And you were told that you had to complete a number of experiments," continues Fr. McKittrick, "including a thirty-day retreat, kitchen probation, or as some like to call it, K.P...."

A moderate chuckle runs through the group.

"...a month at the Indian missions, and hospital probation.

"And you new men, take heart! Because in two short years you may, with the help of God's Grace, commit yourselves to a life in our company with vows as these men are doing today."

"Don't bank on it," I whisper to myself as he continues.

When the Offertory of the Mass begins, I watch the vow men leave their pews to approach the altar and kneel in a big semi-circle, and the first man on the right begins reading his vow formula from a piece of paper that he holds in front of him.

"Omnipotens, sempiterne Deus..." he begins, and I kind of lose the gist of it after that, since it's all in Latin.

***

The day gets better, with a "Deo Gratias" breakfast. "Deo Gratias," or *"Thanks be to God,"* means we can talk. All the vow men are now seated on the other side of the refectory, with the other Juniors. Fr. Rector initiates the event as he calls out, "Tu autem Domine miserere nobis—*But Thou, oh Lord, have mercy on us!"*

Everyone responds in unison, "Deo Gratias!"

Immediately all the new vow men put birettas on their heads. The black, priestly hats had been put on their chairs earlier, long before they sat down. We quickly learn that this is just another little custom that they do after first vows. They still have nine more years to go before ordination to the priesthood.

***

Later on there is morning rec, which we only get on major feast days, and in the afternoon we have "fusion rec," which means rec with the Juniors with vows who live and study on the other wing of the House. This "fusion" only happens a few times a year, on vow days, Christmas, Easter, and a couple of other big feast days.

As we gather outside at the beginning of fusion rec to meet the Juniors, including the new ones who just took vows this morning, I all of a sudden get this cool feeling of unity, or camaraderie or something, with all of these men. And it is pretty strong, I have to admit. It is sort of like in high school, when we were at football games or basketball games and I felt an allegiance to my team and my school and classmates, but it is stronger than that. Even then I did not feel quite so much a part of the group as I do here, all of a sudden. All these young men and all the Fathers are friendly; all of them want to make everyone feel better; none of them has an axe to grind.

And now I notice in particular a Junior who is passing a football around.

"Hey Larry, let's see the ball," someone yells, and Larry throws a long spiral out toward the lake. The guy catches it with ease, then throws it back to another guy who hands it back to Larry so that he can pass it to someone else. Now Larry throws another perfect spiral, and the receiver catches it perfectly, and then the ball is returned to the other guy again so that he can hand it back to Larry. Something's odd about this, but I don't know what just yet.

"So you're Darryl's brother," Larry's sidekick says to me then, extending his hand. "Nice to meet you. I'm Mike Swenson, and this is my brother Larry."

Larry, the guy who has been throwing the football, grins and extends his hand for me to shake. "Darryl's brother," he says, seeming to eye me up and down. "You're one tall drink of water."

"What time is it?" someone asks then.

Larry quickly pops open the face of his watch with his fingers—it is on a hinge of some kind—and he touches the dial, never looking at it, always staring at the distant hills. "Two-fifteen," he says.

I couldn't have guessed he was blind; everybody catches his passes. Now he throws the ball to a Korean Junior who kicks it into the air, jumps and head-butts it to another guy like it was a soccer ball or something, and while it is still in the air the second guy kicks it to another guy who catches it.

"That's Korean football for you," laughs one of the Juniors as everyone applauds.

There's another guy confined to a wheelchair. He's not very old though, probably still in his thirties. He has cerebral palsy, I think. He is Brother Felker, the house librarian, and he has a smile that could melt an iceberg.

I look around for Leonard, and I notice that he and some other new men are chatting with some juniors.

Soon we are heading toward the fields for a fusion game of rag-tag football with the Juniors. Sort of like touch football, but you cannot

Just tag them, you have to pull a rag out of the rear pockets, or belt, of their sweat pants, or wherever they have stuffed it. They are all amazingly nice to me, and I actually remember meeting some of them briefly in years past, when I came up here with our family to visit Darryl. I'm tempted to think that they're nice to me because I'm Darryl's brother, but they're nice to everyone else, too.

As we begin our football game I get this distinct impression that I am living in a different world than the one I left. Here there is equality; the differences between people are minimal. Everybody lives in rooms that are very similar, pretty much; everybody eats the same food; nobody owns anything; nobody makes any money. Yet all our needs are provided for. A perfect world, almost. Communism. But Theistic, and voluntary. And altruistic. And celibate. That last part is the kicker.

***

This evening as we stand for grace before dinner, there is a Junior kneeling in the middle aisle of the refectory. At the end of grace, after we have taken our seats, he says, loud enough for everyone to hear, "Reverend Fathers and beloved Brethren, I accuse myself of using language unbecoming of a religious today at recreation, for which fault holy obedience has imposed upon me the slight penance of kissing the feet of some of the members of the community." He then stoops under the table and kisses the shoes of the two men closest to him. Needless to say, we new men immediately give each other puzzled looks.

This is another D.G. meal, Deo Gratias, and so I am free to talk to Ken Matthews, who is seated right across from me.

"Ken, what's that all about?"

"It's called a *culpa*. Just another one of our little customs," he says with a sly grin, "Another opportunity to mortify yourself."

"What'd he do, anyway?" asks Clark with a grave look on his face.

"Probably just swore at somebody," says Ken. "That's why we try to use the 'crock' word whenever we remember."

"Do we all have to do that? Take culpas?" asks Dubchek. "I mean what if the guy has dogsh...manure or something on his shoes?"

"Actually," says Ken, "it's voluntary."

"Voluntary?" says Clark, his wide eyes relaxing. "So we *don't have* to do it?"

"No. And of course you should *never* do it without asking permission first. But you new novices shouldn't even bother to *ask* permission right now—you can't do it until after your long retreat."

"Don't worry," says Clark, "I most definitely will not bother to ask! *Not one bit* will I bother!"

"So," says Dubchek with a wry smile, "taking a culpa is one of the privileges we can earn only after enduring... uh, *completing* the long retreat?"

"If you want to look at it that way, yes," says Ken.

"Do the priests ever do it?" I ask then.

"No, I've never seen one do it," says Ken, "but we're in formation, and they're done with all of that. Please pass the potatoes?"

ORDO REGULARIS

5:00 AM ....Rise; First Visit

5:30 AM ....Meditation

6:25 AM ....Colloquy (Conversation with God
as I end my meditation)

6:30 AM ....Mass; Thanksgiving

7:15 AM ....Breakfast; Cleanups; Tempus Liberum
(Free time)

8:00 AM ....Manualia (Housecleaning)

8:45 AM ....Tempus Liberum

9:00 AM ....M-W-F: Latin Class
T-Th: Gospel Theology

9:45 AM ....Tempus Liberum

10:00 AM..................Rodriquez (Spiritual Reading)

10:30 AM..................Study Time

11:00 AM ....Ascetical Theology (Rules Class)

11:45 AM ....Tempus Liberum

12:00 PM ....Examen (Examination of Conscience)

12:15 PM ....Lunch; Cleanups/Manualia; Tempus Liberum

1:00 PM ....Lectio Ascetica (Spiritual Reading)

1:30 PM ....Study Time

2:00 PM ....Recreation

3:00 PM ....Tempus Liberum

3:30 PM ....Study Time

T-TH ....Greek Class

4:30 PM ....Rosary; Tempus Liberum

5:00 PM ....Flexoria; Tempus Liberum

5:45 PM ....Litanies

6:00 PM ....Dinner

6:45 PM ....Cleanups; Rec

8:00 PM ....Sacred Silence begins; also Points
  (For tomorrow morning's meditation)

8:15 PM ....Examen (Examination of Conscience)

8:30 PM ....Tempus Liberum;

9:05 PM ....Lights Out

***

The next morning, we have cornbread and stew for breakfast. I have never heard of such a thing, and some of us new men look at each other like this must be some kind of joke. Eventually we learn that it is quite a frequent breakfast offering here, and it's actually pretty tasty. And of course, there are other options available, including a variety of cereals, for the lighter eaters.

Later this morning, I have a conference with Father McKittrick.

I am beginning to like him a lot, because he seems to be very good at quelling my fears and making me feel at ease, as if this whole way of life makes sense.

"Father," I begin, "can a wet dream be a sin?"

"Not if it is a dream. But if you wake up during the dream, you should try not to think about it, try to get it out of your head."

"If you wake up during it, during the ah, the ejaculation, should you try to stop it?"

"Yes."

"Isn't that sort of like... trying to plug a volcano?"

"What?"

He doesn't laugh. I am embarrassed.

"It's... nothing, Father... "

"Simon Peter,
do you love me
more than these? ...

Feed my
lambs..."

John 21:15

CHAPTER FIVE

What is Love?

(From my Ascetical Theology Notes)

Even though we have made something of a grownup choice by entering this place, some of us first-year novices have yet to reach our eighteenth birthday. Right on the brink of adulthood, but not quite. This gives rise to some questions, as Fr. McKittrick kindly points out to us in Rules Class. One of the biggest difficulties for us, and actually for people in general, is trying to understand the concept of "love."

The ancient Greeks actually defined three different kinds, or levels of love. The first level of love was *Eros*, or romantic, sexual "love," love for the beautiful woman, love for the attractive man. But eros, as many philosophers and psychologists have said, is dependent on conditions. It can be jeopardized in a moment if the wrong words are spoken, like a candle snuffed out in the wind. It begins like puppy love, or "movie star love." Some people may say that this is not even love, but mere infatuation, or desire. But however imperfect it may be, this is the kind of love that, when cultivated properly, can lead to a deeper commitment, including marriage, and lifelong happiness. But it takes time and effort for this to happen. Getting married and having children and raising them responsibly is arguably the most positive result of such a union.

The next level of "love" on the Ancient Greek scale was *Philos* or *Philia*, which is friendship, fellowship, or love of those you enjoy being around. While this love is not as romantic or fickle as *Eros*, it is still conditional, because it can depend on perceptions, situations, and "feelings."

But there is still another kind of love that is higher than *Eros* and *Philos*. This highest form of love is called Agape (Ah-ga-pay), which is an unwavering kind of love, an *unconditional* love which gives without receiving in return. It is a choice that is not limited by feelings, sur-roundings, perceptions, or any gifts or favors from the loved one. This Agape includes the love of all mankind, including one's enemies. This is the love that Jesus talks about in His teachings, and it is the kind of love that we are all aspiring to in this religious life. It can be, when all else fails and there is no other reason for it, a pure and simple act of the will, a decision. But it is a lot easier said than done.

For instance, even in a place like this, some of the guys just rub you the wrong way for some reason. No matter how hard you try, it is hard to like them. There's this one guy named Barry Edelfort, for instance, a very light-skinned kid with almost albino-white hair and light blue eyes. He's from some small town in Minnesota and he's good at sports and all that, but he has some funny habits that irk me. Like, when we go to active rec, he walks barefoot down the halls and cloister walks, even though we're supposed to wear shoes or slippers. For some reason, this barefoot thing bothers me. He seems to have no clue about some of the rules, even though he has heard and read all of them, just like the rest of us. And while he is walking barefoot down the cloister walk, he likes to reach his hand around to pinch the zits on the back on his neck, and he has quite a few of them there. And then he brings his fingers around to his nose and rubs them together and sniffs them, as if the zit has an aroma, or something. Weird.

And then there are a couple of other guys who are kind of swishy. You know, like effeminate? They're pretty harmless, I guess, but the other day at rec one of them looked at me and said, "Hello, handsome," and I didn't know how to react, so I just ignored him. But I couldn't forget it.

It's hard to pretend that I like these guys as much as I like Andy or Dubchek, but that's sort of our goal around here, to be equally friendly toward everyone. But now I just had a new thought: Do I have to like someone in order to love him? I mean, there have been people in my life who I really did not like, but maybe I can sort of love them in a way, anyway. Love is definitely a mysterious phenomenon.

***

Every morning we're supposed to meditate for an hour, first thing, at our desks in the classroom. This is where we are to perform our meditation until the end of The Spiritual Exercises, or Long Retreat, which takes place during the month of October. After that, we will be allowed to meditate in the chapel, or in our rooms.

With every morning meditation, we are supposed to start out with an Act of the Presence of God, which is pretty much like trying to make ourselves aware of God's presence right here, right now, wherever we are. When I attempt this, I always try to imagine God's energy, like visible rays of light, beaming down from above. After we do this for a couple of minutes, we are supposed to get into a "First Prelude" and a "Second Prelude," sort of like imagining previews to a movie, I guess. And then we finally get into the content of the meditation itself, which can be a passage from Sacred Scripture, or a prayer, or some kind of important theological concept. We are encouraged to use our imaginations as much as possible, to place ourselves right in the scene. Like, if we are meditating on the birth of Christ, I try to place myself right there in the stable, and picture all the animals that might be there with Mary and Joseph, and try to figure out what exactly happened on that night, and what they, Mary and Joseph, might be thinking and doing and everything.

Dubchek told me he doesn't like to meditate on the Nativity because he can't help but think about the animals in the manger area grunting and shitting and pissing and so forth, and all the odors. And that makes him start to laugh, and that is probably not the best thing to do during prayer, because it pretty much ruins your recollection. But I figure that's okay, thinking about the vulgar aspects, that is, because it's part of the overall surroundings, right? You just shouldn't *concentrate* on those things too much, and try not to laugh too much about it. The birth of Christ is the more important part.

The idea of meditation is interesting, but trying to do it every morning for an hour is difficult. I mean, most of us can meditate on something for a couple of minutes or so, but after that we get distracted, right? I find it hard to kneel for even five minutes, so I sit, which is permissible. But when I sit, I get pretty relaxed and sometimes I fall asleep. So does Dubchek and a couple of the other guys. Dubchek is the most apparent because he snores.

We have been told that meditation is one of the oldest forms of prayer, and that many contemplative orders, like say the Trappist monks and Trappistine nuns, learned it from St. Benedict, who died over fifteen hundred years ago. We have also been told that while we practice many of the rubrics laid down by older monastic orders, our order has a different paradigm, or focus, if you will, on relating to the world. While Trappists and some of the other orders of monks and nuns concentrate on contemplative prayer, or "Contemplation," our order has the motto of "*Contemplation in Action.*" A corollary to this could be, "monks on main street," or something like that. In other words, monks living among the populace and working and interacting with them, as opposed to cloistering themselves away from everyone in a monastery up in the hills somewhere. After these few years of formation that we novices are just starting, we will be sent back out into the world to do our work among the people.

During this morning's attempt at meditation I decide to write God another letter to help me stay awake:

Lord, I feel funny writing to you. Some days I feel pretty good about things, but this morning I'm not sure you are there. Okay, I mean, I actually do think you exist, don't get me wrong. But when I say I'm not sure I believe in you, it's more like someone saying, "I used to believe in this friend of mine, until he let me down." In other words, I still know that the friend exists, but I don't know whether the friend is good and faithful to me, when I am in need. I used to feel that I could trust in you. Until the Accident happened.

So why am I here?

• *I originally wanted to come here because of The Miracle.*

51

• *The Accident killed my faith, almost. Or at least gave it such a kick in the groin that I am still reeling.*

• *But somehow I am still here. Sometimes I get this strange feeling that I'm supposed to be here, and that I am doing the right thing. Does that constitute some kind of faith?*

Man, I'm a walking paradox...

CHAPTER SIX

Quo Vadis?

Mid-September

One of the first things we learn in the novitiate is how to clean up and reset the tables in the *triclinium* (the dining room) and wash all the dishes, pots and pans in *culina* (the kitchen) after a meal. As an added mort—that's short for *mortification*—we have to speak in Latin whenever we give or take orders from the *praeces* (*pray*-sees), the guy in charge that day.

If you are on cleanups, immediately after final grace, you go to the back of the triclinium and ask the praeces, "Quidquid visne me facere (*What would you like me to do?*)?"

He might answer, "Quaeso impone patellas in mensas (*Please set the plates on the tables*)."

Other orders might be, "Quaso ite ad culina, et impone patellas in machina(*Please go to the kitchen, and load the dishes into the dish-washing machine*)." This is actually the most coveted job, because you always try to race the "machina" and load it as fast as you can, but no matter how fast you feed the dishes onto the machina's moving conveyor belt, it always seems to keep up with you. It is almost like feeding dishes into the mouth of a huge, steam-belching dragon, placing offerings onto it's endless, serrated tongue that then draws them into its inner regions and then expels them out the other end, hot, steamy and sterile, for the other men on the crew to stack and store. It's fun to try to load it as fast as possible, because the result is that you and two other unloaders and stackers are able to wash and sort all the dishes and silverware for a hundred-and-thirty-odd men in about twenty minutes or so.

The less enjoyable job is washing the cooking pots and pans in a large sink in culina, which sometimes requires scrubbing. And of course throwing, or "iacens" (pronounced "yatch-ens") all the "gronk"— grease, grime, dirt, garbage—into the appropriate receptacles and wheeling them to the basement elevator and emptying them into the incinerator. Some of the new guys stretch the rules now and then, and start actually making small talk in basic Latin, over and above necessary speech. Like when Harshley started crooning "Est nunc vel numquam..." ("*It's now or never...*") an Elvis hit from a couple of years ago, in Latin, while we were peeling potatoes. He did a pretty good job, too, I have to admit—I couldn't have done better myself. And I doubt if Elvis could, either. At least with the Latin part of it.

Cleanups and the resetting of the tables are usually completed in a little more than half an hour, and then the praeces says, "Tu potes ire(*You may go*)."

Where to? To evening rec in the novice rec room until 8:15 P.M., when the bell rings for points. From the end of rec until breakfast the following morning we have Sacred Silence, which means no talking or whispering unless it is an emergency, or a very serious matter of some kind. After evening Points we have Examen, pronounced "eggs-A'min" (examination of conscience), and then free time until 9:05, which is lights out.

* * *

One night after dinner when we are not on the cleanup crew, Ken Matthews persuades Andy and me to visit the Infirmary with him. He leads us down the steps and through the main doors into a little kitchen with a dining table cluttered with dirty dinner dishes. During this time, we have *Deo Gratias*, or freedom to recreate and talk in English.

"Praise the Lord," says Ken.

"Amen," Andy and I reply in unison.

"A normal kitchen, like the ones back home, in normal houses," I continue as I look around. "I'm almost nostalgic. What are we doing here?"

"Dishes, to start with," says Ken as he hands me a dishcloth and nods toward the sink. "We novices take turns washing them every night. After we finish these, we can visit some of the old Fathers."

Soon I am washing, and Ken and Andy are drying.

"Where's the castle around here?" I ask as I finish and drain the dirty dishwater from the sink.

"Down the hall and to the right."

I head down the hall toward the castle, or lavatory, and walk past a large open door, where I see what looks like a spacious, comfortable dormitory room occupied by an old priest sitting in an easy chair, reading

55

a newspaper with a magnifying glass. Down at the end of the corridor in the rec room, an old brother is watching television. The infirmary wing in some ways resembles a hospital wing, but most of the rooms appear to be more like regular bedrooms than hospital rooms.

I finish up in the castle and turn to head back toward the kitchen when I pass a door that is almost completely closed. I wonder if the occupant is sick, but there is no "do not disturb" sign or anything, so I move right up to the door to get a better look through the crack. It's kind of dark in there, but I see at least one lit lamp, and as I move right up to the crack in the door for a better view, I somehow manage to unintentionally bump the door with my knee, causing a loud "thump," which I immediately try to disguise by knocking on the door.

"Who's a there?" booms a loud voice with an Italian accent, "Come in, come in!"

I slowly push open the door and enter a dimly-lit room that appears to be part library and part museum. Shelves filled with old books and interesting curios line the walls. Under the windows are some flower pots with thorny, almost leafless branches sticking out of them. And in the middle of it all, seated in an easy chair, wearing a biretta on his head and reading a book with a reading glass, sits the old priest who almost ran down Dubchek with his wheelchair a couple of weeks ago.

"Are you a friend or a foe?" he asks without looking up.

"Friend, I guess," I reply uneasily.

He looks up at me and registers surprise. "Who are you, a new man? Sit down, sit down. What brings a you here?"

"I was washing dishes, and..."

"A spirit led you here. Which a spirit was it?"

"I just wanted to say hello..."

"What's a your name? I don't get to meet many novices."

"Wally. Moriarty. Why not?"

"Various reasons. Politics, mostly."

I notice the title of the book he is reading. It is called "The Upanishads." I have to ask myself if that is an actual word. We are interrupted by more knocking, and I look up to see Ken and Andy at the door. Ken is giving me a funny look, and all I can do is shrug.

"More visitors! Whatsa goin' on? Am I dreaming? What have I done to deserve this?"

"Father Lugieri," says Ken to the old priest, "meet Andy Gallagher, and Wally..."

"Yes," he replies, as he puts a marker in his book and closes it, "Wally and I are a already acquainted. You gentlemen may call a me Padre from now on; it makes a me feel more at home."

Ken and Andy find empty chairs and seat themselves.

"Now gentlemen," says the Padre, "I have a one question for you. Quo vadis?"

"Quo...vadis?" I repeat, and then a light bulb goes on in my head.

"Where goest thou?" I say aloud. It was the title of a movie I saw on TV years ago.

"Good," says the Padre with a nod. "Most a new men, they don't know their Latin yet, they cannot translate a simple sentence."

I flush with pride as Ken and Andy smile at me. I want to say, '*Hey guys, it was a fluk*e,' but I keep my mouth shut.

"Now," continues the Padre, "where is it a from?"

Everyone looks at me, and I just shrug. "A movie? Oh, ah... the Bible, of course. I guess."

"When you go back to your rooms, research it," he says with a grin. "That way, you will always remember it, no?"

Andy is eyeing the bookshelf closest to him. "Hinduism?" he says, reading a book jacket out loud.

"Do you believe in a reincarnation?" asks the Padre with a straight face.

"Are we supposed to answer that?" I say with a laugh.

"Think about it," he continues, "the Hindus have a point, there. If you want out, liv a your life so you don't a have to come back."

"What if someone *wants* to come back?" I ask as I notice Ken shift uneasily in his chair.

"If you wanna come back, you are messed up. The Hindus believe that if you are not perfect when you die, you come back in another form, like an animal or an insect, to purge your soul, polish the rough edges, so to speak. We Catholics have a different concept to accomplish that end. What do we call it?"

"Penance?" asks Andy.

"Can you do penance after you die?" I ask.

"*Purgatory!*" says Ken with a smile.

"Bingo," says the old priest. "We do not reincarnate, we just a take a side trip after death to spiff ourselves up for the big party, eh?"

Andy pulls out a book and holds it up. "What is this?" he asks. "It's obviously not in English." He hands it to me and I glance at it before passing it over to the Padre, who takes it and holds it up so we can see the cover. The book has long cloth ribbon markers hanging out of it like a missal or a bible.

"Can a you guess what language it is?" he asks.

I look at the unusual symbols on the cover. "Hebrew?" I ask.

The Padre opens the book to a marker and shows us some lines. "Do you want to know what this says?" he asks me.

"Sure," I say, looking at the script with wonder.

"It says that some angels are telling Mary that she will conceive and bear a son, the Messiah Jesus, and she asks how she can have a son because no man has touched her."

"That sounds like the Gospel," says Ken, "And yet..."

"It is the Qu'ran," says the Padre, "the Islamic Qu'ran."

"Really? I didn't know Muslims believed in Jesus and Mary," says Ken.

"The Qu'ran contains more text about the Virgin Mary than our Gospels," says the Padre, and he looks at me and Ken for a moment.

Andy, still near the shelves, breaks the silence. "May I?" he asks as he points to what appears to be the bowl and the stem of an American Indian peace pipe.

The Padre nods, and Andy carefully picks up the two pieces.

"Do you know the story of a the pipe?" asks the Padre then.

No one answers.

"Long ago," he continues, "the Buffalo Calf Woman brought a the pipe to the Sioux, before they migrated to the Dakotas. The story goes that a two scouts were out a looking for food, when they saw a beautiful young woman in white buckskin approaching them, walking in a sacred manner. One of the two lusted after her and told the other one to wait while he approached her. He embraced her, and a cloud enveloped them both. When the cloud disappeared, the woman was still there, but the other Lakota was gone and there was a pile of bones at the woman's feet. The remaining Lakota was a frightened, but a the woman told him not to fear, because a she knew he did not a have lustful motives..." he goes on to tell us about this holy woman who taught the Sioux seven sacred rites, including how to make a sacred pipe out of just the right materials.

"...and a then, she taught them how to perform a pipe ceremony," he continues with a smile, "...and who's a to say she is not a from God?"

I feel a little uncomfortable, with all of this talk about other religions. I keep wondering whether the Padre believes any of this stuff. So I turn and look at the flower pots under the window.

"What are those for?" I ask him.

"Those are a rose bushes. It has been said that if a you like roses, pray to St. Therese of the Child Jesus, and she will a send you some. But these have been barren for a long time, and I pray to her every day, so sometimes it takes awhile, I guess..."

We three novices look at each other, searching for something to say.

"So," he says, suddenly changing the subject, "what do you learn a so far in the novitiate?"

"Pray, pray, pray," I say with resignation.

"Ah, prayer and fasting can a bring you many blessings," he affirms.

"Fasting?" says Andy.

"Every great religious tradition considers a fasting an important part of a prayer. Jews, Hindus, Buddhists, Muslims, Indians... the Jews have some of my favorite traditions. Have you ever been to a Jewish service?"

"Have *you*?" I ask, feeling uncomfortable again. "I didn't think we were allowed to do that."

"You would be amazed at the similarities between all a the great religions of the world, if a you ever attended some of their services," he says, ignoring my statement.

"But," says Andy, "there are still irreconcilable differences in dogma between all the religions, right?"

"Semantics," he continues, "we always get a bogged down by semantics."

"You mean like, definitions?" says Andy.

"Definitions, yes. Meanings of words and phrases. Sense, reference, implication. And emphasis! You want an example? Many Jewish people will not set a foot inside of a Catholic church for a one reason. You wanna know what it is? Statues. We have a statues in our churches, of a Mary and a Joseph and a some other saints. Why do you think they don't like a the statues?"

"The First Commandment..." says Andy.

"Correct. They think a that we worship the statues like a they were false gods. You and I know that if a the statue falls and breaks, no saint is the worse for it — the statues are a merely visual aids for us, to help us to imagine the saint we are a praying to. We do not actually pray to the statue."

"Very true," says Andy.

"You want another example? If I take a piss while I am saying my rosary, it is a sacrilege. Would you agree?"

I stiffen at his vocabulary. "Well, I..."

"But if I say the rosary while I take a piss, I am a saint, no?"

We all laugh, just as a bell sounds in the distance.

"You must a leave," says the Padre, "a shame. Let's a say a Hail Mary together." He extends a hand, palm down, and Ken lays his hand on top of it. Andy and I follow suit, like our high school football team always did just before a game.

"Hail Mary, full of Grace..." we all begin, "the Lord is with thee..." I sneak a peak at the Padre, and his eyes are closed in peaceful concentration as we finish the prayer.

As we head down the cloister walk to the novitiate wing, I whisper to Ken, "He's pretty weird, isn't he?"

"I knew you'd like him," he answers with a smile as we separate and head to our rooms.

***

As the weeks wear on and I continue to adjust, almost everything here in this new life is getting easier, and almost everybody I have met, including my teachers, seems to give me positive feelings. I'm even feeling better about Barry Edelfort, the guy who walks barefoot down the halls while he pops the zits on the back of his neck.

There are so many new guys here from different walks of life. Some of the new men are older and have college degrees; one is a physicist, and another has a chemistry degree. John Marconi is a mountain climber from Omaha. He's only my age, but he has scaled some peaks in the Rockies and even the Alps. He's experienced some difficult climbs, where you have to move across the bottom of a shelf like a spider on the ceiling, with hundreds or even thousands of feet of thin air between you and the ground, hammering pitons into cracks, threading ropes through them, hanging on for your life. He told us that one summer night back in high school, he and some friends actually tried to scale a building in downtown Omaha with ropes, pitons, the whole bit. But after going up a couple of stories they decided to quit, before they got caught and hauled down to the police station for "illegal ascension" or something.

And then there's Jerome Harshley. He's the guy who brought the scuba tank the day we entered, but his parents wound up taking it back home. It was too much of an "inordinate attachment," he says. He's from Minnesota, but he actually did some reef diving down in Florida before he entered. He's sort of an animal expert, and he has already taught Shanty, the house dog, some new tricks. Shanty is a black and yellow lab who lives in a doghouse out behind the boiler room, right by a vent that blows warm air out of the building so he won't get too cold in the winter. If you want to know anything about wildlife or nature, you don't need to look it up, you just ask Harsh.

And then there is Tom Donavan. He commands the utmost respect from everyone since he actually stole Fr. Doyle's golf stick back in high school, then hid it in his locker so that he could show it to his friends as proof, before returning it days later, without ever getting caught. Fr. Doyle could not give out any swats until he got it back.

If there is one person who does not fit into this "positive feelings" mold just yet, it is Fr. Harrison, who has the title of Fr. Socius, the assistant to Fr. McKittrick, our Novice Master. While I thought Fr. Harrison was fairly personable when I first met him, he has begun to grate on me. And I want desperately to change that, so I sometimes meditate on it to try and figure out what my problem is with him.

Now I have to admit that this religious order is sort of like an army, in some ways. Our founder was a soldier for awhile before he changed his life and started the Order. And our Father Socius — Fr. Harrison — was a soldier, too. In World War II. Since I was born just a few months before the end of the war, I cannot remember a thing about it, except what I have learned in history classes. But I think Fr. Harrison remembers a lot about it. Maybe too much, because I sometimes think he still believes he is in the army, and maybe even still fighting the war, and he considers us novices to be like raw recruits in bootcamp. Rumor has it that he taught in a high school for a short time, but was a little too harsh in disciplining some of the boys, so he was sent here to cool off, so to speak. We call him "The Sarge," but not to his face. Matthews says he does not like to be called Sarge at all, not even in jest by his fellow priests. And he doesn't like women, either. Not even nuns.

The Sarge is our instructor in Gospel Theology, and we meet every Tuesday and Thursday morning. I consider him a fairly good teacher and his courses are okay, and most of the time he's sort of a nice guy, until we try to get him to open up and expound about something, like say, the war.

"What was it like?" Tom Robinson asks him one day in class.

"Oh, it wasn't too thrilling, I'll have to say," Fr. Harrison answers him.

"Did it change your life?" Andy asks him then.

"It changed all of our lives. I wouldn't be here if it was not for the war," he answers.

"Where do you think you might be?" asks Alex Dubchek.

"I don't know, Carissime Dubchek, but I do know that I wouldn't be here. Now let's get back to our lesson."

Oh yeah, that word, "carissime," pronounced *ka-riss'-ee-may*, is a term that our superiors sometimes use when talking to novices. It means, "dearest," or "most beloved." It's kind of antiquated, and most of the priests don't use it very often, except, ironically, for the Sarge. When we learned its meaning, and saw how the Sarge uses it, it almost seems like a joke.

"That scar on your hand, Father," says Alex then, "Did you get that in the war?"

The Sarge completely ignores the question, even though he has this nasty scar on his right hand.

"Now," says The Sarge, "as you should remember from our last class, we are currently covering St. Matthew's Gospel, chapter 25. Carissime Ranier, can you read aloud Matthew, chapter 25, verses 31-40?"

Lou Ranier reads the passage where Jesus speaks of the end of the world where the Son of Man will separate the nations one from another as a shepherd separates the sheep from the goats, and invites those on His right hand, the sheep, to eternal life, "For I was hungry and you gave Me food; I was thirsty and you gave Me drink; I was a stranger and you took

66

Me in; I was naked and you clothed Me; I was sick and you visited Me; I was in prison and you came to Me."

"Then the righteous will answer Him, saying, 'Lord, when did we see You hungry...' and so forth, and He answers, "Inasmuch as you did it to one of the least of these My brethren, you did it to Me.'"

"Good," says Fr. Harrison. "Now, Carissime Wentfogle, could you point out at least one use of metaphor in this passage?"

Leonard is sitting right next to me, and he says, "Well, Father, the sheep represent... ha hah, the sheep..." then he starts to laugh. And sometimes when Leonard starts laughing, he can't stop for a while, and this looks like it is going to be one of those times.

Fr. Harrison just stares at him and says nothing for a moment. Leonard continues to laugh, shaking his head, unable to stop. Then Fr. Harrison's face starts getting a bit pink. He approaches Leonard and bends down over him and speaks very quietly, but I still manage to hear him.

"Carissime Wentfogle, could you leave the room until you get control of yourself? And I want you to see me in my office after class." Leonard gets up and leaves the room, looking very embarrassed, but still lurching with spasms of laughter.

Then Fr. Harrison goes back to the front of the class and says, "Carissime Dubchek, could you please point out a metaphor in this passage?"

"The sheep," Alex Dubchek says, "are the good people, the righteous ones, and the goats are the nasty ones..."

After class, we have ten minutes of TL — that's tempus liberum, or free time — and I watch as Leonard follows Fr. Harrison up to his office. I kind of follow at a distance, and after they go inside and close the door, I walk up to Fr. Harrison's door and pick up the clipboard on the bench outside, as if to sign up for a conference, or something. We usually don't sign up for conferences with Fr. Harrison, because Fr. McKittrick is much easier to talk to.

Now I can hear Fr. Harrison's voice:

"Carissime Wentfogle, look at me. Can you explain what was so funny about that Gospel passage?"

"Father, I don't know," says Leonard, "it was just something funny about the sheep and the goats, I guess..."

"Carissime Wentfogle, I cannot tolerate such immature behavior in my classes, is that clear? I expect everyone in my classes to conduct themselves like mature, spiritual young men. You made a travesty of today's lecture. I will not tolerate that, especially when reading scripture. Do I make myself clear?"

"Yes, Father," says Leonard quietly.

"Enough, Carissime. You may go now."

I quickly duck into the castle, which is located practically right across the hall from Fr. Harrison's office. After I hear Leonard open the door and leave, I wait a moment and then leave the castle and head back downstairs for our next class.

Later on, at rec, I ask Leonard how it went with Fr. Harrison.

"Oh, it wasn't too bad," he says distantly.

"What made you laugh?"

"Just something Alex said last night, about a horse he once saw at the State Fair. Ha hah, he's always talking about how they shit and piss and fart and... and other stuff, and the way he says it is *so funny*! When I read about the sheep and the goats I started thinking about all of that, and I couldn't stop laughing, for some reason. Ha Hah!"

"Thou art Peter,
and upon this
rock
I will build My
church, and the gates
of hell shall not
prevail against it."

Matt 16:18

s

CHAPTER SEVEN

Quid est Ecclesiam?

L ou Ranier and I are taking a walk during Sunday afternoon rec. I was the first one to hang my tag under the "walk" section on the rec sign-up board today, and when you do that you never know who you're going to get for a partner. Okay, so I'm not a saint yet. I try my darnedest not to show it, but I think Lou senses I'd rather be elsewhere. Then he says something that surprises me a little.

"Vince Lombardi has really turned the Packers around."

"Yeah, so I've heard," I say, "I wonder what his secret is?"

"I heard he attends Mass," says Lou, "every day. And he says the rosary every day."

"I didn't know that," I say then. "Do you think it helps?"

"Well, it sure can't hurt," he says.

"I saw him coach a couple of games in Milwaukee," I say then.

"He didn't seem like the daily Mass type. Or the rosary type."

"Well, you don't seem like the rosary type either. But you say it every day, right?"

"I can't argue with you on that one. But of course, we're supposed to do it, around here. So, do you follow football a lot?"

"Well, I did somewhat," he says, "before I entered. But of course around here, we can't. I have to ask the Fathers each week who won Sunday's game. And up here, there're a lot of Vikings fans."

"I have to admit," I say, "that's one thing I miss is listening to the Packer games. Or watching them on TV, when they televise them."

A short silence follows.

"You think I'm a wimp, don't you?" he says all of a sudden.

"Oh. Well, no... what makes you say that?"

"Everybody thinks I'm a pious, intellectual wimp," he continues, and then he takes what looks like a slab of steel out of his pocket and points to an oak tree by the side of the road. "See that twiggy little branch in the trunk? About five feet off the ground?" he says as he raises his arm up over his head carefully. He then brings his arm quickly down, and the steel flashes through the air and sticks in the trunk of the oak, slicing off the twig in the process. We approach the tree, and he pulls the knife, because I now can see that it is, in fact, a throwing knife, out of the tree. He hands it to me and pulls a second knife out of his pocket.

"I bought these in New York City this Summer. My parents took me there for a final trip in the world before entering. They're balanced just right, so they flip evenly. The secret is to judge the distance to your target, and know how many turns it will make during its flight before it hits. You have to practice a lot, and learn how to judge distance."

I wonder for a moment whether he asked Fr. McKittrick for permission to keep these things when he entered. But then I figure they're hardly any bigger than large jackknives, and we're allowed to have those, so what the crock. I try throwing one a few times, and pretty soon I am sticking it into the bark of the tree as if I knew what I was doing.

"En Garde!" comes a voice from behind us, and I turn around to see Dubchek approaching us, with Ken and Leonard following.

"Prithee," says Dubchek, "what clandestine plot be this? Forsooth, should we have brought accouterments of weaponry as well?"

"Check these out," says Lou as he passes the knives around, and after a short lesson, we are all taking turns with them. Even Leonard manages to stick one in a tree once or twice.

Later, as we continue walking, the subject of the Padre enters our conversation.

"So if he's from Italy, what brought him here?" asks Lou.

"They wanted to get him as far away from Rome as they could," says Ken, "they felt he had... unorthodox views."

"For instance?" asks Dubchek.

"He doesn't think you have to be Catholic, or even Christian, to be saved," says Ken.

"Unorthodox is an understatement," says Lou, "'Salus extra ecclesiam non est.'"

"*What?*" says Dubchek with a puzzled look.

"According to Cyprian," says Lou, "and Augustine, 'There is no salvation outside the Church.' If the old man is serious about this, he's in real trouble."

"Who's Cyprian?" Asks Dubchek.

"What kind of trouble?" I ask, "*Lots* of people believe that..."

"...Lots of people can be wrong," interjects Lou.

"He went further," says Ken, "rumor has it that he became a Rabbi for awhile."

"You're kidding," laughs Alex, "While he was a priest? Hah!"

"You know that biretta he wears?" continues Ken, "Underneath it is a yarmulke."

"No way," I say.

"I swear," says Ken, holding up his right hand.

"What's a yarmulkee?" asks Dubchek.

"Ha ha hah," Leonard laughs, and Lou just shakes his head.

"Sounds like he's got an identity crisis," I offer as we walk back onto the novitiate grounds. "Did the Jews know he was a priest? I mean, when they ordained him, or whatever they did?"

"I don't know the details," says Ken, "but they may be as strict as we are when it comes to... loyalties, shall we say."

"This is too much," laughs Alex, "a kosher priest!"

"That's an oxymoron," says Lou, "there's no such thing!"

"Oxy- what?" says Alex Dubchek.

Leonard continues to laugh.

"How could he rationalize being a Catholic and a Jew at the same time?" I ask as we walk past the cemetery.

"He says the apostles were," says Ken, "back when there was no set dogma, when 'the faith was a simpler and a purer,' as he puts it. He says that for years the early Christians went to the synagogue on Saturday — the Sabbath — and then celebrated the Resurrection in somebody's home on Sunday with a reenactment of the Lord's Supper, which eventually became the Mass."

"What's his point?" I ask as we stroll past the duck pond.

"I tried to ask him that once," continues Ken, "and he said, 'I tella you the same thing I tella Roncalli, a long time ago. Roncalli an' I were a having a conversation about a this, and a he says to me, "how can a you talk that way, Ricardo?" and I tella him, '*I find a the keys to the Kingdom!*'"

"Roncalli?" says Lou, "not..."

"That's right," says Ken, "Angelo Giuseppi Roncalli, A.K.A. Pope John the Twenty-Third."

"And he actually *knew* him?" I ask as I wing a pebble out over the duck pond.

"He went to school with him, as far as I know," says Ken, "and they remained close friends after that."

"What does Father McKittrick say about all this?" asks Dubchek.

"He says that we're not supposed to visit him, at least not without permission," says Ken with a sly look in my direction.

"With heretical views like that," says Lou, "he's lucky they don't defrock him and kick him out of the order."

"What," asks Dubchek then, "is 'ecclesiam?'"

"Catholics," says Lou, "baptized Catholics."

"Ah, Bowzo's mother," says Alex, shaking his head.

Leonard and I burst out laughing in unison, almost. "Who's mother?" I ask him. But he ignores me, and turns to Lou.

"Now wait a minute," says Dubchek in a very somber tone all of a sudden, "so you're saying my grandmother, my Lutheran grandmother, can't get into Heaven?"

"'Extra ecclesiam,'" repeats Lou, "outside the church, 'salus non est.'"

There is no salvation."

"With all due respect, Lou," Alex says hotly, "that's a crock of shit!"

Leonard and I laugh even harder.

"I don't make the rules, Alex," says Lou, "and you don't make the rules."

"Gentlemen," says Ken, "we'd best change the subject — none of us are theologians yet."

***

I'm sitting in Fr. McKittrick's office, nervous, as usual.

"You say you've met him?" he says in a way that puts me at ease. I know he could make an issue out of it if he wanted to. "What were your impressions?"

"A little heccentric, lots of curios and stuff," I answer, "and books all over the place. Father, I know he has unusual ideas, but he's not going to change me, don't worry."

He sits back and thinks for a moment. "All right," he says in a kindly tone, "you may visit him, but be careful." He pauses again. "Make sure you have a second-year man with you. Keep things on an even keel, you know? And let me know how it turns out."

"Of course, Father. By the way, while I'm thinking of it, what does 'ecclesiam' mean?"

"Church," he says, "Ecclesiam means, 'The Church.'"

"I know that. I mean, *who* is 'The Church?'"

"Catholics. Baptized Catholics."

"What about other Christians, like Protestants?"

"They've formally broken away from the church, as the word implies."

"But, *they're* baptized..."

He looks at me for a moment. "Let's put it this way: they're 'conditional' members of the Church."

"Under what conditions?"

"That they live like exemplary Christians."

"What about the unbaptized?"

"We can only pray for them, and hope for conversion."

* * *

It's 9:05 P.M. and the Lights-Out bell has just rung. I have to visit the castle just before bed. I notice in the subdued night light that Clark is washing his hands at a neighboring sink, and he exits before I do. When I leave a few seconds later I glimpse, in the faint footlight-glow of the corridor, Clark entering the rec room down at the end. I walk quietly down the corridor after him, sidling along the wall and concealing myself so that I can peek through the windowed rec room door without being noticed. I see him exiting the outside door on the other end, out into the night, closing the door behind him. Where is he going? We're supposed to be inside the building for the night, in bed.

It's a warm night and I decide, on the spur of the moment, to follow him. I let myself out the door as quietly as possible, hoping he cannot hear me. He is wearing dark clothing, and even in the full moonlight I can barely make out his shape walking across the grassy lawn up ahead. Soon I am following him, slowly catching up to him, down the long asphalt entrance drive out toward the highway. We are both clad in street clothes, a simple shirt and black pants, pretty much like what we wear beneath our black robes, the only difference being the sport shirt I have on over my T-shirt. The night is comfortable, with a gentle, balmy breeze. I am gaining on Clark, but he doesn't seem to hear me until I step on a twig, at which point he jumps and turns around.

"Who's there?" he shouts.

"Clark?" I say quietly, "Don't worry — it's me, Wally."

"Wally! Crock, you scared the bejesus out of me!"

"Sorry. Where you headed?"

"On a caper. Into town. Wanna come along?"

"Town? What town? We're supposed to be in bed. Besides, we're not dressed for it."

"What? You think you need a tuxedo or something? We're just goin' into Bonny's."

"St. Bonifacius? What's there?"

"You'll see." We continue walking along the road for about ten minutes until we reach a tavern called "Roy's Place."

I stop dead in my tracks. "A bar? We're going into a *bar*?"

"Just for a little while," says Clark.

"Man, talk about the greasy chute," I say then. "We could get kicked out for this!"

"What's the greasy chute?"

"Matthews says that when you start breaking the rules, it's like sliding down a greasy chute to perdition, or something. You go faster and faster, and it gets easier and easier to break the rules, and pretty soon your vocation is gone."

"Well, let's just say that I'm not sure if I have a vocation in the first place," he says dryly, "so maybe I got nothin' to lose."

We enter a dim, smoky barroom where Johnny Cash is crooning from the jukebox. Two young women sit at the bar, chatting with the bartender and smoking. Otherwise, the place is empty.

"Clark! You're back," says the middle-aged bartender.

"I brought a friend," says Clark, as the two women smile at us. Clark buys us each a beer with money he somehow kept with him when he entered, against the rules, and the bartender doesn't bother to card us. I feel funny, not only from breaking the rules and being "out-in-the-world" all of a sudden, but also because I have never had a drink in a tavern before. Maybe this wasn't such a good idea. But then I quickly manage to rationalize that Clark shouldn't be left alone. He needs a companion, right?

"So this is a caper?" I say as Clark racks the balls on the pool table.

"Yeah. Pick a cue," he says, and I grab a cue off the wall, not bothering to check if it is warped or not. "Wanna break?" he asks then.

"Ah, sure," I say as I try to look like I know what I am doing. I've played pool a couple of times in my life, so I can at least fake it a little bit. I break the set but I don't sink a ball.

"They kicked *me* out," he says as he lines up a shot.

"'They?' Who's 'they?'" I ask, taking a sip of beer.

"My parents," he says as he pokes the cue ball harder than necessary. It knocks in a striped ball and caroms off the side to nudge a second one into a pocket.

"Why?" I ask as he misses his next shot.

"They don't want me to be a priest. My dad wants me to help run the farm. Take it over, eventually."

"Don't you have any brothers who can help?" I ask as I manage to put a solid away.

"Two older sisters, and they're both married already. To other farmers."

"What brought you here?" I say as I miss my next shot.

"You really want to know?" he says as he takes another shot. "At this point, I don't think I can tell you. They—my parents—thought college was bad enough. But while I was there, I got a hankering to try this," he says as he knocks two more stripes in. "Didn't sit well with them at all."

The two young women at the bar get up and walk over to the jukebox that stands, gaudy and bright, a few feet away from where we are playing.

"You don't seem like the type," I say as I watch him make another shot, and another. A new song begins from the jukebox; it seems pleasantly romantic as the beer begins to take effect.

"It seemed like a good idea at the time," he says as he lines up the eight-ball. "What brought *you* here?"

"You wouldn't believe it if I told you," I say as I try to listen to the song that's playing.

"Try me," he says as he puts the eight-ball away and goes to pick up the rack. "But first, get us some more beers," he says as he hands me some change.

I go to the bar and buy another round, feeling a little less uncomfortable, thanks to the brew. When I return, Clark has racked up the balls and is preparing to break.

"So you were saying?" he says as he lines up the cue ball.

"Do you believe in God?" I ask.

"Of course I believe in God, what kind of question is that?"

"Some people don't," I say as I watch him break.

"You guys from around here?" interrupts one of the women at the jukebox then.

"Yes and no," says Clark as I take a shot.

"What's that supposed to mean?" she asks as she lights up a cigarette. She's kind of cute, not a knockout by any means, but my having been away from the opposite sex for over a month definitely makes her appear more attractive.

"We're students," I say quickly, not wanting to start up a conversation with an extern (a person outside the Order). But now I'm really starting to feel mellow, and even though we're not supposed to talk to externs, especially females, the beer definitely eases my concern.

"I'm Marlene and this is Sue," she says, pointing to her friend. "She thinks you look like priests in those black pants," she continues.

"We're definitely not priests," I tell her as I try to listen to the words of the song. I put one ball away and miss a second one.

"Good," she says, "You know, there's a whole bunch of 'em living up the road."

"Oh yeah?" says Clark, "Where'd you hear that?"

"Everybody knows it. That college place up over the hill. Just a bunch of guys living up in the woods, wasting their lives away," she says as I strain my ears to hear the jukebox. It sounds like the Beach Boys, and I start thinking about Malibu...

"Oh?" says Clark as he takes a pack of cigarettes out of his pocket and offers me one. Even though I'm craving it, I decline as he continues to Marlene, "What do you think they should be doing?"

"Havin' fun. Fallin' in love. Gettin' married. I mean, are they a bunch of queers or something?"

"Honey," says Clark as he lights up his cigarette and does a sort of James Dean squint with his eyes and moves closer to her, "let me set you straight on something. They ain't all a bunch of faggots livin' up there, I guarantee it."

"How do you know?"

He takes his wallet out of his pocket, pulls out a snapshot and hands it to her. "Here's a picture of one of them. Does that guy look queer?"

"No... hey, wait a minute. Is that *you*?"

"I cannot tell a lie," he nods as she looks back and forth between the photo and him.

I look at the photo and sure enough, there is a slightly younger Clark with his longer Elvis haircut, sporting a coat and tie, seated in the back seat of a car with a lovely young woman with nice legs sitting on his lap with her arms around him, both of them grinning at the camera.

"So you're one of them?" she asks.

"And so is he," he says, pointing at me.

"You're kidding me. You said you weren't priests!"

"Honey," Clark continues, "If we manage to stay in, it'll take us eleven years to become priests."

"I don't believe you're one of 'em. Those guys wear robes all the time, like a bunch of monks."

"Not all the time," I say as I put the eight-ball away. Then, "What song is that that just ended?"

"Surfer girl. Whatayou wear under those robes?"

"You wouldn't want to know," says Clark gravely.

"Come on," says Marlene, "Whataya *wear*?"

"Well," says Clark, "you know what a union suit looks like? You know, that old-fashioned long underwear that men wore in the old silent movies? Well, we all have to wear that, except it's dyed with all these rainbow colors and flowers and stuff..."

"You're lyin'," she says. "Tell the truth, now."

"Same thing we're wearing now," I say as I rack up the balls.

"Don't *tell* her," says the disappointed Clark.

"Sorry," I say as I break. He wants to shoot the breeze with these women, and I actually just want to go back to the house and hit the sack. After I finish this beer. And maybe one more.

The girls chat with us for a few more minutes, then go back to the bar. Probably figured we were a waste of time. I put in four balls in a row, not bad for my limited skill.

"So, why'd you enter?" Clark asks me again. I freeze for another second or two. Then I line up my next shot.

"Food," I tell him as I take the shot.

"What? Hey, the food ain't *that* great."

"No. It's... to make a long story short, I was having trouble eating..."

"*You?*"

"Yes. But when I came up here, I could eat. I can't explain it. It just..."

"But you couldn't eat at home?"

"Like I said, it's a long story. My brother died, and I just... lost my appetite. My brother was in the Order, and when I came here for his funeral, and they fed us afterwards, I could eat like a horse all of a sudden. Just while I was here, though." I take another shot, miss, and Clark lines one up and makes it.

"So. To Brother Kelley's cooking," he says as he raises his beer, and I raise mine, and we both take a swig, and he makes another shot.

***

I wake up the following morning with a heavy feeling. It is not a hangover, because we really did not drink very much. Rather, it is more a keen sense of guilt for what I did. I feel like I'm tottering on the edge of the greasy chute, all of a sudden.

I go to Fr. McKittrick's room at the first opportunity, in order to go to confession.

"Bless me Father, for I have sinned," I begin. "I went to a bar after lights-out and drank some beers, Father. These are my sins."

"Why did you do this?" He asks with concern. I am not sure if he knows it is me or not, because he is facing away toward the window again.

"Father, another one of the men was going, and I... I know this sounds stupid, but I thought he needed company."

"Wally," he says with a bit of a smile, without even making eye contact, "don't you see the rationalization here? Don't you see that you are trying to find a reason to justify your disobedience?"

"Yes Father," I say, shocked by his candor, "I see your point. But the honest truth is, I have never wanted to go to a bar before and I did not even know that was where he was going when I followed him."

"You followed him?"

"I saw him go out the door and I followed him, just to see where he was going. He heard me, and invited me. I honestly did not want to go, but I just thought... should I have just turned around? I don't know..."

"Your intentions were not evil, Carissime Moriarty, but remember, 'assuming permission' is not a good idea unless it is a matter of extreme urgency. Clark has already told me his version of the story, and it corroborates with yours, so you may go. Oh yes, let me give you absolution..."

He says the Latin prayers of absolution, then says, "And for your penance, figure out the man here, in this house, whom you like the least."

"Okay."

"And say a rosary for him."

"Yes, Father. Father?"

"Yes?"

"What if there's more than one? One man I don't like, I mean? Or three, or maybe four..."

"Include all of them in your rosary."

"Thank you, Father."

As I leave I still feel guilty, especially because he knew it was me.

CHAPTER EIGHT

The Clock is Ticking...

"There are only two ways to live your life...One, as though nothing is a miracle.The other is, as though everything is a miracle."

Albert Einstein

As the days wear on and the countdown to the long retreat, or *The Spiritual Exercises*, as it is officially called, gets shorter, I wonder if I am the only one fearful of this looming month of reckoning. Okay, I know I'm not the only one worried about it, but I still wonder if I am more worried about it than the other guys. But then I look at someone like Alex Dubchek, and I figure if he can get through it, I can. He's an incredible guy, really. He's so funny at rec sometimes, I'll bet he could be a comedian on the tonight show with Johnny Carson. And he plays the piano like Beethoven, practically. And you never know when he will suddenly take on a role like Robin Hood or John Wayne, reciting a line from a film, like, "Well, there are some things a man just can't run away from," or "That'll be the day," or something like that. And everybody assumes he's the one who farts out loud during study time when we are all in our rooms with the doors open, even though it is impossible to pinpoint the source of the echoing sound in the corridor. I call him the "flatulent friar," and he laughs with a red face, but he doesn't deny it.

This retreat looming in our future is the antithesis of almost every instinct of the human animal. Still, a part of me is very curious to get on with it, since it was an important aspect of The Miracle.

***

One morning, we have a visit from two psychologists, who administer a series of written tests. The tests take hours, with hundreds of questions, and some of them are kind of funny, like, "My bowel movements are often black and tarry. True or False?" Or, "I often feel like I have a band around my head. True or False?"

Then, the psychologists spend a couple of days doing individual interviews with each one of us, and Dubchek gets the idea to wear a cloth band around his head when he goes in for his interview. Afterwards he tells us that they didn't laugh, in fact they did not even act as if they noticed it! And so he just took it off and tried to answer the questions as straight as possible. I guess some Psychologists just don't have a good sense of humor.

Fr. McKittrick says that these tests will be administered again in two years. I guess The Order is doing this to see whether there might be any changes in us as we progress in our formation.

***

On an evening just a few days before the retreat begins, Andy, Dubchek and I visit the Padre once more.

"Quo vadis," says Andy, "is from the Gospel of John, when Jesus gives His discourse at the Last Supper. He tells them all that He will soon be going away, and He says to them, '...yet none of you has asked Me, quo vadis? Where are you going?'"

"Good work. That is a one place to find it. There are other places as well. But tell me, where isa He going?" asks the Padre.

"Back to the Father? To Heaven?" says Andy.

"Yes," says the Padre, "He's a goin' back to the Father. And where *is a* the Father? Where *is a* God?" asks the Padre, raising his eyebrows as he seems to stare right into my soul. "In a the sky? In a statue? No... in a *here!*" he says as he taps his finger on my chest. He has a way of speaking that, along with his Italian accent, makes his arguments very convincing.

"You see," he continues, "Our physical world is a corollary fora the spiritual realms. We need to use a parables and a such to explain spirituality better."

He turns and looks around the room for a moment.

"You wanna know what sin is?" he says as he picks up a pen from a small table by his side, holds it out for all to see, and lets it fall to the floor with a clatter. "*Gravity!* You wanna float up to Heaven, what pulls a you down? *Gravity!* Empty your pockets! Get rid of your possessions! Lighten your load, so you can *fly* when a the timecomes!

"Thats a how you get to Heaven, you learn to fly, like a Superman. You read a the comic books? No? Yes? Clark Kent? You wanna know the ultimate Superman? Jesus. He flew away like a Superman, on Ascension Thursday. He conquered gravity. Completely. Forever.

"Holiness," he continues, "is like a invisible balloon floating just above us, attached to our soul by a string, tugging us a gently upward, toward our destiny. Pray, fast, do good works, and the balloon inflates, has a greater upward pull. Commit a sin, and '*Pop!*' The balloon breaks, the gravity is back, you fall on a your face. You have to pick yourself up, go to confession and start over."

"Sort of like the greasy chute?" says Alex as he picks up the Padre's pen from the floor and returns it to his table.

"The greasy chute," says the Padre with a nod, as if he has heard of it.

"Padre," I ask him then, "do you believe in miracles?"

"Miracles, yes! All a the time there are miracles happening all around us, but we seldom even notice them. If the stars came out only once every hundred years, we would all a rush to see, and we would recognize the miracle. But it happens so often, who bothers to look up?

"We are like a dog in a library when it comes to knowing God," he continues. "What does a dog know about all a the knowledge and stories and worlds of insight that books can a give us? The same is true about us trying to understand a God. We do not even know the language, let alone the vocabulary, or how to read all a the signs! When a medical miracle occurs, the scientist or the doctor tries to explain it, but he only knows a what he knows. When a tumor disappears, the doctor has a to fumble for a label, so he calls it 'spontaneous remission.' Not a very impressive term for a miracle!"

***

Andy, Dubchek and I are on a walk the afternoon before the retreat begins. Dubchek is wearing a cap with a feather in it, sort of like a Robin Hood hat, that he found in the shoe room. As usual, he transforms his speech to accommodate his garb.

"Rupert," he says to me, "dost *thou* believe in miracles?" Oh yeah, he has decided to call me his 'second-cousin Rupert,' and sometimes I return the favor by occasionally calling him 'Bowzo,' since that is one of his favorite words.

"I used to," I answer. "I even thought I saw one."

"Explain thyself further, good sir," he replies.

"It happened when I was in the eighth grade. At the time, my older brother was a real assho... uh, character."

"A buttock, forsooth," says Alex.

"Buttock?"

"The closest thing to what you were referring, my good man."

We all laugh. "Okay," I say, "a buttock he was then, and a bully," I continue. "Like the time he gave me a preparatory lesson for high school. 'Disciplinary Conditioning,' he called it. He and Will, my other older brother, held me down on the floor and gave me some swats with an old golf stick."

"A true ne'er-do-well," laughs Dubchek with a foppish frown, "one whose company I would surely avoid."

"And he was almost never on speaking terms with my Dad," I continue. "They had some nasty fights. And he was always getting grounded, or suspended from school, or both. He had like the all-time record for swats from Fr. Doyle in high school. But my Mom never gave up on him. She kept praying, and making novenas, until one day in his senior year something incredible happened."

"Don't tell me," says Dubchek, "let me guess. He decided to enter the novitiate."

"How did you know?" I ask.

"Everybody knows you had a brother in the Order," he shrugs.

"I guess it's not exactly a secret. Anyway, when we came up here to visit him after his Long Retreat, he was a different person. He and my Dad actually went for a walk together, and I sort of tagged along behind them, and I couldn't believe what I was hearing. They talked about a whole bunch of things they had never talked about before, like two adults, two men. That had never happened before. It was..." Suddenly I've got this huge lump in my throat.

"...A miracle," says Andy quietly.

"You call that a miracle?" says Dubchek, with a serious tone all of a sudden.

"If you had seen the way they were before..." I manage to say, "you have no idea..."

"It sounds like a miracle to me," says Andy, "a miracle of faith, a healing of souls."

We pass an abandoned farmhouse, with all the windows broken out and trees and bushes cluttering where the yard once was. "But Darryl's dead now," I continue. "You've probably seen his grave already, out by the Jesus statue. It was a car accident. I was driving. Nobody else even got hurt, Just Darryl. I had a pretty rough time with it — really got pissed off at God. It was so senseless. I'd scream at God for awhile, and then I'd wait for

Him to answer me. I guess you could say I'm still waiting."

We approach a rickety old windmill tower, from a farm long abandoned. Andy walks right up to the bottom of the tower and raises his gaze skyward. "So you've wrestled," he says as he grasps a shoulder-high rung of the ladder that leads up the side of the tower, and lifts a foot to the rung closest to the ground. "The Padre says no one can really begin to know God without a wrestling match. Do you know what the word, 'Israel,' means?"

Alex and I shake our heads as Andy ascends the first rung of the tower. "Go back to your rooms, look it up. That's what he had me do," he says as he takes another step upward.

"You're not going to *climb* that thing," I say.

Ignoring me, he ascends another step.

"Andy?" says Dubchek, "You don't have to go any higher, we know you can do it!"

He continues to climb upward.

"Andy, that thing is falling apart," I yell, "you're gonna get killed!"

"It's rock-solid," Andy says, "I'll be fine."

"Andy," yells Dubchek, "you're making us nervous!"

"What are you afraid of?" He says as he continues upward, "this is perfectly safe. Join me if you like!"

Now Dubchek is reaching for the ladder.

"Alex, no!" I shout.

Alex Dubchek begins to climb, following Andy as he continues upward, at least twenty feet high by now, ascending in brisk fashion.

"Wow!" shouts Andy.

"What can you see?" asks Dubchek, six feet off the ground but still climbing.

The house, the lake, the whole countryside!" Andy shouts from above.

"You guys are nuts, you know that?" I yell angrily as I approach the tower. I reach for a rung of the ladder and grab ahold of it with both hands. I climb a couple of rungs and then stop to look up; Andy is practically as high as he can go, and Dubchek is about fifteen feet up now. There is a weatherworn, cockeyed wooden platform at the top, and Andy is testing it. It is so loose that he can move it up and down with his hand.

"Okay guys, we might as well go down," I say from my lowly perch, four feet off the ground, "this is high enough for me." I start to descend. Then I look up and I can't believe my eyes — Andy is climbing onto the wobbly platform!

"Andy, you're *insane!*" I yell. He climbs onto it and begins seesawing with his feet on the thing, while he holds onto the pointed top of the tower with both hands. After a moment, he lets go the top of the tower and extends his arms outward, balancing on the teetering platform like a circus acrobat!

"*Yee-hah!*" he yells, "this is fabulous!"

Dubchek starts to laugh like a hyena and howls, "Forsooth, Andy, surely thou art a madman!" Then he lets out an elephant call, letting go the tower with one hand so he can extend his arm like a trunk, "phhre-hehehehhhhdddt!" It echoes across the countryside.

I just shake my head and look down, muttering Hail Marys as I lower myself back to the ground, not even wanting to see what Andy will try next.

Eventually Andy and Dubchek descend. "I shall remember this day for many a fortnight to come," says Bowzo.

As we walk back to the house Andy continues to talk about the terrific view he had from up there, while I turn and look back at the old tower, shaking my head and thanking God that Andy is still in one piece.

"In the silence of the
heart God speaks.
If you face God in
prayer and
silence, God will
speak to you..."

St. Teresa of Calcutta

CHAPTER NINE

A Month of Introspection

"In the attitude of silence the soul finds the path in a clearer light..."

Mahatma Gandhi

I t's 8:32 P.M., and we're all seated in the classroom, waiting for the first "point session" of Long Retreat. We have just finished our very last rec until the first break day, which will be about ten days from now. As we silently sit in our respective places and await Fr. McKittrick's arrival, I am keenly recalling an incident that just occurred in the rec room five minutes ago. We were all chatting away, and some of the guys were saying corny good-byes to each other as if they were leaving on a long trip or something, when all of a sudden somebody started passing this polaroid snapshot around. It landed in my lap and I picked it up and saw that it was the photo that Clark displayed in the bar that night of him sitting with a girl on his lap in the back seat of a car. About a second after I picked up the photo, Clark appeared in front of me, grabbed the picture out of my hand and stomped away. Right after that the bell rang, and as we headed out of the rec room, a grinning Dubchek pointed down to the wastebasket by the door. I looked down and saw that the only contents of the wastebasket were fragments of the photo of Clark and girlfriend, torn to pieces.

Now, seated in the classroom in silence, we all begin to hear the faint sound of footsteps from far down the corridor, gradually increasing in amplitude. When one is in a regulated environment such as this, where many of the activities of each day are repeated in the same locales, day after day, one can eventually memorize the oft-repeated nuances of the environment and arrive at conclusions.

Tonight, when we hear these footsteps, we all know that the gait and the shuffle and the swishing sounds of the cassock are combining in such a way that the rhythms of the sounds, along with their unique fluctuations and modulations, can only be those of Fr. McKittrick's gait. And sure enough, folder in hand, the man now enters the classroom, walks to the lectern and kneels down on the kneeler that is positioned beside it. He leads us in the sign of the cross and then says, "Heavenly Father, please give us the help and the strength we need to open our hearts to your grace."

We all seat ourselves, and Fr. McKittrick begins the retreat points. As he talks, I listen to his calm, intelligent words with one part of my brain, but with another part I simultaneously begin to think about other things, the things I believe in or want to believe in, in rapid succession as thoughts go, much faster than a man can talk.

For instance, I really like the idea of the Resurrection. I love the idea that Jesus rose from the dead, and that He had powers such that He was able to enter rooms when the doors were locked and the windows shuttered, and yet had a physical, tangible body, and requested and ate food. These ideas correspond well with my fantastic thoughts and ideas, in some ways even resembling futuristic science fiction stories. The nuns back in Christ King School reinforced these ideas when they told us that

Jesus, ever since His Resurrection almost 2,000 years ago, has a *glorified* body; Perfect, Invincible, Immortal, Eternal.

I also love to ponder the idea that everybody else who chooses eternal life, hopefully every man, woman and child who dies with repentance and goes to Heaven, will some day rise again and also have a "glorified" body for the rest of eternity. I'm not sure exactly what the term "glorified" means, because it is beyond human nature and intellect, and so our words are inadequate. But in my own mind itmeans something like, "really enhanced," or "definitely superior," or maybe, like when we talk of a glass being half-empty or half-full, "glorified" means "beyond full," or "overflowing." Or maybe even "perfect." The word "perfectus" in Latin means, after all, "finished." We are not perfect until we get to Heaven; we are therefore not "finished" until we get to Heaven; here on earth we are still "works-in-progress."

All this is so much better than a fairy tale, and I want to believe it all so badly, even though it seems too good to be true. My problem is that most of the time I'm about ten percent idealist and ninety percent skeptic.

Still, sometimes I've had feelings or dreams that were so special and deep that they were almost glorified, in a way. Like I can sometimes imagine a future, "glorified" earth as if it actually existed right now in some other parallel dimension or universe or whatever, and every once in awhile in my dreams I've been allowed to cross over the vale, so to speak, for a brief glimpse of it. I only wish I could do a better job of recalling the incredible feelings I had in those dreams.

And now I remember the time I drove out to our old house this past summer, just weeks after Darryl died. We had lived in the house until I was five years old, and Darryl was nine, after which we moved a few miles away, to Wauwatosa. But after the move, every now and then on a Sunday afternoon, our parents would take us for a drive out there, just for the fun of it.

But we had not done that for years, until I drove out there alone this past Summer. And although I'm usually a very reserved person, I had to get out of the car and just walk into the yard and explore it, in broad daylight. The people living there probably thought I looked suspicious, and the man of the house came out with a nasty frown on his face until I told him who I was. He and his wife actually remembered me then, from back when they bought the house from my parents thirteen years ago, when I was only five years old. And then, when I told them about Darryl, they were so sad to hear about his death that they were really nice to me after that, letting me wander all over the place. And even though all the trees were so much bigger, and the house had been painted a different color, my mind was flooded with memories of perfect days spent playing with my brothers and sister in a sandbox that was no longer there, or watching the butterflies and bumblebees hovering around the hollyhocks that still bordered the east side of the house.

A little girl named Nancy Drummond with blonde hair and brown eyes lived next door back then, and she was about my age, and she and I would play in the sandbox while the wind whispered through the poplar trees that bordered the fence near the railroad tracks. One morning, as we engineered important roads and pathways for our toy cars and trucks in the sandbox, I told her that I was going to marry her when I was old enough. I did not ask her, I simply told her. And she just said, "Okay."

And when a train passed by on the tracks behind the house back in those days, it was usually a puffing, billowing steam engine, chugging along, bound to or from some distant part of the country. Old 349, with her unique bell tone, was our favorite, and we could recognize her from her bell long before we heard her chugging sound intensify as she drew near and passed our house. But then, in the last year before we moved, when the new, modern, diesel-powered trains began cruising by, we were suddenly so enamored and excited about the beautiful, streamlined shapes of the sleek, powerful engines, that we quickly forgot about old, chugging 349 and her passing era. Suddenly now, the big, orange diesel-powered Hiawatha was the train to see. There was no bell, but a horn that signaled the approaching train. "Here comes the Hiawatha," we would shout, and we would run to the back fence to wave at the engineer as he drove the elegant, shiny engine roaring past our neighborhood.

Belief in God was as easy as breathing back when I was five. And lately, every now and then, for just a brief moment, this present-day, older, more skeptical, heartbroken "me" is able to melt away for a few moments, and I really feel that something extra, something very pure and deep, is seeping up through those memories, something that I should try to hold onto and keep in some way...

Father McKittrick begins his points with a reading from the Gospel of John where Jesus meets the Samaritan woman at the well, John 4, 1-42. When Jesus asks the woman to give Him water, she is puzzled and asks Him where He is from, and then she reminds Him that Jews should not be talking to Samaritans. Then He brings up some things about her past life, including her five ex-husbands and her present live-in arrangement with a male companion, and she is amazed, and she runs back to the town to tell everyone that she has met a prophet.

She was open to Jesus, and He changed her life, and we should open ourselves up to Jesus as well during this time of retreat.

"*The Spiritual Exercises of St. Ignatius*" is the official title of this thirty-day retreat. St. Ignatius of Loyola was actually the founder of another religious order, called The Society of Jesus, or *The Jesuits*. But many other religious orders of men and women, including our own, use his "Exercises" as the basis for their retreats.

***

The Two Standards

As we get deeper into the Spiritual Exercises, we learn that there are two opposing models of life in this world, or Two Standards. Each is, in a very real sense, ruled by a spirit. One of the most important and challenging tasks we have in life is figuring out which of these two spirits is telling us what, and then choosing the best course of action. St. Ignatius of Loyola called this task, or discipline, The Discernment of Spirits.

Like many saints, Ignatius was not exactly born holy. He did not have any great desire to serve God, in his early years. He started out life in a wealthy family, in the Basque region of Spain, and grew into an attractive, albeit egocentric, young man. As a youth he was a page in the court of Queen Isabella of Spain. She, of course, was the one who with her husband King Ferdinand had, in 1492, commissioned an Italian sailor named Christopher Columbus with three ships to go on a voyage of discovery that changed the world forever.

Ignatius became a soldier, the closest thing to an athletic hero or a movie star that they had in those days. He relished bragging about his military exploits to the honorable ladies of the day. Then, during the Battle of Pamplona in 1521, Ignatius suffered a severe leg fracture from a cannon-

ball. After some months of convalescence, he noticed that his leg was not healing properly and it appeared unattractive in the tights that men wore in those times. The doctors told him that the only way to fix it was to re-break it. This was not exactly pleasant news, with no anesthesia back in those days. But he was courageous enough, and vain enough, to choose it.

During his long recuperation, Ignatius was bedridden and bored. He asked his nurses for some reading material to pass the time, but all they could find was a book on the lives of the saints, which he quickly refused. But after more months of boredom, Ignatius finally gave in and started reading about the saints.

It did not take him long to realize that, even with his courageous battlefield exploits, he had nothing on the Saints of the Church. When he tried to compare his bold deeds to theirs, they beat him hands-down. They were nobler in every way, incredibly brave, courageous and loyal to God, even unto torture and death by execution.

And what Ignatius also began to notice during those long months of rehabilitation was that, whenever he meditated on the lives of these saints and martyrs, he felt uplifted and energized afterwards. Eventually, after a lot of thoughtful prayer and meditation, he attributed these feelings of "consolation" to the Holy Spirit.

On the other hand, whenever he regressed to fantasies about impressing the ladies in the Royal Court, he felt vain and egocentric, and he attributed those feelings to The Enemy, Satan.

Later on, he used these early experiences as a basis on which to build and formulate the process which he would call "The Discernment of Spirits."

The easiest way for me to personally grasp this "Discernment of Spirits" concept right now is to imagine what I call the "comic strip" version of it, where the Good Standard is represented by a little angel that sits on my right shoulder. This angel represents the Holy Spirit, there to guide me and tell me the right choices to make. The other standard is represented by a horned, bat-winged imp who sits on my other shoulder. This demon represents the Enemy, and tries to tempt me with the choices that are more exciting and self-fulfilling and "fun." The two spirits offer contradictory approaches to life, and the Enemy's suggestions always seem to be the easier, more convenient, "sexier" approaches to happiness. But is it really happiness? Or just a feeling of contentment that hides something much darker? It's like the Dr. Jekyll and Mr. Hyde story of Robert Louis Stevenson. Maybe everyone has two sides to him, like Jekyll and Hyde, the two personalities, one good and one evil, of a single person.

During meditation I try to figure out how these spirits show up in my life. On the one hand, I know I have this noble, "nice guy" side, where I try to do the right thing with my life and live for other people. But I also have this material, worldly, selfish side where I want to goof off and just live my life for me, do whatever I want and not worry or care about any lofty goals. I call this my "Malibu" side.

So as this retreat moves on, I am gradually learning that my goal in life should be to feed and nurture my noble, or "Jekyll" side, so that it can grow larger, and to starve and shrink my Malibu, or "Hyde" side, into oblivion, as if it was a cancerous tumor on my soul.

***

We are over a week into the retreat and I am doing okay. Funny thing though, whenever Father McKittrick says something new and interesting during our retreat points, my mind starts drifting back to the Padre, and I catch myself wondering whether he would agree with it, or put a new twist on it, or whatever.

This morning Fr. McKittrick repeated something that I've heard him say before. "Man," he said, "has an *almost infinite* capacity for change!" He goes on to say that we have the ability to choose Eternal Life, by living like an adopted Son of God, or eternal strife, by giving into our selfish nature, and winding up in the flaming cesspool of Hell. He looks at each one of us, one at a time, before he continues: "You can accomplish almost anything if you pray and work at it. *Pray as if everything depended upon God, and act as if everything depended upon you!*"

***

During this Long Retreat, we are required to make a General Confession. This is a confession wherein you confess all the sins you can remember from your past life. Granted, we have supposedly already confessed the sins of our past life in previous confessions. Or at least most of them. If we forgot any, they are still forgiven with the broad sweep of Divine Mercy that is the miracle of Absolution. But for some reason, Fr. McKittrick says that a general confession can help us to feel a lot better about ourselves, and to feel like we are really starting anew, with a "clean slate," as it were.

When I go to Fr. McKittrick for my general confession, I try to recall all the great sins of my eighteen-year-old life, including sins of pride and anger against my brothers and sister, sins against friends and associates in school, sins against all my peers during fights and disagreements and other altercations, sexual sins of impure thoughts and words, sins of masturbation, and so forth.

Fr. McKittrick is amazingly kind and forgiving when he thanks me for my openness and gives me absolution. "My Child," he says, "You know Our Lord loves you beyond measure, and He is completely forgiving because of your honesty and your desire to serve Him. Go in Peace."

Even though he knows it was me, I don't care; when I leave his room I almost feel like I am walking on air. Suddenly, I feel that this is where I should be right now; this is my place. For the first time in years, I feel really happy. While this incredible feeling does not last forever, it lasts for a little while. Even days later, it still lingers. And because of this experience, I can truly feel better about being here.

CHAPTER TEN

Whips and Chains

"In this day and age," Fr. McKittrick says one morning during the retreat, "penance is often considered to be an antiquated practice from a bygone era. And while our rules do not require us to perform substantial acts of hardship and denial, we must not entirely rule out works of atonement and expiation."

I sit up, wondering where this is going.

"...Therefore, on Mondays and Wednesdays, we ask that you wear the *chain* during meditation..."

I steal a look to my right; Clark's expression darkens.

"...And on Tuesdays and Fridays, we invite you to give yourselves fifteen strokes of the *discipline* before you retire."

I look to my left; Dubchek looks puzzled.

"We ask," he continues, "that you not discuss or mention these customs with your parents or family, or other externs. These practices should be done with a spirit of love and joyful commitment to Our Lord."

We actually have to go to Fr. McKittrick's office privately to receive our chain and our discipline. There we can, if we feel the need, discuss with him any concerns we might have about these unexpected "customs." After all, nobody warned us about this; during all of our many conversations with the second-year men during recreation, they never hinted at it. For some reason I personally do not have a real problem with it, and so I pick them up from Fr. McKittrick and take them to my room.

* * *

It's fifteen minutes before lights out, and we are all in our rooms, getting ready for bed. I pick up my discipline, a small braided whip with five thinner lashing strands, and examine it briefly. I cannot help but think of the people who manufacture these things. Are they lay people, or monks, or what? Do they test every one of them to see if they work all right? There's a part of me that thinks this is absolutely wacky, but there's that other part of me that concedes that I deserve more than a good whipping for all my transgressions. And after what Jesus went through to merit eternal salvation for all of us, I figure I can take a few little strokes of this.

I take off my T-shirt and pick up the whip. I try to imagine the scourging of Jesus, attempting to picture it like a scene from a movie. After a brief moment, I begin to lash myself. It really doesn't hurt, and it's not supposed to; it's not nearly as bad as when I stubbed my toe on the leg of my desk last night. I guess that I could make it hurt if I really tried, but that is not the point. It is supposed to be a reminder, and that's all.

After fifteen strokes I put the discipline down, put on my pajamas and crawl into bed. After a few moments, my ears become attuned to a faint, repetitive sound coming from the corridor. I creep out of bed and move toward my door, which is slightly ajar, and I open it wider. The corridor is pretty dark, save for the dim floor-level night lights and the room light coming from a couple of transoms, since it is about two minutes until lights-out time. The sound, a repetitive, swishing noise, seems to be coming from one of the lit rooms. I move out into the corridor, and now I realize that the sound is that of someone else using the discipline. But the strokes seem to be harsher than mine were, and greater in number. "Thirty-four, thirty-five, thirty-six..." I count silently, and that is only since I entered the corridor. I figure out that the sounds are coming from Andy's room. Andy, like Leonard, evidently has a side to him that I do not know. After another moment or so of listening to his discipline strokes, I turn around and head back into my room and crawl into bed. Eventually, the noises cease.

***

It's Wednesday morning, and we're meditating in the classroom as usual, and I am very uncomfortable. But I guess everyone else is in the same boat, because we are all wearing our chains this morning. I reach down and pull on mine lightly to rearrange it, because one of the prongs is really poking into my left love-handle in a painful manner. It doesn't take me long to figure out how to move, and how not to move, in order to minimize its effects. I try to concentrate on my meditation points, but it is not an easy thing to do. And now, as a further distraction, I get the sudden realization that, hey, I actually *have* love-handles again! After I lost my appetite they pretty much disappeared, but now, since I'm eating better, they're coming back... and now I regress further, and recall a trip to the beach back in high school, and Sheila Murphy was there, and she was the one who first called them love handles...

"Hey!" I say to myself then, "you're supposed to be *praying*, Moriarty!"

The bell rings, and we all disappear very quickly from the classroom in order to return to our rooms and remove our chain (*would anyone want to wear it even a second longer than what the Holy Rule asks of us?*) before we return to the chapel for Mass.

As Mass begins I feel a definite consolation because I am no longer wearing the chain. It is a bit like finishing a long, grueling test, or a five-mile run or something, where it feels so good when you stop. I am sitting in a pew just behind Andy, and now my consolation gives way to befuddlement, because I notice a slight bulge beneath his cassock, exactly where the chain would be if he were still wearing it.

CHAPTER ELEVEN

Break Day

I t is 10:02 A.M., and I am heading out the shoe room door, football in hand, as fast as my undeveloped concept of religious decorum might allow me. I look at the sky and it is a rich blue — a Malibu day, I'd say.

"Praise the Lord, Wally," says Dubchek as he comes through the door right after me, "Glad to see you're still around!"

"Amen," I say as I turn to see Clark coming through the door.

"Clark,"says Dubchek, *"you're still here!"*

"I got one foot out the door," Clark says in his deadpan style, "and the other one on a banana peel!"

"Praise the Lord," shouts Andy as he exits the door. "Fantastic day, fantastic! Wally, hit me," He shouts as he runs out into the sunshine.

I throw the football hard, but not too hard for him to catch up to it and scoop it out of the air with ease and trot back to us. "Let's pick some sides, guys," he says as he lobs the ball back to me.

"First," says Clark, "we've got to discuss something."

"Okay," says Andy with a carefree grin.

"We've been cooped up for ten days of retreat," says Clark, "and all you want to do is play football? I'm ready to pack my bags, for chrissake!"

Andy loses his grin, spins the ball vertically into the air and catches it.

"Do you guys actually plan to live the rest of your lives like this?" Clark continues as more men, including Leonard, exit the door and join the group.

"Clark," says Andy, "you know it's not for the rest of your life. We're only going to live like this for two years until vows, and after that, things start to get easier. Two years after vows we move on, and by the time we're Fathers, this period will be a distant memory." He spins the ball in front of his face for a moment before he asks, "So what would you rather do? College, or the army?"

"I don't know yet. Let me ask you, Gallagher, do you ever have even the slightest desire to leave this place?"

Andy pauses ever so briefly before he says, "Not yet," and continues to spin the ball.

"The guy ain't human," says Clark as he looks at Dubchek, then me, then back to Andy.

"Clark," says Andy, "what's eating you?"

"Getting up at five every morning, seven days a week. Sacred Silence. Asking permission for everything. No radio, no television, no newspaper. The common room...the common *everything*. Com-mu- *nism*, that's what this is!"

"You've had a year of college, right?" says Andy as he passes me the ball. "If you were there right now, you wouldn't have much time for conversation before morning classes. And if you were in the army in boot camp, you might have to get up at five A.M. or earlier, and you probably wouldn't *want* to talk to most of the guys in your barracks at that hour, anyway. And there wouldn't be much time for news or television, either."

"Crockin' right," says Dubchek as I toss the ball to him. Leonard, right behind him, chuckles in agreement. Dubchek catches the ball and throws it to Clark, who fumbles it. It bobbles over to Andy, who picks it up.

"Give it a few more months," says Andy as he begins to walk toward the playing field. "Think of it as Basic Training. Now let's pick some teams."

"Whose side are *you* on, Moriarty?" Clark says, looking at me. "Is the food still agreeing with you?"

"The food is fine," I say quietly. And I'm wondering, what's this about *sides*? His negative manner is getting on my nerves. Why can't he drop it? If he's having problems he's supposed to discuss them with Father McKittrick, not us guys.

Andy turns around and walks back toward us, still carrying the football, spinning it in the air and catching it. "Do any of you guys know anything about the Trappists?" he says.

"Yeah," says Dubchek, "they're really strict, right?"

"Read Thomas Merton's '*The Seven Storey Mountain*,'" says Andy. "They spend their lives in long retreat. No rec, ever. At least not like we know it. They talk in sign language when they have to communicate..." As he continues, I notice that he is wearing a short sweatshirt that hangs loosely around his waist. At times I can see a patch of bare skin, and there are scratch marks there that are probably from his chain. He must really fasten it tight, because I don't have marks like that.

"...They sleep on boards. They don't eat meat or fish or eggs. But on Easter they can have one egg if they wish. When they die, they're buried in their cowl. They don't even get a coffin."

"So what's your point?" asks Clark.

"Compared to the Trappists, this novitiate is a walk in the park," says Andy.

"I'd kinda like a coffin, when I go," mumbles Dubchek.

"But is this reality?" asks Clark.

"What is reality to you?" asks Andy.

"Just a regular life," says Clark, "A wife, a house, a job..."

"Why are you here then?"

"I don't know. I just didn't think it was going to be so *austere*."

"Do we get coffins?" asks Dubchek of no one in particular.

Leonard laughs again, and some others join him.

"I have to admit," I tell the group, "it's a weird thing not to have some cash in my pocket. Instead, there's a rosary, and an empty wallet with nothing but my draft card in it."

"And *I* have to admit," says Dubchek, "I kind of liked the freedom to shop, now and then..."

"Where did you shop," I ask him, "grocery stores?" Everyone laughs, including Dubchek, and of course Leonard.

"Now guys," says Andy, "does anyone want to play some football? Wally, you and I can be captains. Clark, you're my first pick."

I pick another guy, then Andy chooses Leonard for his second pick. Leonard goes warily over to his team, and I can tell this is something new for him.

We play a good, hard game of touch football. Andy's side eventually wins, due in part to Leonard's touchdown, even though he can hardly run at all. Andy, Stanford-caliber quarterback though he might be, shoved the ball into Leonard's hands when they were really close to the end zone and, since my men were all covering other receivers, Leonard managed to get across unscathed.

"That was my first touchdown, ever!" Leonard proclaims between bursts of crazy, almost maniacal laughter.

* * *

The Spiritual Exercises continue. Everybody seems to hang in there pretty well, including Clark. God seems to bless us, during the two remaining break days, with good weather and other consolations during this spiritual marathon.

As we progress in the exercises, we first-year men continue to grow in our admiration of Fr. McKittrick. As he gives us points and insights for our four daily meditations in the classroom, he exhibits an ambience of holiness and wisdom. When he leads us down spiritual paths, he manages to make his stories inspiring and at the same time sensible. "The saints who performed great penances," he says, "are to be admired but not imitated. Do not do anything to excess; find the middle path and follow it, down the center of the road."

In spite of his common-sense approach to spiritual growth, it is hard for many of us to consider Fr. McKittrick an equal to the rest of us. For example, one of the guys, Pete Torre, told us at the second break day that, while he was relieving himself in the castle one morning, Fr. McKittrick came through the door, walked up to a urinal just two down from where he was, and proceeded to use it. Torre says that he felt shocked to see Fr. McKittrick actually using the same common urinals as the rest of us. But then immediately after, it bothered Torre even more to think that he had had such a reaction in the first place.

CHAPTER TWELVE

Praise the Lord!

It is breakfast time, October 30th, and as soon as everybody is seated, Father Rector says, "Tu autem Domine miserere nobis!"

"Deo Gratias!" everybody shouts in unison, and we all start congratulating each other for completing the long retreat.

"Praise the Lord, Wally," says Andy, across the table from me.

"Amen," I respond, "guess we made it, huh?"

"So far so good," he says. "You doing all right?"

"Yeah, for the most part, I think."

***

"Let me guess," Andy says later that morning as we walk along the rosary path during the rare morning rec period, "You've been thinking about your brother again."

"How did you know?"

"Just a likely guess."

"I still have this guilt," I say as we walk past the duck pond, where a great blue heron is stalking one of the last frogs of the season.

"I remember when, soon after I broke my arm, Darryl wrote me a letter and said, 'Non in solo football vivit homo,' 'not in football alone does man live.' I had sort of been hoping to get one or two football scholarship offers, you know? Especially to a west coast school, near Malibu. But then I thought of entering the novitiate, too, although that was sort of a backup plan, if all else failed..."

"So you were torn between alternative destinies," finishes Andy as we approach the little cemetery beneath the Jesus statue.

"Yeah, I guess so," I concede.

"Yeah, but Malibu? What'd you want to do, just be a beach bum or something?" Andy asks with concern. "When did you finally decide to come here?"

"I *finally* decided in January, during our senior retreat. After the football stuff was no longer possible."

"So you felt positive about it then? The novitiate, I mean."

"Yeah, right up through graduation in May. Then, Darryl came home to visit us for a couple of days on his way to St. Louis. When his visit was finished, I offered to drive him to the train station. I still had the cast on, because they had to re-break and reset the arm, but I could drive pretty well anyway, or so I thought. We were cruising along, and it was a sunny, beautiful summer morning, and I was asking him what he was going to be studying, and he never got to answer me. Because right then a car crossed the center line, and even though I swerved to avoid him, he collided with Darryl's side of the car. Gave him acute head trauma, skull fracture, brain damage... he died three days later."

We're standing at his grave now.

"So," says Andy, "you think *you* caused this accident? You were in the proper lane, and you said the other driver was drunk."

"Well yeah, but... maybe if I didn't have the cast on, I would have been able to steer clear of him enough to..."

"Wally, give yourself a break, for crock's sake! It wasn't your fault!"

***

The Padre peers out at Andy, Leonard and me from beneath bushy gray eyebrows at our next visit. "What's that on a your hand?" He asks Andy.

Andy holds up his arm and reveals the words, "Quo Vadis" written on the back of his left hand.

"Is that a new tattoo?" I joke.

"Nah, just ballpoint. But it's like my new slogan. Some day, maybe I'll have it permanently tattooed on my hand."

"So," the Padre says with a grin, "are you ready for a vows, after all these spiritual exercises?"

"I don't know," says Andy. "I feel like I'm ready for something."

"Ah yes," the Padre continues, "The Spiritual Exercises can a invigorate us! And as a you know, I always like a to compare spiritual concepts to our physical world, make analogies, you know? We all a know that in our world, we cannot excel at sports unless we work a very hard at it for a long time. Who," he continues, "could ever hope to win an Olympic gold medal by diving into a pool just a once, and swimming to a new world record? No, one must a dive into the pool thousands of times and swim laps for a thousands of hours, for years on end, to even hope to approach the record! Our spiritual side needs as a much practice and exercise as an athlete, if we are a to become courageous and a wise."

"Padre," I say then, "I had a good retreat, but on some days, I am still not sure of my vocation. Is that okay?"

"You never stay," he says, "for a the same reason you enter, you see. None of you has a been here for three months, yet." And now the Padre looks at me with a look of admiration, actually.

"You're a wrestler," he says. "Israel. You know what I am a talking about?"

"Kind of," I say as I turn to look at Andy, remembering what he said at the windmill tower.

"I looked it up, Padre," says Andy, "Israel: 'He who wrestles with God.' Jacob wrestled all night with an angel of God, and received the name 'Israel' thereafter."

"Good," says the Padre, "never forget it. Everyone wrestles with God in some way or another. Armageddon, you see, is a going on right now, in a sense. In each of our souls."

Then he looks at me and says, "What you need is a sign. Ask a for one." He says this with such assuredness that I catch myself sitting up straighter. "But don't expect it to happen immediately. And," he says, leaning forward, "Do not assume that you will a recognize it right away."

When we leave the Padre we return to our rooms for points. As I ponder what I should meditate on in the morning, I have to admit that, after our thirty-day retreat, I feel in some ways like a different person. It's like I have this new feeling about myself and my relationship with God and with the world. And I think that even if I left the novitiate — which I don't really feel like doing right now, but just in case I had to for some reason—I would relate to people in a new way. Like I would always be more respectful of my brothers and sister, and probably never get into an argument with them, because I have become a better person. I think I would feel the same way about my old friends, if I saw them again. And I know that I would be much more sensitive and respectful to girls, and how they think. There are even times when I almost manage to forget the guilt I feel about Darryl. Almost. And every day I can feel a little more confident that that guilt will gradually fade into the background, as time goes on. That's what Fr. McKittrick tells me, and I am coming to believe that he may be right.

The other guys seem to feel the same way that I do about themselves, because we talk about it at rec. Everyone is more charitable toward one another, and the foul language that a few of the new men used in the beginning has all but vanished. I remember how, when we visited Darryl soon after his long retreat, he and Dad took that walk together, and I can understand it much better now. I think that if everybody in the world made a long retreat, it would truly be a much different, and much better, world.

After points and examination of conscience I get into my pajamas and, just before I get into bed, I kneel down at my kneeler and ask for a sign.

* * *

Over and above the regular novice scholastics, we have some novice brothers here as well. The Order calls the brothers "coadjutors," which can be broadly translated as "assistants." They do a lot of the menial work around the House, including maintenance, repairs, tailoring, grounds-keeping, and so forth. They have to be "postulants," or "candidates," for six months before they can even begin their two-year term of novitiate, but we are still allowed to recreate with them, which is good, because they are cool. One of them, Brother Mueller, is from my high school class, and his conversation always abounds with unexpected delights. Like he will say, "today I had to install a new herper into one of the house cars, and it wasn't easy, because the old herper had a broken herper on the left side of its herper, so I had to make sure the new herper had a perfectly functioning herper on the left side of its herper before I replaced it. You understand what I'm saying?"

"Well, Slip, I'm not sure. What do you mean?"

Oh yeah, his nickname is Slip, because one day he disappeared from a tree planting detail for a couple of hours and no one knew where he was, so when he returned, his Brother Superior started calling him "Slippery." Turns out he actually wound up planting twice as many trees as everyone else on the detail, and he was commended for that. But back to the question I put to him. His answer:

"What do you mean, what do I mean?"

I can only respond, "What do you mean, what do I mean, what do you mean?"

"What do you mean, what do I mean, what do you mean, what do I mean?"

It could go on for as long as we wanted, until one of us gave up or slipped up.

One day Bowzo and I, his "second cousin Rupert," are on a walk with Slip and he shows us a sling he made out of rawhide and leather. It is the same kind of sling that David used to kill Goliath, and Slip can really whip a stone a long way with it.

He shows me and Bowzo how to make one, and later, while on a walk, we run into Harshley and Andy, and we proudly display our new ancient weapons to them. Then Harsh pulls his own sling out of his pocket, which he evidently made before any of us made ours, and he whips a stone into the trees so that we can hear it hiss through the air before snapping some branches in its path. He claims he killed a bird with it once, but there must have been some luck involved, because it is really hard to aim these things with any accuracy. I'm sure David must have had some Divine Assistance against Goliath. But accuracy aside, it just goes to show how reading Sacred Scripture can enrich one's walks through the woods.

"You are not a human
on a spiritual
journey. You are a
Spirit on a human
journey."

Pierre Teilhard de
Chardin, S.J.

CHAPTER THIRTEEN

The Glorified Kingdom

A ndy and I are trudging through a marshy area in rubber galoshes, examining dried rushes. "What do you think 'ecclesiam' means?" I ask him.

"The church?" he answers. "All Catholics?"

"Don't you think that still leaves a lot of people out?" I ask.

"I guess I'll leave that up to God, for the time being," he answers as he reaches for a reed. "Look, here's one."

I come over to look. There on the reed is the husk of a dragonfly nymph. It has a consistency similar to delicate, dried paper, sort of like a hornet's nest, and Andy proceeds to carefully remove it from the reed.

"Look, there are more of them over there," I say as I point to a nearby stand of rushes. We slosh on over and begin to remove more of the crumbly exoskeletons from the reeds and drop them into a paper bag.

***

\

Later in the afternoon, there is a sign on the bulletin board:

I will give points in the rec room tonight.

Andy Gallagher

Points from fellow novices are nothing new; Fr. McKittrick occasionally allows a second-year novice to give points for the following morning's meditation, if the novice is so inspired. What is unusual is that Andy is a *first*-year novice.

After the bell at 8:30 P.M., we wait silently in our chairs until Andy enters the room, carrying a folder and the paper bag from the swamp. He sits down in an empty chair facing everyone.

"Let's start with a prayer," he says, bowing his head. "Father God, please help us to understand Your Kingdom that is to come."

He smiles and continues, "I am going to try to tie together several different trains of thought tonight. You may have to perform some cerebral acrobatics in order to follow my points."

Then he takes the bag of insect husks and begins to pass it around, inviting everybody to take one. Some of the guys don't want to touch them at first, but most don't seem to mind.

"Kingdom..." says Andy with a pause, "...phylum...class...order... family...genus...species. If you took biology, you will recognize these groupings. And most of you probably also know that, biologically, we humans are all members of the same species, called 'Homo sapiens.'

"With that in mind, I have to say that I was struck by a quote from

A well-known scientist that I read before entering. He said, and I quote: *'It is not the strongest of the species that survives, nor the most intelligent that survives. It is the one that is most adaptable to change.'*

"Now," he says, "take a look at this little husk in your hand. A nymph," he continues, holding up one of the fragile exoskeletons, "lives for three or four years on the bottom of a pond before it crawls up out of the water, onto a reed, and dies. But then something incredible happens. Do you wonder why it's so light and hollow? Check out the big hole in its back. It bursts open right there, and a wet, wrinkled insect pushes out, unfurls its wings and tail, dries off, and... what kind of insect am I talking about?"

"A... dragonfly?" says Leonard.

"Yes," says Andy, "this underwater creature totally transforms itself into a winged dragonfly, and flies away."

I examine the nymph husk in my hand and it sort of resembles a more primitive insect from an ancient era, nothing at all like a dragonfly.

"If you are an entomologist, this raises a lot of questions," continues Andy, "including, 'Did the nymph evolve from some other form of insect that was unable to do this transforming act?' And, 'At what point in history did nymphs suddenly start transforming into dragonflies?' 'Is this an example of Darwin's 'natural selection' theory?'"

This, to me, is already insightful enough, and food for thought for several meditations. But Andy is not finished.

"Now I am going to attempt to bring in a whole new level of thought, here. According to biologists, we are all members of the 'Animal Kingdom,' as opposed to the 'Plant Kingdom.'

"If you have read Teilhard de Chardin, the Jesuit Paleontologist, you know how he tries to explain our universe, and our planet's evolution, in terms of 'spheres,' or 'degrees of consciousness.' He says that consciousness is somehow related to spirituality, and that the more our world evolves, the more conscious it becomes. And the more conscious our planet becomes, the closer it gets to God's Kingdom, which is the highest possible consciousness. While I was reading Chardin's 'The Phenomenon of Man,' I all of a sudden remembered something from scripture. Specifically, what Jesus said to Pilate the night before His Crucifixion."

He opens his bible and continues, "John 18, 33-38: I will just paraphrase it to emphasize the words that struck me the most: When Pilate asked Jesus, 'Are you the king of the Jews?'...Jesus answered him and said, '...My kingdom is not of this world.' I started to think about those words and tried to figure out what He meant, in terms of definitions, practical explanations, semantics, and so forth. To start with, what does 'Kingdom' really mean? In biology, a Kingdom is a major grouping of biological life-forms. Biologically, you and I belong to the same 'kingdom' as every monkey, rabbit, elephant, alligator, sparrow, snail, octopus, oyster, cockroach or mosquito on this planet. The only other biological Kingdom is the Plant Kingdom.

"Now, let's get metaphysical and jump to the spiritual realm. Spiritually, our souls are of a totally different nature. And these souls of ours are our truest, deepest selves. In other words, our souls are what is left after the death of our bodily 'husks,' so to speak. And we have all been invited to exchange this earthly 'Kingdom' for another one that is beyond imagining, a Kingdom that knows no sorrow or death, thanks to Our Lord's incredible act of salvation.

"Each of our souls is, in a sense, a *chrysalis of consciousness*," he says, turning the nymph husk over in his fingers. "We each have the ability to evolve until we can finally take off and fly away to our true destiny, which is Eternal Life in God's Kingdom of the very Highest Consciousness.

"According to some Evolutionists, the survivors of a species are those that are most adaptable to change. We, as humans, have an *almost infinite* capacity for change. We can, with God's help, change not just our spiritual species, but our genus, family, order, class, phylum, and ultimately our Kingdom, to the eternal Kingdom that, as Jesus told Pilate, is '*not of this world.*'

"Let's ask God to help us to better understand the miracle of our existence here and now, and our eventual spiritual metamorphosis into a perfect, glorified, eternal Kingdom, as we pray:

"Our Father, Who art in Heaven, hallowed be Thy name..." we all join in as he continues the Lord's prayer, "...Thy *Kingdom* come, Thy Will be done, on earth as it is in Heaven..."

As I meditate on his points the next morning, and for some mornings after that, I keep realizing more and more that Andy is just one of those guys who seems like he was made for this place and for this life; he appears to have a higher spiritual IQ than most of us first-year men.

∗∗∗

"Non-violence,
which is the quality
of the heart, cannot
come by an appeal
to the brain."

Mahatma Gandhi

CHAPTER FOURTEEN

A Tragic Day

I ascend the basement stairs to the bulletin board area on a Friday afternoon just after choir practice to see four of the guys standing around the bulletin board, whispering in English. This is unusual. They stop whispering and watch me as I draw closer to the board, and now I see a new typed message from Fr. McKittrick. It says:

SOME VERY BAD NEWS

President Kennedy was shot today while riding in a motorcade in Dallas and was rushed to a hospital. Mrs. Kennedy was with him and was not injured. Texas Governor Connally was also shot; no further information is available at this time.   Fr. McKittrick

I immediately enter the chapel and begin to pray for the President. After a few minutes I go back out to the bulletin board and see another note pinned beneath the first one. It says:

"John F. Kennedy is dead."

Later, at rec, Clark, Barry Edelfort, Alex and I, along with a few other guys, are exiting the shoe room for afternoon rec. We signed up to play a game of touch football. Andy was signed up but he does not show up. This is unusual.

"Guys," says Clark as we stand around outside the door, "I know it's uncharitable, but I'd like to take that s.o.b. who did it and put him on a rack. You know, the rack? As in the *Tower of London rack*? And stretch him until..."

"Clark," interrupts Alex, "I hate to admit it, but I am tempted to agree with you..."

"Guys," I butt-in, "where's Andy? The sides aren't even."

"I saw him in the chapel as I was coming out," says Alex. "He was still in his cassock."

"Maybe he'll show up," I say. "Let's start the game without him."

We try to start a game, but we can't get it together. Whenever someone throws me a pass I drop the ball or something. "Son-of-a *bitch!*" I yell after a fumble. "Sorry guys," I say immediately afterward.

When it's my turn at quarterback, I throw a long one to Edelfort and he drops it. "Shit!" he yells.

None of us is in the mood for football. We stop the game and just sit by the side of the field, talking about the President.

"So what's going to happen now?"

"The Vice President will take over."

"Johnson? What does he know?"

"We'll find out..."

After rec, when I enter the chapel for a visit, I see Andy, still in his cassock, kneeling up near the altar; he never changed into his rec clothes.

At dinner time during first grace, I notice Alex kneeling in the center aisle. When the communal prayer is over he says: "Reverend Fathers and beloved brethren, I accuse myself of using language unbecoming of a religious at rec today, for which fault holy obedience has imposed upon me the slight penance of kissing the feet of some of the members of the community." He then leans over and kisses my shoes and those of Andy, who is seated across from me. I am feeling pretty guilty, because I used worse language than Alex at rec today, but I did not even consider taking a culpa. So much for my post-Long-Retreat fervor, wherein I thought I was finished using such language.

***

Over the weekend we learn more details about the assassination, and then we hear that Lee Harvey Oswald, the apparent assassin, was himself shot and killed by someone. On Monday we are allowed to watch the President's funeral on television.

That night, after evening rec, Andy once again gives points in the rec room. He enters, sits down and says, "Brothers, I have a real difficulty to share with you tonight. I always assumed that forgiveness was something that I was capable of. But right now, I am having trouble with the idea that God wants me to love my enemies, and pray for them, and forgive them, even if that includes Lee Harvey Oswald. If any of you feel the way I do, let's continue to pray for one another, and for our country and our world, in the coming days."

He rises to leave, and one by one the other guys follow.

Except for me. I just sit and stare out the tall windows into the darkness for a long time, until the manuductor — the "head novice" —comes and turns out the lights. I wonder if he sees me, but whether he sees me or not, he just shuts off the lights and leaves. I sit there in the dark for a long time, staring out across the countryside to where a single light illuminates a distant barnyard.

* * *

The following night, Ken and Leonard and I visit the Padre again.

"Padre," I say, "is it always necessary for us to forgive? Like say, are we required to forgive Lee Harvey Oswald for killing the President?"

He pauses for a long moment, lost in thought.

"It is a good question," he finally says. "First, let us make sure we understand what forgiveness is and a what it is not. Forgiveness is a not saying that what someone has a done is in any way excusable. Forgiveness for a you and me is a letting go the terrible burden of anger and loss and injustice and even desire for vengeance that a weighs us down. Handing all a that over to God, you see. There is in everyone's a life a lot of a psychological baggage that accumulates over the years because of all of our sins, but also because of the *sins of those who wronged us*. To get to Heaven we must a lighten this load, get rid of this terrible ball and a chain around our ankles, this *gravity* of sin, as a much as possible. And understand that even if it is another's sin against us, it can a still weigh us down. It is a not an easy task, not an easy task..." as his voice trails off, he seems to be distracted, deep in thought.

***

On Saturday, five days after the President's funeral, I have my first visit from home. My parents and my younger brother and sister all show up; my older brother Will stayed home to watch the house and study (and maybe have a party, unbeknownst to Mom and Dad) because he is in his sophomore year of college.

It is a nice visit, and I have to admit that I am glad to see them. Any old sibling issues are forgotten, at least for now. It is a good time, and we sit and snack on cheese and sausage and crackers, chat, take pictures, and go for a walk around the grounds. And of course we visit Darryl's grave.

When we say our goodbyes, I feel pretty content, once again feeling like maybe I do sort of belong here, after all.

***

"When you realize how perfect everything is you will tilt your head back and laugh at the sky."

Gautama Buddha

CHAPTER FIFTEEN

Nightmares and Dunghills

I t is past midnight, and I wake up with a start. I think I heard a muffled noise, like someone shouting. Then I realize that I have to visit the castle—the men's room—so I get out of bed. The corridors of each floor are such that the castles are directly across the hall from the Novice Master's and Socius' rooms, Fr. McKittrick's on the first floor and The Sarge's on the second. My room is on the second floor, right next to The Sarge's room. He actually has a suite of rooms, and the office part of it is right on the other side of my wall. The bedroom part of his suite is on the other end, with one wall separating it from the room of a novice named Dennis Sarafini. As I walk quietly to the castle, I hear another muffled shout coming from The Sarge's room, like the one that woke me up. I enter the castle, do my business and return to my room, straining to hear any more noises. But there are none, and soon I drift off to sleep.

***

The following week there is a small, typed note on the bulletin board. It reads:

"Clark Upton has left the novitiate.
He asks that you remember him in your prayers."

Fr. McKittrick

Just like that, Clark is gone. No warnings, no blatant hints. He's about the tenth new guy who's left so far. It always shocks you a little, because you might have had a great conversation with him at rec last night, little knowing that he would be gone before breakfast, and your paths may never cross again. Still, most of us pretty much knew it was coming. With some guys it's hard to tell, but it wasn't with Clark.

Part of me envies him a little, because the grass always seems greener on the other side, and all of us sometimes yearn for the "reality" we left behind for this new and different world. And yet, something makes me want to stay in this place, which is not only a world of Truth, but also the realm of Ruperts and Bowzos and Slips with our herpers and our fortnights and greasy chutes, and all the other necessary "accouterments" that make this life and this place more bearable.

***

We are required, during our spiritual reading periods, to read some biographies of the founder of our order. We are also required to read a three-volume work entitled "The Practice of Perfection and Christian Virtues," written over three hundred years ago by a man named Alphonsus Rodriguez. We have to read these volumes not once, but twice. This Rodriguez guy writes about a number of ways we can attain spiritual wisdom and insights and perfection and everything, and he does it, shall we say, in a very sixteenth-century manner. And he includes some "true" stories about stuff that happened even hundreds of years before his own time. Like he will relate a story about a monk in a monastery back, say, eight hundred years ago in Europe somewhere, who was a kitchen chef, and, when a few peas fell on the floor during dinner preparation, he simply reached down and picked them up and ate them. This may not seem like a big deal, but it was in fact an incredible breach of obedience to the strict monastic rule, which says that a monk should eat only at the allotted mealtimes, and only when at table. His companions reminded him of this, declaring, "Thou hast committed a great transgression — thou must hie thyself to shrift (confession) forthwith!"

But the monk defiantly decreed, "No, I *will not* confess it!" Immediately, according to Rodriguez, the impenitent monk was stricken with a grave illness, and within hours he lay dying on his deathbed. But even then, despite the urgings of all his monastic brethren, he *still* refused to confess the eating of the peas at the wrong time, and so died in his sin. Because of this grave sin and his *refusal to repent*, according to Rodriguez, the monks could not give him a Christian burial, and could only throw his body on the dunghill, to rot there like a dead dog and be devoured by vultures.

Rodriguez has many tales like this in his volumes, and he repeatedly tells the reader about the importance of following every rule religiously, no matter how insignificant or bothersome some of them might seem. And he never fails to illustrate the grave consequences suffered by those who broke said rules.

Occasionally during Rules Class we tell Fr. McKittrick that it is hard to take some of these stories seriously, and he agrees with us, and he promises to appoint a committee of novices to decide what passages are worthy to keep, and what passages could be eliminated for future classes of novices.

And often, during our conversations at rec, if anyone admits to a little transgression that he might have committed, such as heading down to the shoe room a minute early before the rec bell rings, or some such equivalent impropriety, Dubchek will be quick to ask, "Art thou suddenly feeling a bit out of sorts? Is the devil about to pluck thee anon from our midst, for thy grave trespasses? 'Twill be the dungheap for sure if thou dost not repent... confess, or *get thee to the dungheap!*"

***

The next time we visit the Padre I have to ask him a question that has been on my mind for a while lately. I ask, "Padre, what about those people who, uh, who don't believe as we do?"

"How do you mean?"

"Okay, I mean, 'Salus extra ecclesiam non est.'"

"Ah, Cyprian," says the Padre, "and Augustine. Well now, what do you think?"

"I think... crock. I like to think that everyone should have a chance at salvation. Jews, Hindus, Muslims, Buddhists, Pagans, everybody. Even if they never heard of Jesus."

He looks at me warily. "That is a nice thought," he says, "but it is a very idealistic. The Church can a be very strict when it comes to who is a saved and a who is a not."

In themselves, his words would seem to convey a heavy sentence upon mankind. But as I watch him, his demeanor and facial expression seem to betray something different. A bit of tongue in cheek, perhaps?

"Can a you substantiate your ideas with a Scripture?" he says after a moment.

"Um, I don't think so," I say meekly.

He leans forward for a moment, deep in thought.

"The Gospels say many things, have a lots a clues. But we must a read them over and over again quite carefully, to glean all a that we can from them."

There is a moment of silence.

"You asked," says the Padre then, "whether Jews and other non-Christians can a be saved. Go back, examine the evidence. You must become detectives, Lads. What would a Sherlock Holmes do? Our Lord tells us to 'ask, seek, knock. Ask and you shall a receive, seek and you shall a find, knock and it shall a be opened to you.' You can a discover many things, but you have to look for them first."

He pauses for a moment, then says, "Do you want a hint? Let us have some fun with this. Listen carefully," and he bends forward and says slowly, "In primo de quattuor, quintus caput octo tenet."

"What?" I ask him, taking a pen and notepad out of my pocket, "Could you repeat that?"

"He looks at me with his kindly, grandfatherly demeanor and

repeats slowly, so that I can write it down, "In primo de quattuor, quintus caput octo tenet."

* * *

The next day I spend all of my tempus liberum — free time, which usually comes in bursts of ten to fifteen minutes after manualia periods — looking at the words and translating them. I am a little disappointed that the Padre did not say more than he did. I guess I assumed that, since Ken Matthews inferred that he, the Padre, believed that the unbaptized can be saved, he would come right out and admit it to us. But instead, he decides to send us on a scavenger hunt, so to speak. Maybe Ken was really just spreading a sort of rumor or something. I think he even said, "rumor has it that..." such and such, or whatever.

The Padre's little hint is very basic Latin, really, and my first attempt is simply a word-for-word translation: *"In first of four, head five eight has."* First of four what? And caput can mean more than just "head." I go and see Andy and he is a little mystified too, because *caput* has a lot of translations, including: "head," "person," "chief," "origin," "summit," "status," "paragraph," or "chapter." We agree to write out all possible translations to see what makes the most sense.

* * *

My next attempt is to discover what "first of four" means. What is the significant meaning of the number "four" in the Bible? It does not take me long to realize that, if we are dealing with the New Testament – the Gospels and the Acts of the Apostles and the epistles of Paul, Peter, James and John, and the Apocalypse — the "first of four" may very likely be the first of the four Gospels, or the book of Matthew.

144

As I am exiting the shoe room door for afternoon rec, I see Andy and he says, "So, can you recite the Beatitudes?"

"What are you talking about?"

"Hah! You mean you didn't get it yet?"

"The Beatitudes?"

"Yeah! In the first of the four Gospels, Which happens to be Matthew, of course, chapter five has eight. Matthew chapter five contains the Eight Beatitudes!"

I look at him with admiration. Then he says, "Leonard actually figured it out, too."

***

"'Blessed are the poor in spirit,'" says Andy to the Padre at our next visit, "'for theirs is the kingdom of Heaven.'"

"'Blessed are they that hunger and thirst for justice,'" says Dubchek, "'for they shall have their fill.'"

"'Blessed are they who mourn,'" says Leonard, "'for they shall be comforted.'"

The Padre nods, and waits for another one.

"'Blessed are they...'" I say, trying to remember, "'...Who suffer persecution for justice' sake?'"

"May I use your Bible, Padre?" Alex asks, "my memory is rusty."

"'Blessed are the meek,'" says the Padre then, "'for they shall a possess the earth. Blessed are the merciful: for they shall obtain mercy. Blessed are a the pure of heart, for a they shall see God. Blessed are the peacemakers: for they shall a be called children of God.' Next time," he continues, "I want you to remember each and every one."

"Okay," I tell him, "We'll memorize them. Now, as to my question about salvation for everyone?"

The Padre just looks at me and smiles.

"Wait a minute. The Beatitudes...?"

The Padre continues to smile and says, "It is time for our Hail Mary."

***

"So," I ask Ken Matthews the next evening at rec, "why is he so clandestine and secretive?"

"I'm not sure," says Ken, "but I think it is because he has to be very careful. He may have some enemies, right here in this house."

"Enemies? *Here*?"

"Well, in the theological sense, at least," he says. "But we should also understand that we can learn a lot from him by just discussing the passages he has pointed out to us."

***

The following afternoon, Andy, Leonard and I are on a walk during afternoon rec.

"I've got a question for you," says Andy. "Did He say, 'Blessed are the *Jewish* meek? Or Blessed are the *Christian* peacemakers? No, He just said, 'Blessed are the meek... Blessed are the peacemakers, Blessed are those who mourn."

"So," I say then, "you're saying that *everyone* who is meek or makes peace or hungers for justice or is merciful or pure or... any of those other things... is saved?"

"What do you think?" asks Andy.

"Well, maybe because he was only talking to Jewish people at the time, and they were God's chosen people, it was understood that the Beatitudes were only for them. At first, anyway."

***

During our next visit to the Padre, I tell him that we are puzzled, not because of any difficulty, but because of the incredible *simplicity* of the Beatitudes. Our Lord never mentions anything about ethnicity or religious background; he only describes those who are blessed in the broadest terms possible. And the Padre never says anything; he just nods and smiles, and lets us go on and on about what we think.

"Are there any more passages like these?" I finally ask him.

"Yes," says the Padre, "and here is a your next clue: In viginti quinque de publicanus, oves et capri."

He repeats it slowly as I diligently write it down for all of us to work on later.

The Padre smiles and says, "Until a next time, Lads. Let's a say our Hail Mary."

***

We take the passage back to our rooms to study it in our free time. Again the translation is simple: "In twenty-five of the tax collector, sheep and goats." The tax collector. Matthew again, I am presuming. At rec I learn that the other guys agree with me.

During evening points I look up the passage and prepare to meditate on it the following morning.

I find:

> "All the nations will be gathered before him, and he will separate the people one from another as a shepherd separates the sheep from the goats. 33 He will put the sheep on his right and the goats on his left.

> "Then the King will say to those on his right, 'Come, you who are blessed by my Father; take your inheritance, the kingdom prepared for you since the creation of the world. 35 For I was hungry and you gave me something to eat, I was thirsty and you gave me something to drink, I was a stranger and you invited me in, 36 I needed clothes and you clothed me, I was sick and you looked after me, I was in prison and you came to visit me.'

> "Then the righteous will answer him, 'Lord, when did we see you hungry and feed you, or thirsty and give you something to drink? 38 When did we see you a stranger and invite you in, or needing clothes and clothe you? 39 When did we see you sick or in prison and go to visit you?'

"The King will reply, 'Truly I tell you, whatever you did for
one of the least of these brothers and sisters of mine, you
did for me.'   Matt. 25:32-40

This is the passage the Sarge got upset with Leonard about. Funny, but I've heard this passage, and the Beatitudes, so many times, but never really thought about them in this way.

On our next visit, Andy reads the passage aloud to the Padre while we all listen.

"So now," says the Padre, "What did you notice?"

"Again," says Leonard, "we notice both what He says and what He does not say."

"When a you make points tonight, read it over again, meditate on it tomorrow," says the Padre.

We say our Hail Mary and return to our rooms for the night.

✳✳✳

"No one saves us but
ourselves. No one can
and no one may.
We ourselves must
walk the path."

Gautama Buddha

CHAPTER SIXTEEN

More Clues

C hristmas comes, and with it several days of feast-day order, which includes a whole week of morning rec and longer afternoon rec. We receive presents from our families, clothing like new socks and underwear and black sweaters, and snacks like cookies and cheese and sausage and crackers and, for Dennis Sarafini, an electric toothbrush. Most of us laugh at this newfangled gadget, and we are surprised when Fr. McKittrick lets him keep it.

"My father is a dentist," Dennis says defensively, "and he says there is proof that it cleans your teeth better than a standard toothbrush. Some day everybody will be using these."

***

One morning during the Christmas holidays, Alex Dubchek and I are in the rec room playing Hearts with Pete Torre and Lou Ranier, when the subject of the Padre comes up.

"How often do you visit him?" asks Lou as Alex takes a trick with a high card.

"Well, pretty often," I say. "Maybe a couple of times a week."

"A couple of times a week?" repeats Lou. "We're only supposed to visit the infirmary a couple of nights a month. To give all the novices a chance, you know? And of course, we're supposed to visit *all* the priests and brothers there. Do you take turns visiting all of them?"

"Actually,' says Alex, "we want to make the rounds with the other priests, but I have to admit, the Padre is the most interesting."

"What do you talk about?" Asks Pete.

"Lately, we've been talking about the Beatitudes and the Works of Mercy," says Alex.

"Yes," I say, "they seem to be all you need to do to be saved."

Lou looks at me in an odd way. "You're kidding, right?"

"Well, okay," I say then, "the Padre doesn't come right out and say it, but if you read the scriptures he recommends, and meditate on them, you start to get the picture."

"Sounds like he's really simplified our theology," says Lou. "Does he ever mention the Sacraments? Specifically, Baptism?"

I sense a sarcastic tone, but I let Alex take the ball.

"Oh, yeah," says Alex, "Um, well, I mean, we've talked about Baptism a little, but we really haven't talked about the Sacraments much yet. We're talking about how you can be saved without them."

"Getting saved without the Sacraments? Are you guys letting an eccentric old priest dupe you into forgetting what Catholicism is?" asks Lou as he drops his hand on the table.

"No, I don't think so," says Alex, giving Lou a cold stare. And now Alex abruptly starts to shoot the moon, taking one heart trick after another.

"What are you doing?" says Pete, suddenly concerned.

"What does it look like I'm doing?" says Alex, "I'm shooting the moon!"

He continues to take trick after trick, and Lou and Pete are puzzled. I want Alex Dubchek to win, and I especially want Lou Ranier to lose, if at all possible. I think Lou is waiting with a high card to take maybe one trick near the end, just to foil Dubchek. But the Queen of Spades is still out, and Lou suddenly tosses the Ace of Spades into the mix, so he won't be forced to take the thirteen-point Queen with the higher Ace. He must be assuming that Alex has the Queen of Spades. Alex already threw in a card this round, and I know he doesn't have the Queen, because I do. And I am in the right place at the table to send the Queen of Spades to Lou, if he has the king. The opportunity presents itself, and that is what I do.

"Oh, CROCK!" Lou says with a look at Alex, "I thought you had the Queen! Why would you shoot the moon without her?"

"I dunno," says Alex. "I like to make the game interesting, and I just had this compulsion to shoot the moon."

"Yeah, but you should still try to win, for crock's sake," complains Lou. "Why would you deliberately want to lose?" Then he looks back and forth between us and says, "If I didn't know better, I'd almost think you guys were conspiring against me."

Alex gives me a veiled look of satisfaction. "But Lou," he says with a grin, "that would almost be uncharitable, wouldn't it now?"

"Hey, it's just a game," I say with a smile. "The consequences are minimal."

✳ ✳ ✳

The following night, Dubchek, Leonard and I bring the Padre some Christmas cookies for a present.

"I should a eat just one," he says, and takes one and offers the rest of them to us.

"Padre," Dubchek asks him, "do you like living here? In this house?"

"Well, let's a say I go where the Order sends a me without complaint. And of a course, my active days are over. But I would not mind a being back in Italy, or perhaps a South Dakota, at the Indian Missions... but I feel at home here. *You* lads a make me feel at home. And I think this is a my last assignment, if you know what I mean."

"Padre," I say then, "the last time we were here, you said that the Beatitudes and the Works of Mercy were all that we need to be saved."

"Did I?" he says warily. "I don't a recall saying any such thing."

"Wally," says Dubchek, "maybe the word should be 'inferred.' The Padre *inferred* something not unlike what you describe, by giving us clues as to where we might find certain scriptural... arguments."

The Padre looks at each of us, and says nothing.

"Okay," I say then, "I guess you really did not actually say it, but somehow we have been led to believe that salvation might be possible by just practicing the Beatitudes and the works of mercy. But I have to ask you, Padre, if such is the case, then why does the Church insist that we have to be baptized to get to Heaven?"

"Because we do. Everyone must a be baptized to get to Heaven," says the Padre.

"Well," I say, "that's what we've been hearing and thinking all along, since kindergarten."

"But," says the Padre, "now I have another question for you. And it is a most important question. Are a you ready for it?"

We all just look at him, and I nod a little. He looks at each one of us in turn, and when his gaze falls on me I feel as if he is staring into my soul. "What," he finally asks, "is a baptism?"

"An outward sign," says Dubchek, "instituted by Christ to give Grace."

"Isn't that the definition of a sacrament?" asks the normally quiet Leonard.

"I think," I interject, "the definition of baptism is something like, 'A Sacrament which cleanses us from original sin, makes us Christians, children of God and heirs of Heaven.'"

"Bravo," says the Padre with a clap of his hands, "You remembered your catechism! Now, let's a dig deeper. Tell me, how is a one baptized?"

"You have to pour water over the person's head," says Dubchek, "and say, 'I baptize you in the name of the Father, and of the Son, and of the Holy Spirit.'"

"And if a you do not do it that way, what then?" asks the Padre.

"The person is not baptized," I say.

"And so..." says the Padre, looking at each of us.

"The person does not inherit Eternal Life, cannot be saved," says Dubchek.

"Well a now," says the Padre, "Do you really believe that?"

"Well," says Alex, "isn't that what we're *supposed* to believe?"

The Padre's gaze seems to take on an air of learnedness then, resembling more the professor that he once was. "'In Evangelium secundum Matthaeum,'" he says, "'caput octo...' You must a continue to ask, seek, find. Time for our Hail Mary."

✳✳✳

Since we have more free time and rec time right now over the Christmas season, it should not take us long to figure out this next clue.

But I actually had such a good meditation this morning on the last clue that I continue my meditation on it the following morning. During this meditation, I start wondering about all the good people in the Old Testament, the patriarchs and the prophets, who were born and lived and died long before Baptism was instituted, and I wonder where they are now?

Later on, at morning rec, while I am playing sheepshead with Pete Torre and Dennis Sarafini, Alex comes barging into the rec room with his Bible saying: "Matthew again, chapter eight, where the centurion asks Him to cure his servant. When Jesus says 'I will come and cure him,' the centurion says, 'Lord I am not worthy to have you enter under my roof; only say the word and my servant will be healed.' Then," continues Dubchek, opening his Bible to read aloud, "'When Jesus heard this, He was amazed and said to those following Him, "Amen, I say to you, in no one in Israel have I found such faith. I say to you, many will come from the east and the west, and will recline with Abraham, Isaac and Jacob at the banquet in the kingdom of Heaven..."'"

"So," says Alex, "Jesus is saying that Abraham, Isaac and Jacob will be at the banquet in Heaven."

Dennis and Pete are looking at us questioningly.

"So?" asks Pete.

"So they are saved, even though they were never baptized."

"I don't know..." says Dennis, "baptism is essential, isn't it? Maybe they got a special break, because they were Patriarchs?"

"Come on," says Alex, "You can't tell me that nobody who lived before Christ is saved?"

"'*Extra ecclesiam...*'" says Dennis, "'*salus...non...est.*' Didn't Augustine say that?"

"Maybe they're in Limbo?" says Pete Torre with a twinkle in his eye.

"Limbo?" says Alex.

Pete shrugs with a grin and says, "Hey, it's where people go when they're not baptized, right? The Bosom of Abraham. It may not be Heaven, but it sounds a lot better than hell," he says as he looks back at his cards.

"We should ask Fr. Harrison," declares Dennis Sarafini, "I believe I heard him say that Augustine's quote is valid..."

"But guys," says Alex, "Jesus says right here that Abraham, Isaac and Jacob will all be at the banquet in Heaven. And if they're going to be there, a lot of others from that era might make it as well."

***

"So," says Andy at our next visit to the Padre, "Abraham, Isaac and Jacob lived more than a thousand years before baptism was instituted, but are considered saved, according to Jesus. Are there more clues like that?"

"Caput novem secundum Medicum," says the Padre. "Let us say our Hail Mary."

***

"Medicum is Luke, the physician," says Leonard on our next walk, "and chapter nine describes the Transfiguration."

"The Transfiguration," says Dubchek, "that's one of my favorite passages. That's when Jesus takes Peter, James and John up the mountain with Him and allows them to see His True Colors, so to speak."

"That's right," I say, "and I, for one, haven't been seeing the forest for the trees."

158

"How do you mean?" says Dubchek.

"I mean, during the Transfiguration, Moses and Elijah appeared and conversed with Jesus. We have all read or heard this Gospel account many times over the years, but did any of us stop and wonder how Moses and Elijah could appear there on the mount with the transfigured Lord if they were not baptized?"

***

"Padre," says Dubchek at our next visit, "What is limbo?"

"Ah," he says with a smile, "I was a wondering when you would bring that up. First of all, what do you know about limbo?"

"Well, we were told that that is where the unbaptized go, for one thing. It isn't hell, but it is not Heaven either."

"Limbo," says the Padre, "Is a place where all a the just, unbaptized people from the beginning of time have a been waiting."

"Waiting for what?" asks Dubchek.

"What do you think?" asks the Padre.

"Salvation?" I ask.

The Padre smiles and shrugs, and I don't like it.

"You're not going to tell us?" I say then.

"Officially, I cannot. And over and above that, I have a to tell you that it is a not a doctrine, limbo is a speculative idea that is a believed by some more than others."

"So the Church doesn't even know what happens to the unbaptized?"

"Not officially," says the Padre.

"Padre, what do *you* think?" asks Dubchek.

"I cannot a tell you what I think," he says matter-of-factly, "but maybe you can a find out for a yourselves."

We all sit and stare at each other for a moment.

"I brought up a question during an earlier visit," says the Padre then.

"What is baptism?" I say then. "Didn't we answer it?"

"No," says the Padre, "you did a not. I tell a you what, this is not even the tip a the iceberg. For a reasons we cannot discuss, I am a not allowed to teach you. Or anyone else, for that a matter. But, I can a not stop you from a teaching yourselves, no? 'When the student is ready, the master appears.' You know the meaning of that little saying?"

"I think," Leonard says hesitantly, "it means that, when you are ready to learn, you sort of become your own master?"

"You are a smart lad, Leonard. For now, I shall a drop one more hint about what we are getting at, so you can a be like a Sherlock Holmes one more time. Your clue... is a right there on a the desk."

We all look at the desk and it is the same as it has been since we began our visits to the Padre: empty of any papers or clutter, save for a small card with a holy picture on it, sitting in the corner. The holy picture is of the crucifixion, with Jesus on His cross in the middle, and the two other men who were crucified with him, one on either side of Him, on their crosses. Our Lady, and Mary Magdalene, and John the Apostle are standing beneath Jesus.

"The crucifixion?" I say.

"You have all done the Spiritual Exercises, you all know how St. Ignatius instructed you to meditate. Put a yourself in a the scene! What do you see? What do you hear? What do you feel? Let's a say our Hail Mary."

✱✱✱

The following afternoon, during Spiritual Reading time, I hear a knock and look up to see Fr. McKittrick at my door.

"Wally," he says with a somber look on his face, "I just want to tell you, I think you should limit your visits to Fr. Lugierri for awhile. Spend more time with the other Fathers and Brothers when you visit the Infirmary."

"Okay Father, of course," I say. "Could we still visit him once in awhile?"

"Perhaps. But I want you to ask me for permission each time," he says before he leaves.

Fr. McKittrick has never knocked on my door in the past for any reason, and so I am quite surprised by this request, but I try not to show it. After he leaves, I can't help but think that somebody has said something to him about our visits to the Padre.

In the following days and weeks, we spend some time on the Padre's latest "commission." As for me, I keep remembering what he said about St. Ignatius' method of meditation. I picture it as if the Padre is telling me in his own words: "Look it up, put yourself in a the scene, imagine you are there, and a use all of a your senses! Reread the accounts!"

I read and reread all four evangelists' accounts of the crucifixion several times, and then I go to the novice library and find some books that offer commentaries on the Gospels.

The more I examine everything and meditate on the whole scenario, the more I tend to home in on the two thieves, or "revolutionaries," who were crucified with Jesus. I confer with Andy and Leonard and Alex, and we begin to figure out what we think the Padre is getting at.

CHAPTER SEVENTEEN

The Dismas Factor

After a month, I obtain permission from Fr. McKittrick to visit the Padre again.

"So," says the Padre, "it has a been awhile since I have a seen you lads. I was worried that maybe you did not like me, or worse, maybe you gave up this incredible adventure and a left the novitiate?"

"Padre," I say then, after we grab chairs and take seats around him, "we were instructed by our superiors that we should also visit some of the other fathers down here in the infirmary, and spend some time with them."

"Ah, that is a very acceptable reason," he says. "But now, what have you uncovered with your latest investigations?"

"Well," says Andy, "it is common knowledge that there were two other men who were crucified with Jesus. And the Church says that one of them, the 'Good Thief,' was saved for sure."

"Dismas," says the Padre. "And how was he saved?"

"He said to Our Lord, 'Jesus, remember me when you come into Your Kingdom,'" continues Andy.

"And?"

"Our Lord then said, 'Amen I say to you, today you shall be with Me in Paradise.'"

"So, why did Our Lord save him?"

There is a long pause.

"Because..." says Leonard, "He... asked?"

The Padre smiles. "So then what?"

"Well," says Andy, "since this good thief — Dismas, you say his name was — since he was saved without any sort of baptism, or at least the kind of baptism everybody is familiar with, the Church developed the doctrine of Baptism of Desire."

The Padre beams at him with a look of hope and approval.

"So if you want to be baptized," continues Andy, "but there is no one around to baptize you, you still have Baptism of Desire, and so you are saved!"

"Okay," I chime in then, "I remember hearing about that once or twice, a long time ago in early Catholic grade school, but it sure wasn't emphasized very much." I turn and look at Alex and Leonard. "Do you guys remember anything about it?"

"Yes," says Leonard.

"Yeah, vaguely," says Alex. "But they hardly ever talked about it. All we ever heard was about how incredibly important baptism is. Traditional baptism, I mean."

"Baptism is *very* important," says the Padre, "and it should a never be understated."

"Okay," I say, "But now I've got another question: what if someone never even heard of baptism? How can he desire it? I mean, was Dismas really *even asking* for baptism? He just wanted to be saved."

"It would appear," says the Padre, "that your detective work is a still not a finished. You are all willing and able students. Please a understand, as I have a said before, I cannot a be your teacher, for reasons that cannot be discussed. But perhaps you can a continue on your own. Until a then, let us say our Hail Mary."

***

I am extremely curious as to why the Padre cannot instruct us, especially when he adds "for reasons that cannot be discussed." But I have a strong hunch that eventually I will find out more; I just have to be patient.

***

Another month goes by. Fr. McKittrick, who seldom informs us about new fads out-in-the-world, tells us one morning during Rules Class about a new rock band from Britain called The Beatles, who are taking over the music world by storm. "They have long hair and bangs," Fr. McKittrick says with somber resolution. "They wear high-heeled boots, and their music is not exceptional."

In our letters from our siblings at home, we soon get inundated with news about how these "Beatles" have become an incredible overnight sensation across the country. Some of the second-year guys returning from Hospital Probation tell us that, while working in their wards, they managed to see them on the Ed Sullivan Show. The fact That Fr. McKittrick is not excited about them is to be expected, because after all, he's in his forties, born the same year as President Kennedy. Most of our parents are of that same generation, and they couldn't stand Elvis when he hit the big time a few years ago, so why should they let these Brits off any easier?

***

I have this weird dream one night, where I am near the back of the chapel in the middle of the night for some reason, climbing over the pews, naked. It is incredibly embarrassing, as dreams can sometimes be, and I cannot figure out what is going on. Luckily, there are no other people around to see me in this incredibly mortifying state.

The next day at rec I actually tell a couple of the guys about the dream, because in hindsight, it's pretty funny.

Later, I find a letter in my napkin box from Fr. Rector, the Father Superior of the entire House. I open it and read,

Dear Carissime Moriarty,

This morning some clothes and underwear with your nametags on them were found on some of the pews near the back of the chapel. Perhaps you could come and see me to explain how they got there.

Fr. Rector

I am shocked! How could this happen? Was I actually sleepwalking last night? I walk back down the cloister walk toward the bulletin board area, reading the letter over and over again, my heart pounding, wondering how I am going to explain things to Fr. Rector, when all of a sudden I look up and see a grinning Dubchek standing by the bulletin board, watching me and futilely trying to suppress a laugh. Then I look at the letter again, and upon re-examination I notice that it is typed, and Fr. Rector did not sign it—it just has his name typed in at the bottom.

I look at Dubchek again, and he cannot contain his mirth. "Tu scis ubi tu potes ire," I say to him ("You know where you can go,"), "Ite ad montem fimum!" ("Get thee to the dungheap!")

The letter is such classic Dubchek that I put it away and save it as a sort of souvenir.

"Those who are
patient in
adversity and
forgive wrongs
are the doers of
excellence."

The
Prophet
Muhammad

CHAPTER EIGHTEEN

The Blame Game

We visit the Padre again in another month, after Andy gets permission from Fr. McKittrick. None of us has made much headway concerning our inquiries into Baptism, and so Alex brings up another issue.

"Padre," says Alex, "some people think that the Jews are sort of responsible for the Crucifixion of Jesus, and so they hold that against them. What should we tell them?"

The Padre looks at him for a moment in silence.

"I will answer your question with another question," says the Padre. "Who executed Joan of Arc?"

"The French?" says Andy. "No, the British?"

"The... I don't know," says Dubchek.

"You did," says the Padre.

"What?" says Alex in utter confusion.

"Well, you're a *Catholic*, aren't you?" continues the Padre with a straight face.

"What... how..." says Alex Dubchek, "What are you *talking* about?"

"Okay," says the Padre as he breaks into a smile, "let a me clarify things. A Catholic bishop condemned this holy, pious, nineteen-year-old French girl to be burned at a the stake."

"Why?" asks Andy with a pained look.

"He believed she was a witch, and a heretic," says the Padre. He pauses for a long moment and regards each of our quizzical, uncomprehending faces. "And, five hundred years later," he continues, "who *canonized* Saint Joan of Arc?"

"The... Catholic Church," says Leonard.

The Padre nods.

"That sounds unbelieveable," says Andy.

"We must understand," says the Padre quietly, "that those who condemned Joan of Arc were a not of the same frame of mind as those who canonized her later on. Those in power at the time influenced the outcome of the trial to suit their corrupt purposes. And without Papal approval, I must admit. But the moral of the story is that every religious sect has some corrupt leaders from time to time. And corrupt Jewish leaders were responsible for the crucifixion of Jesus, not all their relatives and descendants."

"Plus," says Andy, "Didn't Jesus *have* to die, in order for mankind to be saved?"

"Yes, that is a true. He had to die by *someone's* hand," says the Padre. There is another pause as he regards us with his extraordinary stare.

"With that in mind," I say then, "I have to ask you once again, Padre, what is the meaning of 'ecclesiam?'"

"I'm a going to let you ponder that one for awhile," says the Padre with a wink. "Meditate on it!"

I look at my watch, and it is time to go. We say our communal Hail Mary and depart.

***

That evening I look at a list I have been developing. I have a title at the top: "Unbaptized Saints." The list includes:

Abraham, Isaac, Jacob, Moses, Elijah; The Wise Men(?); Mary's cousin St. Elizabeth, and maybe her husband Zachary (the parents of St. John the Baptist); St. Simeon, who prophesied about Jesus when they brought Him as a baby to the temple; the prophetess Anna, who was there with Simeon; the two hundred or so Holy Innocents murdered by Herod in his attempt to kill the infant Jesus; St. Joachim and St. Ann, the parents of Mary, the mother of Jesus; St. Joseph, the husband of Mary and foster father of Jesus. Most if not all died before the institution of Christian baptism...

The list is a work in progress, and it may contain errors, because I am doing it on my own. We are not allowed into the main house library until after vows, and so I cannot do adequate research and vouch for its accuracy. But I keep it handy so that I can add to it when I think of new names.

Now I write another note to myself and hang it on my bookshelf with a piece of tape, where I can see it every day. It says:

> "Could God's definition of Baptism be broader than man's? Could God's definition of *Ecclesiam* also be broader than man's?"

With all this so-called evidence, my heart says "yes," yet I still have that skeptical side of me that begs for some concrete, absolute *proof*...

***

I get up in the middle of the night to go to the castle, once again because I hear noise coming from the Sarge's room, another muffled shout. I hear it again when I walk out of my room, across the corridor to the castle. I guess he just talks in his sleep a lot, or something. But it's more like he is yelling in his sleep. I just can't make it out, but I'm sure Dennis Sarafini hears it too, because he is right next to the Sarge's room on the other side, and only separated from his sleeping quarters by one wall.

***

The next day at rec, I make a point to ask Dennis Sarafini about the noises.

"Yes," he says with a sad grin, "I have heard him a number of times. I can't wait to change rooms, because sometimes the shouts keep me awake."

"I wonder if he has a problem?" I say then.

"I think it must be a recurring dream," he says. "It's hard to under-stand what he's saying, but I can definitely pick out one word. He says 'water' every now and then. Maybe he's dreaming about a trip across the desert or something."

"God
sometimes
does try to the
uttermost those
whom He wishes to
bless."

Mahatma Gandhi

CHAPTER NINETEEN

In the Beginning Was The Word
John 1:1

T he courses we take in the novitiate include Speech and English Composition, and, during our otherwise silent meals in the refectory, we are all expected to take turns reading aloud at the podium for the whole group. The juniors read during dinner in the evening, but we novices take turns reading aloud during the shorter noon lunch period. It is a bit nerve-racking the first couple of times you do it, because most of the people here already are, or will eventually become, speakers and orators or high school teachers and college professors themselves, and you feel sort of like a cabin boy auditioning in a room full of admirals.

When a reader mispronounces a word in these readings, he is corrected by a priest at the Fathers' Table at the far end of the refectory, who has his own little microphone so that everyone can hear the corrections. Let's say the reader mispronounces a word like "caravan" in a sentence. The Father in charge, who is often also our speech teacher, will click on his microphone and say, "Repitet, (repeat), that word is *caravan*," and the reader will read the sentence over again, pronouncing the word correctly.

One day during lunch it is Leonard's turn to read, and I think he does a pretty good job, considering he has always had a hard time emphasizing certain phrases and words. He has come a long way since entering, I think, although there is still room for improvement.

After lunch I notice Fr. Socius, The Sarge, who was in charge of the correcting microphone today, talking to Leonard at the podium. After The Sarge departs, I go up to Leonard and say, "Good job!"

"Really?" he says quietly.

"Yeah," I say, "really!"

"The Sarge thought it was awful," he says. "He said I was the worst reader he's ever heard."

"Are you serious?" I say.

"That's what he said."

"Well, I think you did great," I say, "and I'm sure a lot of the guys will agree with me."

"Thanks, Wally," he says, "I appreciate that." He turns and goes to the table to eat his lunch with the novice waiters.

I walk away shaking my head, wondering what the hell is wrong with The Sarge.

***

After another month or so, Alex Dubchek is the next one to get permission to see the Padre, and Andy and I join him.

Andy asks, "Padre, what is the worst kind of sin?"

"The worst kind?" He scratches his neck and thinks for a moment. "It has often been a said that pride is a the worst of the seven deadly sins," he begins, "but in a nineteen a seventeen, Our Lady of Fatima said that there are more people in hell for sins of the flesh than for any other kind of a sin. So, as far as a the most *frequent* kinds of sins, sins of the flesh may be the worst."

"Sins of the flesh? Sexual sins?" says Andy.

"Yes, sins against the sixth and a the ninth commandments are considered sins of the flesh. Although gluttony may be in a that category, and a some others as well."

"Our Lady of Fatima?" says Alex.

"Of course you've a heard of Fatima," says the Padre.

"Yes, we've heard of it," I say then, "but are we supposed to believe it?"

"The Church said, in a nineteen-thirty, that the apparitions at Fatima were a deemed *worthy* of belief. So we are allowed to believe them, but no, we are not *obligated* to believe them." He pauses for a moment.

"And a now," he says, "some say that there have been more appearances, in Spain."

"Really?" I ask.

"To four children, in Garabandal."

"Gara who?" says Alex.

"What do they... what has Our Lady told them?" asks Andy.

"It is purported that she says there will be a great chastisement, unless we all begin to pray more."

"Chastisement?" asks Andy.

"A punishment," says the Padre, "a consequence for sin."

"For whom?" asks Alex.

"For a the whole world," says the Padre.

"What kind of punishment?" I ask.

"The children have not revealed that," says the Padre.

"When is this going to happen?" asks Andy.

"They cannot tell, but sometime in a the future. Perhaps within the lifetime of the visionaries."

"Padre," asks Andy, "do you believe in these apparitions?"

"Look up Fatima," he says, ignoring the question. "Most a the predictions of Fatima have already come to pass, just as Our Lady told a the children there. Including World War II."

"World War II was predicted at Fatima?" I ask.

"Yes, it was a predicted there."

"Padre," I say, repeating Andy's question, "do *you* believe in Fatima?"

He looks at me for a moment. "I was a there," he says quietly.

"*You* were at *Fatima*?" says Andy. "In nineteen-seventeen?"

"During the miracle," he says.

"The miracle," repeats Andy.

"Our Lady appeared every month for a six months, and before the sixth and a last apparition she promised a miracle. I had heard of it, and I was in a Spain at the time, not far from a Portugal, and so I went."

His voice becomes quieter. "It was a terrible day! Pouring rain soaking everybody. Muddy, sloppy... there were not a many automobiles in those a days, or paved roads, so most came on a foot or horse-drawn wagons. Seventy-thousand people waiting around in a the rain!" His voice thickens as if he is trying to hold back his emotions. "But just when everybody was about to give up and turn around and a go home, the miracle occurred." He is quiet for a moment, as if trying to regain his composure.

"And I," he continues then, "I became a believer that day." He stares at each of us with moist eyes.

"What was it like?" asks Andy.

"The sun began to move and a spin and a many colors came out of it. It seemed to grow a larger, and hotter, and most of us bent down, covering our heads, because we were very afraid it would a come down to the earth! But within minutes it dried up all a the rain, and all our clothes were dry! It was a beautiful sight, all right..." He pauses again. "But..."

"But what?" asks Andy.

"The most significant part of it all for a me was the *feeling* that I had at the time. I have a seen beautiful natural events before, eclipses and rainbows, and impressive fireworks displays, but they can a never give me such a *feeling*, a feeling of a holy presence, of a God's Presence, as I had a that day in Fatima!"

We sit in silence for a moment.

"Have all of the prophecies of Fatima come true?" I ask him then.

He pauses for a moment. "All a but one," he says.

"You mean, it has not come to pass?" I say.

"It is still in a the future, yet to be fulfilled," he says quietly.

"Is it as bad as World War II?" I ask.

"I think it will a be worse."

"Worse than the war?" asks Alex.

"Roncalli and a Pacelli both read it, but they said they would not reveal it just a yet, and now both have passed on. It may have something to do with the chastisement. Whatever happens, I think that the Church, and the world, may be in for a great trial, a great trial..."

CHAPTER TWENTY

Spring Fever

The winter months go by, and Spring is in the air. Lou, Alex and I are washing castle floors during Long Manualia, a Saturday afternoon work detail that lasts for hours. Since there is no active rec on Saturdays, we are allowed to chat in English during this work time to lessen the intensity of this "mort," which is house slang for "mortification," or "penance."

Lou Ranier, our *praeces* (group leader), says, "Wally, you soap. Alex, you rinse, and I'll do the showers and meet you back here in a few minutes. By the way," he adds as he is walking out the door, "did anybody see Andy yet? He's supposed to be in our work crew."

We all answer "no," and so Lou leaves, pushing his mop and wheeled bucket ahead of him.

Just as I begin to soap the floor, Pete Torre barges through the door, enters a stall by the window, and latches it behind him.

"Pete," I say, "your timing's bad, we're doing the floors in here."

"I'll be out soon. Do the rest, and save this stall for last."

"Alex," I say, "open some windows so the floor will dry faster."

Dubchek opens one of the frosted bathroom windows, peers out and says, "Looks like Robinson has a visit. He's out there taking a walk with his family, it looks like. Is that his *sister? Wow!*"

"Bowzo," I say as I notice him lingering at the window, "we've got work to do." Then, "How old is she?"

"About our age, I guess," he says as he walks to his bucket and wets his mop.

"That must be Christina Robinson," says Torre from his stall, "I heard Andy dated her in high school. Crock, I wish I could see out of this window! She's a *basilisk*, right?"

"Andy *dated* her?" says Dubchek as he opens another window and looks out again. I head over there to join him, just as Lou re-enters the castle.

"You guys aren't even done yet?" says Lou as he surveys the unfinished floor. "What are you looking at?"

"What's a basilisk?" asks Dubchek of no one in particular.

Lou approaches the window and looks out. "*She,*" he says, "is a *basilisk!*"

I finally approach a window and look out to see, strolling along the rosary path, our fellow novice Tom Robinson, a second-year man, with his parents and his sister. Robinson's sister, on this mild April afternoon, even at a distance of fifty yards or so, is lovelier than a spring day, perhaps all the more so because most of us have not laid eyes on a member of the opposite sex for months.

"What the crock," says Dubchek, looking over to the right, toward the main door at the front of the building, where a young man in a cassock has just exited and is walking rapidly toward the Robinson family. "Who's that? Is that Andy?"

"Yes," says Lou, "that's Andy. He's supposed to be working with us!"

Andy catches up with the Robinsons, shakes hands with all of them, and *receives a hug* from the glamorous Christina! She smiles fondly at him as he talks to everyone.

"How did he wangle permission?" asks Lou. "Didn't Fr. McKittrick know that she was his girlfriend, out-in-the-world?"

"What's she look like?" says Torre from his stall.

"You don't want to know," laughs Dubchek, "I mean like, she's already destroyed my recollection for the rest of my day, if not my life!"

"Wait, look," says Lou, "Isn't that Father McKittrick, coming from the Porter's Lodge?"

"Sure is," I say as I watch Father McKittrick in his cassock, walking rapidly down the path, catching up to the group. He says something briefly to the Robinsons and then puts his hand on Andy's shoulder and they both turn about and walk rapidly back to the Porter's Lodge as Christina waves goodbye to Andy.

Just then a toilet flushes, and Pete Torre bulldozes out of his stall and rushes toward the window. He arrives just as the Robinsons move around the side of the novitiate wing, out of view.

"Crock," he says, "missed 'em!"

"What's a basilisk?" asks Dubchek once more, as the atmosphere begins to cool.

"According to Greek mythology," says Lou with studious flare, "'tis a beast that can kill by its glance.' St. John Berchmans says in his writings that beautiful women are to be regarded as basilisks, and you should avoid looking at them, because they can, by their very glance, kill your vocation."

"But what a way to go," laughs Dubchek as he returns to his mop and bucket. "Sometimes the greasy chute can be quite appealing, ha hah!"

"Yeah," says Lou, "until you get to the dungheap at the bottom..."

"Lou," I say then, "I just remembered something I have to do — I'll be back in a minute," and I rush out the castle door and down the corridor.

Okay, sometimes I get this burning need to know what's going on, and now I rush down the stairs into the bulletin board area, admitting to myself that this is one of those times. I know that Fr. McKittrick and Andy will have to pass this way if they are going where I think they are going.

I stop at the bulletin board and act like I'm fixing a message to it, just as Father McKittrick pushes through the door from the Porter's Lodge and passes by. He is staring straight ahead, resolute. Andy is directly behind him, eyes downcast. They rush right past me as if I were invisible and continue through the open doors into the first floor corridor of the novitiate wing.

I turn and watch as they go down the hall and enter Fr. McKittrick's room and close the door behind them. I quietly and quickly move down the hall until I arrive outside Fr. McKittrick's door, where I pick up the clipboard and pen from the bench by the door and pretend to be signing up for a conference, just in case I'm caught. As I do this, I bend closer to the door, straining my ears and at the same time apologizing internally to God for eavesdropping. But hey, it's not sacramental confession, so I won't go to hell for listening, right?

"...Old family friends..." I hear Andy say.

"...Should have asked permission..." says Fr. McKittrick.

"...Couldn't find you..."

"...She's going through some difficulties...better not to remind her of the past..."

"...Wasn't aware of that..." Andy says then, "...I acted without thinking...no more than a sister to me now..."

"We're located out here, away from distractions, for a reason..."

The conversation is quieting down now, and I quickly set down the clipboard and hurry across the corridor and push open the castle door, ducking inside just before I hear Fr. McKittrick's door opening. I wait inside the castle until I hear Andy's footsteps recede down the corridor.

***

It's dinner time, and during first grace Andy is kneeling in the middle aisle of the refectory. After the Latin prayer, he says, loud enough for all to hear, "Reverend Fathers and beloved brethren, I accuse myself of visiting some externs without permission, for which fault Holy Obedience has imposed upon me the slight penance of kissing the feet of some of the members of the community." He then stoops and turns and, still on his knees, leans under the nearest table and kisses the shoes of the two men nearest him.

***

The next morning in Rules Class Fr. McKittrick begins class with a resounding statement.

"Let me make something clear," he says, "once and for all. There is no such thing as a Platonic relationship between a man and a woman." He scans us all with his eyes for another moment, then says, his voice booming louder now throughout the room, "I repeat, there is *NO SUCH THING as a Platonic relationship between a man and a woman!*"

I glance over at Andy, and he is just looking down, taking notes.

Dubchek raises his hand. "Father," he asks, "what does *platonic* mean?"

"An intellectual relationship without any sexual attraction."

"Father," asks Pete Torre, "what if she's like... a nun?"

"I don't care if she's a nun," Fr. McKittrick booms, "underneath that wimple, she is *still a woman!*"

"Father," asks Dubchek, "what's a wimple?"

"The white headwear that nuns wear beneath their veils, to hide their hair."

"Oh."

"I will repeat it one more time," says Fr. McKittrick, "There is *no such thing* as a Platonic relationship between a man and a woman!"

I notice the faintest twinkle in his eye as he says this.

***

Dennis Sarafini and I are admonitions partners this week, and I am glad of this, because he is a likable guy. Admonitions is something we do every week with a different partner. We are assigned partners by Fr. McKittrick and we pair up and try to tell each other, in as nice a way as we can, what each thinks the other's faults might be. This is supposed to be done in a very gentle, positive way, but it is still not easy to do, even if you don't like the guy that much. Perhaps *especially* if you don't like the guy that much, because you don't want him to know that you don't like him, right? Whatever. But if you are still here after six months, you really start liking almost everybody pretty much. Or at least you love them. Wow, that sounds kind of paradoxical, I have to admit. But it's like you're all in this corps, this battalion of men, this group of young soldiers who are all trying to focus themselves more and more on a life of service and dedication to God and to their fellow man and everything. And Dennis has always impressed me as a wise person, even though sometimes he is a bit hard to read.

As we approach the sewage treatment pond, I pick up a stone from the side of the path.

"I don't really have much on you, Dennis, so you can go ahead and lay into me any time you want," I say in a light-hearted way as I skip the stone across the pond.

"Well, I really don't have much on you either, Wally," he says casually as he also picks up a stone and examines it. "But wait," he says as he stares at the stone, "I have an idea. In order to make this time productive, tell me what you think is the hardest thing for you about this life, so far."

"That's easy," I tell him, "no girls. No women. The whole chastity thing. And of course, that's why we're stuck out here, far away from them, to *'lead us not into temptation,'* so to speak."

"Does that work for you?" he asks as he tosses his stone, "Being far away from the source of the problem?"

"Well, only to a point," I say, "because I still think about them a lot, even though I try not to. And in some ways it even makes it worse because, as they say, 'absence makes the heart grow fonder.' I mean, sometimes I have these dreams... man!"

"Uh huh," he says, and he keeps looking away.

"Is it pretty much that way for you, too?" I ask.

"Well, yes and no," he says then, picking up another stone. "Yes on the chastity thing being the most difficult," he continues as he pelts the stone out across the water, "but as for the second part of your question, no... the temptations are not so far away."

I sort of hesitate before I pick up another stone.

"Do you understand what I'm getting at?"

"You mean... I mean, you're..."

"And please don't use the word '*homosexual*.' I hate that word!"

I am speechless for a moment or so.

"What word should I use?" I ask then.

"I don't know. I don't think I like any of the terms that are in use right now," he says as he throws another stone, hard, across the surface of the pond. It skips five times.

"Does Father... I mean, have you talked to anyone about it?"

I am rapidly discovering what an inadequate counselor I would make right now.

"Fr. McKittrick," He says as he throws another stone.

"What does he say?"

"He tells me to keep praying about it. He says there is no sin in temptation. *Yielding* to the temptation is wherein the sin lies."

"That's exactly what he tells *me*!" I say, and I actually laugh a little as I pick up another stone and skip it across the pond.

An awkward silence follows.

"I don't know what it's like to be in your shoes, Dennis," I continue, "but I'm sure that there must be a number of, say, guys like you in the order, in the priesthood."

"Guys like me?" he says, and he sounds angry, frustrated.

"I'm sorry Dennis, I just don't know what word to use."

"Let's just say that I don't know what word to use either, or what to think or what to feel or *anything*!" he says, and now he is almost in tears. "I just know that I hate myself for being this way!"

"You can't *do* that," I tell him. "Look, I don't know what it's like, but it's *not* bad, it's *not* sinful, as long as you don't *yield* to the temptation..."

"Yeah. That's easier said than done. And you heteros have an out, you can get married, at least."

"Heteros?"

"Study your Greek," he says as he skips another smooth disc across the water.

I take a moment to throw a couple of more stones as I ponder this dilemma.

"Okay," he says all of a sudden, "I'm sorry for being so short with you. 'Hetero' means 'other,' and 'homo' means 'same.' I just get practically overwhelmed with these temptations some of the time, and I am hoping it won't always be this... severe."

"Understood," I say. "I have to say that I like to think that, because I chose this life, God will give me some extra Grace to make it less difficult. But the further I progress—if I can even use that word, because sometimes I feel like I'm going backwards, or at best treading water — the longer I'm here, the more I keep thinking that God *isn't* doing me any favors just because I chose this life. In fact, it actually is harder than what I left behind. Harder, but... I know that this sounds awfully trite... it's harder, but somehow better."

Dennis looks at me for a moment, and I know that he has a deep respect for me, as I do for him. "Yeah," he says, and we just look at each other for a second or two. "Yeah," he says again, "I think I can see that. You're right... I think you're right about that."

We start walking again.

"See that lily pad?" I say as I point across the pond, and I skip another stone and it flies and romps and bounces across the surface a few times before it hits a lily pad, square on.

"Is that the lily pad you were talking about?" says Dennis with a wry grin.

"Well, to tell the truth, no. But, I could have lied, right?"

"You're so damned honest," he says as he makes another toss, and his stone seems to follow mine to the same lily pad.

"You said we heteros can get married," I say, "and out in the world, that's true. But here in this order, we all have to give it up. You and me both. It's in the constitution of our order. It's one of our three vows. Even if the Pope came out and said priests could get married, we still could not."

We both throw a couple of more stones.

"Do you ever... *can* you ever get some relief by praying?" I ask him then.

"A little." He pauses for a moment. "But it's not easy."

"In that sense, I can agree with you completely," I say with a wry grin. "Prayer helps, but never as much as I would like."

The bell rings, and we walk back to the building in silence. Just as I open the door for him, I whisper once again, "Harder, but better."

"Harder, but better," he repeats as we enter the building.

CHAPTER TWENTY-ONE

Extraordinary Time

"We do not want riches. We want peace and love."
Red Cloud (Chief) Oglala Lakota

Ninety-five percent of the time here in The Order is spent in *Ordo Regularis*, or "regular order." The schedule is very ordinary, to the point that we know exactly what we are going to be doing on a specific day at a specific time better than just about anybody else in the world. I know that I am going to be rising at 5:00 AM seven days a week, rain or shine, Monday or Thursday or Sunday or whenever, no matter what. I know that at 10:00 A.M. next Tuesday, I will be opening a Spiritual Reading book. I know that at 4:30 P.M. on Wednesday, or just about any other day of the week, I will be saying the Rosary, and afterwards I will be doing Flexoria, a half hour of afternoon meditation, followed by Litanies and dinner. I know that on every Thursday morning and every Saturday afternoon we have *Long Manualia*, or work detail, since we novices are the cleaning brigade for most of the entire House. And almost every other Thursday, about twice a month, we have villa from 11:30 AM to about 4:00 PM, which starts with a walk to villa, followed by a picnic lunch and then recreation, during which time we can, weather permitting, take a hike, play football or handball or soccer or, if the weather is bad, play basketball in the gym or something, before returning to Ordo Regularis at 4:00 P.M. to act like monks again.

Villa day is just about the best escape that we first-year men have during the regular year, because of the relaxed lunch and subsequent conversations around the fireplace or hikes or whatever before returning to the house in the late afternoon.

I know that, aside from villa days and Sundays, unless there is a major feast day during the week when we get longer active rec in the afternoon, we will have one hour and only one hour between 2:00 and 3:00 PM to get some form of physical exercise. Human nature being what it is, we novices all try to squeeze every possible second out of this brief hour of active rec, occasionally cheating a little by starting to change into our rec clothes a minute or two before the bell.

During this first year of novitiate, we almost never get to go anywhere save for a trip into the city to see the dentist. Bizarre as it sounds, these trips to the dentist are relatively exciting for most of us because, during this first year, it is not just an escape from Ordo Regularis, but we can also actually *leave the House* for a couple of hours, driving into town in a regular automobile while wearing regular clothes (well okay, not *exactly* regular, because we have to wear coats and ties) and act and feel almost like normal college freshmen while we get our teeth worked on. Of course, we are not allowed to listen to the car radio or read magazines, and it is, after all, a trip to the dentist, but it is still a great, albeit brief, vacation from *ordo regularis*.

But we know that there is something a lot better than a brief trip away from the house looming on the horizon, thanks to the second-year men having primed us for it since the day we entered, practically. We have all been told about it during the dreary January nights of sub-zero cold, and during the long afternoons of Long Manualia when we have sought out any kind of consolation possible.

And soon we will have it: the hands-down, far-and-away, absolute best, most incredible escape of the year: the July trip to the Indian Missions in South Dakota.

***

I am at Malibu again, and it is a beautiful sunny day, and I am sprawled flat on my back on a towel, listening to a radio, and the girls are just down the beach playing volleyball again. I sit up and watch, and now they are approaching me, six swimsuited, dreamy feminine beauties. Marcia kneels down close to me, and then Sheila Murphy approaches and stops right in front of me, almost glowing with loveliness, and she reaches down and takes my hands and tugs at me and says, "Come on, it's time for my piggyback ride!"

I obediently get up and she hops onto my back, and I grab her warm, smooth legs as the other girls all come over and swarm around me and shout, "Come on, it's my turn!" Then I look out toward the water and I see The Surfer standing there again, holding his board and waving. I have that same funny feeling that I know him, but once again, he is just a little too far away for me to recognize him. The girls are gently coercive, and now Sheila is kissing my neck, and Marcia is standing in front of me and she holds up her hands and pushes against my shoulders and stops me. Then she leans forward and plants another kiss on my lips...

I awaken, breathing hard, taking a moment to remember where I am. Ah...my dark, austere novitiate room. I want to be back in the dream, I loathe the reality of reality...

Now I become aware that there is water running in some distant place. A faint light shines on my ceiling through the transom above the door, and I turn toward the window where I can see the morning light leaking through the slats of the drawn blinds. I grope for my watch on the desk. It is almost 5:00 A.M.; very soon, the three long wake-up bells will ring.

And now I suddenly remember what day this is, and I jump out of bed, eager, for once, to greet the day before the bells. Because today we novices are heading out on our Mission Experiment, four weeks at the Indian Missions near Rosebud, South Dakota. It is the first real probation, or experiment, for the first-year-men, and a happy repeat for the second-year-men before they take vows in August or September.

After rising and dressing we attend early Mass, not in our black robes, but in jeans and casual shirts for a change. We throw our packed duffel bags into the back of a rented yellow school bus. Then in silence we board the bus and make our morning meditation during the first hour of the drive. Afterwards we have a Deo Gratias (talking allowed) breakfast of juice, coffee and sweet rolls at a wayside, and more Deo Gratias for the rest of the day except for our fifteen minutes of Examination of Conscience at noon and again at night before bedtime. On the bus we chat, play cards, tell stories and even have a hootenanny since we have some guitars and talented players in our midst. We are normally not allowed to play guitars in the novitiate except during feast days and special events, but this trip is one of those events, and so we can have at it for the next month, when time permits. A couple of the guys are great at folk songs like *500 Miles, Michael Row the Boat Ashore,* and *Blowin' in the Wind.* Some of us with decent voices are able to quickly learn the tunes and harmonize with one another.

It is almost a five-hundred-mile drive from eastern Minnesota to our mission base in St. Francis, South Dakota. Around noon we stop for a picnic lunch at a pig farm, owned and operated by the family of Sean Hanson, a first-year-man. Due to some of the aromas in the air that are a part of the pig farm ambience, most of us have marginal appetites, at best. This is because we are totally unfamiliar with the daily routines of our grandparents' generation, to whom, as young adults before the automobile replaced the horse, the stench of animal manure and urine was as common as the more present-day stench of exhaust fumes and smog is to our nostrils.

After lunch we re-board the bus and continue our drive through the plains of South Dakota, following the sun toward its western bed until we cross the Missouri River at Pierre. There we head into the swollen, bulbous hills that lie to the west and south of this state capital, and after more hours of driving we finally arrive at St. Francis, where we enter the aging wooden dorm buildings of the mission boarding school to claim our cots for the coming weeks.

These mission buildings are old and ramshackle, yet still pictur-esque in their own unique way. They are dated, timber structures from another era nestled amidst the dusty, windblown prairies and grasslands of the reservation. Architecturally and structurally, our building back in Minnesota is ages newer than these edifices, and yet the *otherness* of this whole area is attractive to us novices, after almost a solid year of living in The House.

Our work at the missions is varied according to our seniority. We first-year men have to work in the mornings at house-painting, earth-moving and maintenance projects around the mission buildings, while the second-year men teach summer Bible school to the Indian children here and in surrounding towns.

In the afternoons we first-year men are encouraged to go for walks around the area and visit Indian families. After supper in the evenings we are expected to continue these pursuits until examen and bedtime.

* * *

On our second evening at the missions we visit an Indian settlement on the outskirts of St. Francis, and I am amazed. While some of the Sioux actually live in real houses, with wood floors and running water and flush toilets, many more live in buildings which are not much better than the scrap-wood clubhouses my friends and I threw together in vacant lots when I was a kid. Some of these hovels have dirt floors and glassless windows that are loosely covered with worn, tattered blankets that flap and fray in the breeze. Kitchens and bathrooms are unaffordable luxuries for most of these folks. Mongrel dogs roam about, some of them with huge dark marble-sized protuberances bulging out of their fur that upon closer inspection turn out to be blood-gorged ticks. And while the weather is warm enough now, what happens in winter? Some of these shacks have stoves, some don't. I never realized this kind of poverty existed in the here and now, in the USA, even as we are spending billions to launch men into space.

We quickly learn that, while the Sioux do not trust white people in general, due to the many wars and broken Government treaties over the past centuries, they surprisingly do not think of us as white men. To them, we are "The Fathers." Even if we are first-year novices, barely a year out of high school, they all address us as "Father." Even if we are blond-haired, blue-eyed Nordic types, they treat us with more respect than they do many of their fellow Indians, because of what we stand for. A child might approach one of us and say, "Father, can you give me your blessing?"

We in turn are supposed to politely tell them that we are not able to do that yet; we are not ordained priests yet, and won't be for a number of years. But due to so many requests from so many children, Pete Marconi has come up with a kind of solution. He makes the sign of the cross over a child and says, in Latin, "Quidquid non habeo, non possum dare tibi," which translates, "Whatsoever I do not have, I cannot give you." The child always leaves happy.

While it feels good to be in this honorable position among the Indians, I am uneasy about it, because I know I did not earn it; it was earned by the many heroic, ground-breaking Fathers who toiled and suffered and died here long before I was born.

We learn many Indian customs. For instance, the Indians seldom, as a rule, make eye contact with us, or each other, during conversations; it is considered disrespectful. Most of us have to get used to these practices. Leonard, however, has never been big on eye contact anyway, and so he fits in well that way with the Sioux.

There are numerous stereotypes that we try to get past in our first few days here. For instance, we grew up on a diet of western films where cowboys and Indians battled it out with each other in gunfights, range wars, and so forth. Now, in this place, where one of the main industries is ranching, almost all of the cowboys *are* Indians!

During our second week at the missions there is a huge Sioux pow-wow, or national celebration, and all of us "Fathers" have been invited to the various activities. People go to different areas around the reservation and stand around in the yards, listening to the chanting drummers, talking with one another while they cook huge, open-fire caldrons of *shunka-wahumpi*—dog stew—and eat and tell tales. Most of the guys do not want to try the shunka-wahumpi, but I figure, *"When in Rome, do as the Romans do."* I discover that it is not bad, and it has a hint of woodsmoke flavor from the open fire.

There are other festivities, including rodeos scheduled at the fairgrounds. As I walk along a road one afternoon with Leonard and Dennis Sarafini, an Indian-cowboy rides up to us and extends an amazing invitation.

"Hey, Fathahs," he says as he reins in his horse, "any of you do any ridin'?"

"No," says Leonard.

"Oh yeah," I answer, "once in awhile."

"I have three broncos in this afternoon's rodeo," he continues, "and I'm still lookin' for riders. Ya wanna do it?"

It is a question that catches me completely off-guard.

"What do we have to do?" I ask cautiously.

"Well," he says, "just hang onta this rope with one hand," he says as he shows me the bridal rope on his horse, "and try not to fall off."

"That's it?" I say.

"Well, pretty much, yeah. We tie a cinch around 'is middle, right by 'is rear legs, so he'll try to buck it off, but you jis' hang on as long as you can! If ya stay on long enough, you win a prize!"

I feel an incredible rush, because not too many years ago I would have practically sold my soul to do this kind of thing. But that was when I was an invincible ten-year-old. I turn and look at Leonard, and he has a look of excitement and hope in his eyes that I haven't seen before. Dennis, on the other hand, looks wary. And alas, with all of my recently-acquired wisdom, I know I have to decline the invitation.

"I would have to ask permission first," I say with a kind smile to the Indian, "and I don't think I would get it. But thanks for the offer."

He just grins and says, "Permission? That's okay, take care, Fathahs," and he rides away.

Leonard watches him ride away and says, "So you've done some riding before?"

"Yeah. A little."

"I'd sure love to ride a horse," he says then. "I never rode one."

"You wouldn't want to ride *his* horse," says Dennis, "you might wind up with a broken neck."

"He's right," I say to Leonard, who appears a bit sad. I silently pray that he will be able to ride a horse some day.

✳✳✳

Here at the missions we are allowed to make our morning meditations outside, if we wish. One morning I slowly amble through the cemetery next to the parish church. Not many headstones, but a lot of homemade wooden crosses mark the graves. My eyes come to rest on a simple white cross with words painted on it: "Emily Robedeaux, November 17, 1963—February 7, 1964." And then I see another child's grave, and another. Soon I am overwhelmed at the number of babies and young children who are buried here. All so young, Lord. Soon I get the impression that half the people born on the reservation die before age five. That was sort of how it was for the population of our country as a whole, a hundred years ago, before all the medical improvements of the twentieth century. But these folks are way behind the rest of the country in terms of medical care. Once again, I am reminded of what a different world this is from the one I grew up in, and how well off I have been my whole life, without even realizing it.

***

Later that week we have a softball game in which the Indians challenge the "Fathers." Since a number of the second-year guys are out of town teaching catechism at various mission stations, and some of the first-year guys are not back yet from a trip to one of the smaller mission outposts up north, we have a shortage of good players on our side. Our best man is Andy; he is our best pitcher *and* hitter, but we know our Indian foes may have more depth in those categories.

A half-hour before the game we are still one player short. We only have three guys to choose from, and two of them have injuries. Dubchek has a sprained finger, and Ranier has a sort of twisted ankle. And neither of them like to play softball anyway. The only guy left is Leonard, and he is not at all excited about playing. "I'm no good," he says, "I almost never played baseball or softball or anything."

"That's okay," I tell him, "just go out there and do the best you can." I hand him a glove, and he puts it on. He looks around for a moment, then awkwardly pounds his free hand into the pocket of the glove. I know he is working hard to accept his plight and to mentally get into this game that he does not want to play. He really does not care much for sports in general, but he does not complain. We give him right field, because we don't think a lot of balls will come that way, and we quickly learn that it is a good decision, when he drops the first easy catch that comes his way.

Soon enough, Leonard has to take his turn at bat. When he is on deck, I hand him a bat. He takes the neck of the bat into his fingers as if it was a dead rat or something, letting it dangle loosely.

"Have you ever swung a bat?" I ask him quietly.

"Oh yeah," he says, "yeah, maybe a little."

He begins to swing it back and forth a little bit, just warming up. Then he actually starts swinging it harder, with a look of grave concern on his face. He seems to be upset or something. He gets so intense that his eyes actually moisten up a little bit, and he is really swinging the bat hard, almost like he's really angry about something.

Now Leonard is up to bat, and he just stands there as he lets one pitch go by, then two, then three. The Indian pitcher is good, with a very fast underhand delivery, but Leonard is either better than I thought at discerning pitches, or he is just lucky, because the pitcher walks him. Then our team scores a run, and maybe we could have scored another, if we would have had a faster man than Leonard on base. But hey, it's just softball.

It is now the bottom of the ninth, and we are behind three to two. We have one man on base, and Leonard is up again. He stands over the plate again, holding the bat up and behind, in an awkward stance. His face appears very concentrated, and again he looks angry. One pitch crosses the plate, and the ump, Dennis Sarafini, yells "Strike!" The second pitch crosses the plate, and Sarafini again yells "Stee-rike!" Then the Indian pitcher does something a little different. He pitches the ball a little slower, sort of lobbing it across the plate, as if he is confident that Leonard won't swing at anything, because he hasn't swung at anything yet for the whole game. Either that, or he's being kind, and hoping Leonard will swing at it and at least get a little baby hit. Then, all of a sudden, Leonard takes a swing and connects with the ball. It actually sails over the head of the center fielder, who had come in close, expecting a bouncing grounder, if anything. The fielder turns and chases the ball while Leonard begins a slow, limping jog around the bases, and the man ahead of him scores. By the time the center fielder gets the ball, Leonard is rounding first base. The fielder throws the ball to second, but he throws it wide and Leonard winds up safe at second. The score is tied, and Andy, our best hitter, is up. Andy knocks a fly ball into right center field, right between and beyond the two fielders, and by the time they get to it, Leonard limps across home plate, and we win!

Leonard is the man of the hour, and he grins with embarrassment as everyone, including our Indian rivals, heap praises upon him for his accomplishment in the game.

***

A couple of nights later, we listen to a talk by one of the elders of the tribe, Fred Points-at-him. Fred reiterates themes that we have been hearing and seeing since we arrived here, telling us stories of the poverty and the domestic abuse and the alcoholism in the area.

After the talk, Fred sits down with me and Leonard and Ken Matthews, and the conversation moves around to a ten-year-old girl named Therese who is in Ken's catechism class.

"What do you think of her?" asks Fred. He actually makes eye contact with us when he talks, and so we feel a little more comfortable with him.

"She is definitely a handful," says Ken. "Hard to manage. She does not have a lot of respect for adults."

"What else do you know about her?" asks Fred then.

"Not very much," says Ken, "I just know that her mother is dead."

"Her father killed her mother. Ran over her with the car. Therese and her brother were in the car with him when it happened."

"What a terrible accident," says Ken.

"No," says Fred, "It wasn't an accident — he drove back and forth, several times, to make sure she was dead. He was in a drunken rage."

Ken looks down at the floor; I feel a sudden chill.

Then after a moment of silence, Leonard says, "I know what it's like. My father tried to kill me."

I feel like somebody just hit me with a club; I cannot believe what I have just heard. By the look on his face, neither can Ken. Even Fred looks stunned.

"With a baseball bat," continues Leonard. He pauses for just a moment, and looks away. "He broke my leg in two places. That's why it's shorter than the other one."

"Leonard," I manage to say, "I had no idea..."

"That's okay. I'm not very good at talking about it," he says quietly. "My little brother almost got away from him. But he jumped out of a window, and died from the fall."

Another moment of silence follows.

"My father is in prison," he continues. "For the criminally insane. My mother died when I was six, before all that happened. So my grandmother took me in and raised me. I never went to church until my grandmother brought me there when I was ten years old."

I don't know what to say.

"My grandmother," he says then, "is the most beautiful person in the world. I would not be here without her."

"Leonard," I manage to say then, "I honestly don't know what to say. I'm so sorry."

"When things are not going well," he says then, "my grandmother always says, 'Say a little prayer for me, Leonard, and I'll say one for you.'"

***

That evening I spend some time in the chapel, trying to process what I have just learned about Leonard. And I actually thought, for a good part of this past year, that I knew him. I knew that his Grandmother pretty much raised him, and his mother was dead, and his father was in a mental hospital, but I never knew about this terrible abuse in his young past. I can't help but feel guilty for all of my own childish self-pity, when I compare my life to his.

***

With all the sadness among the people out here in South Dakota, in one of the poorest areas in the entire country, these days at the missions still manage to have their own kind of serene beauty. Most of the Indians really appreciate the Fathers, because they know that these priests and brothers do not have to be spending their lives in their midst, and they understand the sacrifice. Even most of those Indians who choose not to practice Catholicism or Christianity have some respect for us. Most, but not all.

One afternoon Andy, Dubchek, Leonard and I have a caper of sorts. It starts out with a long walk over the rolling hills of the prairie. We find a little valley with a stream running through it, and spend some time climbing pine trees, perching in their branches, swaying silently in the breeze, meditating.

After that, we take a circuitous route back to the Mission complex. On the way, after hiking over a small rise, we come across some Indians in a ravine below us, setting up poles, building a structure of some kind. We sit down in the grass and watch with fascination as some Indians on horseback drag long poles into a level area. Other Indians take the poles from them and begin to erect the timbers into some kind of a large, circular structure.

"This looks like something out of a movie," I say. "What's going on?"

"Beats me," says Andy.

"Some sort of ceremonial area?" offers Alex.

Leonard just stares silently at the goings-on.

Then we hear a snorting noise behind us, and turn around to see three Indians approaching on horseback. They are clad in more traditional vests and feathers, not the everyday jeans and shirts of the "Cowboy-Indians." One of them is holding a rifle across his chest. They seem to be glaring at us; they are not happy.

"I am Lone Eagle," one of them says. "Who are you?"

"We're... fathers from the mission," says Andy guardedly.

"Fathers," Lone Eagle repeats. "Are you here to spy on us?" He is large and swarthy, with long braided hair.

"We were just out walking," says Andy, as congenially as possible.

"Why did you come this way? You are on reservation land, our land. We are doing things here that are private."

"We did not know anything about that..." continues Andy. "We were told we could walk freely around here."

One of the other Indians, an older man, leans toward Lone Eagle and says something quietly to him.

"You are the young fathers? The new ones?" says Lone Eagle then.

"Yes," says Andy.

"You may go," says Lone Eagle, "but do not bother us again."

They turn their horses as if to ride off. And then something amazing happens.

I notice, out of the corner of my eye, that Leonard is taking something out of one of his large pockets. It is an Indian pipe; it looks exactly like the Padre's pipe.

"*Wanblee Ishnala?*" Leonard calls out, holding up the stem and the bowl in his two hands. Lone Eagle reigns his horse back around and stares at Leonard with a look of surprise.

"May we smoke the pipe with you?" Leonard asks.

I look from Lone Eagle to Leonard. Then I turn to Andy and Dubchek, who return my gaze, incredulous.

***

"My Grandmother is part Sioux," says Leonard during our walk back to the town, to the pipe ceremony. "She taught me some of their customs and language."

"So you're part Sioux then?" I ask.

"I'm not sure. My mother was adopted."

"Is that the Padre's pipe?" I ask.

"Oh, yeah. He said I could take it along on the trip, in case we needed it."

"*Needed* it?" laughs Dubchek. "Yeah, I guess we did need it. So far, it's come in handy."

To get to the pipe ceremony we have to walk for a while overdusty, unpaved streets. We enter a building, then walk down a hall into a large room where some Sioux are gathering. There are a number of chairs arranged in a circle, and everyone is invited to sit down. Soon Lone Eagle enters, and he is clad in ceremonial clothing, with feathers and buckskin. Then an older man enters. We are told that he is a Medicine Man—a Holy Man—of some renown. These men are not members of our mission church in St. Francis; they practice the Native American religion.

The Medicine Man then speaks. "We welcome you young fathers to our ceremony. Let me tell you a little story that my grandfather told me when I was a child. The story is this: 'There are two wolves inside of me, fighting for my heart. The first wolf is kind and compassionate and respectful, and it always tries to do good and put others before itself. The second wolf, however, is mean-spirited, harsh, vindictive, and it cares for no one but itself.'

"I asked my grandfather then, 'Which wolf wins?' And he answered, 'The one I feed.'"

I turn to Leonard and I whisper, "The Discernment of Spirits." Leonard nods slowly.

"Now," continues the Holy Man, "Let me tell you the story of the Buffalo Calf Woman, who first brought the Sacred Pipe to us."

He continues with a more detailed version of the story which the Padre told us already, including how the Buffalo Calf Woman taught the Sioux to conduct a Pipe Ceremony.

Then he begins the sacred pipe ceremony by offering the pipe to the first of the six directions, the East. He stands and holds the pipe in two pieces, the bowl in his left hand and the stem in his right hand, and points the stem toward the East. He sprinkles some tobacco on the ground, then loads a small amount of tobacco into the pipe and says, "The East is Red, where the star of knowledge, the morning star, rises... we pray for knowledge..."

Then he turns to the South, sprinkling more tobacco on the ground and loading some more into the pipe, saying, "The South is Yellow, the color of Spring... we give thanks for growth, strength and healing..."

He turns to the West and continues, "The West is Black..."

Then to the North: "North is white..."

Then he touches the stem of the pipe to the ground, saying, "Green is the color of Mother Earth..."

He then points it to the sky and says, "Father Sky and Mother Earth are our true parents..."

He holds the stem straight up and says, "Great Spirit, Creator of us all, Creator of all things, of the four directions and of Mother Earth and Father Sky, we offer this pipe to you."

Now the pipe is lit, and passed around the circle from east to south to west to north. As each of us in the circle takes the pipe, we offer a prayer if we wish. I notice that they do not inhale the smoke, and so I don't either. The smoke from the pipe is said to carry our prayers upward to Wakan Tanka, the Great Spirit.

"I ask for world peace," I say, then smoke the pipe and pass it to Leonard.

"For all the people here on the reservation," says Leonard, "we ask for healing and mercy."

After we finish the circle, we talk quietly.

"We did not mean to spy on your Sun Dance preparations today," says Leonard, "we had no idea."

"I am sorry I was so short with you," says Lone Eagle. "Many Fathers in the past forbade us to do the Sun Dance. The government still does not allow it. Some of us prefer to do it, and find great meaning in it. It is our way of giving thanks to our Creator, and asking the Creator for healing."

The Holy Man observes each of us "Fathers," one at a time. I feel a little uncomfortable when he looks at me, and as soon as my eyes meet his, he lowers his gaze.

"I can sense that you young Fathers have no malice against us, and you are honest men of integrity," the Holy Man says. Then he looks at Leonard and says, "Father Leonard. I know that you are a unique person, and that you have been chosen by the Great Spirit for special tasks."

Leonard glances at him as he says this, then lowers his gaze to the floor. I can only wonder what the Holy Man means.

Now the Holy Man caps the pipe with some leaves of sage. Then he separates stem from pipe bowl again, and sets them aside in a special pouch until the pipe is smoked again.

We chat with them for a while afterwards. Leonard sometimes speaks simple phrases in their tongue, and I can tell that they really like that. Then Lone Eagle tells us that he served as a fighter pilot in the Marine Corps.

Later, as we walk back to the mission buildings, Andy says, "The Buffalo Calf Woman reminds me of Our Lady."

"Really?" says Dubchek. "But the Buffalo Calf Woman appears to be an Indian woman."

"When Our Lady of Guadalupe appeared to an Indian in Mexico, in 1531, she looked and dressed like an Indian," says Andy.

"I wonder what the Padre thinks?" I say then.

∗∗∗

The following week we return to the House and *Ordo Regularis.* Needless to say, it requires some readjusting.

"The greatest jihad
is to battle your
own soul, to fight
the evil within
yourself."

The Prophet
Muhammad

CHAPTER TWENTY-TWO

Year Two: More Experiments

A new crop of first-year men arrives, half in August and the second half in September. The second-year men take vows and move over to the Juniorate Wing of the House, and all the members of our class become the new second-year men. Because of our order's rule of Division between the novices and juniors, the men with vows will now sit on the other side of the refectory, worship on the other side of the chapel, and can only socialize with us during "fusion" rec on special feast days.

The day after vow day, we novices are all permitted to go over to the Juniorate side of the house to bid farewell to the men who are beginning their fifth year, leaving for St. Louis to begin their "Philosophate," or study of Philosophy and other college courses, for three years. As I am saying goodbye to some of the guys, I notice Brother Larry, the blind junior brother, saying goodbye to his brother Mike. Even though Mike is the younger of the two, Larry is the one staying behind because he is actually a brother, while Mike is moving on in his studies to become a priest. Larry wanted to be a priest, but the Church will not allow him to be ordained because he is blind. This is another one of those Church laws that make people wonder. Technically, a priest can be blind if he had his eyesight at the time of ordination, and lost it, say, an hour afterwards in some kind of accident or whatever. But he cannot be blind at the *time* of ordination. Larry is a good student, and in my opinion would make a great priest. I can see a great bond between him and his brother as they say their emotional farewells to each other.

Regarding our new first-year men, I was a little surprised when Fr. McKittrick picked out the Angels, the guys who introduce the new men to our way of life, because Andy was skipped over, and in my opinion he is a stand-out novice. Except of course for maybe a little transgression here and there, now and then. I was also passed over, as were Dubchek and Leonard. Lou Ranier was picked as the Archangel — the head of all the other angels — and that did not surprise me. I mean, he's quite intelligent and studious and everything, and you can tell he gets good grades, even though we are not even allowed to know our grades in the novitiate. That would make it too worldly and competitive and everything. And he is definitely good at retaining information and regurgitating it when called upon to do so. With little, if any, personal interpretation of said information.

***

Now it is October, and the new first-year men are in Long Retreat. We second-year men have some more Experiments, or as we like to call them, "Probations," to work through at various times during this year. The first one of course was the Mission Experiment, when we went to the Indian missions this past summer. And we get to do that one a second time, next summer, before we take vows. Another probation is teaching Catechism on Saturday mornings to elementary school children in various parishes in the surrounding towns, and we have already started doing that. And another, the second-best one after the Indian Missions from what I hear, is Hospital Probation, where you have to spend a month in an elder care facility and take care of old people, get them out of bed and dress them in the morning and give them baths and wait on them at table and all that. For some reason this one still does not excite me at all right now. And the last one is Kitchen Probation, where you have to do kitchen duties all day long for a month. This is the worst one of all, because you get no active rec for a whole month.

* * *

Leonard continues to amaze me every now and then. He is so quiet and unassuming, and yet so intelligent, and he has such fascinating interests and facts that he all of a sudden just brings up and tells us about, without warning.

For instance, one clear, starlit night, he takes me and Andy outside during evening rec and points out the Great Spiral Nebula called M-31 in the constellation of Andromeda.

"That," he says, "is the farthest away object visible to the naked eye."

"How far away is it?" I ask.

"At least one and a half million light-years. Maybe more."

"And how far away is *that*?" I ask again, with a laugh.

"Okay," he says, "a light-year is about six trillion miles. That may not seem like a lot, but when you figure the sun is ninety-three million miles away, and yet it's light only takes about eight minutes and twenty seconds to reach us, a light-year is pretty far. So," he continues, "the light that you see there, coming from that galaxy, left the galaxy at least one and a half million years ago."

"So essentially," says Andy, "we are looking back in time, at a galaxy as it was back before man first walked the earth?"

"Essentially, yes," says Leonard. "And theoretically, if you had a powerful enough telescope, you could check out the solar systems in that galaxy, and even see whether there is life on any of the planets. Keeping in mind, of course, that whatever you are seeing actually took place at least one and a half million years ago."

"Could we ever build a telescope that powerful?"

"Not with our present technology. Probably not ever."

"I can't believe the universe is that big," I say then.

"Actually, that galaxy is very close to us," says Leonard, "it is a member of the 'Local Group' of galaxies. There are thousands more, maybe millions more, almost all of them much farther away than the Andromeda galaxy. And each one has billions of stars in it, and many of the stars may have planets like earth."

"Stop! that's enough," I say, "I can't handle any more of this right now! You've already given us points enough for hundreds of meditations!"

When evening rec is over I return to my room, wondering how many of the kazillion planets in our universe have intelligent life on them, and if they do, whether any of those intelligent races of beings are fallen, like we are, and in exile, groping their way back to God.

CHAPTER TWENTY-THREE

Perilous Capers

"Where love is, there God is also."
Mahatma Gandhi

I t is the middle of the night, and I hear water running again. It's pretty common around here, so I am not too alarmed by it. But it sounds like someone is doing more than just washing his hands after visiting the castle. I reach for my watch on the desk, and discover that it is 3:30 A.M. I decide to get up and visit the castle myself.

As I walk across the corridor to the castle I discover that Andy has his light on, and the running water sound is coming from his room. After I finish in the castle, just as I cross the corridor back to my room, the running water ceases, and I turn to see Andy's light go out and his door open. I impulsively duck back into the darkness of my room just in time to avoid detection. I hear him leave his room and begin padding down the corridor, very quietly. I peer out just enough to see him walking toward the bulletin board area, dressed in his suit and carrying shoes, an overcoat and a gym bag; he is walking in his stocking feet. As soon as he disappears through the doors at the end of the corridor, I quietly but rapidly try to catch up to him in my pajamas, slippers and robe. I have to open the doors carefully, just a crack, to see if he is looking in my direction or not. I glance down the cloister walk by the chapel to see if he is heading for the garage. I do this because I figure when a novice leaves the novitiate—I mean,

219

leaves for *good*—he probably heads straight for the garage and a priest or brother drives him into town to the bus depot or whatever, all before anyone else is even awake.

The chapel cloister walk is empty. Now I turn around and go through two more sets of doors before I carefully open the door to the Porter's Lodge. I am just in time to see Andy on the other end of the long, cavernous foyer, exiting through the main front doors of the building. I walk through the Porter's Lodge to the doors he just passed through, and open one of them as quietly as possible to peer out. It is a dark night, but in the faint light from the building I can just barely make out Andy's coated figure walking rapidly down the entrance drive toward the highway. Lord, what's going on? He cannot possibly be leaving... can he? Because if he is, why is he walking, with no driver and no suitcases or anything? As the damp, chilly breeze cools my face, I almost shout out his name before I think better of it. I have to remember that the house is under Sacred Silence at this time of night, and I don't want to awaken or alarm anyone. So I utter a quiet prayer for him as I close the door and return through the various corridors toward my room.

Before I get to my room I stop at his door, enter it, turn on the light and open his armarium. I heave a sigh of relief when I see underwear folded on shelves, shirts and pants hanging on hangers, slippers on the floor. Wait a minute, what's this? On a hanger in the back I see what looks like a vest woven of very coarse, rope-like material. I run my fingers over it, and it is rough, sort of scratchy to the touch. It takes a moment or two before I realize that it must be a hair shirt, a bristly, scratchy undergarment worn by some ascetics since medieval times as a form of penance. Where did he get it? Does he really wear this thing? Isn't the chain for two hours a week enough? This is way beyond that, since it comes into contact with much more skin, and is meant to be worn all day. I wonder whether he wears it regularly. Of course, if I ask him about it, he'll know I've been snooping. I'll have to figure out a way to bring up the subject, or maybe let somebody else do it. I close the armarium and turn to the sink in the corner and open the medicine cabinet. Toothbrush, toothpaste, razor and shaving cream are all in place. He'll be back, I'm sure of it. I return to my room, crawl into bed and try to sleep.

***

I do not see a trace of Andy all day until dinner time, when he appears and takes a seat next to me.

"Where'd you go?" I whisper as we sit down after Grace.

"I pulled a caper," he says quietly as he passes the bread plate. "I'll tell you later."

***

"A *synagogue*?" I repeat as I walk with Andy at rec that night along the rosary path under a new moon.

"What did Fr. McKittrick say?"

"He doesn't know."

"So you didn't ask permission for this? You just snuck out of the building..."

"I thought it was important."

"I almost thought you'd left, for crock's sake! I never thought *you'd* sneak out and hitch a ride into town."

"At least my intentions were not to go to a tavern," he says with a sly grin.

This gentle barb finds its mark, and I return his grin. "How long did it take to get a ride?"

"First car. I was there a lot sooner than I thought, so I sat on a bench in a nearby park and meditated."

"I just can't believe... why did you do it?"

"I wanted the experience. You know why. Do you want to come with me next time?"

"Next time?"

"To a Bar Mitzvah. Seriously."

✳ ✳ ✳

Two weeks later we are up very early on a Saturday, hitchhiking in our coats and ties into town, each of us carrying a change of clothes in a gym bag. It does not take long to get a ride, even though there are very few cars on the road at 5:00 A.M. People are friendly around these parts. And of course, we are not exactly dressed like vagrants; "vestis virum facit," as our Latin textbook tells us: "clothes make the man."

The synagogue service does not start for awhile, so we manage to find a church and attend an early Mass, then spend some time meditating in a park near the synagogue. When Andy hears my stomach growl, he produces a package from his gym bag and opens it to reveal a large piece of cornbread, which he splits with me.

"Do you feel okay about this?" I ask as I take a bite.

"Yeah. How about you?"

"I'm not sure. I feel sort of guilty."

Our main reason for getting up so early was not so much our timetable, but the fact that we had to leave the house without being seen. This bothers me, because of course we're not supposed to do anything without permission. But since both of us have bent the twig pretty much already, and our *intentions* are not bad, I figure it's okay to rationalize again.

When we enter the synagogue, we are each given a yarmulke, or *kippa*, and we put them on our heads and sit near the back in order not to draw attention to ourselves, since we do not know any of the customs. It strikes me that this kippa very much resembles the little white beanie that the pope wears when he does not have his miter on.

After awhile I have trouble staying awake, due in part to our early wakeup time. I nod and catch myself a few times, hoping that no one notices, and happy that we are sitting in the back. Evidently Andy doesn't notice my yawns, because he's still watching the ceremony in rapt attention.

Afterwards we eat cookies and drink punch and chat with some of the young man's family and relatives. When people ask where I am from, I just say "Milwaukee," and that seems to quell their curiosity enough. One thing that surprises me is that, when I meet the Rabbi, he smiles at me as if he already knows me.

"We would love to have you young men visit us more often," he says as he shakes my hand. "You can bring your friends as well!"

Andy smiles, and I can tell that he and the Rabbi are already acquainted.

* * *

On the way back to the House we hitch a ride with a farmer in a pickup truck.

"You boys have to hitchhike all that ways to go to church?" he asks as we ride west on the highway back to St. Boni's. "We got some fine churches out in our area, closer to where you live at."

"Yeah, but no synagogues," says Andy.

"Oh," he says, turning to observe us, "so you fellas are Jewish then?"

"No," says Andy, "We're Catholics."

"Catholics. Yer Catholics, but ya wanna go to a synagogue," he says as he turns again to check us out, looking us up and down.

Feeling a little nervous, I ask him, "May I ask if you have a religious affiliation?"

"Well, I'm Catholic, but I sure never been to a synagogue."

"Well, that's okay, it's not required," I assure him.

"Yeah, I know it's not required," says the farmer. "Why do you wanna go to a synagogue, anyhow?"

"We like variety," says Andy.

He thinks for a moment, then turns and looks at us again and says,

"Well after all, variety is the spice o' life," nodding several times before repeating, "the spice o' life." He becomes quiet after that.

We have a plan figured out so that we will return to the House during afternoon rec, wearing our walking clothes. This requires a change of clothes, which we carry in our gym bags. It sounds subversive and clandestine, and I am not crazy about it, but it seems to work. Andy managed to schedule this whole affair during a feast day when we had long rec in the afternoon, with a two-and-a-half-hour window of opportunity to casually return to the house, as if from a long walk. We just change clothes in the woods before heading back to the House in our rec clothes, having stuffed our coats and ties as neatly as possible into the gym bags.

***

In the ensuing months, changes continue to occur in the Church and in our Order. While we still have to study Latin and speak in Latin during our days of *Ordo Regularis* when we are not at recreation, we are starting to celebrate our house community Masses in the vernacular, which for this part of the world is English. And we have a new hymnal and now must learn English hymns that used to be sung in Latin, and in Gregorian Chant music. These changes have been happening quickly, and Church music people are busy translating and rewriting all the Latin hymns and the Chant, and composing new melodies that work better with the translations. And of course there are other sources of good Christian hymns in English: the numerous hymns of the many Protestant Christian denominations.

One day at choir practice, Fr. Puetz, our choir director, says, "Today, we're going to try something new," and he bends down to the floor by the lecturn and pulls a guitar out of its case! Soon we are singing a folksy sort of hymn to the music of his guitar. He is pretty good on the guitar, I might add. For a priest.

On another day, he teaches us a new hymn called, "A Mighty Fortress Is Our God," and Dubchek, standing next to me, holds up the hymnal to me and points out the fine print at the bottom of the page. It says that the author is Martin Luther. Dubchek grins at me and does a "thumbs-up" sign, and I smile and nod. When we were growing up we would not have sung a hymn written by the leader of the Protestant Reformation, let alone include it in our hymnal; the ecumenism of Vatican II is changing our world.

***

Christmas comes and goes, and we have tried to continue our monthly visits to the Padre. And Andy and I manage to get into town a couple of more times, to a Buddhist meditation center and a Muslim religious center. We get Alex to come with us, but Leonard is not interested. He doesn't think it is a good idea to sneak out like we have been doing.

When Alex learns the lotus position for meditation at the Buddhist center, he says, "I'm not going to fall asleep in this configuration — it's too crocking uncomfortable."

At the Islamic center he proclaims, "Now these people really know how to *kneel*!"

CHAPTER TWENTY-FOUR

Forbidden Fruit

"Padre," I ask him at our next meeting, "What is the Church's teaching on evolution?"

"Pacelli said, in *Humani Generis*, that there is a no intrinsic conflict between Christianity and a the theory of evolution, as long as we believe that each a man and a woman has a unique soul created by God."

"Padre, how about you?" asks Leonard. "Do you believe in evolution, or creationism?"

"Yes," he says with a matter-of-fact look.

"Yes? I mean, which one do you believe in?"

"Both of them, as a far as they go."

"Which means...?"I ask.

"Evolution is a kind of ongoing part of the creation process. Creationism is a how evolution started. But," he adds, "even though mankind shares some similarities with a the primates, it is quite possible that we humans did a not just evolve from a the apes. There had to be a great intervention, a kind of a helping hand, so to speak."

"How do you mean?" Leonard asks.

"If there was a mutation, shall we say, of a type of ape into a human, was it gradual, or could it have been more sudden, and dramatic?"

"Like... Adam and Eve? Is that what you mean by 'sudden and dramatic?'"

He takes a moment to gather his thoughts. "There are," he says, "many dissimilarities between the surviving ape species and men. Apes do not really have anything but animal intelligence, the kind of intelligence that a number of mammals have. And it is not just our human intelligence that is a so much greater. We have unique traits that no other animals possess."

"For instance?" I ask.

"For instance, why do we humans rely on visual and tactile sensation for sexual arousal, rather than scent? People go to great lengths to create false realities, or fantasies, with environment, revealing clothing, and perfumes that eliminate repulsive body odors.

"You want another question? Why do we have hair on our heads that keeps on a growing, when no other ape or mammal is a like that?

A third question. Why do we have a so much less body hair, especially women, while apes, male and female, have a so much more?

And a fourth question. Why, if we have so little body hair, do we have a so much pubic hair, and armpit hair, when a no other primate or mammal seems to have it? Those are the parts of their bodies with the least amount of hair."

We just look at him.

"You want a fifth question? Why can a you see the whites, the sclera, of my eyes, and I see the whites of yours when we look at each other straight on, and a no other primate or mammal is a like that?

"More questions: Why do people have chins? Why do we walk upright? Why do we have such long legs? And why are we so much weaker in muscle strength and in endurance, than any primate? A one hundred fifty pound chimpanzee has a the strength of the strongest humans, who have to work out for many years to achieve such strength. You might say, 'They get more exercise, living in the wild.' But even the ones that grow up in zoos and get little exercise are incredibly strong.

"And as far as intelligence goes, we are not just twice as intelligent as apes, or even five or ten times as intelligent, we are hundreds of times as intelligent. Look at all the products of human culture, all the knowledge and books and a libraries from antiquity, and understand that if you took an ape into a library, he wouldn't know what to do, he would just a want to jump around and screech, poop and piss on the floor, then leave, go outside and a find a banana or something.

"If you spend the next twenty years of a your life trying to teach him to read, he may, like a smart dog, learn a number of words, but only very basically, with a no nuances. Will he ever be able to write, or to talk? Can he ever be house trained? Some people will tell you that horses and pigeons can a count to ten or twenty or higher, as well as an ape."

I am silent for another moment, as is Leonard. We cannot answer him. But of course, We are not paleontologists or biologists.

"I challenge you or anybody, if ayou think man truly evolved from a primates, to *try to breed* a man out of an ape. Why don't we try to breed some primates like a we breed dogs? Let's a do it for a number of generations, and a see what we can a come up with. Breed some chimpanzees together, take the smartest offspring and breed them, and breed their smartest offspring, and on and on, and a see what happens. Or how about some gorillas? Or maybe some bonobos? Orangutans. Baboons. Temple monkeys. Whatever you want. Let's see if we can a come up with a human being."

"You think we will?"

"I think not."

"How can you be sure?"

"If you are willing to take a leap of faith, Our Lord said so."

"Where?"

"In the writings of Maria Valtorta."

"Who?"

"Her greatest work is 'Il Poema dell 'Uomo Dio,' The Poem of the Man-God."

"May I ask what it is about?"

"It is an extension of the Gospels."

"An extension? Have you read it?"

"Yes. In fact, it is right there on a my bookshelf," he says, pointing.

I get up and go over to the shelf, and soon I find it, a set of five volumes. I pull out the first volume and open it, and my excitement quickly turns to disappointment. "I was just about to ask you if I could read it, but it is in Italian."

"Which is just as well, because I could a not let you read it anyway. It is on a the Index."

"What index?"

"Index Librorum Prohibitorum, the Church's Index of Forbidden Books."

"Darn, now I *really* want to read it," I say with a laugh. "Why is it forbidden?"

"Soon after it was finished, in a the nineteen-forties, Pacelli — Pius the Twelfth — said that it should be published as is. But some other officials in the Vatican read it and quickly condemned it, saying it did not sound like a their idea of a Jesus. They decided, among other things, that Jesus did not talk as much as is written there. They banned its a publication, but someone managed to publish it anyway."

"Reminds me of the Joan of Arc story. Couldn't the Pope override them? It sounds like he has less power than I thought."

"Often the one with a the most power in our world seems to be the Enemy. God tells us how to live, then Satan takes His words and symbols, twists them to suit a his ends, and gets many of us to believe his lies. Look here," he says as he takes a piece of paper from his desk and draws something on it. "What does this symbolize to you?"

I look at the drawing; it is of a simple cross. "The ultimate symbol "of Love," I say.

He then takes the paper back and adds a little something to the drawing. "Now what does it symbolize?"

"Hatred," I say as I look at this new drawing of a swastika, "a twisted, distorted cross." I ponder this for a moment.

Then Leonard holds up the book and asks him, "Is there more in 'Il Poema' that is objectionable?"

"Our Lord dictated the book to her, and says some things that may surprise or shock you. Among other things, He tells her that the forbidden fruit of Paradise was not, in fact, the fruit of an actual tree."

"Well," I say, "I always thought that could be the case. What was it?"

He looks at me for a moment. "Sex. Sexual pleasure. It was the one thing truly forbidden to our first parents, the fruit of the tree in the middle of the garden *of their bodies*, so to speak. But the serpent caressed Eve, and she, instead of turning to God and repenting of her sin, took this new-found experience to Adam, and they sinned together."

"Well, but if sex was forbidden, how were they, and how are *we* supposed to reproduce?"

"God had another way. Virgin Births, perhaps? But since the fall of our race, and our exile from Paradise, God *does* allow us to have sex, but only with strict guidelines. It is the marriage act, and it should only be done between a man and a woman joined in marriage, with an openness to procreation. No birth control of any kind, you see?"

There is a moment of silence.

"Okay Padre," says Leonard then, "but if we did not evolve from apes, what about all the evidence of ancient, man-like creatures that have been discovered by paleontologists?"

"These also are lower forms of men, but they did not precede Adam and Eve, they *came after* them. It is revealed in Genesis, after the second great sin of our race, the First Murder."

"When Cain killed Abel, his brother?" says Leonard.

"Yes. Here," he says, picking up his Bible, "look it up and I will a show you. Start with Genesis, chapter four."

I take the Bible and open it to chapter four of Genesis.

"Do you see," continues the Padre, "that God put a mark on a Cain because of his sin? He effectively made Cain the father of a new race, and said that no one would kill him on sight. And a now, go to chapter six. Read verse two."

"'...the sons of Heaven saw how beautiful the daughters of man were, and so they took for their wives as many of them as they chose.'"

"The sons of Heaven," says the Padre, "are the sons of Adam and Eve, and the daughters of men are the daughters of Cain and his wife. Then the Nephilim appeared, the great, powerful men of old. But, according to the notebooks of Maria Valtorta, there also appeared aberrations and monstrosities, due to the mixing of a the races, the now imperfect, fallen race of Adam with the even more corrupt, bestial, unrepentant race of Cain. These are a the sources of a the distorted early man fossils that have been discovered."

This entire conversation has become difficult for me. On the one hand, I find myself beginning to question the Padre's wisdom, but on the other, most of what he is saying, save for the actual definition of the Forbidden Fruit, seems to be in accordance with Church teachings. And the Church has never really defined the forbidden fruit of Paradise as far as I know.

"Do you think her writing is... authentic?" asks Leonard. "I mean, could it all be true?"

"I do not a know. Some of her work is a difficult to accept, but I have to say that when I read "Il Poema," I often feel inspired, and nothing she says about Jesus or any of the other people in her work, which includes Mary, Peter, and all a the apostles and many more people never mentioned in a the Gospels — seems contrived in any way. They all have a personalities that are much more defined than in a the gospels. The Virgin Mary is an amazing woman, very educated, very beautiful, holy and a wise. Peter is amazing in another way. He is so human, you say to youself, 'if a he can a get into Heaven, I can a do it too!' More fleshed out, more developed, but so human. It fills in a lot a gaps in the Gospels, and expands a them, you see.

As we say our Hail Mary and leave for points, this new information both puzzles and enthralls me. According to this Maria Valtorta, we did not evolve from lower animals, but rather we, through the Original Sin of our first parents, *devolved* from immortal, Heavenly beings into a lower, mortal nature, as is related in the book of Genesis. And our interbreeding with the race of Cain pulled us even further away from the Glorified Perfection of Paradise. Because they chose to partake of the fruit of the tree of *carnal* knowledge of good and evil, they lost Paradise for themselves, and for all the rest of us.

I wonder if this 'Poema' is at all legitimate. But then when I think about it, the Church has always talked about sexual sins as being very serious. And why was Mary's virginity so important? And why have priests and nuns and members of religious orders been asked to take vows of celibacy, and chastity?

"An eye for an eye makes the whole world blind."

Mahatma Gandhi

CHAPTER TWENTY-FIVE

Icing on the Cake

I t is 1:55 PM, and outside my window the entire countryside is covered with a blanket of snow. I am trying to concentrate on Homer's Odyssey, "...*And seated in order...they beat the sea...white with their oars*," I translate, between frequent glances at my watch as the time creeps slowly, agonizingly toward 2:00 PM.

Even though I am anticipating it keenly, the abrupt, staccato clanging of the two O'clock bell makes me lurch involuntarily. It is rec time, and I must not tarry. I jump from my chair, close my door and whip off my cassock in a matter of seconds, even as I hear a dozen other door-closings echo up and down the corridor. In a matter of moments, I change from black pants and T-shirt to rec clothes, then reopen the door and walk rapidly down the corridor, joining others on our silent but brisk march toward the stairwell to the basement shoe room. We duck into the chapel for a very short visit to the Blessed Sacrament before continuing on down to the lower level. In the shoe room many of us pick up ice skates, hockey sticks and jackets, and head out the door into the cold.

"Praise the Lord," says Leonard as I exit the door to join him.

"Amen," I say as we walk rapidly toward the hockey rink. "So you're going to try hockey?" I ask him.

"Andy talked me into it," he says. "We found a pair of skates that seem to fit me."

"Have you ever played before?"

"No, but I'm going to sort of observe and maybe play goalie a little."

The hockey rink is adjacent to the pump house, where we get our well water. The rink is a simple but adequate home-made structure, fashioned out of scrap two-by-sixes and other old lumber by some of the brothers during the warmer months. Now, thanks to a couple of Juniors going out under the frigid starscape last night and flooding it with a fire hose, there is a new, smooth layer of ice for our game. It is much easier than shoveling out a rink on the lake, and it is closer to the house, and the ice quality is much smoother.

"Lou," I say as I notice Lou Ranier walking behind us, "you're going to play hockey?"

"Yes," he says, "Andy talked me into it."

"You ever done it before?"

No, but I might play goalie a little."

We do not have a great quantity of hockey enthusiasts in our midst, and Andy is one of the best recruiters for new players.

Soon we are skating around the rink, warming up and checking the ice quality. Neither Leonard nor Lou are very good skaters, and that is why they are both picked for goalies on the opposing teams. Andy and I are captains, and we square off in the middle of the rink. Andy knocks the puck toward Alex Dubchek, who is one of his teammates, and I manage to skate over to Alex and steal the puck away from him and slap it toward Andy's goal. The puck ricochets off the edge of the cage and comes to rest right in front of Lou Ranier, Andy's goalie. Lou manages to bat it toward Andy, who now maneuvers it out and away toward our goal. One of my men, Pete Torre, nabs it away from Andy and knocks it toward me, but Barry Edelfort snatches it away from me and knocks it toward our goal. Leonard stands in front of the goal, stick in hand, as Edelfort thwacks the puck toward him. The puck sails through the air toward Leonard and hits him in the chest. He grimaces in pain, but he has saved us from a goal.

"Way to go, Leonard!" I shout, and his mouth breaks into a smile.

The game is fast and intense, and verbal interjections abound. The "crock" word is frequently forgotten, replaced by harsher, cruder expletives.

Now I send the puck back toward Pete Torre, and he knocks it toward Lou's cage, narrowly missing Lou... and a goal. Andy swoops in, snatches the puck and pops it out toward mid-rink, and Edelfort once again takes control and skates it down right in front of Leonard. Edelfort hits it, knocking it toward the edge of the goal, but Leonard performs an unlikely hand-save and the puck is ours once more. But not for long, because Edelfort and Andy commandeer it and steer it right toward Leonard again, and Leonard attempts yet another save amid waving, clacking sticks. Somehow, between Andy and Edelfort and a couple of other guys in the fray, a stick comes up from below and hits Leonard right in the groin. He falls to the ice and curls into a fetal crouch for a minute, groaning in pain, halting the game.

Soon Andy and Pete Torre are helping him back up, and they volunteer to assist him back to the house.

"Are you kidding?" Leonard says, "this is fun!"

And so the game continues. Now the puck cruises into their goal — Ranier's goal—and we score!

I can almost feel the desperation of the guys on Andy's team — they are behind, and there is not a lot of time left. They recklessly try to make a goal, and miss.

Soon enough, we have control of the puck again, and I make a desperate, strong slapshot toward the other goal. Edelfort intercepts it and slaps it vigorously back toward us. The puck takes off and sails, almost in slow motion, it seems, straight toward Leonard, and stops, absolutely, perfectly almost, in his mouth. There is blood.

"Leonard!" Edelfort shouts. "Oh my Go... Lord, I'm sorry!"

Leonard falls and lies on the ice for a moment, then gets up. He has a strange sort of twisted smile on his bloody, misshapen mouth, and upon closer examination we see that his two front incisor teeth have been broken off.

Andy and I assist him back to the house, his arms hanging over our shoulders.

"Ith thith... what they mean by...contemplathion in acthion?" Leonard blurts between laughs as he gingerly limps between us, spitting up blood and still limping from his earlier groin injury.

"That's a good one, Leonard," says Andy, "I'm not going to forget that one."

We take him to see Brother Ritchie in the Infirmary, who checks him out and makes a doctor's appointment for the groin slap, and an Orthodontist's appointment for the broken teeth. "Leonard," says Brother Ritchie, "I want you to stay in the Infirmary tonight, and tomorrow. And maybe longer. And I think you should swear off hockey for awhile."

That evening, before first grace at dinner, there are five novices kneeling in the center aisle to take culpas. Three of them are for "using language unbecoming of a religious at recreation," and two are for "carelessly causing injury to one of my brothers at recreation." All were participants in the hockey game.

***

"The unexamined life is not worth living."

Socrates

CHAPTER TWENTY-SIX

Lost in Translation

One morning, there is a new note on the bulletin board, the style of which we have become accustomed to:

Barry Edelfort has left the novitiate.
Please remember him in your prayers.

Fr. McKittrick

We get notes like this every so often, about once a month or so on average, and it is always a kind of a shock, because after living with someone for a year or more, you think you know him pretty well. And when a man leaves there is never any warning; it happens so early in the morning that no one sees it, and the guy who is leaving is instructed not to tell anybody beforehand. Once in awhile they do, though, due to very particular friendships. Which of course we are not supposed to have. I personally started to like Barry Edelfort after my initial snobbishness, and everybody already knew that he was having trouble learning Latin. Even though he had tutors and extra help, he was still far behind the rest of us. Still, I was surprised when I heard, through the grapevine, that that was the reason he left. Surprised because I figure that if the Mass is moving over to English, what's so important about Latin any more, anyway? Then I heard that he never had any other languages in high school either, and so he was having trouble with Greek, too. I would like to assume that maybe language studies were not his only reason for leaving, but I guess I'll never know for sure.

***

In late January Andy and I go to the synagogue one last time. On the return trip we get a ride from a man named Sam. We get out in St. Boni's at the juncture of highway seven and route ninety-two, about a mile from the house, but somehow Sam seems to know where we're from.

"Say hello to Fr. McKittrick for me," He says as we get out of the car.

"Fr. McKittrick?" Asks Andy uneasily. "You ah... you know him?"

"He says Mass at our parish church here every now an' then," he says. "Say, what's your names, anyhow?"

"Omygosh," I say, looking at my watch, "we'd better go right now —gotta mind the rules," and we head up the highway.

"Hey," yells Sam out of the car window, "if you're late, I can give you a ride up to the door," but we wave him off.

"You've been too good to us already, Sam," Andy yells as we continue up the highway.

A little later, as we approach the building, I catch a glimpse of a face staring at us from a second-floor window in the novitiate wing, and it gives me an uneasy feeling.

When we return to the house and Ordo Regularis, we have to keep mum about our little "caper," because we know that some of the men might report us if they knew.

I am just donning my cassock and tightening my cincture when I hear a knock on my door and look up to see Lou Ranier. My stomach tightens; he is definitely one of the people I do not want to inform about our little adventure.

"Wally," he says quietly, "where were you? We missed you at manualia after breakfast and lunch. We were worried about you."

"Well... I had some unforeseen difficulties that I had to..."

"...Don't worry about it—we managed pretty well without you. Not perfectly, but pretty well." He begins to walk away, and I sigh with relief. Then he turns around and says, "Oh yeah, and Fr. Harrison was looking for you. He said that if I saw you I should tell you to go and see him." I feel a renewed tightening in my stomach as he departs.

I decide that maybe I should head down to the Sarge's office and see what's up. I'm not sure what this is about, but I want to at least try to be on the up-and-up. As I climb the stairs and head down the corridor, I notice Fr. McKittrick's silhouette up ahead of me, knocking on the Sarge's door. He enters and closes the door behind him. I continue down the corridor until I am at the Sarge's door. I decide to wait until Fr. McKittrick leaves, then I'll knock. As I approach the door, I can hear the Sarge's voice, louder than normal, from inside the office:

"...The old coot is a madman, and he shouldn't be here, in contact with novices during their critical stages of formation. I personally think he should have been defrocked a long time ago. And in any case, he should not be in the same county, let alone the same building, with novices."

I get this sudden realization that he must be talking about the Padre! Then I hear Fr. McKittrick's voice: "Now Jim, I think you're being a bit harsh. He may be eccentric, but he is not unbalanced. And from what I hear of the catechetical discussions at Vatican II, in Rome, he may be ahead of his time in some ways..."

"I don't know what to say about that. I still think we need to do something. I've already talked to Bernie, and he's concerned. He's going to get back to me..."

"Bernie" must be Fr. Bernard Kemper, our current Fr. Provincial. It sounds like the conversation is winding down, so on impulse I cross the hall and enter the castle door, just before I hear the Sarge's door open and Fr. McKittrick walk away, down the corridor. Needless to say, after I leave the castle I decide not to knock on the Sarge's door. My mood has changed drastically, and I head down to my room, hoping that he doesn't come looking for me.

* * *

That very evening Andy, Leonard and I visit the Padre again. Leonard asked for, and received, permission yesterday. I haven't yet told anybody about the conversation I overheard between Fr. McKittrick and the Sarge, mainly because I haven't been able to talk to anybody until just now. I am wrestling with all of this psychological baggage, wondering whether I should tell Andy and Leonard before we arrive at the Padre's room. I decide to bring it up while we are visiting with the Padre.

When we enter his room, the Padre is sitting in what appears to be an electric wheelchair.

"Padre," says Andy, "is that a new wheelchair?"

"Yes," says the Padre, "Brother Mueller built it for a me. It's electric, with a two car batteries; he says it can a run for hours on a charge."

"Padre," says Leonard then, "Tell us a parable."

"Did I tell you the one about the wise old Rabbi?"

"No, I don't think so."

"Once there was a Rabbi," the Padre begins, "who was famous for his great wisdom. One day in class one of his students asked, "Rabbi, tell us a wise saying."

The Rabbi looked at a the class and a said, "On the day before you die, repent!"

The student smiled and said, "Thank you, Rabbi!" and then the class continued. But after a few minutes the student raised his hand again and a said, "But Rabbi, *every* day could be the day before I die."

"Exactly!" said the Rabbi.

Now the Padre asks, "Can any of you give me an example of a one difference between human nature and Divine Nature?"

"Human nature says, 'seeing is believing,' says Andy, "and Divine Nature says 'believing is seeing.'"

"Very good, Mr. Gallagher!"

"I've got one," says Leonard, "human nature says, 'Me first,' while Divine Nature says, 'God first.'"

"The Greatest Commandment," says the Padre, "love the Lord thy God above all else, and a love your neighbor as yourself."

"Padre," I say, finally getting a word in edgewise, "there's something I think we all need to talk about..."

Just then, there is a knock at the already-open door, and in walks The Sarge, followed by Fr. McKittrick. They are not smiling. Once again, I have a very strange feeling in my stomach; I did not speak soon enough.

"Hello, Reverend Fathers," says the Padre with a smile.

Fr. McKittrick nods and says somberly, "Hello, Father Lugieri. We are sorry to interrupt your visit, but we need to talk to these young men here. Carissimes Gallagher, Wentfogle, and Moriarity, please come with us."

As we stand up the Padre says, "Brothers, let us say our Hail Mary!"

We all put our hands in the circle and say the Hail Mary, and I wonder if the others notice that my hand is shaking. Fr. McKittrick stands back a bit and recites the prayer with us quietly; I do not see or hear The Sarge, but I feel his presence behind me somewhere.

As we leave, I glance back at the Padre, and I see what I can only describe as a look of sad resignation on his face.

As we walk down the corridor to Fr. McKittrick's room, Leonard is dismissed and told that he can go to the rec room to join the other novices. Now I am certain that it was Fr. Harrison, the Sarge, who saw Andy and me coming back to the House from that second-floor window.

Andy goes into the room first, with both of the priests. I am told to sit and wait on the bench outside. I try to strain my ears to hear what is being said, but they are talking quietly and there is just enough noise from the novice rec room at the end of the hall to drown them out.

When Andy leaves he heads down the hall in the opposite direction from the rec room, toward the chapel, without looking at me, and Fr. Harrison sticks his head out the door and asks me to enter.

I walk into the room and he closes the door after me.

"Carissime Moriarity," says the Sarge, "we know where you were today."

"Yes, Father," I say, and I feel terrible, not because I did something terrible in itself, but because I deceived my superiors, in a sense, by not asking permission or informing them of my whereabouts.

"I'm sorry, Father, I just thought it was an experience we could not pass up."

"Once again," says Fr. McKittrick, "I do not understand your intentions, Carissime Moriarity. By this time in your formation, you know that you are supposed to obey the Holy Rule and follow orders, rather than just disappear into town for a day without permission. Obedience is one of the three vows that you will take this coming August, if you are still here then." His tone is ominous.

"Father McKittrick," I say in my defense, "our original founders were all Jewish. I wanted to see what they do, how they do it, why they do it."

"That is all well and good, Carissime Moriarity, but there is a time and a place for that, and it should not be done at this stage of your formation. If it is that important to you, it can be done at a later time. Now is the time you should be concentrating on novitiate concerns, and the Holy Rule!"

Fr. Harrison has been listening the whole time, but now he adds, "We know that Fr. Lugierri is responsible for this."

"Oh no, Father," I say, "he did not put us up to this at all!"

"Carrissime Gallagher informed us that Fr. Lugierri gave him the name of the synagogue and the rabbi. Whether or not he suggested you go and see him, I consider him responsible, because I know he is filling your heads with subversive ideas."

"Subversive?" I repeat, as I look at Fr. McKittrick. He is watching Fr. Harrison talk, and I sense a slight hint of disagreement on his face.

"Yes, subversive," repeats Fr. Harrison. "We will do whatever is necessary to correct this problem," he continues. "Understand that you and Carissime Gallagher are on probation, and no more escapades like this will be tolerated. Are we clear?"

"Yes, Father," I tell him, and I mean it. Sort of.

"And of course, you are not to visit Fr. Lugierri again, under any circumstances. Understood?"

"Yes, Father."

He opens the door, and holds it open for me as I exit.

***

We have a fusion rec with the Juniors on a feast day near the end of January. Andy and I and Leonard take a fusion walk with Ken Matthews, hiking on a trail around the shore of the lake during afternoon rec. It is a mild, overcast afternoon in the low twenties, with little wind, and the countryside is cloaked under a shroud of snow.

"I recently visited the Padre," says Ken, "and I learned some more about him. It would be good for you to know, considering your present situation."

"We're all ears," I say then.

"First of all, did he ever tell you about his mother?"

"No."

"The Padre's mother was a Jew. His father was Catholic and wanted her to convert to Catholicism, but she considered it a betrayal to her family. She went to the synagogue every sabbath, but every Sunday morning, she got her little Ricardo out of bed, dressed him and sent him off to Mass while his Catholic father was sleeping off his wine.

"So then he asked me, 'Now, which of my parents do you think was a more pleasing to God?'"

None of us says anything.

"He says that he asked Roncalli the same thing, and Roncalli said to him, 'Ricardo, you are either a heretic or a saint. Maybe both, eh?'"

"So his mother was Jewish? That could explain a lot..." says Andy.

"Prior to the war," continues Ken, "the Padre was an outstanding scriptural scholar. Theologians, bishops, cardinals, and even the Pope would solicit his opinions. He did not tell me this part, by the way, he doesn't like to brag about himself. I learned some of this from other reliable sources. Then the war started, and some time during the war his mother died. The Padre changed after that. He was very saddened by his mother's death. After the war he took a sabbatical and went to the village where his mother had grown up, and he stayed with the local parish priest."

"What's a sabbatical?" I ask.

"Just taking some time off, sort of like a long vacation," says Ken. "One day while he was there, he entered the Jewish part of town and visited his mother's former synagogue. He learned that the rabbi had died, and they had not yet replaced him. Now the Padre was incognito; these Jewish people did not know who he was. He dressed like the rest of them, and they considered him one of their own. And then he went into the synagogue and began to interpret and explain the scriptures to the congregation."

"Sounds a little clandestine," says Andy as we head down a ravine, dubbed "George's Gorge" by one of the Juniors, and approach the shore of the frozen lake.

"He was so good," says Ken, "that soon everyone was coming to the synagogue to hear him, even some Gentiles. Since the Jews had no idea who he was, and they assumed he was Jewish, they asked him to join their synagogue. He graciously declined, but continued to teach them."

Now we are closer to the lake shore, moving southward across a small rise. "Then," says Ken, "the gronk hit the fan. The local parish priest with whom he was staying found out what he was up to and he informed the bishop. Very quickly, the Padre was summoned back to Rome."

"Just for preaching?" I say as we turn around and head back toward the House.

"The Vatican wanted to question him in detail," continues Ken. "After they learned everything, they demanded an apology. There was even talk of dismissing him from the priesthood, but the Padre did not understand why. To him, these people needed a shepherd, and so he stepped in and shepherded them in a way that made them comfortable. The Padre argued that he never really disobeyed any orders, and he never stopped saying Mass every day or helping out the Catholics in town; he just spent some of his time in the Jewish part of town as well. He never forsook his Christianity. On the contrary..." he pauses.

"On the contrary what?" asks Andy.

"...he insisted that he became a better Christian because of it," says Ken.

Now we are approaching the House, crossing a stream that leads from our lake to Mud Lake, and eventually to Lake Minnetonka, a few miles to the northeast.

"So," I say, "it sounds like they were really strict. What about the Order? He's still a member of our Order."

"His superiors were in disagreement about it," says Ken. "But then an old friend of his stepped in... Roncalli. He talked both the Church and the Order into a milder discipline. They simply asked him to leave Rome, and they removed him from his position as a theologian, and a professor."

"Why couldn't they just forgive him?" asks Andy.

"It's not so much a question of forgiveness," says Ken, "it's a question of appropriate behavior as a member of the priesthood... and as a theologian. Some thought he lost his direction after his mother's death. But did he really do anything wrong? People are still arguing about it. And I don't know all the details. So here we are, a few novices and a junior in our religious order, trying to figure it all out."

"Where did you learn all this?" I ask him.

"I learned some of it on my visits to him, but I also heard some from other sources. I can't really tell you who they are right now," he says. "Let's just say the Padre has some allies around here, and leave it at that."

***

I spend my points time tonight wondering why everything has to be so complicated. Why can't we just stick to the fundamentals? Tell people about the Beatitudes, and the works of mercy? And repentance? I mean, guys like Dismas get to Heaven, and what did he know?

***

The very next morning, in Rules Class, Fr. McKittrick has an announcement. "Fr. Lugierri is going to be transferred from our Infirmary to the Missouri Province Infirmary near St. Louis."

Alex Dubchek raises his hand.

"Yes, Alex?"

"Father, did the Pad... did Fr. Lugierri request this transfer?"

"No, but as you all know, in this order we go where we are assigned, without question."

Leonard raises his hand.

"Yes, Leonard?"

"Father, will you need help packing his things?"

"If Brother Ritchie needs assistance, I will let you know. Now," he adds, "we will continue our discussion on the vow of obedience...

"Therefore I tell
you, whatever you
ask for in prayer,
believe you have
received it, and it
shall be yours."

Mark 11:24

CHAPTER TWENTY-SEVEN

Another Kind of Prayer

Illumine your hearts with hunger, and strive to conquer
yourself with hunger and thirst; continue to knock on the
gates of paradise by hunger.

The Prophet Mohammed

We are seated at dinner in the refectory, listening to a Junior reading "The Making of the President, 1960," over the P.A. system. Platters of meatloaf, bowls —or "deeps" as we call them—of green beans, potatoes and gravy, and plates of bread are passed down the table. I notice that Andy, across the table and two down from me, is passing everything on and not taking anything save for some bread. He takes two slices and passes it on down, then pours himself a glass of water. His face is expressionless as he listens to the reading. I have already taken some meatloaf and beans, but now I forego the potatoes and gravy for some bread. I do this in part because I am not particularly hungry this evening, but also because I have a sort of compulsion to follow Andy's example, and I know that cutting down on food is a type of fasting. But what am I fasting for? Well, there are at least a million good causes out there, but right now I am upset about the Padre's situation, and so that's a really good cause to start with.

***

The following morning, I notice Andy taking only some toast, and passing up the eggs and sausage. No juice, cereal or milk, just water. Unsure of his motives, I decide to do the same, after I recall the Padre's words about prayer and fasting. I have a special intention I am praying about, and I am guessing that Andy has a similar idea.

At lunch time, Andy and I are at the same table again, and we both pass up everything except the bread and the water. Then I notice Pete Torre down at the end of our table, and he is doing the same thing.

During afternoon rec, Andy and I and some of the other guys play a heated game of basketball in the gym. Just before the bell rings, I ask him, "Are you praying for a special intention?"

"Oh yeah," he says, "how about you?"

I don't want to say more than I should, so I just nod and leave it at that.

The next time I pass the bulletin board, I notice a brief, hand-written note that says:

> Brothers in Christ, could you please say some prayers
> for a special intention of mine?
>> Andy Gallagher

Dinner time comes, and a few more of the men are just eating bread and water, and the platters of meat and vegetables sit at the ends of the tables, for the most part untouched. The dessert cake comes out, and it is passed down and most of it is returned to the waiters, uneaten.

As the waiters collect the platters of cake, I glance at the Fathers' table and notice the Sarge and Fr. Minister, who is in charge of all our meals, whispering to one another.

The next morning, few novices are eating any of the breakfast food except for the toast, and some water. I can see a number of deeps of pancakes and bacon and full pitchers of juice and milk returning, untouched, to the carts.

After the opening prayer at Rules Class Fr. McKittrick says, "Fr. Harrison wants to see each of you in private in his office, starting immediately after this class."

So now I am standing outside The Sarge's office, next in line after Andy, and he goes in. There are three more guys behind me, and I try as best I can to overhear Andy's conversation and at the same time try to pretend that I am not eavesdropping. The main reason I want to hear is because I honestly have not even asked Andy the specific reason for his fast and, while I have a pretty strong hunch, I want to find out for sure.

"...I don't think you understand the spirit of the novitiate, Carissime Gallagher," I hear The Sarge say through the door. "If you persist in this direction," he continues, "You may be asked to leave the novitiate."

"May I ask why?" asks Andy, and his voice sounds shaken, almost frightened.

"Because you are wasting food, you are making a mockery of Holy Obedience, you are making a travesty of the Holy Rule, and you may even be endangering your health. And all of this on top of your recent hitchhiking escapades... need I continue?"

"Father, I can only tell you the honest truth. I began fasting because of a special intention...(muffled)...had no idea anyone else was doing it.

I never mentioned fasting to anybody...I didn't think that my little fast would waste any food, because it always winds up in the stew, anyway..." Now his voice becomes too quiet to hear, and I back away from the door.

Andy comes through the door, his face a map of defeat; I enter the Sarge's room.

"Carissime Moriarty, I want to ask you one question," The Sarge begins as I sit down. "Why have you been fasting?"

"For a special intention, Father."

"Who put you up to it?"

"No one, Father. Honestly."

"Do you understand the seriousness of this transgression?"

"No, Father. And I did not think it was a transgression."

"Once again, you have elected to do something above and beyond our regular order, without asking permission first. Do you understand that, if necessary, I am prepared to ask you and some other novices to leave the novitiate?"

"I had no idea..."

"What is your intention?"

"For the welfare of the Pa... Fr. Lugierri."

"Did he suggest this?"

"No, Father. I haven't talked to him since... you forbade us to."

"Carissime Moriarty, I am going to order you, right now, to start eating again. Do you understand me?"

"Yes, Father," I say quietly, and there is an awkward moment of silence.

"Father, may I ask one question?"

"Ask."

"Does the Church recognize fasting as a form of prayer?"

"What are you getting at?"

"Our Lord fasted when He prayed. The apostles fasted when they prayed. Trappist Monks... nuns... Jews... Buddhists... Muslims... American Indians... Hindus... they all consider fasting an important part of prayer."

"What is your point?"

"I just wonder what it's going to look like if you kick me out of the novitiate for..."

"For what?"

"For praying." With that, I rise from my chair and walk to the door.

"Carissime Moriarity?"

I begin to open the door. "Father?"

"You are excused."

"Holding onto anger is like grasping a hot coal with the intent of throwing it at someone else; you are the one getting burned."

Gautama Buddha

CHAPTER TWENTY-EIGHT

A Desperate Move

I am lying awake in my bed, unable to sleep. My real intention for fasting and praying was not exactly just for the Padre's welfare; I have been praying specifically to keep the Padre from being transferred away from here, to Missouri or anywhere else. I keep thinking that maybe, after we take vows and move over to the Juniorate side, we will be allowed to visit him again. I reach over to the desk to pick up my watch and see what time it is. 1:20 AM. I turn over and look up at the crucifix on the wall, barely visible in the dim light coming through the transom from the night lights in the corridor. *Should I attempt a rosary?*

Now I notice a subtle change, the briefest flash of red across the ceiling, then another. The pattern continues, getting brighter, and it is coming from the window. I hop out of bed and look out of my window to see, moving along the entrance drive, a police car with emergency lights flashing, followed by an ambulance. I jump out of bed, pull on pants over my pajamas, don slippers and cassock, and trot down the corridor as quietly as possible toward the chapel. I manage to see, from the windowed cloister walk, the two vehicles pulling up to the garage. I rush down the cloister walk and down the steps by the refectory, then into the basement corridor.

Now I see four people wheeling a gurney from the garage entrance into the basement corridor. They turn the corner and guide it directly toward me. I step to the side to let them pass, not caring at all if they see me. There are two ambulance attendants, and Fr. Minister (Fr. Gebhart is his real name) and Brother Ritchie, the Infirmarian. And prostrate on his back upon the gurney, eyes open, staring up into space, lies the Padre, with a black kippa on his head.

Fr. Minister and Brother Ritchie notice me as they pass by. "Shouldn't you be in bed, Carissime?" asks Fr. Minister quietly.

"I... wanted to help, if possible," I blurt out.

"Don't worry, we've got things under control," says Brother Ritchie.

I watch them wheel the Padre into the Infirmary and close the door behind them. After a moment of silence, I ascend the steps to the cloister walk and return to my room, wondering what the crock is going on.

It takes me some time, and at least three rosaries, to get back to sleep.

$$* * *$$

The following morning in Rules Class, Fr. McKittrick appears concerned. "Fr. Lugierri was discovered out on the highway last night," he says slowly. "A motorist saw him and managed to avoid hitting him, so he was not injured."

"Father," asks Alex, "how did he get out there?"

"He managed to drive out there in his electric wheelchair." He pauses for a moment. "The sheriff called an ambulance and they brought him home late last night, and this morning he was taken into the hospital in Waconia for tests."

"Father," asks Andy, "Do they... do you know why he was out there?"

"I cannot answer that question at this time, Andy. We will do whatever we can to find out."

I look over at Leonard, and he stares intently at Fr. McKittrick.

* * *

While the Padre is in the hospital, a signup sheet appears on the bulletin board for volunteers to help pack his things for his transfer to St. Louis. Since he is not around, and we won't actually see him, I figure it's all right to sign up. So do Andy and Leonard and Alex.

When the four of us arrive at the Padre's room, Brother Ritchie is there to meet us.

"You can retrieve his trunk and some packing boxes from the trunk room," says Brother Ritchie, "he has a lot of extra curios and things that won't fit into the trunk."

Alex and Andy depart for the trunk room, and Leonard and I have a look around while they are gone. We start opening drawers and cabinets, just to get an idea of what we might have to pack.

Then Leonard goes to the rear corner of the room and tries to pull open a closet door. It seems to be locked or something, and I go back to help him. After a couple of real hard jerks, the door gives way.

"Holy crock," says Leonard, looking up, and I follow his gaze up to the top shelf, and there, lined up like props in a costume shop, are a number of different hats and headpieces. A biretta, a Sikh turban, a couple of kippas, a bishop's mitre, an Islamic Kufi, and some others I cannot identify.

Leonard and I stare at each other for a moment.

"He's a man of many hats," I say quietly.

Then Brother Ritchie re-enters the room. Just as he starts to say something, Andy and Alex come in behind him, pushing a dolly with the Padre's trunk and some packing boxes on it.

"Men," says Brother Ritchie, "I just received a phone call from the hospital. You can return that stuff to the trunk room."

We all stare at him as he continues, "Fr. Lugierri is returning from the hospital this afternoon. Doctors' orders are that he rest for at least a month before he can be transferred to St. Louis."

"How is he, Brother Ritchie?" asks Andy.

"He suffered some exposure," says Brother Ritchie, "because he was out there in the elements for awhile, with nothing more than a sweater over his cassock."

"Did he tell you why he was out there?" Andy asks.

"The Doctors say that he could have had a mild stroke, maybe became disoriented, but he hasn't exhibited any stroke symptoms, other than aphasia."

"Aphasia?" asks Alex.

"Inability to speak," says Leonard.

"So he can't talk?" I ask then.

"That seems to be the case," says Brother Ritchie.

"When... when was he told about his transfer to St. Louis?" asks Andy then.

"A few days ago," says Brother Ritchie.

"How did he take it?" Andy asks. "I mean, when you told him about the transfer?"

"Actually, Fr. Harrison came and told him," says Brother Ritchie.

"The Sarge," I say quietly.

"The Padre just nodded, and didn't say anything," says Brother Ritchie.

***

"After undergoing some tests," Fr. McKittrick says at Rules Class the following morning, "Fr. Lugierri has been returned to the Infirmary."

Lou Ranier raises his hand.

"Yes, Lou?" says Fr. McKittrick.

"Father, how long will he be around? Before he is transferred, I mean."

"It would not be wise to transfer him right now, in his present condition, so his transfer has been postponed indefinitely," says Fr. McKittrick.

I look over at Andy, and he grins and gives me a little "thumbs-up" sign.

CHAPTER TWENTY-NINE

In Pursuit of Eloquence

We second-year novices have some other special tasks, over and above the "experiments," to prove that we are worthy of being "company men," so to speak. For example, each of us has to give a speech about Mary, called a "Marianum," to the entire community. We must do this in the refectory, during lunch, no more than one speech per day, on various days throughout the winter. We are each given a slightly different topic about Mary to develop and expound upon for a few minutes during the lunch period. It is not an easy thing to do because, as I have said before, practically everyone in the audience either already is, or will soon become, an orator, a teacher, or a preacher of God's word.

In a way it's like trying out for the Green Bay Packers in front of Vince Lombardi, Bart Starr, and all the rest of the team. You know that every word, every gesture, every eye movement is going to be critically analyzed.

The Sarge, Fr. Harrison, is our mentor and our "coach," so to speak, and in some ways he can be as formidable as Vince Lombardi, if not more so.

We have to give our Marianum while standing on a little riser, about the height of a chair, fairly close to the rest of the community, without the use of a microphone. We first of all write our speech, then fine-tune it and memorize it, then practice it with the Sarge looking on. He will then tell us how to emphasize certain points, what gestures to use, and so forth.

My theme is about Mary's "Openness" to God's calling. I am able, with research and practice, to make an acceptable go at my topic. The Sarge gives me passing grades, and I feel good about my efforts.

Leonard is up the week after me. I know he has been working extra hard on his speech, because he is not good in this area. I actually walk past the empty refectory one day when he is practicing there with the Sarge, and he sounds okay. Not exceptional, but sort of acceptable. For Leonard.

Then, on the day Leonard gives his Marianum, there is a problem. Maybe it is because his speech just happens to be on a certain topic — Mary's Humility — or maybe it is something else that triggers it. He starts out okay, when he talks about the Annunciation, when the Angel Gabriel appears to Mary and tells her that she is to become the mother of Jesus. But then when he gets to the birth in the stable, he begins to fall apart. It is embarrassing, not just to him, but to all of the audience, because we want so badly for him to finish. He just winds up his speech with a lot of self-conscious laughter, and an assertion that Mary is really a humble, loving mother. "She really loves us all, more than we can imagine," he says before stepping down from the platform.

Later, at rec, he starts out by saying that his downfall is once again because of the stable problem. The idea that Jesus was born in a barn, so to speak, somehow distracted him at the wrong time.

"Is that really the reason, you think?" I ask him.

He pauses, looks at the landscape for a moment.

"Okay. When I think more about it, I think it's more of a... 'trust' issue."

"Trust issue?"

"Do you remember when those psychologists came, soon after we entered? They told me that I had answered some of the questions on the tests in such a way that I seemed to exhibit a trust problem. I was amazed at that, and I guess it goes back to... to my father. I'm sure that I could profit from some psychoanalysis, but... Fr. McKittrick has been a pretty good listener, even though he's not a licensed psychologist, you know? But back to my Marianum speech, it seems like I can't really concentrate on what I have to say when I feel there is someone in the room I can't trust."

"Okay," I say then, "that's really interesting, actually. May I ask who it is in this house you don't think you can trust?"

"I'll give you one guess."

"The Sarge, right?"

"Yeah. I just get the feeling that he doesn't like me, and he's out to get me. And that, combined with my nervousness from speaking in front of a room full of people, made me fall into a laughing fit at the worst possible moment."

271

"The best way to
find yourself is to
lose yourself in the
service of others."

Mahatma Gandhi

CHAPTER-THIRTY

Sisters in the Cities

S pringtime comes, and with it, my turn at Hospital Probation. This is the one I've been worried about. Because, as I have said more than once, I've never been excited about getting old men up out of bed in the morning, helping them get dressed, emptying their urine bags or giving them baths. But all the guys have told me that it's less of a problem than it sounds like, and the nuns we work with are helpful and inspiring.

Leonard is my partner for the month. Near the end of April we are driven into Minneapolis by one of the fathers, to St. Joseph's Home for the Aged, run by an order of nuns, "Les Soeurs de Pauvres," or "The Sisters of the Poor," who specialize in caring for poor people. Both Pete Torre and John Marconi, the two probationers stationed here for the previous month, seem a bit dejected when we show up.

"What's wrong with you guys?" I ask. "You look sad."

"We don't want to leave," says Torre with a wry smile.

"You guys are gonna love it here," adds Marconi. "Just don't get used to it; the days go by awfully fast."

They start showing us around the place, and the first person we meet is Tom McFinn, a ninety-five-year-old Irishman, taking short little steps down the hall with his walker. "Hail Mary....Hail Mary..." he says as he inches along, his rosary clenched between his fingers and the walker handle-bars. "Hello Brothers, nice ta meet ya. Ya'd be saprised at some o' the things these beads 'a brought me, ya'd be saprised... Hail Mary..."

Torre and Marconi spend the next few hours teaching us the lay of the land. "Everyone here calls us 'The Brothers,'" says Pete as he and John show us our sleeping quarters in the old mortuary building, across a small parking lot from the main building. We set down our suitcases and look around. It is a large room with dividers and curtains separating it into two bedrooms and a living room. There is also a bathroom with a shower.

"They used to have all their funerals here," says Torre, "until they changed their policy and started holding them in regular funeral parlors."

"How many... how many funerals do you think they had here?" I ask.

"Hundreds," says Marconi, "they did it until just a couple of years ago, and the place was built in the eighteen-eighties."

"Hundreds?" says Torre, "I'd say more like thousands. None of the patients leaves here alive, and if they average only two funerals a month, for eighty years, that's almost two thousand since the place opened."

I look around the room once more; it is stately yet simple. Thankfully, I don't believe in ghosts. Most of the time, anyway.

After Marconi and Torre show us the ropes, they catch a ride back to the House from another priest.

There are a few old men we have to help out of bed and dress every morning. One of them is a man named Ferdinand Grumman, but he prefers to be called "Grandpa." He is not a very large man, and of course he was probably taller in his youth than he is now. His "youth" took place in the eighteen-eighty's, a while before the automobile and the airplane were invented. He was born in eighteen sixty-eight, three years after Lincoln was shot. He was in his mid-teens when both my grandfathers were born in eighteen eighty-two, and they both died before my fifth birthday. He is ninety-seven years old, so he was probably a teenager when this ancient building he now dwells in was erected. This old guy has seen a lot, and he frequently reminds us of that.

"I seen more than enough," he wails on our first morning as we wake him up at five-thirty a.m., "I was in the Indian war at Wounded Knee. But I never fired a shot. I couldn't shoot women an' children. By the time the first World War came along, I was too old to go, I was forty-six. I seen enough, an' I wonder why God don't jes' take me. Ohhh, it hurts sa bad, the artritis jes' hurts sa bad..."

Every morning at five-thirty, we manage to get him to sit up on the side of his bed, already clad in his white "union suit," the old-fashioned long underwear that men of his generation wear for both pajamas and underwear, and dress him in shirt, pants, suspenders and shoes, and get him up off the bed and into his wheelchair. Then we push him out into the hall, and park him there to sit and wait until Mass. Within minutes he is fast asleep again, leaning sidewise in his wheelchair like a listing ship. We wonder why he has to get up so early when he is going to fall asleep again anyway, but the sisters say it's healthy for him and his peers to get them up and get their blood circulating, and keep them alive and as healthy as possible until God decides it is time.

***

In a matter of days Leonard and I adjust to our new schedule. And I have to admit that the guys were right; I actually do enjoy it, and I can tell Leonard does too.

For one thing, there is a spirit about this place that is hard to put into words. These nuns spend their whole lives serving the old people and trying to make them happy. If anyone has a complaint, the nuns really try to fix things as best they can. And some of them, like Sister Jacqueline and Sister Bernadette, are really getting to me, almost like I have a little crush on them, or something. Sister Bernadette speaks with a French accent. John Marconi told her she was *gentille*, which means nice or kind in French, I think, and it made her blush. Okay, I know Fr. McKittrick said that there is no such thing as a platonic relationship between a man and a woman, but I did not really understand what he meant until I met these nuns. Even though they wear these religious outfits to sort of minimize sexual attraction and all that, when you start understanding where they are coming from, and where their hearts are, and you look into their eyes, they're all of a sudden incredibly beautiful. And that's when you begin to realize more than ever that all the shallow gronk that Hollywood and the media throws at us, just emphasizing how women look in a swimsuit, or less, just becomes laughable; some people in Hollywood know less about real beauty, and real love, than a pig. At least that's my opinion.

This morning I have to help another old guy, Harry Martin, put on his shoes. This seems simple enough at first, but Harry has had a significant stroke, and so he has about a three-word vocabulary. The only thing he ever says is, "Trees an' trees," and it seems like that phrase can have a variety of meanings to him, because he uses it in greeting, departing, and in every other situation that requires speech. I try to put one of his shoes on his foot, and he keeps resisting me and shaking his head and saying, "Trees an' trees!"

"What?" I say, "Don't you want me to put your shoes on?"

He shakes his head and says, "*Trees and trees!*"

"I'm sorry, but I'm not sure what you mean," I say, trying to be as patient as possible.

He looks at me as if I am very thick-skulled and says, slowly and emphatically, while pointing at the shoes, "Trees...and... trees!"

"Um... okay, you want me to ah, polish them or something?" He just shakes his head and points at the shoes and repeats, with less patience than before, "*TREES...AND...TREES!*"

Finally, after several more moments of frustration, he turns and points to a drawer behind him, repeating his mantra. I get up and open the drawer and find a second pair of shoes in there, and I pull them out, and he smiles. "Trees and trees," he says with a nod and a happy smile. I slip them onto his feet and tie them.

"Trees an' trees," he repeats, pointing to the other, unwanted pair of shoes, and then pointing to the drawer. I put the other shoes into the drawer and he beams and nods, saying "trees and trees," one more time with a wave as I depart from his dormitory ward.

Later that morning, we learn that Joe Gustafson has pulled out his catheter. He does this fairly often, and Sister Jacqueline asks us to assist her in replacing it.

"Now Joe," she says with a smile as we wheel Joe into his dorm area, "remember, you're not supposed to pull out your catheter."

"I don' like it," he grumbles.

"Well, you'll be happier if you keep it in," she says in a kindly way.

After everything is prepped, she undoes his trousers, takes his penis in her gloved hand and methodically pushes the lubricated tube up into his urethra with the other hand.

"There are balloon catheters available," says Sister Jacqueline to Leonard and me, "and they stay in place better, but they can be dangerous when these fellows try to pull them out, so we seldom use them."

"There Joe," sister Jacqueline continues kindly, "now remember, keep your catheter in this time."

Joe grunts and looks off into space.

✳ ✳ ✳

Even with daily meditation, Mass, and the various chores around the place, including serving meals in the old men's dining room — the sisters take care of the elder ladies in another wing of the home — we still manage to have some nice stretches of free time on certain days. That, along with the mild spring weather and two ancient but functioning bicycles, allows us some enjoyable excursions into the world we have been away from for so long.

On our first day of extended TL, or free time, on one of the first really warm days of spring, we ride the bikes downtown and stop at the Foshay Tower, the tallest building in town. We enter the building and ask the elevator operator if we can ride to the top, but when he tells us it will cost us fifty cents apiece, we politely decline and go back outside and point our bikes toward the University of Minnesota campus. We don't have fifty cents!

We approach the dark red brick buildings and ride between two of them to discover a stately campus surrounded by more such buildings, with students by the hundreds lounging around on the quadrangles of fragrant green grass. I have never been to a secular college campus when classes were in session before, and it is pretty interesting just to check this place out. I get the feeling Leonard is a little scared, but does not want to show it.

"What's that tune you're whistling?" he asks me when we stop riding for a moment.

"Oh, yeah," I say, "it's called 'Whistle a Happy Tune.' Did you ever see 'The King and I?'"

"No..." he says quietly.

"Just whistle a happy tune, and no one really knows you're afraid," or something like that.

"Do you think I'm afraid of this place?"

"I don't know. Are you?"

"Well, I just really feel like I'm out of my element, you know?"

"I can totally agree with that," I say with a laugh. "I mean, this isn't exactly *ordo regularis!*"

We continue the ride along a sidewalk. The girls are prettier than ever, and the hemlines are more revealing than when we entered the Order almost two years ago. It seems like the attractiveness of girls in general has increased dramatically in the past two years, almost like it is directly proportional to the amount of time that I have spent away from them. Which is significant, to be sure. There are basilisks by the score, and it is hard not to stare at them.

We pull up at the physics building because Leonard thinks he might want to major in physics, or even astronomy, after we get out of the Juniorate and move on in our studies. I, on the other hand, would prefer History or English Literature. I sit and wait on the steps outside the physics building, guarding the bikes and inhaling the incredible aromas of Spring, while Leonard takes a quick tour inside.

A little ways away, some of the male students are tossing a football around, and I feel some kind of camaraderie with them, even though I am on such a different career path than they are. How many of these students are my age, I wonder?

There are some lovely damsels sitting in the grass nearby, and I try to appear as if I am not listening in on their conversations, even though I am.

"Hey Silver," one girl says to another, "how was your French test?"

"It blew," says 'Silver,' "I didn't know half the vocabulary." The girl's hair color appears closer to gold than silver, and so I wonder how she acquired that nickname. Unless it's her real name, of course. But if that's not the case, maybe she collects silver. Or maybe her father owns a silver mine. Probably not, though...

Leonard returns shortly. "It's mainly a lot of classrooms and labs," he says, "and I didn't know what to look for. They have that observatory dome on the roof, but I couldn't get in to see the telescope."

"You're back pretty fast," I say. "How did you cover that whole building?"

"Well, I didn't really. I've got a headache, so I cut it short."

We hop onto our bicycles and head back to the home.

***

The next morning is Saturday, and we have to wheel some bins of bed linens down to the basement laundry. There we meet three high school girls who help out in the laundry, as well as in the ladies' dining room and other places around the home. Their names are Catherine, Lesley and Janet. They wear special blue and white striped uniforms, sort of like candy-stripers in regular hospitals. One of them, Catherine, is blonde and sort of pretty. Of course, the other two are cute, too... all girls are cute in some way or another, from my current perspective. They have a portable radio playing as they work. A song comes on that I never heard before, and it is really good: two guys singing, *"Hello darkness my old friend...I've come to talk with you again..."* I continue to listen to it as long as I can until the girls turn around and say hello to us.

"Hi," I say, "I'm Brother Wally, and this is Brother Leonard." I assume it's okay for us to talk to them, as long as it is sort of work-related and is not just socializing. But because I like this song, which I also should not really be thinking about, I have to ask, "Do you know the name of that song that's playing? Is that the Beatles, by any chance?"

"The Beatles? Oh no," says one of them, "That's not what they sound like. I never heard this one before, but it's pretty cool, isn't it?"

"Yeah, definitely. So," I continue, "what year are you girls in school?"

"Lesley and Janet are juniors, and I'm graduating in three weeks," says Catherine.

"Oh yeah?" I say, realizing she is only two years younger than me, "Congratulations!"

Leonard, meanwhile, is grinning and laughing a little bit, not really taking part in the conversation.

"And, she's valedictorian of her class," says Janet all of a sudden.

"*Maybe*," says Catherine, blushing a bit. "We won't know for sure until just before graduation."

"Sounds like you're doing well," I say then.

"She's got scholarship offers, too," says Lesley.

"Well, congratulations again," I say.

"Yeah," says Leonard finally.

"So, where are you going to college?" I ask.

"Nowhere just yet," Catherine says. "Actually, I'm going to become a postulant, with the Sisters here. And if it works out, I'll become a novice."

"Really?" I say, probably with more surprise than I intended.

"Yeah, really," she says with a smile. "Does that surprise you?"

"Well, yeah, I mean, it's nice to hear," I say then.

Then Sister Jacqueline shows up. "Brother Wally and Brother Leonard, we need you up in the kitchen," she says.

"See you later, girls," I say, wondering whether I've been too talkative as we head up the stairs.

When we get to the kitchen, the Good Mother — the Sister Superior here at the home—greets us.

"Sure an' we don't think we need you now, after all," she says in her Irish accent.

"Oh, really?" I say.

"Yes, the freezer is workin' again. It broke down, but I fixed it, same way I fixed it before. We were goin' to ask you brothers to move some things out of the bad freezer, and put them in another one, but it's okay now."

"Well, how did you fix it?" I ask, marveling at her apparent technical know-how.

She looks at me for just a moment before she says, "Come an' see," and she opens the freezer door. "Right inside, on the left."

I peek inside, and there, standing on the shelf, about eight inches tall, is what appears to be a statue of St. Joseph.

"You're kidding, right?" I say with a grin. But as I study her face, I can tell she is not.

"Look," she says, as her eyes grow larger, "I have no idea why it works, but it does. This isn't the first time I've tried it!" She has this funny smile on her face, and I just turn from her to Leonard and notice that he is as perplexed, if not as amazed, as I am.

"Well," I manage to say, "it's a lot quicker and cheaper than calling a repairman, I'll grant you that!"

"Sure an' he *is* our patron saint here, this bein' St. Joseph's Home," she says with a wink before we leave to do some more chores.

"Ahhh!" I say to Leonard when we get back upstairs to swab the men's room, "St. Joseph in the freezer? I mean, there are a lot of weird miracles I've heard about, but this one takes the cake!"

"What other sort of weird miracles have you heard about?" asks Leonard.

"Okay, I mean, here's just one. You ever heard of St. Don Bosco?"

"Yeah, isn't he the guy who had a school for juvenile delinquents or something?"

"Right. In Italy I think, about a hundred years ago. Well, I heard that Don Bosco did not have enough bread to feed a large group of hungry boys one day, and he blessed this basket of about twenty rolls and started handing them out to everyone, and there were more than enough rolls to feed four hundred boys!"

"I never heard that one," he says.

"And of course, there's the Padre with all his stories of Lourdes and Fatima and other visions of Mary. And now this! I mean, don't you have trouble believing this stuff?"

He just grins and shrugs.

"Faith is not some-
thing to grasp. It is a
state to grow into."

Mahatma Gandhi

CHAPTER THIRTY-ONE

Believing is Seeing

The next morning, after we wake Grandpa and dress him and seat him in the hall before Mass, I notice, parked in the corridor nearby, another old man in a wheelchair. One of the older nuns is assisting him. The nun doesn't seem to be much younger than the old man, and her fingers are bent with arthritis, but she is washing his face and helping him blow his nose. He is grumpy, like most of the old men this time of morning, and she is just being so sweet and nice to him.

"There you go, Albert," she says, "see, now don't you feel better?"

Albert frowns.

"Albert, don't you want to go dancing tonight?" she continues. "I thought you were gonna take me dancing."

"You can't dance," says Albert, "Yer a *nun*, fer chrissake."

"Oooh, Albert, now don't you go using Our Lord's name in vain. And I can too dance. Watch!"

Now she starts to do a sort of demure little jig, as another nun starts clapping her hands in time.

Albert grins and begins to laugh loudly.

"See now, Albert? Doesn't it feel good to laugh?"

After that, Leonard and I introduce ourselves to the "dancing nun," and learn that her name is Sister Margaret. Then she pulls us aside and quietly tells us, "Some of these men don't have much faith. We just want them to know that they are loved."

Later on, at Mass, we are surprised to see Catherine, one of the helpers we met yesterday, in attendance. It is Sunday, so she doesn't have school, and we learn that she is here to help lead the singing. She invites Leonard and me to sing with her, since we know the musical parts of the Mass.

When Mass begins, Catherine picks up a guitar and starts playing it and begins to sing the Kyrie Eleison — "Lord Have Mercy" — and I am stunned. She sounds like an angel, practically. And even though Leonard and I and some of the sisters sing along with her, her voice practically drowns the rest of us out.

***

That afternoon, Leonard and I ride the bikes to Minnehaha Falls, where we have a little picnic in the park with sandwiches, chips, and soda. Then we walk near the base of the falls, and Leonard kneels down by the edge of the stream and starts fishing around in the water with his hands. He picks up a stone from the bottom, examines it, and drops it back in. He does this several more times, until he finds one that he likes. He wipes it off with a paper napkin, rolling it around in his hand.

"This would make a good wotai stone," he says, as he hands it to me.

"What's a wotai stone?" I ask as I examine it.

"According to the Lakota, it's a stone that comes to you at an important time in your life. It may contain a pattern that has a unique, personal meaning with special significance for its owner."

I continue to inspect it, and it does have pretty lines and shapes in it. I hand it back to Leonard and look down at the stream, then bend down and run my fingers over some of the stones there, picking up a few of them to inspect them. But I cannot find one that compares to Leonard's stone in color and beauty.

"Your stone almost seems like it should not have been here," I say, "it's so different from the other stones."

"According to the Lakota, Wakan Tanka, the Great Spirit, meant for me to find this stone here from the beginning of time," says Leonard. "Or, maybe He meant for you to have it." He hands it to me again. "You can keep it. I already have one of my own that I found a couple of years ago."

"Thank you, Leonard," I say as I put the stone in my pocket. We head back over to the bikes. I notice that the sky is clouding up, and I wonder if we will make it back to the home in time before it rains.

We are riding down a city street when we hear a crack of thunder, and it begins to pour. We pull over to the curb where some people are gathered under a marquee, filing into a building. We have locks for the bikes now, since the nuns decided we needed them. The nuns have a network of helpful people who like to give them things, and so when they mention anything they might need, as long as it is not an unreasonable request, someone always provides it for them. We quickly lock the bikes to a parking meter in the pouring rain, and duck into the building. As we enter I notice a sign on the door that says: KTXZ TV.

We find a men's room down a hallway and dry our hair and our faces with some paper towels. When we exit, we notice more people filing past along the hallway.

"Right this way, gentlemen," says a woman in the hallway, and I notice she is looking at us and beckoning. "There are plenty of seats," she continues.

We follow the crowd, and soon we enter a brightly-lit television studio, with all kinds of big theatrical lights hanging from a grid on the ceiling. There are three large TV cameras on the floor of the studio, manned by cameramen wearing headphones and microphones.

Ushers direct us to seats. The studio layout is that of an amphitheater, and in the central staging area where all the cameras are focused, there is a dark wood table and three empty chairs.

"A TV show," says Leonard. "Do you think we should stay?"

"Why not?" I say, "it's probably still pouring outside."

We take our seats and look around the studio. Most of the people in the audience are somewhat older than we are, conservatively dressed, and many of them appear to be holding Bibles. I cannot help but notice several large TV monitors placed at intervals around the studio for the audience and others to watch.

"What kind of a show is this?" I ask the woman seated next to me.

"You don't even know?" She asks. "A religious debate. I hope you're up on your Bible verses."

Suddenly we hear some music, and on the TV monitors we see the opening titles for a show called, "Sunday Afternoon." Then a well-dressed, middle-aged man enters from a side door and leads two other people out to the table and chairs in the central area.

One of them is an older, distinguished-looking gentleman, and the other is a well-dressed, middle-aged lady. The gentleman and the lady are also carrying Bibles. They all take seats, and the middle-aged man, evidently the host, seats himself between the other two.

"Good afternoon, Ladies and Gentlemen," says the host, looking at one of the cameras as he holds up a magazine with a cover on it that reads, in large white letters across a black background, "Is God There?" One of the cameras zooms in on it, and we see a closeup of the magazine cover on the monitors.

"I am sure many of you have seen this week's American News Magazine," the host continues, as he turns slowly around with the magazine held high, so that all of the audience members have a chance to see the cover. "Today we will be hosting a debate between Mrs. Lillian Marshall Kennedy, president and founder of the National Atheists' Association, and the Reverend Francis Marion Huston, a well-known minister of the Church of Christ the Lord.

"Now I want to remind you that you audience members are invited and encouraged to participate and ask questions, if you feel so moved. If you have a question, please raise your hand and we will offer you a microphone, so that our viewers can hear you. Lillian, would you like to begin?"

"Hello everyone," says Mrs. Kennedy, and there is a slight rustling, or perhaps a murmur, among the audience. "I am so overjoyed to see this article," she continues, "although I did not like everything I read in it regarding religion. But regarding atheism, I have to say that our wonderful association has been growing by leaps and bounds. More and more people in this country and around the world are beginning to see the light, and to understand that religion in all its forms is biased, it is a pack of cruel lies, and it is a system of brainwashing that stifles the growth of its followers..."

The audience begins to murmur again, and groan.

"With that said," she continues, "I want to ask the audience for a show of hands. How many atheists are here today?"

A few hands go up, in various parts of the audience.

"Uh oh, I guess we have an uphill battle," she says with a smile. "Do any of you atheists have any questions?"

"Yes," says a young man of college age, raising his hand as a man approaches him with a microphone, "I want to ask Mr. Huston, if there is a God who is all-good and all-loving, why do little children get cancer and suffer and die?"

"Because we are in exile," says the Reverend Huston without hesitation. "When those children get to Heaven, they will forget all about the pain that they had to suffer from cancer, and they will have eternal life and eternal happiness with God in Heaven."

The audience applauds.

"Well," says Mrs. Kennedy, "I have a different answer. There is no God, there is no Heaven, and there is no exile. Life is what it is, and you have to make the best of it."

The audience murmurs.

"And now Mr. Huston," Mrs. Kennedy continues with a forced smile, "I would like to ask you a question: what fables did you tell your congregation this morning?"

"I did not tell my fellow church members any fables, Mrs. Kennedy," says the kindly older gentleman, "I seek only the truth, as do the members of my congregation."

"Then how can you believe in this book of fiction?" she says as she holds up her Bible.

At this, I turn to Leonard and ask, "Is this woman serious?"

He just shrugs. I am really bothered by her hostile attitude, and I can tell Leonard feels the same way. She is apparently trying to rile up her opponent, and the audience as well.

"Why don't you read something from the Bible, Mr. Huston," she continues, "and I will point out to you how phony it is."

"Well, let's start with Genesis," says the Reverend Huston, in a kindly, grandfatherly way, as he opens his Bible and reads: "In the beginning, God created the Heavens and the earth..."

"Oh, Mr. Huston," says Mrs. Kennedy in a patronizing way, "most so-called *believers* don't even agree with the creation myth. Haven't you heard of evolution?"

"I believe what the scriptures say," says the Reverend Huston, "and they do not mention evolution."

Leonard leans over and whispers to me, "I was just thinking you should make a comment. What would the Padre say?"

I nod, and I start waving my hand in the air.

"Of course not," Mrs. Kennedy continues, "the scriptures are antiquated. They are completely eclipsed by modern scientific discoveries."

"Wait a minute," I yell out then, and a man approaches me and hands me a microphone. "You are both right, insofar as semantics will allow," I say.

Everyone looks at me, and the cameras turn in my direction, but I don't think about that as I continue, "The evolutionists believe that, billions of years ago, this lifeless ball of rock we now call earth, through a combination of elements, water and perhaps lightning and other phenomena, eventually spawned and nurtured living organisms. Over time these organisms evolved into higher life forms."

"Crude," says Mrs. Kennedy, "but essentially correct."

"And Genesis says," I continue, "Ah, let's see, Reverend Huston, what does Genesis say?"

Reverend Huston looks at his Bible and reads: "'In the beginning, the earth was a formless wasteland...'"

"Thank you, Reverend Huston. Now Mrs. Kennedy, what evolutionist would say that that is not a good description of the 'Lithosphere,' or the early, lifeless earth?"

"All of the verses following," says Mrs. Kennedy then, "are completely inaccurate. God did not form man out of clay..."

"Mrs. Kennedy," I say then, "Where did your breakfast come from this morning?"

"What kind of question is that?"

"What did you have? Eggs? Bacon? Or maybe cereal and milk? Fruit?"

"What difference does it make?"

"Whatever you ate this morning came from the earth. It did not come from outer space, it came from this planet. Everything you have ever eaten has come out of the earth. You and I and everyone else are made out of the clay, or dust, or dirt of the earth, because that's where our food comes from. That's where every living creature's food comes from. Therefore, how can you not believe that we humans, along with every other creature on earth, are not formed out of the clay of the earth?"

"Well, if I believe it, I don't believe that a God made it happen."

Leonard whispers something to me.

"Mrs. Kennedy," I say then, "did you ever read a poem that said, "'The fog comes on little cat's feet...?'"

"Yes," she says, "Carl Sandburg wrote it. But what's that got to do with anything?"

"Do you think that Sandburg really meant that fog really has feet like a cat?"

"No, of course not..."

"Let's read that passage from Genesis," I say then. The lady sitting next to me hands me her Bible, and I read, "'...Then the Lord God formed man out of the clay of the ground... and breathed into his nostrils the breath of life...' Now, if Sandburg wrote something like that, you would not object, would you?"

"If? Well, he didn't," she says then.

"What is your point, sir?" asks the host.

"My point," I say, "is that we don't need to demand that every word of the Bible has to be scientifically accurate. It is still essentially correct. And concerning the evolution theory, is it not reasonable to believe that what we call evolution could actually be God's creative process at work?"

A lot of the people in the audience are looking at me now, murmuring quietly, and I just turn to Leonard and wait for his next cue.

"Let's take a commercial break," says the host, "and we'll be right back."

"Who are you?" asks the lady sitting next to me during the break.

"We're two seminarians," I say to her, "we just came in out of the rain. And thanks for lending me your Bible."

"Well," she says, "You seem to know what you're talking about. Nice job!"

I thank her, and then the music comes back up.

"Let's take up where we left off," says the host.

Mrs. Kennedy looks right at me and asks, "You there, in the audence. How can the theory of evolution correspond with God creating man on the sixth day?"

"Okay, Mrs. Kennedy," I say, "what is a day? Twenty-four hours?"

"I should hope so," she says.

I look at Leonard.

"What if you were on the moon?" he whispers.

"What if you were on the moon?" I ask her.

"I'm not on the moon. What kind of a question..."

Leonard continues to inform me, and I repeat his words as I say, "A day on the moon is almost a month long... and a day on the planet mercury is almost three months long, which is also equivalent to a year on that particular planet. There are probably millions, if not billions, of planets in the universe, and probably no two of them have 'days' of identical length."

"What are you getting at?" Asks Mrs. Kennedy.

"I just want to know," I tell her with the most sincere voice I can muster, "if anyone can tell me what planet God was standing on when He created the universe?"

There is a loud reaction from the audience, including some laughter.

"Well, *I* sure cannot tell you," Mrs. Kennedy says, "because God wasn't even there!"

"And *I* cannot tell *you*," I return, "not because I believe God was not there, but because it is a big, wide universe, and a day could last for a million years, somewhere out there!"

The audience murmurs and laughs a little bit.

Mrs. Kennedy doesn't say anything, nor does the Reverend Huston or the host, as Leonard thumbs through the Bible the lady lent us and hands it to me, pointing to Psalm 89.

"Listen to this," I say, "Psalm 89: 'For a thousand years in Thy sight are as yesterday...' The psalmist is addressing God, who lives beyond time. Conclusion? God's days are not like our days; they could last for a very long time."

"Now Mr. Huston," she says, ignoring my statement as she turns to the Reverend, "I ask you once again to show me some proof that God exists."

He looks her straight in the eye and says, "I don't know if I can prove it to you... I just know that He exists."

"You *just know?*" she repeats sarcastically.

"My faith tells me that God exists."

The audience applauds.

"Your *faith?*" she says with the same air of sarcasm.

The audience murmurs, and many of them begin talking to each other. Leonard whispers to me again, and I raise my hand and shout, "Mrs. Kennedy!" The microphone man trots over to me and holds his mic close. 'You will never get 'courtroom proof' that God exists... God does *not want* us to have proof! If there was such proof, it would take away our gift of free will..." I pause to listen to Leonard... "because we would automatically choose Him and reject everything else. God wants us to have faith, to believe in something we *cannot see or prove*. Over and over again in the Gospels, Jesus says to those who have been healed, '*Your faith* has saved you...*Your faith* has healed you.' He also says, 'Blessed are they who have not seen and yet have believed.' Faith is something totally invisible; it is from the heart."

A round of applause erupts from the audience.

"That sounds like a lot of sentimental gibberish," she answers when the applause dies down.

Then the Reverend Huston suddenly speaks up. "You don't seem to have much faith, Mrs. Kennedy. Do you ever wish you had faith?"

"Absolutely not," she says with defiance.

"Mrs. Kennedy?" The Reverend Huston says then, "You will never have faith if you do not open your heart and ask for it. If you lack faith, you have to want it and ask for it in order to get it. With any kind of openness on your part, God will eventually grant you faith. But you, Mrs. Kennedy, will never have faith if you do everything in your power to suppress it. I will pray for you, and ask my congregation to do the same, to change your heart."

The audience applauds.

"I don't want your prayers, or anyone else's. Faith," she repeats, "is sentimental gibberish."

The audience is murmuring again.

"Mrs. Kennedy?" I say then, "Can I ask you one more thing? Have you ever met a person who was blind from birth?"

"Yes. I should think everyone has, at one time or another."

"According to your belief system, a man born blind should not believe in the existence of a sunset, because there is no way he will ever see one or sense one in any way; he has no proof."

"Well, he should listen to those who can see the sunset, and believe them."

"Do you believe people who say they've seen something you haven't? Like say, God?""

"Nobody," she says defiantly, "has ever seen God."

And all of a sudden, I get an inspiration. "Oh yes," I say then, "I saw God this morning. Clear as a bell."

"So, what did your God look like?" she asks with her now habitual tone of sarcasm.

"Like a nun, a sister." The feeling is even stronger now, and there is a lump in my throat. "She was washing the face of an old man, and he was complaining, and she was doing her best to cheer him up. And then she danced a little jig, and made him laugh. And I know she will be doing this again tomorrow, and the next day, and for the rest of her life until she's too old and tired to move."

The audience applauds again.

"She sounds like an ordinary caregiver to me," says Lillian.

"She's far from ordinary," I say, trying to keep my emotions in check, "She doesn't get paid a dime, oftentimes doesn't even get a 'thank you.' She does it out of love."

The audience begins to applaud louder than before, including the Reverend Huston and the host.

"You've got quite an imagination, thinking you saw God in her," Lillian says when the applause dies down.

"Mrs. Kennedy," I say then, "your problem, as the Reverend Huston has pointed out, is not that you don't have faith, but that you *don't want* to have faith. I have learned that, in the end, belief is actually an act of the will. Not a feeling, not a hunch, but a decision. And do you want to know why I choose to believe?

Because when I see all the terrible things in this world, all the pain and the suffering, I *want* there to be some happiness at the end, some reason for putting up with all this. When I see the little child dying of cancer, I refuse to believe that death is the final end for her. I refuse to believe that my friend's father who died in an accident while working hard to support his family will not have eternal life. I refuse to believe that the beautiful young woman killed by the drunk driver is not going to live on forever in some better place. I refuse to believe that the mother who died giving birth to her son is not waiting to be reunited with him somewhere. I want all these things to be true. I want them so badly that somehow, when I pray enough, I can actually believe that they are true. And you, Mrs. Kennedy, what do you want?"

"I demand proof!"

"You'll never get your proof, Mrs. Kennedy. Because the proof lies in faith, not faith in the proof. With God, believing is seeing, not the other way around."

Everybody applauds again, as Mrs. Kennedy smiles defiantly, shaking her head. The music comes up, and suddenly the program is over. I see Mrs. Kennedy get up and quickly leave, while the Reverend Huston hangs around and talks to a number of people.

Leonard and I go over to shake his hand, and he thanks us for our insights and invites us to attend his church. We chat for a moment, then try to leave as quickly as possible, but it is not easy because many audience members continue to approach and thank us.

When we reach the street, the rain is over and the sun is starting to come out, and we unlock the still-dripping bikes and begin our ride back to the home. I am feeling light and giddy as we bicycle down the misty, steaming streets, and in some indescribable way, I all-of-a-sudden realize that maybe this could be the sign I asked for, so many months ago.

When we return to the home, Catherine and the other girls are there, helping out in the kitchen. Catherine gives me and Leonard a long look, and says, "I saw you on TV, and you were amazing. I thought you did an incredible job!"

"I'm glad it came off all right," I say then. "And I've got to give credit to Leonard—he told me what to say, most of the time." Leonard just grins and turns red.

I'm sure that if I would have known ahead of time that we were going to be on that show, and known what the show was going to be about, I would have been much more nervous and reticent to raise my hand to comment.

Later on, as we serve dinner to the residents, old Tom McFinn says, "Saw ya on TV. You told that woman a thing or two! What were ya talkin' about? I couldn't hear it, but it looked interestin'... Hail Mary... Hail Mary....Ya'd be saprised at some o' the things these beads ha' brought me... ya'd be saprised..."

✳✳✳

"Your work is to dis-
cover your work and
then with all your
heart to give yourself
to it."

Gautama Buddha

CHAPTER THIRTY-TWO

Back to Reality

After our month of hospital probation is over, we drive back to the House and marvel at how green and lush the countryside is. At rec that evening we learn that some of the infirmary priests, as well as Brother Ritchie and Alex Dubchek, who was working in the infirmary at the time, managed to see part of the TV show with Mrs. Kennedy and the Reverend Huston.

"You were great," says Alex, "and I have to tell you, the Sarge even chanced by and saw some of it!"

"Oh yeah? What did he think of it?"

"He said, 'Technically, they're not supposed to be there, but he *is* doing a good job…'"

It is almost June, and Summer Order is around the corner. And the best news of all is that the Padre is still in the Infirmary, and since he does not talk any more, and so cannot fill our heads with "subversive ideas," I have permission to visit him again and read to him on some evenings.

I haven't seen Andy in almost two months, since he started his hospital probe almost a month before me, at another elder care facility in

Winsted, a town some twenty miles west of the House. Because he is from the Twin Cities area, he was sent to Winsted, in the opposite direction from his home town, to minimize any temptation to visit his old stomping grounds. During formation, this is standard procedure. He did not return from there until after Leonard and I left for the Twin Cities, so we have some catching up to do.

When I finally see him, I give him a reserved hug as I shake his hand. We have the rule of "tactus" — Latin for "touch" — which forbids us to touch one another except in greeting, at which time handshakes and reserved hugs are acceptable. I notice a slight reticence in Andy's demeanor, and I am wondering what to make of it. He seems a little more serious and withdrawn than usual, but hopefully there is a positive reason for it.

***

My life is more peaceful now, and I believe it is due in great part to the "sign" I witnessed while on hospital probation, when I related the story of the old nun, Sister Margaret, dancing for the old man.

I have thought about it often since it happened, and I have been thinking back over all the years of Catholic elementary school and all the thousands of days I have spent around nuns, and how often I just took them for granted, until all of a sudden, out of the blue, I was inspired by this one little incident with Sister Margaret.

And I also recall how, back when I broke my arm in the football game, and the doctor reset it, it hurt so badly that I almost passed out and I almost threw up. But I did not come close to tears. Yet in the TV studio that day, relating the story about Sister Margaret and the old man, Albert, I came closer to tears than I have in a decade. Which, at age twenty, is half of my lifetime.

*** *** ***

In July we make our annual trip to the Indian Missions in South Dakota. On the bus ride, we learn to sing more songs that have been released in the almost two years since we left The World. We have actually listened to tapes of some of these songs that have been 'smuggled in' by some of the first-year men, and by some of our own family members and siblings on visits. We have tape decks in our little speech practice booths at the house, where we listened to some of these when time permitted. Songs by Peter, Paul and Mary, Joan Baez, Bob Dylan, and Simon and Garfunkel. Andy and I have taught ourselves the harmony of "The Sounds of Silence," and, accompanied by Alex Dubchek's guitar prowess, we perform it during some of our little hootenannies. And we even take it a step further. We—that is, Andy, Dubchek and I—actually write a few of our own songs, and perform them for the guys, who are generous to a fault with their praise.

At the missions, we second-year men focus on teaching catechism to Indian children. We are divided into mission teams of about five or six guys each, and we are sent out to different mission sites around the Rosebud Reservation. Fr. Dan Faragan is in charge of my team, and he drives our group, in a small van, to Our Lady of Victory Catholic Church in Kadoka, South Dakota, which is our mission base for the next eight days. There we teach catechism to kids around the area at several sites during the day, and sleep in sleeping bags on the floor of the church basement at night. Father Otis Grinwald, the pastor there, has filled a refrigerator in our living quarters with some food and snack items, including a variety of bottled sodas, and several six-packs of beer.

It turns out that most of us are not interested in the beer, and I tell Brother Mueller, one of our novice brothers stationed here with us, that he can have my share. Little do I know at the time that most of the other guys have told him the same thing. Consequently, at dinner time and after, while the rest of us are guzzling coke, root beer, pepsi or whatever, he is quaffing beers and becoming tipsy. I finally decide that maybe he has had enough and I ask if I can drink some of the beers after all.

"Hey Wall, of course, I mean, yeah, they were yours to begin with, anyway."

One evening, Father Grinwald receives a telephone call from the local hospital that a woman has miscarried her baby and she and her husband would like him to come and baptize the child. He invites those of us who are there to join him, and so we do. The hospital is within walking distance of the church, and when we get there, Fr. Grinwald leaves us so he can spend a few minutes talking to the distraught mother and her husband. Then he returns and we enter another room with him, where a nurse is standing over a cloth-covered stainless steel dish. She uncovers the dish and exposes the tiny, red-orange body of a little boy, just a few inches in length, lying on his back, with crimson arteries visible beneath his transparent skin.

"They have named him Marc Antony," says Fr. Grinwald, as he fills a glass with tap water.

Then, he picks up the dish with the child in it and says, as he pours water over the child's head, "Marc Antony, I baptize you in the name of the Father," then pours more water over the child's chest and says, "and of the

Son," and pours water over Marc Antony's tiny feet and says, "and of the Holy Spirit. Amen."

***

The day we get back to St. Francis and the big dorms, I notice Leonard and Lou Ranier together, as if they were the best of friends. This is good, because I always assumed these two did not have a lot in common.

"So," I say to Leonard that evening, "How was your mission site?"

"Oh," he says, "that was okay, I guess, but we got back three days ago, and it's been interesting."

"What's that supposed to mean?"

"Well, Lou is my new hero."

"If there's a story behind this, I'm all ears."

"First off," he says, "you have to meet Baxter."

"Baxter?" I say as he leads me into the rec room to a terrarium on a table. Inside it is a little landscape with dirt, some rocks and a small log, and a pan of water. A gopher sits in the middle of it all eating some sunflower seeds.

"Where'd you find him?"

"An Indian girl gave him to me. She just kept him in a big box. I got the terrarium from the science classroom in the school building. The story starts about a day after I received Baxter. One of the Indians, Joe Killsin-water, gave Harshley a bull snake for a present. Harsh has no fear of snakes, and he figured he should not refuse the gift, since that might offend Joe. So he took the snake and kept it in a terrarium in the science classroom, but didn't tell everybody. At that time, I was also keeping Baxter in the science classroom, in another terrarium. Harshley's snake was in another part of the room, but I didn't know it was there. I assumed the other terrariums were empty.

"So anyway, that afternoon I went into the science room to feed Baxter, and as I approach his terrarium I see the bull snake there, out of its terrarium, crawling up the side of Baxter's terrarium and pushing up the screen on top, sticking out its forked tongue, sticking its head into Baxter's den. I honestly froze; I didn't know what to do because I hate snakes! I just started shouting 'No God, no!' I couldn't go any closer, because it was a snake..."

"My gosh, I don't blame you. But obviously, Baxter is still alive and healthy. What happened?"

"I was so petrified I didn't hear Lou coming up behind me, and all of a sudden I saw a flash of metal, and the snake falls onto the floor, writhing, with a knife stuck in its neck. I turn and there's Lou standing just behind me. 'I don't like snakes,' he says."

"So. Lou saved Baxter's life."

"Yeah. But he paid a price. That night he found the snake's carcass in his bed. Harsh had warned everybody that if someone killed his snake, he would put its carcass in the perpetrator's bed. Although he did wrap it up in an old vinyl shower curtain so that it would not stain or smell up the bed. Still, Lou moved to a different bed in the dorm."

***

During our last week there, a couple of things happen that I will remember for the rest of my life. The first one is just a simple stop at a hospital in Rosebud, where Fr. Faragan and I go in to visit the maternity ward. Here we watch as a nurse is spoon-feeding an infant, and I am amazed at how much the child is eating.

"Periodically, the nurses go out into the hills and bring these babies back to the hospital, to fatten them up," Fr. Faragan says. "Some of the mothers often don't get enough nourishment themselves, and do not produce enough breast milk, and so they feed their babies sugar-water. We bring them in here for a few days every month or so to give them some nutrition, before returning them to their families."

As I watch the baby eat, I am once again amazed at how lucky I have been my whole life, always getting enough food, and all the other necessities of life that I always took for granted.

The second thing I will always remember is when Fr. McKittrick takes us on the bus to Wounded Knee. It first appears, as we drive over the prairie, to be just another bleak hill in the middle of the vast South Dakota rolling prairies, but it is different because it has a small chapel on top of it. When we arrive at the top of the hill we get off the bus and walk to an area near the chapel that has a long, fenced-in section with hundreds of ribbons and bows of various colors tied to the wires of the fence. We gather around this fenced-off area, which is the mass grave of hundreds of Lakota, many of them defenseless women and children, who were massacred there in December of 1890 by the U.S. Cavalry.

The ribbons are prayer ribbons, signifying a fraction of the many thousands of prayers that have been said here. We stand around the mass grave and listen to an Indian lady, Maria Walking Eagle, narrate the story of the massacre. Her grandmother, at age fifteen, was shot in the chest twice, but survived and married and begat Maria's father.

She points to a nearby hill and says, "On New Year's Eve, the anniversary of the massacre, many of us have seen lights moving along that ridge, and we have heard the sad weeping of many women and children. You may find this hard to believe, but we know these are their souls, lamenting this terrible event."

I stare at her as she tells the story, to a point where I wonder if I am making her uncomfortable.

"I'm sorry," I say when she finishes.

She smiles and says, "That's all right... many people do not comprehend the horror of those days until I tell them."

"I can't help but wonder... how it must be to walk in your shoes," I say then.

"You weren't even born yet, Father. Nor was I. We cannot go back to the past... we can only learn from it. My job is not to hold a grudge, but to educate young people so that we do not repeat the mistakes of history."

CHAPTER THIRTY-THREE

A Visit From the Sisters

Just a few days after we get back from the Indian Missions and into Summer Order (a slightly different Ordo Regularis with History and French classes instead of Latin, along with a little more rec), some of the nuns from St. Joseph's Home come out to visit us on a Sunday afternoon. Even though she is still a postulant, or a sub-novice, as it were, Catherine is allowed to come with them, and she wears a postulant's veil and dress, including black stockings and shoes that look like they are from another era. Somehow, the clothes don't really do the job of making her appear unattractive.

Leonard and I go for a walk with her, out along the rosary path. She has to wear these clothes for awhile before she can even become a novice, a lot like the postulant brothers in our order.

"So," I ask her, "how long before you become a novice?"

"Actually, a few more months," she says.

"But even so, you sort of still have to live like the other sisters, right?"

"Yes. We pray, do chores, follow the rules and the daily order, those kinds of things."

The conversation drifts around to things we all have had to give up, including television and movies.

"So who's your favorite movie star?" I ask her all of a sudden.

"Well, I really like Julie Andrews in 'The Sound of Music.' I saw it just before I entered."

"I'd love to see that! But we won't be allowed to for at least a couple of years yet..."

"Oh, that's too bad, because it's really good, and Julie Andrews is great. But I have to say, I like Dolores Hart even more."

"What film of hers was your favorite?"

"I never saw her in a film."

"Then how can she be your favorite movie star?"

"Because she left Hollywood to become a nun," she says with a laugh.

"That's right, I remember that now. So, your favorite movie star is one who quit the business?"

"Yep. Threw in the towel, at the height of her career."

"Do you think she'll stay in the convent?"

"Good question... one never knows, I guess."

Leonard smiles and nods in agreement. I have this vague feeling of competitiveness with Leonard, like I had every now and then at St. Joe's Home whenever the high school girls or the younger nuns were around. It's a kind of feeling where I want the girls to like me more than they like Leonard, and I am feeling it again now with Catherine. I actually don't like this feeling, but I can't seem to shake it.

We are walking near the duck pond now, where a mallard hen is swimming along with her six ducklings following behind her all in a row. "Look at the ducklings," she says, "they're almost half-grown, sort of like teenage ducks!"

I cannot help but feel, in spite of her garb and mine, a bit of romantic attraction. In the middle ages, during the time of Romeo and Juliet, all women dressed even more conservatively than she is dressed now. And even during the colonial times in this country. I can see how Romeo could be "smitten." I wonder what Leonard is feeling, because he is so quiet and shy around her. "If young ducks are ducklings," I ask, "and little geese are goslings, what are we?"

"Well, you have to be a... priestling. But for me, nunling doesn't ring right. How about, sisterling?"

Leonard suddenly says, "How about sisterette? Or wait, 'petite soeur!'" he says, remembering our French classes.

"That works," she says with a laugh, "little sister."

"Can I ask you something a little... personal?" I say then.

"Sure, Brother Wally. Ask away."

"Why did you enter the convent?"

"Oh, that's a big one. I guess I just felt very drawn to it, for a number of reasons. I started coming to the home to help out while I was a sophomore, and I was overwhelmed with this positive feeling about the place. I mean, here these women were doing God's work, performing the works of mercy more clearly than anywhere else I have seen. And they seemed so happy!"

"Did you ever think about getting married?"

"Oh yes," she smiles. "I had boyfriends here and there. And I was even getting a little serious about one guy for a time."

"So what happened?"

"I just didn't feel good about it. The relationship, the future. And he seemed like a nice guy at first, but then one day he said something that really floored me. I thought I knew him well, and that he was a caring person, but one day he started telling me about someone at his school, a guy named Willard who wanted to be his friend, and he described him as 'somebody not worth knowing.' And I was so shocked I could only say to him, '*Everybody* is worth knowing!' After that I started recognizing a lot of holes in his 'nice guy' image. I called it quits with him not long after that."

I pick up a stone and skip it across the water. "Some people think that what you're doing... what *we're* doing, is an escape from reality."

"What is reality?" she asks. "We are in *exile*. If you study our Faith, if you really look at what it's all about, we are *supposed* to escape from this... this impoverished reality of our world, and our faith is the pathway out.

You could say people who avoid our kind of commitment are the ones in denial. When we escape from this *lacrimarum valle*, this 'valley of tears,' as the Salve Regina prayer calls our fallen world, when we get back to Paradise, that's when the *real* party begins."

"You have a point there," I say as we continue our walk right up around the Jesus Statue, where Darryl is buried. I stop for a moment and look at his grave.

"I'm sorry about your brother," she says.

I look at her with surprise, because I never mentioned him to her.

"I told her," says Leonard quietly.

I nod to Leonard, wondering where they both were when he told her, before I realize how weird I am being.

"In high school," I continue, "he was just a goof-off. He liked to break the rules and draw attention to himself. He was suspended three or four times, at least. He actually wanted to quit high school and go out to the West Coast and become a surfer. But somehow, he changed his mind and applied to join the order instead. And they *accepted* him!"

She just smiles at me and says, "Oh, the depth of the riches and wisdom and knowledge of God!"

Leonard looks at her and says, "Romans eleven, thirty-three!"

I just look at the two of them and nod. I've heard the quote, but never knew the book or the chapter and verse.

After a moment, we continue our walk. "What about college?" I ask her then. "You were valedictorian of your high school class. Did you ever think you could do the world some good, say, by going to school?"

"That may be true. And I've actually thought about going into medicine. Which is quite possible for me to do as a nun, once I get through my novitiate. But for now, my place is right here."

"So you have no regrets?"

"Let's just say that out there—out in the world, as we like to put it —it was always a struggle to do everything that was required. No matter how busy you were, there was always more to do, never enough time for doing it. Here, I find that the more I think about others instead of my own pursuits, the more I try to serve other people as they approach death, the more I am at peace."

"Yeah. I mean, I agree with you. It's just sort of amazing to hear it from..."

"A girl? Ah, a *blonde!*"

"Well, I... yeah. You're awfully... you seem to read my mind."

"If you ever read the writings of Maria Valtorta, you would know that Our Lady was also a blonde."

"Maria Valtorta? Our Lady? I thought Maria Valtorta was... on the Index. How did you manage to read her?"

"I didn't, really. But one of our older nuns had permission to read her works, and told me that when she met me the first time."

We pause for a moment. Then she turns and looks at me with a funny smile. "I love you," she says, "platonically, of course. And you too, Leonard."

Then Leonard starts to say, "Fr. McKittrick says that there's no such thing as a pla..."

"I have to say the same," I say to her, cutting him off, "for you."

"Me too," says Leonard, as he shrugs and tries to suppress a giggle.

***

Later on, we have a lemonade and cookie haustus with the nuns in the triclinium (dining room), followed by a hootenanny. Catherine has her guitar, and she leads us in *Where Have all the Flowers Gone?* She sings it like an angel, and I notice that Leonard listens in rapt attention. I also notice, looking down the cloister walk from where I am sitting, the Sarge is approaching our little get-together as Catherine sings. Before he gets too close he stops to listen for a bit. After we sing, "...where have all the soldiers gone, gone to graveyards everyone..." he turns around and goes back where he came from. I don't know if anyone else even saw him, because he was pretty far down the cloister walk when he stopped.

Then Andy and I lead everyone in *Blowin' in the Wind* with Alex accompanying us on his guitar, after which we all sit around with the nuns and drink punch and eat cookies.

Then Fr. McKittrick asks Sister Margaret if she would like to offer us young men a few words of advice. I begin to move to sit as close to Catherine as I can, until I realize how silly this all is. Have I learned nothing since I entered the novitiate? If I am looking for some kind of relationship with a woman, I should get the hell — crock — out of here right now, right? I change my mind and sit down, but then she turns and looks at me, and comes over to me. My heart begins to beat faster as she leans over and practically whispers into my ear, "I have to add one more reason about why I chose this life. Sister Margaret. She is amazing. She has so many stories and pieces of wisdom..."

"We have a guy like that too," I tell her, "the Padre. But he can't talk any more. Still, you'll have to meet him some time."

"So," Sister Margaret says to everyone, "some of you young men are getting ready to take vows next month. I have a little story to tell you, if you'd like to hear it."

"Yes sister," I say, "absolutely. Tell us, please!"

"A long time ago, during my novitiate, I was having a bad day," she begins. "Sound familiar?"

A communal laugh ensues.

"We were situated way out in the farm country, in France," she continues.

"France," somebody murmurs.

"Yes, it was France, but it was still a novitiate," she says, and we all laugh again. "I decided that I had had it, so I just took off. Just walked out the door and started hiking over the fields and the hills, across the countryside. I did not have a destination or a plan, I just wanted out. So I walked and walked, for hours it seemed, in my novice's habit and my clunky shoes. They were not much different from these shoes," she says as she shows us the granny shoes that she is wearing.

"After what seemed like a long time," she continues, "I came upon a churchyard. A little cemetery next to a small old country church. Nobody was around, so I opened the gate, walked in and sat down in the grass amid the tombstones. And then I started to talk to the dead people. I told them how lucky I thought they were, because they didn't have to put up with anybody any more. They didn't have to put up with Sister Agnes, our associate novice mistress, who was an old battle-axe if there ever was one!"

More laughter.

"Well, I continued to talk to the dead people for quite some time, and after I did so I began to feel better. I guess you could say I was praying, in a way, and I didn't even realize it at the time. It was like therapy, believe me! Then I slowly started to change the direction of my prayer, and soon enough I was praying to Our Lord, to give me guidance. And I asked all the dead people in the churchyard to pray to the Lord for me as well. Then, after enough of this I began to feel relaxed, and pretty soon I felt so peaceful that I just fell asleep right there on the grass, amidst the graves in the churchyard, for a little while. And when I awoke I felt really refreshed. Then I stood up and said good-bye to them all, and began my hike out of the churchyard, back over the hills and valleys to the novitiate, back to my novice life.

"A year and a half later, just before vows, I went back there again, and had another nice long talk with the dead folks. And then I returned to the novitiate and I took my vows."

"Sister Margaret," I say, "may I ask what year that was?"

"Well, I entered the novitiate in ought-two, and I was a postulant for awhile, so that was in ought-five, I guess. Yes, I took vows in nineteen-ought- five."

"Sixty years ago," I say, and the room erupts with applause.

* * *

After the sisters leave, I have the same problem I had when we left St. Joe's Home and returned to the House and Ordo Regularis — I cannot get Catherine out of my mind. I can see once again why we are kept away from women in our formation... they have incredible powers that they are not even aware of.

Later on at rec I go for a walk with Leonard and when I ask him what he thinks of Catherine, he just turns red and starts to laugh.

"I can understand what Fr. McKittrick meant about the platonic thing," he says, and then we do our best to change the subject.

* * *

I am with the beautiful volleyball girls again, and as I walk along, giving the girls piggyback rides as before, Catherine appears in front of me, looking beautiful and majestic, not in a swimsuit, but in a long, white robe, and tries to lead me toward the ocean, while the other girls in their swimsuits try to turn me in the opposite direction. Suddenly I am torn, enjoying the volleyball girls, but looking at Catherine and wanting to follow her. And once again the surfer is standing there on the beach, holding his surfboard, waving...but I still cannot recognize him before I wake up...

* * *

The next day I notice that Leonard is really down. He has been down before, now and then, but I think he looks worse this time. "What's wrong?" I ask him.

"Just a headache," he says, and he tries to laugh it off, but his laugh is hollower than usual.

"Did you see Brother Ritchie about it?"

"Yeah, he gave me some stuff to take, but it doesn't always work too well. But I'll be okay, don't worry."

"Hate the sin;
love the sinner."

Mahatma Gandhi

CHAPTER THIRTY-FOUR

A Dark Secret

T he following morning, there is a note on the bulletin board. As I approach it, I see that it begins: "Andy Gallagher..." and for a fraction of a second, my heart stops. As I get closer, I read the rest of it and have mixed feelings of relief, but also sadness for Andy.

> Andy Gallagher's father died suddenly last night, of an apparent heart attack. The funeral will be Saturday. Please pray for Andy and his family.
>
> Fr. McKittrick

I walk to Andy's room, but he is not there. He is evidently already back home in the twin cities with his family members as they gather for this sad event.

The following Monday, I am washing windows with Alex in the Father's Rec Room, and looking out across the tree-lined entrance drive, when a sportscar appears on the drive. A sportscar shows up on our entrance drive about once a year, or less, on average. "Take a look at this," I say to Alex, and he stops washing and looks.

I recognize that it is the same Porsche convertible, or cabriolet, that Andy arrived in on the day we entered. The top is down, Andy is driving, and a young woman is sitting next to him, her hair blowing in the wind. They are both wearing sunglasses.

"That's Robinson's sister, again," says Alex.

The car pulls up into the parking lot just below us, and Christina Robinson reaches over and pulls Andy closer to her, but he gently pushes her away. They both get out of the car, and while he takes a suitcase from the small trunk, she hops into the driver's side. She is tanned and gorgeous, but he only puts his hand on her shoulder as he says his final goodbye.

"The guy's got will power," says Alex as we watch her start the car, back it out and drive away into the trees that line the entrance drive.

I see Andy at rec that evening and I welcome him back and tell him we're all praying for him and his family, but a number of the other guys also want to pay him their respects, and so I don't get a chance to really talk to him at length.

***

Later on, after lights out, I am tossing and turning a little bit, when I hear a faint knock on my door. "Wally?" comes a barely audible whisper. "Wally, are you awake?"

"Yeah," I whisper back, "yeah, I'm awake."

"Wally, it's Andy. May I come in?"

"Yes, of course," I say, and I am really worried all of a sudden, because nobody around here visits anybody during Sacred Silence, in the middle of the night.

He gently closes the door and then lies down on his back, right on the floor. In the faint light from the corridor through the transom, I can see that he is still in his cassock.

"Wally, I have something to tell you."

"What?" I say, but I already think I know the answer, and I steel myself for what is to come.

"Wally, I'm going to leave the novitiate. I'm not going to take vows."

There is a moment of silence as I let the words sink in. The soft sound of his voice, the matter-of-fact way he says it, and all the hours and days and weeks and months, almost two years worth, that we have spent together here, all of these times that I will remember as long as I live, add an incredible weight to his words.

"I guess this comes as a surprise," he says then.

"Yes, it is definitely a surprise." I try to grope for something to say; this news is sort of paralyzing, in a way. After a moment I say, "May I ask if there is any one really big, overriding factor in your decision?"

"Christina. Christina Robinson. I...Wally, there's a lot that's been going on that...well, if what I just said surprises you, you're gonna be even more surprised. When I was on hospital probation in Winsted, I called her. She came out to see me, and I found out that she had a baby. My baby, Wally."

He pauses for a breath, and I am glad, because I need to grasp what he is saying.

"I'm a father, Wally, and I didn't even know it. We slept together

327

before I broke up with her, three months before I entered. It was stupid, it was crazy, but I was in love with her. I'm still in love with her. I mean, we were going together during senior year of high school, and I had a real hard time breaking up with her. You're probably wondering why we broke up in the first place. I had these feelings for her, but I also had this incredible need or urge to enter the novitiate. Especially after my senior retreat in high school. It was pretty difficult, because I knew I had to choose between her and the novitiate. She was amazingly okay with it, when I said that I had to try this. Of course, the fact that she had a brother who had entered the year before didn't hurt either, I guess. And when we broke up, she didn't even know she was pregnant yet. So I tried it. The novitiate, I mean." He pauses again.

In my mind and in my heart, I cannot believe that this person talking to me is the Andy I have known for almost two years. How could he have had all these experiences, and never mentioned them, and appeared as if he had been such a straightforward, intelligent, well- rounded, even *gifted*, religious novice? How could he have hidden these facets of his personality, during all those retreats and conversations and discussions about... everything? It's like he almost seems not to be Andy, all of a sudden. And yet I have to remind myself that we have been told from day one not to dwell on or talk about our past, if it is not conducive to improving our present state in life, so in a way I can understand his silence.

"This is definitely a major shock," I say. "Out of everyone who entered with us, you would be the last one I would pick to leave. But regarding Christina, how..." I ask, trying to find the words, "how did you keep everything so quiet? And how did she keep it from you? I mean, her pregnancy? And how did *Robinson* keep it from you? I can't believe that they could all just not *tell* you!"

"Wally, it's complicated. Remember that time when Tom Robinson had a visit, and I went out there and Fr. McKittrick came out and hauled me back in? I only had about two minutes with them before he came out, and I asked them how they were all doing, and I had a funny feeling the way Mr. and Mrs. Robinson were looking at me, and how they responded, that there was something odd going on. Christina seemed fine, though, or so I thought, and Robinson was okay too, it seemed. And to this day I honestly don't know if he knew it yet at that time. If he did know about her being pregnant, he may not have known it was me, you know?"

"Wow," I say, trying to absorb it all. There is another moment of silence.

"So where is the kid now?" I finally ask.

"Christina dropped out of school to deliver her, and now she has been taking care of her, along with her mother's help. Her name is Maryanne. Christina was going to give her up for adoption, but then decided against it. Wally, I saw her when I went home for my Dad's funeral, and I absolutely love that little girl. I knew right then and there that I would have to leave and marry Christina. Wally, it's not only what I want to do, it's my moral obligation. I know this is all so sudden, and I know that I may sound like a... a different person, in a way, with all of these new issues right out of the blue. I'm kind of shocked at myself, actually. I've been blindsided by all this stuff the last two months, but I've had to make a choice, and I believe it's the right choice."

Another silence follows.

"This is a lot to swallow," I say. "Have you talked to Fr. McKittrick about it?"

"Tomorrow, Wally. You're the first person I've told. Please pray for me... I need it." Now he gets up from the floor and comes over to my bed. In the faint light, I can see his hand extending. I reach out and shake it.

"Please pray for me too," I say, with a lump in my throat.

"God bless you, Wally," he says, and he turns and exits, quietly.

I try to say a rosary, but my thoughts are moving along at the speed of lightning, and prayer is difficult. It takes me hours before I calm down enough to fall asleep.

CHAPTER THIRTY-FIVE

Men in White Coats, and Black Holes

T he shrinks are back. They were here for a short time during our first year of novitiate, before our Long Retreat, and now they're back. They do not really wear white coats, but we still like to refer to them as "the men in the white coats." They are not actually shrinks, either, because shrinks are psychiatrists and these guys are psychologists, but what the crock, they're in the same ballpark.

They give us a series of written tests similar to what they gave us last time, with many similar questions, including some occasional funny ones like the ones about black and tarry bowel movements, bands around the head and whatever.

For some reason it is not as big a deal as it was the first time, and when they see us individually, we don't talk about it among ourselves as much. Maybe because we've been there before, or maybe because we are more mature. Whatever the case, we know that the Order just wants to have some kind of record of any patterns or differences between the guys who stay and the guys who leave. And of course, just because a number of us will take vows, there is no guarantee that we will all be lifers. We have a lot of years ahead of us, and sadly, there may still be some difficult adjustments for some of us as we move along in our lives in the Order.

One thing I notice is that, when Leonard returns from his conference with the two psychologists, he is withdrawn at first, more like he was back when we all entered the novitiate, almost two years ago. At rec, he tells me that he did not feel comfortable with their questions.

"They asked me," he says, "if I still had a problem with anyone here that I felt I could not trust. I admitted that I still felt that way about the Sarge. When they asked me why, I said that he reminded me of my father. And then, when they tried to find out more about my relationship with my father, I started feeling like I couldn't trust them either, and I reverted to my old habit of excessive laughter. And they just sat there, as if they didn't understand what was so funny. To tell you the truth, I didn't understand it myself. It was pretty weird."

***

It is time for our annual eight-day retreat. Andy left a couple of weeks ago, and I think I'm starting to accept it, actually. I have been thinking about it a lot, of course. I have also talked to Fr. McKittrick about it, and about Andy coming to my room and telling me all these things that seemed so out-of-character for him. Fr. McKittrick said that these kinds of things happen in life to everyone, not just people in religious orders. And even though we are not supposed to cultivate "particular friendships," we still manage to do so. I even told him that Andy was one of the main reasons I stayed for the first few months; he was like a role model, or something. And Fr. McKittrick seemed to understand.

On the morning Andy left, I saw, when I awoke in the pre-dawn light, an article of clothing on a coat hanger hanging on my transom. When I turned on the light, I saw that it was his hair shirt, with a note attached. The note said:

> Wally,
>
> You're the only one I can think of who might really appreciate this. Except maybe for Leonard. Use it wisely, and please pray for me.   Andy

After praying and meditating on it for awhile, I realize that the long and the short of it is that my vocation is my vocation, and nobody else's. My final commitment to this life is between me and God. And amazingly, even though Andy's leaving was a bolt out of the blue, I am getting over it, I think. Slowly but surely.

* * *

The night before our vow retreat, I go for a short walk under the stars with Leonard and Alex.

"Have you ever heard of a Schwarzchild Singularity?" Leonard asks the two of us.

"A who?" asks Alex.

"A number of years ago a mathematician named Schwarzchild came up with a mathematical hypothesis in which a star of a certain mass can collapse in on itself, due to gravitational forces. If the star is massive enough, the star's material becomes so dense that its gravitational pull is increased to the point that nothing, not even light, can escape from it."

"I didn't know that light was influenced by gravity," I say then.

"Only slightly," says Leonard. "But the gravitational pull in some collapsed stars is incredible. In fact, some scientists have started to call these phenomena 'Black Holes.'

"These black holes have a spherical region surrounding them called an 'event horizon,' that is actually like a point of no return. Some scientists theorize that if you were flying through space and were to venture too close to this event horizon, feet first, gravitational waves would begin to stretch you and pull you apart, because the gravity at your feet would be so much more intense than the gravity at your head and shoulders. This stretching would cause unbelievable pain. But that would not be the worst part..."

"What could be worse than that?" asks Alex.

"The worst part," says Leonard after a moment of silence, "would be that you might be frozen in time forever. You would be in eternal agony, because even time itself would seem to stand still at the event horizon."

"That sounds incredible," I say. "So do these 'singularities,' or 'black holes,' actually exist?"

"Oh yes," Leonard says. "The math works, and therefore, they exist. We may not have discovered any yet, but they're out there."

"So," says Alex, "somewhere in the universe there may be a black hole or two. But how can this matter to you and me?"

"Remember," says Leonard, "how the Padre always tried to correlate the spiritual world with our physical world? Sort of like Jesus did with parables?"

"Yeah," says Alex, "but how..."

"Especially when you consider sin to be like the force of gravity," continues Leonard, "the Singularity, or Black Hole, with its incredibly powerful gravity and impenetrable darkness, and eternal agony at the event horizon, may be the closest thing in our physical universe to Hell."

***

During our eight-day retreat we get big chunks of free time, including an hour and a half of it right after lunch. I like to go out and take solitary walks, and today I'm heading up the hill right to the windmill tower that Andy and Alex climbed, and I sort of half-climbed along with them. I've actually come back here more than once since then, when no one else was around, and each time I try to climb it, I get a step or two higher. Today I'm able to get up over halfway, before I decide that I'm high enough. It's weird, but I have this sort of fear of heights. I didn't think I had it when I was younger, but that's because I never climbed anything very high beyond a few shorter trees and things. It's interesting, though, that I am able to get up this high and it doesn't bother me nearly as much as that first time.

Andy once said that the ultimate challenge would be to climb it in your cassock, and stand on the seesawing platform on top, with your arms free and clear, spread-eagled, and then try to look straight up, and keep your balance. In a wind.

In some ways he's nuts, I think.

***

It is almost lights-out time, and Leonard is still not in his room. We change rooms, and sometimes floors, every few months, and he lives right across from me now, so I cannot help but notice. I know that he sleeps with his door slightly ajar, and he has not been around, in or out of his room, for several hours. I cannot imagine Leonard leaving the order, so I just assume that he is doing some special assignment with Fr. McKittrick's blessing.

The next morning when I arise at the bell, I look across the corridor and I see that Leonard's door is wide open, his bed made. It appears that he has not been in there all night. Now I'm worried. I make first visit to the chapel and return to my room to meditate.

After meditation, I head back to the chapel for Mass, and after Mass we have breakfast. My eyes search the dining room for Leonard, but I do not see him anywhere. Fr. McKittrick is also gone.

I head back to my room and get ready for manualia, and I walk down the hall toward the stairwell to the verrator shop—verrator means "sweeper" or "mopper"—when I see Fr. McKittrick coming toward me and Leonard a little ways behind him.

I feel a surge of both relief and concern, because Leonard is dressed in disheveled rec clothes and looks very tired, and Fr. McKittrick is dressed in his black clerical suit, which he wears when he has to leave the House and drive into town.

"Leonard," I whisper to him as he passes, "quid est fabulam te-cum? *What's the story with you?*"

He just looks at me for a moment, then looks down, as if he has done something terribly wrong.

"Ubi erasne? *Where've you been?*" I ask.

"Est fabulam longam, *it's a long story*," he says. "Postquam... *Later.*" And with that he enters his room.

I continue my trip to the verrator shop and get a mop to clean the basement corridors. I know that Leonard is also assigned to the verrator shop this month, and I wonder if he will show up this morning. Knowing him like I do, he probably will. He is resolute about doing his part, taking responsibility for his assignments.

I spend the next forty minutes pushing a wide floor mop up and down the long corridors, then return to the shop to shake out the mop and vacuum it. I hang around for a couple of minutes to see if Leonard will show up. Finally, after what seems like ages, Leonard enters the shop to vacuum his mops.

I look at him and I am sure that my eyes speak volumes, and he just repeats what he said before, "Postquam." Still a stickler for the rules, no matter what happens.

There is no rec during our eight-day retreat, and so "later" really winds up being a lot later than I would prefer. But finally, after the fourth day, he tells me. "I can't wait until the end of the retreat," he says, "because we have vows and all that stuff to ponder, so I'll just tell you. I was in jail."

"Jail."

"I had had a bad headache, and I went out after lunch for a walk. I cjan't remember many details, I just know that I couldn't sit still, and so I went out toward the highway and just walked along for a little while, when a sheriff's car pulled up. He asked me why I was walking funny. I said, 'One leg's shorter than the other.' He just said, 'Get in the car.'

"He said he knew I was drunk, with the way I was walking and my funny speech." Leonard pauses at this and looks away. I have seldom seen him get emotional, except maybe at the missions that time when he was up to bat.

"He took my fingerprints, my wallet and all that stuff, and I spent the night there."

"You spent the night there? He presumed you were drunk?" I am feeling very angry all of a sudden. "So he just locked you up?"

"It's okay. Don't worry, I'm okay. He apologized when he found out that I was actually from here."

"Didn't you tell him that you were from here right away?"

"Well yeah, but he didn't believe me. Thought I was just a drunk, making up a story."

"Did he bother to check your reflexes? Smell your breath?" I am getting angrier by the second. If this would have happened to anybody else, we would have all had some great yuks about it. But Leonard? Somehow, because it happened to Leonard, I don't even want to tell anybody about it, don't want to bring it up even, because it will probably cause him more agony.

Whether Leonard was in the Order or not is beside the point; what happened to him was very, very unfair. I can hardly control myself. But then all of a sudden I get an inspiration.

"Leonard," I say then, "I can only think of one thing to say."

"What?"

"Could I ask a favor?"

"What?"

"Could you just... say a little prayer for me?"

He grins all of a sudden. "Of course," he says.

"And of course I will reciprocate," I tell him as I slap him on the shoulder, then turn and walk away.

Sometimes I am tempted to think that God is picking on Leonard. I know that isn't a good thing to think, and it is only a temptation, after all. I have to pray about it some more, I guess.

After the retreat, a number of new novices enter the novitiate and begin their First Probation. My class continues our preparation for vows. It is a very big deal, actually, since it is what we have been preparing for since the day we entered the novitiate two years ago.

"Suscipe, Domine,

Universam

meam libertatem..."

"Take, Lord, all my liberty..."

St. Ignatius Loyola

CHAPTER THIRTY-SIX

The Day of Commitment

I t's Vow Day. We get up at the normal time, 5:00 AM, and meditate for an hour before Mass, as we have been doing faithfully for two years. Then we head into the Chapel and take our places at Mass on the right-hand, novitiate side of the chapel, in the first two pews. We are seated in our order of seniority which, for us, corresponds with our numerical birth dates. Two years ago, a number of us entered on August 14th. A second group entered on September 1st. Altogether, in our class, forty-seven men entered the novitiate that summer. Today, there are twelve men left from the August group and fourteen from the September group. Twenty-six total. Almost a fifty percent dropout rate for our class. I've heard that this is pretty close to the norm.

At the Offertory, at a given signal, the twelve men of our August group, including me, stand up and walk into the center aisle and turn toward the sanctuary in a line to form a semi-circle around the altar. We kneel down on the stone floor, facing the altar and the priests who are standing there. Fr. McKittrick, our novice master, is among them and watches us intently. He is our Spiritual Father, mentor, and chief role model, the man whom we have come to know and trust as our guide in this new way of life. For two years, in preparation for this event, we have been learning from him about the religious life and the meaning of the three vows of poverty, chastity and obedience.

I have to admit that when I entered, there were times when I did not think I would last a month. But here I am, two years later, taking this next big step.

Rick Abrams is up first. He's an older guy who already had a degree in physics before he entered. He raises his vow formula and reads from it, saying aloud for all to hear, "Omnipotens, sempiterne Deus, *Almighty, everliving God*, Ego, Ricardus Petrus Johannes Abrams, *I, Richard Peter John Abrams,* licet undecumque divino Tuo conspectu indignissimus, *though altogether most unworthy in Thy divine sight..."*

I watch the priests who are watching us. I am sure they are remembering their own vow days from decades ago, most of them before we were even born.

Now Marconi is up; he's the guy who climbed the outside of a building with some friends in Omaha one summer night back in his high school days, when he had an urge to climb and there were no mountains available... "...fretus, tamen, pietate ac misericordia tua infinita, *relying, however, on your infinite mercy and love..."*

Now it's Harshley's turn. I recall how he brought me into his room one night after dinner recently to show me "Harvey," his new pet. Harvey was a huge wolf spider Harshley found in the woods and let loose *in his room*, where the sizable arachnid proceeded to spin a great concentric web between the curtain rod and Harshley's armarium. Harshley would catch flies and toss them into Harvey's web every day to keep him fed, before he finally got tired of it and returned Harvey to the woods.

"...Et impulsus tibi serviendi desiderio *and driven by a desire to serve you...*"

Now Tom Donavan is up. I remember how he and his friends would climb a watertower during the hot summer nights in high school, open the hatch on top and jump in to take a swim. "It was really dark and really, really cold," he recalled... "...voveo, coram sacratissima Virgine Maria et Curia tua coelesti universa ...*I vow, before the most holy Virgin Mary and your entire court of Heaven...*"

Dubchek is up. I think of my recent month of kitchen probation when I had to make a nightly walk-through before lights-out, and noticed one night that the interior light in the walk-in refrigerator was still on. I opened the door and there was Dubchek, standing in his cassock in the cold, caught in mid-bite as he shoved a piece of leftover meatloaf into his mouth with one hand, holding a saltshaker in the other hand... "...paupertatem, castitatem, et obedientiam perpetuam in Collegio Domini...*perpetual poverty, chastity, and obedience in the Company of the Lord...*"

Now it's my turn. I state my vows with sincerity, looking from my vow formula page to the tabernacle and back to the page, trying to comprehend every word of the formula I am reciting, and trying to imagine in some way the Face of the Creator I am addressing.

Now George Winzerling is up. He, along with Dennis McFadden, the next guy after him, are two of the most balanced guys in our class. If I had to bet on who would make the best priests, I would put my money on them, hands down. Along with a few others as well, of course.

And now it is Leonard's turn. Unlike the rest of us, he holds his vow formula down at his waist and stares at the altar and recites it from memory,.. "...et promitto eandem collegium me ingressurum, ut vitam in ea perpetuo degam... *and I promise to enter into this company, to forever spend my life therein...*omnia intelligendo juxta ipsius collegionis constitutiones... *understanding all the constitutions of this same order..."*

Soon enough we are all finished, and we rise and move to the pews on the other side of the chapel, the Juniorate side.

After Mass, the rest of the day is Major Feast Day Order, a day of celebration, with Deo Gratias breakfast, morning rec, afternoon fusion rec, and good times in general.

Our parties are not very intense. There is no booze, of course, but as brand new Juniors we are allowed to have a soda haustus in the morning, in the Juniorate rec room. And there are no families or relatives or special guests to celebrate the day with us, as some orders, especially some orders of nuns, might have. The only observers of the vow ceremony are the other men of the order who have been living with us, including the brand-new novice candidates who just received their cassocks.

During fusion rec in the afternoon, I go for a walk with Brother Larry. I have never really talked to him much, in part because it could only happen on fusion rec days, and I look upon this as an opportunity, because I have come to learn that he knew Darryl pretty well, back when Darryl was here. In fact, they both entered about the same time.

We start walking along the paved rosary path, because he knows it so well that he does not even need a stick to guide him.

"Your brother was really a good friend of mine," he says with a smile. "I really miss him, sometimes."

"Well, I can appreciate that," I tell him. "You know, we were never

344

very close when we were growing up. It was only after he left home and entered the order that I really began to admire him," I say then.

"Yeah," says Brother Larry, "he actually talked about that a little. I remember him telling me once that he really disliked his dad — your dad—and he wasn't too happy as a teenager."

"Yeah, that sounds pretty accurate," I say to him, and then I tell him all about The Miracle, and how all of a sudden Darryl had announced that he was joining the order, and how when we came and visited him he and my dad had a long talk, and it changed the whole dynamic of our family. "I often wonder how he would be doing if he hadn't... I mean, if he had lived, you know? I mean, what his future in the order would have been like?"

Brother Larry just reaches up and scratches his head a little. I notice his feet as we walk along the pavement, and his steps are shorter and more careful than mine.

"Well," he says, "that's an interesting question."

"Did he ever tell you anything? Like whether he had any preferences? About what he would like to study, where he might want to be assigned?"

"Do you really want to know?" he says, and the way he says it makes me a bit uneasy.

"Well yeah, if you know something about it."

He stops for a moment, and I stop and look at him. "Darryl was going to leave," he says quietly.

"Oh," I say after a moment.

"Yeah. He almost left sooner, but when he heard that you were interested in entering, he decided to stay for a while longer."

"So he... told you this?"

"Yeah, he wasn't real happy here. Not as a Junior, anyway. He really loved the novitiate, though. He really got over a lot of his teenage angst, I guess you could say, in the novitiate. He was just having trouble later on, when he got into the Juniorate. Not with studies, but more with some other aspects of the life, I guess."

"Wow, that's... that's interesting," I say then. An awkward silence follows.

"So," says Larry, "maybe we should head back to check out the football game."

I am at a loss for words, so I just say, "Okay." It takes me awhile to absorb this news, and so I just walk with Larry over to the football field without really saying much. The news is shocking at first. But after I think about it, Darryl has been dead for over two years, and so this news is not nearly as bad as his actual death was back then. But it sets me to thinking again about why God "allowed" things to work out the way they did.

***

After vows we have two weeks of relaxed schedule called "Long Order," wherein we are allowed to sleep until 6:00 AM. We eat lunch at villa every day, and sometimes even breakfast, and we have both morning and afternoon rec, and we can even go outside for our morning meditation. One morning, when there is a breakfast at villa, I take out a canoe and paddle it around the edge of the lake to villa during my meditation.

An exceptional art teacher, Sister Angela of the Sisters of St. Joseph, is brought in from the Twin Cities to give us some painting and sculpture lessons. These are days of rest and relaxation, and everyone seems to be having a good time.

Then we hear some disconcerting news. A priest who taught some of us in my high school back home, Fr. Jared Morris, was arrested and charged with some sort of "sexual misconduct." That is all the news that we hear at first, and we are left hanging about the details.

At almost the same time, I have noticed that Leonard has become a bit absent-minded. On two different days he has failed to show up for art class, and one morning he did not manage to get up in time after the morning bell. And once, at evening recreation, after I asked him a question, he just sat for a moment, not even shifting in his chair, and would not answer me. He just stared into space for the better part of a minute. I had to repeat the same question two more times before he finally responded.

I have been thinking about all of these incidents, and I don't know what to make of them, and I try to figure out how to approach Leonard about them.

Then he breaks the ice himself. "Wally, I've been having problems lately," he says quietly. "I sometimes just tune out completely. I get very absent-mined, and I don't even know where I am, or what's going on, sometimes." He pauses. "And I'm still getting headaches. Sometimes I can't handle them, and so I just take some medication, and go to my room, and try to relax."

I can only say the first thing that pops into my mind. "Does the medication help?"

"A little. Most of the time."

"Leonard, I will pray for you. I know we're not supposed to have particular friendships, but I consider you one of my two best friends here. You, and Alex."

"Thanks, Wally. I appreciate your prayers."

***

In the ensuing weeks, we become immersed in Juniorate studies: English and History courses, Greek Tragedies — in the original Greek, of course — and Virgil's Aeneid in the original Latin, and some Calculus courses for the guys who will be pursuing scientific disciplines later on.

One morning we learn that our Father General in Rome has appointed Fr. McKittrick to be our new Provincial for the next six years, and he has also asked Fr. McKittrick to pack his bags and come to Rome for some weeks to attend some sessions of Vatican II with him. This is very positive news to everyone, because we all, to a man, respect Fr. McKittrick, and applaud his being chosen for our next Fr. Provincial. Fr. General has also invited Fr. Hillard, the present Rector of the House, and some other priests from our province to come to Rome with him.

The upshot of all this is that, in their absence, Fr. Harrison, the Sarge, has been appointed both Acting Provincial and Acting Rector of the House.

"But I tell you, love
your enemies, bless
those that curse you,
do good to those who
hate you, and pray for
those who speak evil
about you, and
persecute you..."

Matthew 5:44

CHAPTER THIRTY-SEVEN

An Underhanded Blow

The Sarge announces that, as acting Provincial, he has to interview each of us recent vow men, to see how we are doing and how we are adjusting to the Juniorate. This happens every year, where the new vow men meet with whomever the current Fr. Provincial happens to be. Ken Matthews says his class went through it last year at about this same time. I manage to get through the Sarge's interview all right, and it is my assumption that everyone else does, too.

***

A few days later, in early October, Leonard asks me to join him for a walk. We head out over toward the other side of the lake, and climb the hill beyond "George's Gorge."

"Wally," says Leonard all of a sudden, "I have been asked to leave the Order."

I stop in my tracks. If it was someone like Dubchek, I might have expected a joke, and I'd wait for a punch line. But Leonard is too serious for that kind of thing. "Why?" I manage to ask fairly quickly, without too much of a pause.

"I have some mental problems. I've been losing my concentration, and the headaches have been getting worse."

"Well, okay," I say, "but why should you have to leave the Order? I mean, why aren't they taking you to the hospital, and giving you tests?"

"Well, they gave me some tests in the infirmary. And the tests were inconclusive, so far." He becomes silent for a moment. "I guess I..." he hesitates.

"You what?"

"I've... sort of fallen into the category of guys who..."

"Guys who what?"

"Guys who can't adjust to the Juniorate, after they take vows."

"Are you serious? You're saying that this is the result of your interview with the Sarge?"

"In part, I think. He called me in this morning and told me that, as a result of the interview and some other issues and difficulties, it was his conclusion that I should leave."

"What other issues?" I am surprised at how relatively calm I am able to be.

"Well, I'm terrible at giving speeches, you know that. And when I'm nervous, I laugh too much. And remember those psychological tests? I did not do very well on them."

"How... how do you know that?"

"The Sarge told me. He said that I was in a different category than almost everybody else. I was, they said, very asocial and... some other things. I can't seem to relate to people very well."

"I think you relate just fine."

"Well, maybe I relate to you okay, and to Alex, but I'm not good with most people. I have to know people really well before I can feel comfortable around them."

We stare out at the lake in a long moment of silence.

"How do you feel about this?" I ask.

"I don't know. I just... I'm kind of in shock. I've been praying about it, and even though... even though it's hard, I guess I just have to accept it."

All of a sudden it hits me, and I almost feel sick. I am in a state of disbelief. What is it that makes some people — people like me — prefer this way of life? When I first entered, I was way out of my comfort zone... and yet I could still feel secure here, in some way. I regained my appetite, for one thing. And over time, I got to know and love the truth that this life stands for, as well as some incredible people. Including Leonard. And now? Now I'm in a new comfort zone, I guess. And so is Leonard. And after all we've gone through, this has to happen? Lord, why?

"Do you have any idea what you're going to do?" I ask as we turn around and head back to the House.

"I'm not sure yet. Probably go back to live with my Grandmother, at first. And get a job of some kind, I guess. Maybe try to finish school, if I can."

I feel a gradually increasing anger toward the Sarge, as if he has really made some kind of bad mistake, here. But he holds all the cards. One of our vows is that of Obedience, and so if a superior asks us to do something, even to leave the Order, we have to comply.

"How long... how long do you have?" I ask him then.

"He wants me to leave the day after tomorrow. Early in the morning. Actually, he doesn't want me to tell anyone. I just felt I should tell you."

I am all of a sudden experiencing a powerful attack of what we in formation have come to call "desolation." The direct opposite of "consolation." After all we have learned here for the two years before vows, I feel that this is a new, unprecedented, blind-sided kick from somewhere unknown. Somehow, with the speed and unexpectedness of a lightning bolt, Leonard has been bomb-shelled, rudely thrust outside the embracing arms of the Order, and I can neither understand it, nor do anything about it. Except pray. I actually feel an urge to go and confront the Sarge about all this, and tell him what an asshole he is, and tell him where he can go, and on and on, but then I quickly realize that this is of course a temptation, and that I must be more discreet, and pray about these matters.

***

The next morning, I put on Andy's hair shirt for meditation. It is so uncomfortable, I cannot concentrate on my points. All I want to do is take it off, and after half an hour, I do so.

***

Later in the morning Leonard gives me a hand-written diary which he has entitled, "The Laws of Gravity."

"What's this?" I ask him.

"Every time we visited the Padre, after I got back to my room, I wrote down notes about what he said. This is a notebook of that, with some of my own insights and interpretations."

"Okay, but why aren't you keeping it for yourself?"

"Oh. Well, I figured maybe you needed it more than I do. You're staying and I'm leaving, after all."

"For crock's sake, Leonard, keep it! You're the one who compiled it!"

I open it and glance at some of the pages. There are all kinds of little sayings and comments, like:

> "Never forget, *'With God, all things are possible...'"*
> Matt. 19:26; Mark 10:27; Luke 18:27.

"Tell you what," I say then, "Let me borrow it and copy it, then I'll mail it back to you when I'm done."

"Okay, that'll work," he says.

✳✳✳

It is better to conquer
yourself than to win
a thousand battles.
Then the victory is
yours. It cannot be
taken from you."

Gautama Buddha

CHAPTER THIRTY-EIGHT

A Sad Farewell

Leonard left very early on Friday morning. As I helped him haul his trunk and suitcases down to the garage, I kept having this feeling, or this conviction or whatever it was, that this scenario was all wrong, and none of this should be happening. I kept thinking that God really wants Leonard here, even though things were not working out that way.

When I said good-bye to him, I had this strange combination of feelings of both desolation, and consolation. Like I was saying good-bye, and at the same time, I was not. Whether or not these feelings were honest and true, at least they kept me from breaking down. I've never really broken down since about age ten or eleven or so, when I started reaching puberty and became more masculine, or hardened, or whatever. At least not totally; I just sort of teared up a little, these past two years, in a quiet sort of way. But I figure there's always a first time, and I am probably getting closer to a breakdown every day. Crock, sometimes I feel like I'm almost as emotional as a woman, in some ways. But then I have to ask myself, what's wrong with that?

***

And now there is more news. We hear that Fr. Jared Morris, the sex pervert, or whatever one might call him — Okay, I'm still not a saint yet— was a buddy of the Sarge. And perhaps because of this, the Sarge, as Acting Provincial, has simply transferred Fr. Morris to another assignment in another province. We hear all this through the grapevine, and we are not supposed to discuss it, at least not publicly.

I have been thinking about this, and when I compare the Sarge's handling of this Fr. Morris situation with the way he handled the Padre's situation, and Leonard's dismissal, I become livid. I get feelings of anger where I have trouble controlling myself. I have terrible thoughts, including thoughts about leaving the Order. I had, over the past two years, come to believe that this Order is a wonderful, blessed way to live one's life, in accordance with God's plan. And yet, what I have now been seeing here in the Sarge's handling of these three different situations is a biased, unfair approach.

Two weeks after Leonard leaves, I receive a letter from Andy. Oh yeah, after vows they don't open our mail and read it any more; Andy's letter has not been opened or censored. In the letter Andy says that he has been visiting Leonard and assisting him, including taking him to the hospital for more tests. They have learned that Leonard has an inoperable brain tumor, and he has a few months left to live. I am shocked to hear this, and I have to stop reading for a bit, just to reflect and to let this sink in. But then, Andy says that Leonard has requested to be reinstated into the Order, so that he can die as a member of the Order. That is such an uplifting thought, it would be incredible! And very understandable, because I am sure the medical news would explain his absent-mindedness, headaches, and so forth. He really should not have been asked to leave, for a medical condition outside of his control. At least, that's my opinion.

Another week passes, and I receive another letter from Andy. He says that the Sarge, as Acting Provincial, has decided that to reinstate Leonard would take months of red tape, and he says it is absolutely unnecessary. This news is difficult to believe, much less understand.

I am not sleeping well because of this, and I have been praying a lot. I think I have been praying more than I ever did in the novitiate, outside of the Long Retreat. And after some days of prayer, I have decided that I have to do something about it (*Pray as if everything depends upon God, Act as if everything depends upon you...*). So, what can I do? I guess the best thing is to at least talk to someone. In the novitiate, that would have been Fr. McKittrick. But that was when he was novice master, and I was a novice. Now I am supposed to have a different Spiritual Father, Fr. Sheridan, our Spiritual Father here in the Juniorate, but I do not want to talk to him, because I really don't know him very well yet. Instead I have this feeling, and even though it is a confrontational, adversarial kind of feeling, I truly believe I have to go with it. And the feeling says to me, loud and clear, that the Sarge is the man I have to see.

***

I walk to the open door of the Rector's office — the Sarge's office for now — and knock.

He is sitting at his desk looking over some papers. He looks up at me and says, "Yes?"

"Father Harrison? Can we talk for a moment?"

He nods curtly.

I enter his office and pull up a chair and sit down in front of him. "I heard about Father Morris. It was really sad, what happened. You know, he taught me sophomore English, back in high school."

He just looks at me.

"I mean, they say he did something sexually improper? In public? That's just unbelievable."

He puts his hands on top of his desk and continues to look at me. "I am not at liberty to discuss it," he says quietly.

"That must have been a hard decision, what to do, where to send him? I mean, technically, couldn't the man go to prison? If they convicted him of something?"

He just gives me a look that is hard to interpret.

"But you, because of your philosophy of life, and because of what our order stands for, you decided to give him another chance, send him to another province."

"Yes..." he says quietly.

"That's quite an act of forgiveness. A lot of people might think that you were too kind. You know, if there was a victim, say, and the victim's family?"

He just continues to look at me.

"But forgiveness is important. And second chances are important, we both know that. Especially for a man like you who's been through the war. Iwo Jima, right? That's where you were, right?"

He straightens up, almost as if to assume a different role for a moment.

"Yes."

"I'm sure the war was a difficult time for you. But you also learned how to watch the backs of your men, and they watched yours. You took care of one another. And I know that you and Fr. Morris go way back, and he was your buddy, so you made sure you could do everything possible for him, right? Even though he deserved worse, you did him a favor, pardoned him, so to speak?"

"Can you tell me what you're getting at?"

"You pardoned him. You let him stay in the Order."

He just stares at me.

"Forgiveness," I say quietly, "seems to be the defining quality of our Christian Faith. I mean, everything we do here, every thought we think, is subject to examination. Twice a day. We are expected to live and act and breathe the words of Jesus, the words of the Gospel."

"Mr. Moriarty, I have to ask you once again where you are going with this?"

"I'll tell you where I'm going." I can feel my voice begin to shake. "I have been here in this house of formation for over two years, and I have had the most amazing revelations. I came here feeling almost abandoned by God. I had trouble believing He was even there. But then I met Fr. McKittrick, and he presented this order and everyone in it, and everything it stands for and strives for, as the most loving, compassionate and holy and Christ-like group of men I could ever hope to meet. And yet, right now, at this moment in time, I am convinced that I am seeing the *antithesis* of that in you."

He reinforces his cold exterior. "I am sorry to hear that, Mr. Moriarty. I'm still not sure where you're going with this, but you must realize that he and I have different jobs to do."

"*Jobs*? In other words, he was what, a good-will ambassador? A salesman? Getting me to buy into all this? And now that I've committed myself to the order, I have to readjust my thinking and roll with the new punches, so to speak?"

"Mr. Moriarty, life in this order is not all roses. There are many hard decisions to make, and those of us in charge have to make them, whether they are pleasant or not. Remember, Our Lord wasn't always pleasant — like when he threw the money-changers out of the temple, for instance. Sometimes I have to make difficult decisions, like it or not."

"Is that your preferred image of our Lord? The day He threw the money-changers out of the temple?"

"What is your point?"

"That was only one moment in the Gospel, one wakeup call for greedy people with hardened hearts. His biggest, most frequent virtues were kindness and compassion."

"You still haven't answered my question."

I pause for just a second. Then, "Why did you kick Leonard out?"

He is taken aback for the briefest moment. "We did not kick him out. We should never have accepted him into the novitiate, but that mistake did not become apparent until later. We came to the conclusion that he was psychologically unfit for the priesthood, and we acted accordingly."

"Why did you take so long to come to that decision? You led him to believe that he was accepted, that he could be a member of the order and do the work of a priest. You let him go through the entire novitiate, with all the probations, and you let him take vows! Why did you take so long to dump him?"

"Mr. Moriarty, I don't like your choice of words. We did not 'dump' him. We don't always perform our tasks quickly. We have priorities and limited resources, and this decision was given a lot of careful thought."

"I take it that he's not the only one, that this is not a new direction for you, and that there are other people on your hit-list? Like say, Fr. Lugieri?"

"That has nothing to do with this issue."

"Doesn't it? I heard you want him out of the order, and the priesthood. And for what? All he ever did was love and serve people. People of all races and creeds. And yet you want him gone, *and you let a sex pervert stay?*"

"You don't know the circumstances!"

363

"But of course, The Order accepted the Padre long before you were even born. Maybe the priests of his day were just not clever enough to discern whether *he* was a company man, before they accepted him? Or maybe they were more charitable and open-minded back then?"

"I told you, we don't always have time to commit to such issues. And I find your attitude offensive."

There is a crucifix standing on his desk, and I pick it up.

"This didn't happen," I continue, holding the crucifix right up to his face, "because he refused to offend people. This happened because He spoke the *truth, whether or not it offended people.* Maybe you *need some* offending. Some *serious* offending!"

He looks astonished, for once.

"Don't you think it a bit strange, Father, that Jesus, even with His Divine Nature, still managed to let a flawed, vile man like Judas Iscariot slip into the fold of the original twelve? And even when Judas chose to betray Him, He *still* did not just *kick him out*? I mean, Jesus was so willing to put up with, say, the rabble, the commoners, the *vulgar* of society. The apostles were rough wage earners, fishermen, maybe some were illiterate..."

"Mr. Moriarty, what are you getting at?"

"Leonard deserved to stay in the order! He is brilliant, in some ways. And even if you didn't think he had a suitable personality for a priest, couldn't you have let him stay in as a brother? We're not all on the road to priesthood, here."

"We made our decision, and that's the way it is."

"And now that he has cancer, and would like to return and die in the order, you still won't let him back in?"

"We don't let people back in, as a rule. There is a lot of red tape to be gone through, and it isn't worth it. Besides, it would be expensive. He would need medical attention..."

"Isn't *worth* it? You know who you remind me of when you say that? Remember when the repentant woman opened an expensive bottle of nard to pour over Jesus' feet, one of the apostles said it was a waste of money? Wasn't *worth* it? What was that guy's name? Oh yeah, I just mentioned him a minute ago. Judas Iscariot. And you talk as if the order is short of funds right now? Yeah, like maybe you can save some money here, so you could buy another country club membership for one of your university presidents?"

"Those are donated, Mr. Moriarty, by generous alumni."

"Donated or not, they're still money, money that could feed the hungry and shelter the homeless, and... wait a minute. You said 'we' don't let people back in. Who is 'we?' I just thought of something else. I'll bet Fr. McKittrick doesn't even know about this, does he? He's our real Provincial, but he's way off in Rome, out of sight, out of mind. Did you even bother to make a long-distance call to him about all this? Oh yeah, transatlantic calls are expensive. I'll bet you didn't."

"Mr. Moriarty, you are out of line here, and I have other business to attend to. Are you finished?"

"Almost. Just one more thing, Father. I am curious about you, as to what it is you meditate on every morning, when you supposedly rededicate your life to God, and to the work of Jesus Christ, as we novices and juniors are required to do, every day. And I am curious as to what you think of when you examine your conscience every day, *twice* a day, as you must do, as all of us are required to do. Do you ever really think about the *compassion* of our Lord? Do you ever think of what it must have been like for this God-man, this member of the Blessed Trinity to come down to earth, choose to take on our disgusting, puking, farting, defecating, sinful human nature — this Creator of the stars of night, and the galaxies and the planets and moons and the winds and the seas and the storms, this King of Kings, what it was like for Him to come into this f****d-up, exiled world and, when He had every right to condemn us, *He knelt down on the floor and washed our feet?*"

I am almost screaming at him when I say this, and he looks down. "That's the God-Man *I* will always try to emulate!"

He is quiet for a moment. "Are you... finished?" he almost whispers.

"Just about. Tomorrow morning I'll be out of here. You won't have to buy me a ticket home. That's expensive. I'll be more than happy to hitchhike. Save the order a little money." I get up and walk to the door.

"May I remind you, Mr. Moriarty," he says now, "that you cannot just walk out of here — you have sacred vows?"

"So did Leonard! Until you decided to play God!" And with that I go through the door and close it, very quietly.

I go back to my room and try to think straight. Then I sit down at my desk and try to compose a letter to Fr. McKittrick, our actual Provincial, asking for a release from my vows. It takes me awhile to write it, because I am having a terrible time thinking of what to say.

> *"Dear Father McKittrick,*
>
> *"I am very sad to have to write this letter, but I cannot see any other way out of it. I have come to the conclusion that I am not really fit for life in this Order, because of certain irreconcilable differences I have had with one of my superiors..."*

I decide to stop writing for the time being and just wait for nightfall. I do not feel like praying, so I don't try. For some reason, I feel like God has totally abandoned me, once again. After these years of formation, where I had thought I had left such extreme emptiness behind me forever, I feel as badly as I did when Darryl died. If not worse. This is the worst feeling of all...I feel so empty, I don't even want to live.

***

It's dinner time, and I am kneeling in the middle aisle, still feeling terrible. At the end of first grace, I say out loud for all to hear, "Reverend Fathers and beloved brethren, I accuse myself of talking disrespectfully to one of my superiors and using language unbecoming of a religious, for which fault Holy Obedience has imposed upon me the slight penance of kissing the feet of some of the members of the community. And, and I... I love all of you."

I lean under the table and kiss the feet of the two men nearest me, then take my seat at table. I am wondering why I am even still here. I could have actually packed and left before dinner, but somebody might have seen me. Best to do it under cover of darkness. I am not making much eye contact with anyone, just looking down at my plate, taking a little food from the deeps as they go by and then passing them on, even though my appetite is totally gone once more..... but I have to force myself to eat this repulsive fare on my plate, so as not to appear suspicious.

During evening rec, I sneak away and walk down the basement halls to hide in the trunk room. Again, I do not feel like praying, and when I am like this I am at my worst. Every minute lasts for hours, it seems. "Lord," I say aloud, "I want to pray, but I cannot. I feel as if you have abandoned me. I feel terrible. Is there any way out of this?"

I remember the words of Jesus, on the cross, "Eloi, Eloi, lama sabachthani..." *"My God, My God, why hast Thou forsaken Me..."* and I say them over, and over, and over again...

That night, after everyone else is asleep, I finish the letter to Fr. McKittrick, then seal it and leave it on my desk. I pack my bags as quietly as possible, in the dim light of my desk lamp. We do not have a lot of personal possessions here, and so the two suitcases I brought in with me when I entered are enough for underwear, pants, socks, shirts. And Andy's hair shirt, sort of as a souvenir. Of course I am leaving behind my black robe, black suit, chain, discipline, and all the other clerical attire I have acquired. After one last check of my armarium, I shut off the lamp, open my door and, in the dim night-lights of the corridor, quietly make my way down toward the Porter's Lodge.

I push open the great wooden doors and exit into the night. After all this time, it still surprises me that none of the doors are locked at night. I mean, the doors should always be openable from the inside, for fire safety and that kind of thing, but aren't they ever worried about intruders from the outside?

As I head out the curving drive toward the highway, I am still having spasms of anger and emotion. On impulse, I walk off the paved drive and start crossing over the lawns and the fields. The grass and the fields are not dewy yet, but even if they were, I would not care. I approach some woods, and enter into a kind of clearing amidst some copses of trees. On a small rise, I stop and set down my suitcases under the moon. There is a knot in my stomach, worse than I had the day I entered, over two years ago. I look up at the stars, and even though the moonlight is overpowering the dimmer stars, I find the constellation of Andromeda that Leonard first pointed out to me.

"Why," I cry out, "do You have to make it so hard?" I am panting, more from anger than from hauling these suitcases over a half a mile of countryside. "Just when I thought I could handle this life, You throw all these curve balls, these f***ing obstacles! Sorry, but the crock word doesn't cut it here. Leonard wanted to serve You here, so what do You do? *You kick him out!* The Padre tries to teach us to love everyone, so what do you do? *Disgrace him!* The Sarge hates everybody, shouldn't even be here, so what do You do? *You put him in charge!* Do You know how shitty I feel right now? I hate this life, I hate my life, I hate everything! *I wish I was never born, that's how I feel!*" I am shocked at myself for saying this, but it is how I feel.

Something in my pocket is poking into my leg and I reach down into the pocket and pull out a stone...my wotai stone. I want to fling it away, into the deepest woods or swamp or whatever, as far as possible, along with every other memory of this place and this life. I raise my arm to throw, then stop. It was, after all, a gift from Leonard. I look at it again, in the light of the full moon. I can actually see that the hues, the maroons and purples and browns, are not the same in the moonlight, and because of this the darker parts of the pattern, almost colorless in the dim light, seem to take on a different shape. *An animal?* I sit down on a suitcase, then sink down into the long grass of this little field and I close my eyes. I don't know why I have to feel like this. I wish I could just disappear...

After a little while, I hear a rustling sound. I open my eyes and see, a short distance away, a shadowy moving figure. Then I hear a low growling sound. The figure is moving toward me, and it is some sort of large dog, skulking along close to the ground as it approaches, pushing and stalking through the taller blades of field grass. "Shanty?" I call out, but it's not him... it's not the house dog. I can see its eyes flash every now and then, and it is still grunting, snarling. Can this really be happening? This is downright scary! "Dear God," I say then, "I am really sorry for all the things I said, for all of my anger. I just really have trouble understanding You sometimes. Do You know how I feel? And what is this dog all about? Holy crock, it looks like a wolf!"

The animal is hard to see clearly in the moonlight, but it is definitely glowering at me, slinking on its belly practically, as it continues to move toward me. Now it stops a few feet from me, and it is low to the ground, but its rump is still a little high; it almost gives me the feeling that it is guarding me, and will spring at me if I make the slightest move. I can see its teeth glaring in the moonlight. I am afraid to stir, so I just sit there, petrified, watching it.

"Dear Lord, I know I may not be worth saving, but I'm asking, please help me to get away from this damned dog."

All of a sudden a new, louder rustling sound comes from off to my left, and a second animal comes charging over the hill. It barrels right into the wolf-dog and they begin to fight, snarling and snapping at each other. The second animal appears to be wolf-like as well, much darker in color than the first, and now there is a great, savage brawl, and a din of yelps and growls and snarls. Very quickly, the second wolf gets the upper hand and chases the first one away. I cannot believe I am seeing this. As soon as they disappear over the rise I stand up and pick up my suitcases. I begin to walk away, in the opposite direction from which they went, when I hear rustling again in the tall grass behind me. And now one of the animals, the second, darker one, returns and approaches me. "Oh no, here we go again," I say to myself. But then I notice that this wolf is not skulking on its belly, but walks high at the shoulder, and it approaches me slowly, with little whining sounds and submissive moves of its head. It is mild and almost seems friendly! I set the suitcases down and sit down on the larger one again. This is unbelievable. This wolf, or very wolf-like dog, whatever it is, comes up to me, slowly and submissively, and nuzzles me!

"Well hello boy, or girl, you're a friendly animal. Thanks for chasing off that other nasty fellow," I say as I pet it and scratch it behind the ears. It honestly looks just like a black wolf, in the dim moonlight, but why is it so friendly?

"Would you like a piece of cornbread?" I ask as I open my smaller suitcase and take out a foil-wrapped package. I open it up to reveal a square of cornbread and I break off a piece. The animal takes a bite and eats, but it does not appear to be very hungry. But of course, how many wolves like cornbread?

"You sure are a dark one, aren't you? Midnight, that's what I'll call you." I scratch Midnight behind the ears, and he — or she — turns and licks my hand. I'm starting to feel like this animal is my best friend! I sink back down to the ground, my back against the suitcase. I continue to rub Midnight's

neck, and I begin to relax, and I start to feel a little better. Midnight lies down right against me, a big, warm, furry oasis of comfort on this cool night, and eventually I doze off.

Later on I open my eyes, and the moon is in a different part of the sky. Midnight is still here, lying right up against me, keeping me warm. Then he gets up, takes a few steps, turns back and looks at me, almost as if he wants me to follow him.

I shake my head, rub my eyes and look around. I stand up, stretch, pick up my suitcases, and begin to walk in the direction Midnight went. The sky is beginning to brighten, and I am wondering where the time went. I was a little disoriented in the dark, but now, as I go over a rise, I see that I am actually heading back toward the house. My lupine friend seems to have disappeared, but for some reason, I now feel a need to return to the house, which I do.

As I open the big oaken doors, I think of the Padre, and I hastily carry my suitcases back to my room, change into my cassock and hurry down the corridors and steps to the infirmary wing. I enter the infirmary and head to the Padre's room and open his door to find him sound asleep, in bed.

"Padre," I whisper as I kneel down, "I have sinned... I have shouted in anger at God, and I beg of you to give me absolution. I am sorry Lord, I am so sorry..." I am kneeling right next to him, head bowed, when I feel the soft touch of his old hand rest on my head. Tears run down my face. After a moment, I raise my head, and I see that his eyes are still closed. I gently lift his hand from my head, move it back onto the bed, and leave.

CHAPTER THIRTY-NINE

Deo Gratias!

My room is on the front side of the Juniorate wing, overlooking the parking lot, and I have my window open. And now, as the sunlight continues to brighten across the countryside, I hear a sound through the window, the sound of a car approaching. But it is not just a regular car sound, it sounds more like a sportscar. I turn and look, and there, coming along the entrance drive, is that familiar Porsche convertible with the top down! I watch with fascination as it pulls into the parking lot, squealing its tires a bit as it comes to a stop. But who is driving it? My mouth drops open as I see, not Andy Gallagher, but *Leonard* at the wheel! He is grinning and laughing with Andy, who is seated on the passenger side! Now Andy is getting out of the car and pulling a portable wheelchair out of the back.

I jump up from my kneeler and head down the hall as quickly as I can toward the Porter's Lodge. I trot along toward the main doors and reach them just as they are being pulled open from the outside.

"Andy? Leonard?" I say quietly as I hold the door open for Andy to push Leonard through in the wheelchair. Leonard is holding a small suitcase across his lap. "What's going on?"

"Leonard, why don't you tell him?" says Andy.

"I'm coming back," says Leonard. "The Sarge called me yesterday and told me I could come back!"

"He called you yesterday?" I say, trying to grasp all this. "When?"

"Six O'clock, actually. Around dinner time. Never underestimate the power of prayer!" He says with a grin.

All at once, I have trouble breathing, and I feel a lump forming in my throat, and my eyes are tearing up. That was less than an hour after I left the Sarge's office.

"Wally," says Andy, evidently not noticing my problem, "We're going to Mass with you guys, then Leonard is going to get a room in the infirmary. I'll bring more of his things out here later on."

***

That very day, Leonard gets situated in the Infirmary, and during my noon Examen, in the quiet of my room, I take the letter I wrote to Fr. McKittrick and think for a moment. I am amazed that my venting to the Sarge may actually have influenced this whole turn of events, and I thank God profusely. I am just about ready to tear the letter up and throw it in the wastebasket, but I reconsider and for the time being put it in the large pocket of my cassock.

***

That afternoon, during rec, I tell Alex about the talk with the Sarge, the walk through the fields at night, the wolves, everything.

"You actually packed up and left?" he says, staring at me. "Wally, that's hard to believe."

"Well I was really upset, you know?"

"Yeah, and I can't blame you. The Sarge is an enigma of the first magnitude, and I have spent many an hour trying to figure him out. But this whole thing with the wolves, are you sure it wasn't a dream?"

"Good question. I think we should try to find the area, see where it happened."

We head over the fields to the northwest of the House, and after a little searching, we find some disturbances in the grass, and figure that some of them could have been caused by me sleeping among the suitcases. They could have also been caused by the wolves, but the evidence is inconclusive. There do not seem to be any little tufts of fur, or other signs.

"Is there any other possible evidence?" asks Alex.

"I'm not sure," I say. "Wait! The cornbread!"

"What cornbread?"

"Didn't I tell you? I gave the wolf a piece of cornbread. I still have the rest of it in my room; let's go back and see what it looks like."

After rec Alex and I head to my room and I take out the foil-wrapped package of cornbread. I unwrap it, and indeed, a piece is missing!

"Are you sure you didn't eat any yourself?" asks Alex.

"Yes, I only gave some to the wolf. And it was a small piece, just about this size."

Alex gives me a funny look. "Well, you know me... I'm a skeptic. And this wolf story sounds a bit, shall we say, imaginative? I mean, should we call them Romulus and Remus, or what?"

This is typical Alex, bringing up the legendary twin founders of Rome from our classical studies, who were suckled by a she-wolf as babies.

"Look, Alex," I offer, "I'm as skeptical as you are. Let's just let it go for now. But I will tell you, dream or not, it has been etched in my mind, to the point that I'll never forget it."

That evening, as I walk down the hall to litanies before dinner, the Sarge sees me and pulls me aside. "Mr. Moriarty, can we talk for a moment?" Oh yeah, after vows we are no longer called "carissime;" from now until ordination we are called "Mr."

"Yes, Father, of course!" I have trouble suppressing a grin; I feel as if we are allies, all of a sudden.

"I see you're still here. You changed your mind after yesterday's tirade?"

"...Yes," I say, quickly taken aback by his choice of words and his attitude.

"I just want you to know that, first of all, I did not appreciate your lack of respect toward me as your superior, and I am going to make a note of it and keep it in a file. Your file."

"Okay," I say as a new knot begins to grow in my stomach.

"Secondly, do not assume, in any way, that our chat yesterday influenced my decision to allow Mr. Wentfogle to return to the Order. That was my decision, and my decision alone."

"Yes, Father."

"That's all, Mr. Moriarty," he says as he turns toward the chapel.

Needless to say, this takes some wind out of my sails. But Leonard is back, and that's the important thing.

***

"Pain is certain;
suffering is optional."

Gautama Buddha

CHAPTER FORTY

Leonard's Illness

Leonard's infirmary room quickly becomes popular, with many of the men coming to visit him nightly. Frequently, Andy drives out with Leonard's grandmother, a sweet older lady with a sad but beautiful face, and she works hard to console him. However, as the days go by, his condition begins to deteriorate and his visiting hours are restricted.

On the positive side, the Sisters from St. Joseph's Home have volunteered to help us out with round-the-clock care, since Brother Ritchie has other patients to take care of, and the sisters would like to "pay us back" a little for all our novices' help for them on their hospital probations. Sister Bernadette comes out and moves into the infirmary wing, and they actually let Catherine, the Postulant candidate, come as well, to assist Sr. Bernadette and be trained in a newly developing concept called Hospice Care for the terminally ill. The nuns are housed in vacant infirmary rooms, which are outside the papal cloister that is implemented in the main residential wings of the House.

I head into the Infirmary one evening, in part to read a little to the Padre, but hopefully to see Leonard as well. And maybe even see Catherine, if possible.

I have not seen the Padre for awhile, since those who wish to read to him have to take turns, and there is a waiting list. I approach his door and I am about to knock when I hear a muffled voice. "Okay Padre, it's time for me to go," says a voice quietly. Then I hear a very quiet sound, almost like someone else talking. It is so quiet that I cannot even be sure it is really that, and I raise my hand and knock.

"Come in," says a voice, and I recognize it as Brother Larry's. When I enter his room, the Padre is seated in a large easy chair, and Brother Larry is standing up in front of him. The Padre slowly turns and regards me with a knowing smile, just as Brother Larry sets down a Braille book on the nearby desk. I have been here three times to read to him since he lost his ability to speak, and every time I come here, I wonder how much he remembers, and how well he can still think.

"Good evening, Padre," I say as I reach out to shake his hand. "Remember me? Wally?"

He squeezes my hand in both of his, and nods with a smile.

"My relief pitcher is here," says Brother Larry with a grin, and he shakes the Padre's hand and says, "I'll continue this on Thursday."

"What have you been reading?" I ask, staring at the Braille book.

"Just some theological essays," says Brother Larry, "pretty boring, actually," he says with a laugh as he departs from the room.

The Padre laughs a little himself, and I am glad to see his smile.

"Padre," I say, "I can continue reading from the latest book you were listening to, other than the Braille one. What was it?" I say as I look at his desk, where I see a copy of Steinbeck's latest work. "Steinbeck's Travels With Charlie?" The Padre nods.

I pick up the book from his desk and sit down on a chair in front of him, and he looks at me intently.

"How've you been, Padre?" I ask quietly, almost forgetting that he cannot say. Then he turns his head to look at the door, which is slightly ajar, and turns back to look at me.

"Quo... vadis?" he whispers, and my mouth drops open.

"You... you can speak?" I blurt it out softly, because he spoke so quietly, and it is so unbelievable. "How... how long have you been able to..."

He puts a finger to his lips. "I figure," he says quietly, "that if I keep a my mouth shut, everyone will a be happier."

"Holy crock," I say, perhaps louder than I should, "this is, this is incredible. I..."

Suddenly there is a slight rustling sound, followed by a soft knock at the slightly ajar door. I quickly open the book and turn toward the door in one movement, to see Brother Ritchie peering in.

"Everything okay?" asks Brother Ritchie. I nod, and he turns and disappears down the hall.

"Quo... ivisti?" says the Padre now, very quietly, after Brother Ritchie leaves. "Where have a you been?"

"Oh, I've been around," I say with a chuckle.

"You try a to leave? You left a the house in the middle of the night?" he whispers.

"It's a long story, Padre, but I'm back. Who told you all this?"

"You did! Remember? You came a to my room," he says with a wink. "So, I have a not talked with you in awhile. Do you remember what we used to talk about? I never got a satisfactory answer, for my question."

"Your question..."

"What is a Baptism?"

"Well ah... I guess we never got to the bottom of it."

"Here is a your last set of clues. Do not a worry, they are so easy, they are not even real clues, they give it away," he says as he hands me a folded-up piece of paper. I unfold it and read:

Summa Theologica, 3, 69, 4

Lumen Gentium 16

I fold the piece of paper up again, and put it into my pocket.

"That reminds me," I say, "I had a nagging question myself. Do you remember?"

"What is Ecclesiam?" he says as he looks into my eyes. "I can tell a you this, the answer to your question is... related to mine, shall we say."

"I'll keep that in mind," I say then.

"So," he says, "how is a Leonard doing today?"

"I haven't seen him today yet. I'll check on him when I leave you tonight."

"Go, and a check on him now," he says authoritatively, "I will a be fine."

I nod, get up and leave the Padre's room and head down the hall to Leonard's room. I knock quietly on Leonard's closed door, and I hear a woman's voice say, "Come in."

I enter to find Catherine seated at Leonard's bedside, washing his face with a damp washcloth. I can tell Leonard is in pain. I cannot imagine what it must be like. He is barely conscious. Catherine looks at me as I pull another chair close and sit down.

"Leonard," I say as I sit down and clasp his hand, "It's me, Wally." He turns his face slightly toward me, opens his eyes for a moment, smiles a little, then closes them again.

"Hello, Wally," he whispers quietly.

Catherine daubs his face again with the wet washcloth, then puts it down.

"Leonard," I say, "I don't know what this is like for you, but I want you to know that we are all praying for you, every day."

He opens his eyes and tries to smile again, then closes his eyes. "Do you think..." he says slowly, "...do you think... it's boring up there?"

"Do I think what's boring?" I ask.

"Heaven," he says slowly. "Do you think it might be boring? Alex said he worries about that."

And now Catherine takes Leonard's head gently in her hands, and he opens his eyes again. She says to him, "Leonard, Heaven is *not boring!* If and when I get to Heaven, you and I, we'll have a party that lasts for ten thousand years. And as soon as that party ends, we can start another one!"

"I never was at a party... with girls before," he says as he closes his eyes again, and she strokes his cheek with her hand. "Wait," he says, opening his eyes again, "except when you nuns came here, in August. When we had lemonade... and you sang, 'Where have...where have all the... flowers gone...'" then he seems to slip into unconsciousness again.

Even though I shouldn't be, I am envious of Leonard, when I see how she dotes on him. Then, almost as if she senses this, Catherine turns to me and says, "I'm sorry. Whenever somebody is sick, I develop feelings for him. It's one of my faults."

"Felix culpa," I say then.

"What?"

"Happy fault," I say. "I would not call it a fault. It's more of a virtue than anything else."

She continues to dampen his face, and I watch her. She looks at me again and says, "You're not...?" but stops in mid-sentence.

"Jealous?" I say, finishing the sentence for her. "Well, put it this way. If I am, it's *my* problem, you know?"

She turns back to Leonard, as if she doesn't want to look at me all of a sudden.

"What?" I say.

"That's the most mature thing I ever heard come out of the mouth of a twenty-year-old male," she says quietly. She continues to cool Leonard's face, and I watch her in the light of the lamp, and her blue eyes, and a tassel of her blonde hair that hangs a little outside her postulant's veil. I really should not be staring at her like this. And she actually thinks I'm mature?

"Do you want some more water?" I ask then.

She nods, and I go and fill another pan, and bring it to her.

"Thanks," she says, then she steals a look at me and says, "Perhaps your novice master was right."

I just look at her.

"About the platonic thing, you know?" She says with a brief, funny smile.

I suddenly have the strangest feeling of warmth and giddiness. "Who told you about that?" I ask.

"Leonard," she says quietly, and she is silent for a moment. I look at Leonard, and his closed eyes cannot hide his discomfort; I wonder how terrible his pain can be.

"You're invited too," she says then, all of a sudden.

"Where?" I ask.

"To our party," she says. "That's all it is up there, just one big party, you know? Jesus calls it a banquet..." She turns back to Leonard then, but that's okay, because I don't feel envious any more, when I try to comprehend what he is going through.

"Do you know he hero worships you?" she says as she turns to me. "You're all he talks about."

"He must not know me very well," I say, shaking my head.

"I think he does," she says with a smile.

"I'm going to leave now," I say, "see you tomorrow," and I exit the room with the strangest mixture of regret and light-headed bliss. But within moments, reality begins to seep back in as I ascend the stairs and enter the chapel to say another prayer for Leonard.

***

The next chance I get, I go to the main house library and, with the Padre's latest clues in hand, I find the first volume I am looking for. I open it, a volume of Summa Theologica, written by St. Thomas Aquinas, arguably the most brilliant Doctor of the Church. I find what I am looking for, (3, 69, 4), and put a marker in the book. I then seek out and find the second book containing Lumen Gentium 16, a recently-published volume from Vatican II. This will take some time to read, so I take it and the volume of Summa Theologica, check them out, and head back to my room.

That evening and the following day, whenever I have time, I peruse Lumen Gentium 16 until I find exactly what I think the Padre was talking about. Then I go and find Alex, tell him about the two clues, and give him the volumes to corroborate my findings.

Alex opens the old volume of Aquinas and reads: "'*As stated above (1, ad 2; 68, 2) man receives the forgiveness of sins before Baptism in so far as he has Baptism of desire, explicitly or implicitly...*'"

"Wow," says Alex, "here it is, in Aquinas' Summa Theologica. Implicit Baptism of Desire. When was this written?"

"About seven hundred years ago," I say quietly.

A moment of silence follows.

"What does Lumen Gentium 16 say?" asks Alex then, and he opens it to my marker and reads:

"'*Nor is God remote from those who in shadows and images seek the unknown God, since he gives to all men life and breath and all things (cf. Acts 17:25-28), and since the Savior wills all men to be saved (cf. 1 Tim. 2:4). Those who, through no fault of their own, do not know the Gospel of Christ or his Church, but who nevertheless seek God with a sincere heart, and, moved by grace, try in their actions to do his will as they know it through the dictates of their conscience — those too may achieve eternal salvation.*'"

"Okay," says Alex then, "but... I mean, if that's true, you're saying that all the unbaptized — Jews, Buddhists, Muslims, Hindus, and even agnostics — can be saved if they just *ask*?"

"Ask and you shall receive. Whoever asks for salvation with sincerity, yes."

"Crock," says Alex, "this is a lot to swallow all at once."

"Yeah," I say, "but I like the taste of it, you know?"

"To understand
everything is to
forgive everything."

Gautama Buddha

CHAPTER FORTY-ONE

Leonard's Final Weeks

A few days later, I manage to visit the Padre again by getting someone to relinquish his spot on the readers' waiting list. I begin to read aloud to him and, when I know there won't be anyone listening, I interrupt my reading.

"Padre, I think I found the answers to your clues."

He looks at me with a hopeful stare.

"In the broadest sense," I say, "Ecclesiam is... all the baptized." He continues to watch me, once again refusing to agree or disagree. "But," I continue, "who does that include? Since Baptism of desire can be not only explicit, but also implicit, according to Aquinas, Baptism of desire can include the desire to be saved. Therefore, Ecclesiam is... all those who wish to be saved."

He continues to look at me, and he just smiles.

"With God, all things are possible," he says quietly.

"Thank you, Padre. You've made my life happier."

"Likewise," he says with that sincere smile. "I must emphasize," he continues, "that traditional baptism by water is *very important* and must be employed whenever possible. It is only when it is *not* possible, due to physical resources or other circumstances, that one can and should, with fervent prayer, rely on God's infinite mercy."

"I'll remember that," I say quietly, as I let this sink in.

"Padre," I ask him then, "I'm having trouble forgiving someone. One of my superiors, to be more specific. I'm praying about it, but I don't know if I am making progress."

He thinks for a moment before answering. "Superiors? Ah, we all have a run-ins with them." He hesitates for a moment, then continues. "Years ago, during the war, I had a problem with Pacelli."

"You're talking about... Eugenio Pacelli? *Pope* Pius the Twelfth?"

"Yes, '*il Papa.*' We were a having a discussion about some theological matter, and a he could a see I was a very upset. Don't you know, I wanted to a take him and a *shake* him, I was so upset. Not a good thought to have about a the Holy Father, you know? And a he could see it, he could a see I was upset, so he asked me, 'Ricardo, you are not happy. What is a wrong?' And I tell a him, 'Your Holiness, I cannot understand why you are a silent about the Nazis, when they are a killing so many innocent Jews in a their camps!'"

"And a he says a to me, 'Ricardo, we are a doing all a we can, but it has to be under the table, you know?' I ask a him, 'Why?' 'Because,' he says then, 'when a we speak out, they take it out on a the prisoners in a the camps!' 'How do you know this?' 'Because some men have escaped, and a told us so! They come to me and a say, "Keep a you mouth shut! Every time you say anything, those devils take us outside and a torture and shoot some of us, and a starve some more of us!" So we have a to do it quietly, you see.'

"And then I meet some of those escapees, and a they say that Pacelli is right, so I have a to forgive him."

He hesitates for a long moment. Then he says in a low voice, "And there are some people who are a much harder to forgive than a superiors. I have told Our Lord many times that, try as I might, I cannot forgive the Nazis for taking my mother's life, you see."

"The Nazis... your mother?" I feel the knot in my stomach again. "Padre, I had no idea... I am sorry!"

"That's all a right, you did a not know." He puts his old wornhand on my arm.

"Sometimes I think I make progress," he continues, "but then the darkness returns. I keep praying, but it is not easy. Still, I must work at it, because as I have said, we must a lighten our load as much as a we can in this world of gravity in order to rise up to Heaven.

"Understand," he says, with a piercing depth in his eyes, "forgiveness does a not excuse the Nazi, does not get him off the hook. It gets a you and *me* off a the hook! The Nazi still must answer to God."

I nod in agreement, and then he changes the subject.

"There is a news from Garabandal," he says.

"What news?" I ask.

"Our Lady says many priests and bishops will be lost, unless we all pray more."

"Priests and bishops? Lost?" I ask. "How?"

"I cannot say for sure," continues the Padre, "but never underestimate the power of The Enemy. Judas Iscariot spent years with our Lord, listening to His every word. He saw Him raise people from the dead, witnessed him multiply loaves and fishes, calm the winds and the seas, and even walk on water! And yet The Enemy was still able to persuade him to betray the Master, for thirty pieces of silver."

***

I visit Leonard again, and he is not doing well; the cancer is slowly but surely sucking the life out of him. He is sleeping, and so I cannot talk to him. Catherine is there again, spelling Sister Bernadette as she does every two hours or so.

I have a question I have wanted to ask Catherine, and I figure this is as good a time as any. "Catherine, do you ever wish that women could be priests?"

"Well, I've certainly thought about it," she says with an air of quiet humility. "I once said to Sister Margaret that the Church appeared to be very male-centric, and she said, 'Oh no, Catherine, you've got it all wrong. Men get to be priests, bishops, and a few might even become popes. But women? We get to be *nuns!*' And then she just looked at me for a long moment with her funny little smile. I'm sure I appeared confused, because then she said, 'If what I just said is puzzling to you, meditate on it. Sometimes it takes a girl some time to figure that one out.'"

"That sounds like a riddle to me," I say then. "I'm going to have to spend some time thinking about it, myself."

I pause for a moment. "But just for the record," I say then, "I don't know if I want to be a priest, myself. I just want to do God's work, and if priesthood is part of that, if it's His Will, so be it."

"And how do you know if it's His Will?"

"I don't. Not yet, anyway."

I leave and head once more to the chapel.

***

After I leave the chapel, I head down the corridor and enter the rec room about five minutes before the bell for points. Lou Ranier and Alex Dubchek are having a discussion, and I grab a chair and join them.

"I still can't believe... Aquinas? Implicit baptism of desire?" says Lou.

"No?" says Dubchek. "Didn't you learn that in the minor seminary?"

Lou says, "Well, ah, we didn't learn everything there... just like here, most of our theology courses were saved for the last three or four years before ordination..."

Alex brings forth the large old volume of Aquinas that he has been holding in his lap. "Try Summa Theologica 3,69,4," he says, handing Lou the book.

Lou looks at him for a moment, then opens the book and finds the passage, and begins to read it out loud. Then he turns and looks at me for a moment, ignoring Alex.

But Alex is not finished; he hands the other book to Lou and says, "This is from Vatican II. Open it to the bookmark, and read."

Lou opens it and reads.

At that moment, just for a second, Alex sticks his tongue out at Lou like a five-year-old, but immediately resumes a normal expression just before Lou turns to look back at him.

"I am going to have to..." says Lou as the bell for points interrupts him. "Can I keep these for awhile?" he whispers to Alex.

"Just return them to the library when you're done," says Alex, winking at me.

***

On another evening, I visit Leonard, and Catherine, again, and Leonard seems somewhat better. He is awake and unusually talkative as Catherine checks his vital signs.

"Catherine," says Leonard in a slightly halting fashion, "Tell Wally about the hands of Jesus!"

"You tell him," she says, appearing slightly embarrassed.

"Okay," says Leonard, "when I was ten, and my grandmother first started taking me to church, I had this nun, Sister Anne, for a religion teacher. On my first day, while we were sitting at our desks, she had us all cover our eyes and she said, 'Now, when you take your hands away from your eyes, you're going to see the hands of Jesus!' So then she gave us the signal, and we all pulled our hands away from our eyes, and she said,

'Now, can everyone see the hands of Jesus?' And everyone was kind of puzzled, but I just looked at my own hands, right in front of my face, and I just kind of murmured to myself, 'I can see *my* hands.' And Sister Anne heard me and said, 'Leonard, you are absolutely right; your hands *are* the hands of Jesus!' I was amazed. I really didn't answer the question properly, but Sister Anne made it seem like I got it right, even though I had never been to a religion class before."

"Sounds like an interesting story," I say to Leonard, wondering why he never told it to any of us before.

"But I'm not finished," says Leonard, "Just today I was sleeping, and Catherine was washing my face, and I began to wake up and saw just her hands, right in front of my eyes, and I somehow thought they were the hands of Jesus, and I said, 'Thank you, Jesus!' And then I woke up a little more, and I saw that they were her hands, and... well, I laughed, because it was funny, sort of."

I am watching Catherine, and by the look on her face I can see she has been touched by this little incident.

And now I have this feeling, or insight, or enlightenment that I had a number of times before when I was at St. Joseph's home, a realization that these sisters may, in some way, be called to a greater kind of holiness than we men are. And I cannot explain how or why. I just get this idea now and then, when I am around the sisters.

Now Leonard is starting to appear troubled, and I assume he is getting another headache. He closes his eyes, and I can tell he is in pain.

"Leonard, do you need anything?" asks Catherine. He does not respond, and she turns to me and says, "Could you get Brother Ritchie on the intercom? I think he needs some morphine."

I try the intercom, but when no one answers, I jump up and leave the room, and I find Brother Ritchie down the hall, and I bring him back to Leonard's room, and then I have to leave.

***

Leonard is in his last days now, and none of us can do anything other than try to keep him comfortable with painkillers and pray for him. His cancer has progressed more rapidly than any of us had expected, and we are all trying to cope with it. We all try to find positive reasons as to why God is letting this happen to Leonard, of all people, and why it is happening so quickly.

On a sunny, mild Friday morning in early October, Leonard stops breathing. Sister Bernadette checks his pulse, and he has none. Brother Ritchie also checks, and confirms that there is no pulse.

Everyone knew this was going to happen, everybody was prepared for it, so nobody is very shocked or upset. I myself am very resolute and somber, knowing that this is, after all, God's Will.

Even though he has received Extreme Unction, or the Last Rites, in the past few days, the spiritual father for the Juniors, Fr. Sheridan, comes in and administers the Sacrament one last time.

After he is finished, Fr. Minister calls the undertaker to come and take Leonard's body to prepare for his funeral. The funeral will be here in our chapel, of course, and the burial will take place in the cemetery on the hill, beneath the Jesus statue. Almost right next to Darryl.

CHAPTER FORTY-TWO

An Incredible Journey

I volunteer to assist Brother Ritchie and the sisters in putting Leonard in a body bag, as soon as the undertaker arrives. Lou Ranier is here as well, and Alex is on the way. It will not be an easy thing to do, but somebody has to do it. And he wasn't just my friend, he was everybody's friend. As soon as the undertaker comes, we will zip him up.

I am standing in the hall outside Leonard's room with Brother Ritchie, and now Andy is approaching with Leonard's grandmother. Brother Ritchie says, "The undertaker should be arriving shortly..." when there is a sudden commotion from Leonard's room.

"Oh!" comes a shout, followed by a gasp. We all rush into the room to see the sisters staring at Leonard, who is sitting up in bed, very much alive!

"Oh, no," says Leonard, "oh, no..."

"Leonard," I yell, "you're *alive!*"

"No... no..." he repeats, shaking his head. Brother Ritchie, Andy, Leonard's grandmother and the sisters are agog, but Leonard is morose.

"Leonard," I say to him, "we thought you were dead!"

"I can't... this can't be happening," Leonard says, shaking his head.

"What can't be happening?" I ask. "You're *alive*! For crock's sake, you should be happy!"

"It's incredible... it's so incredible... I just... what's going on? Why am I here?"

"What's incredible?" I ask.

He looks down, rubbing his eyes. "The greatest... the greatest... " he repeats, and he leans back on his pillow with his eyes closed and continues, "... one, Corinthians, two... nine..."

I see a Bible on the desk bookshelf and frantically page through it, just as Alex Dubchek escorts the undertaker through the door into Leonard's room. Alex's jaw drops, but the undertaker, who has never met Leonard, is merely confused.

"He's not dead," says Brother Ritchie.

"I... guess not," says the undertaker.

Just then I find the passage and read aloud: "'However, as it is written: eye has not seen, ear has not heard, and no mind has imagined what God has prepared for those who love Him...'" I close the book and stare at Leonard. "What... what happened just now?"

He sits in silence for a moment. "Indescribable beauty," he begins, and his voice starts to quiver and his eyes begin to tear up. "Beautiful gardens...flowers like you've never seen...trees... colors... endless colors that no eye has ever seen, beyond description... mansions. Music, a thousand different melodies all at once, somehow blended together in perfect harmony... voices singing, choirs...more beautiful than you can imagine. Radiant beauty, and a feeling beyond description, a feeling of completeness, of belonging, of incredible happiness... beyond words. Completely beyond explanation..." He is still looking down, slowly shaking his head back and forth. He seems to be sobbing a little.

"Did... did you see any people?" asks Catherine as she daubs his eyes with a moist cloth.

"Yes," he says as he looks at Catherine, "I saw lots of people. I saw my mother, and my little brother," he says as he turns to his grandmother, "And they are beautiful, and happy, and I want so much to be with them..." he lowers his eyes again and covers them with his hand.

I have never seen Leonard this emotional. Then suddenly he raises his eyes to Catherine again.

"I saw your grandmother. She says hello. She is beautiful!" Catherine's eyes become moist, and she reaches for some tissue. "And Sister Bernadette, your mother says hello, too!" Sister Bernadette appears incredulous. "Wally," he says as he turns toward me, "Darryl has a message for you."

Suddenly, my heart jumps. "What? You saw Darryl?"

"Yes! He says... this may sound odd, but he says, 'Surf's up!'"

I have a sudden flashback to my beach dream, and suddenly I comprehend that the surfer, standing with his board, is Darryl, clear as a bell!

"Alex," Leonard continues, "your grandfather is there!"

"My *Lutheran* grandfather?" says Alex, and he begins to cackle with laughter. "Wait'll I tell Lou! Wait, Lou, you're *here*!"

Lou Ranier is standing near the doorway, with a blank look on his face.

"Brother Ritchie," continues Leonard, "Your mom and dad are both up there, waiting for you! They send their love."

Now Brother Ritchie gets quiet and reflective, and the undertaker turns to leave. "I guess you won't be needing me right now," he says to Brother Ritchie as he walks out the door.

Leonard looks at the departing undertaker and says, "Your little sister says hello!"

The undertaker stops for a moment, then turns around and sticks his head back into the room and says, "How did... thank you."

Leonard seems to be in a better mood since he started communicating all these messages. "Where's the Padre?" he asks, "I have to see the Padre."

"I'll go get him," says Brother Ritchie.

"Leonard," asks Alex then, "I have a question. What about... purgatory?"

"I didn't see it," says Leonard.

Alex nods somberly. "Maybe because you had it here already..."

Now Brother Ritchie is wheeling in the Padre. This could be interesting, because most of these folks do not know that the Padre can talk.

"Padre," says Leonard, "Your Mama says she misses her Ragozzino!"

The Padre's eyes get wide. "You... you saw my Mother?"

"Yes! She is beautiful, and she is happy!"

"You say she is a happy?"

"She is full of joy," says Leonard, "she is waiting for you!"

The Padre becomes visibly elated, and he takes out a handkerchief and wipes his eyes. "Deo gratias, Deo gratias..." he repeats to himself.

I notice that Brother Ritchie is no longer in the room. I stick my head out the door and see him on the phone down the hall. I turn back to the room, and Brother Ritchie quickly returns and approaches Leonard's bedside. "Leonard," he says, "how are you feeling? Do you need some rest?"

"I feel... okay, Brother Ritchie. I mean, physically, I have no pain right now. But psychologically..."

"Psychologically?" repeats Brother Ritchie.

"Psychologically I am trying to be upbeat, but it is hard because... I want to go back."

"Back to..."

"Heaven. I cannot explain how difficult it is, after you've been there, to come back here. They told me I had to come back here, and I pleaded with them..."

"Who is 'they?'" asks Brother Ritchie.

"Just... my guides. People who were guiding me up there."

"Leonard," I say to him, "Did you see... did you see The Lord?"

He looks at me. "The Lord? Yes, oh yes, I saw Him."

"Well? What was He like? Did He say anything?"

"Yes, He... first of all, I can't describe how totally different it is there, how perfect it is. I can only use words, and words cannot begin to describe Heaven. It was like, when I first got there, I was standing in this bright place, and there were all these other people around me, and there were so many others who were not people, really... they were beautiful, elegant beings of all kinds. And I just knew that some of them were angels. And then there was this great, powerful singing, and in the distance, we could all see moving toward us thousands... tens of thousands... millions of beings, other than men, Angels I guess, and maybe other kinds of beings, more than I could ever count, and then... I saw Him. He was actually leading them all, and He was mounted..."

"Mounted?" asks Alex.

"...On a horse. An incredible, magnificent horse. And riding toward me, with all of them following. And then I became aware of that term, 'Son of Man,' because He was, even though He was Lord of all those magnificent beings, and of the whole court of Heaven, He was still one of us, He was a

Son of Man. And I felt so overwhelmed at this vision that I could only kneel down on the ground, or whatever seemed to be the ground, because I don't know if you could call it 'ground' up there, even though it was sort of solid, I guess... and I lowered my face to my knees, and I just heard this great legion coming closer to me, and they were singing hymns of praise, incredible, glorious singing, and there were millions of people all around on either side and behind me and above, as if they were in a stadium that was miles in circumference with uncountable numbers in the stands, all praising and singing and worshipping... I felt like the only thing I could do was bow down and kiss the ground. And I could hear sounds, like the horse's movements and breathing as he came closer, along with all the incredible music and singing, and all of a sudden I heard a snort, and I felt something, and it was the horse, nuzzling me. And I heard the Lord say, 'Leonard. Look at Me.' So I looked up, and there He was, the Lord, astride His majestic steed, and He was reaching out His hand to me, and even though I don't like to look people in the eye — you all know that — I looked at His eyes and they were so beautiful, I could not stop looking at them, they were mesmerizing... and I just reached my hand up to His, and the wound in His hand was glowing and sending out beams of beautiful light, and just as I touched it, touched His hand, I was all of a sudden up and sitting behind Him, on His horse, as if... as if..." he is having trouble controlling his emotions.

"As if what?" I ask.

"...as if there was no gravity," he continues with difficulty. "And then, I am riding there with Him, astride His horse, and the thousands, the millions of smiling, beautiful people, the legions of angels are behind us, and before us, beyond number, beyond number... and I am sitting there with the Lord, feeling so incredible that I will never be able to explain it, and then He turns to me, He turns around and says, 'Leonard, would you like to take a ride?'

"'Yes, Lord,' I say to him. So He says, 'Put your arms around my waist.' So I wrap my arms around His waist and He leans forward and says into the horse's ear, 'Christopher...'

"Christopher?' says Dubchek with a laugh, "of course! Christopher!"

"...so He says, 'Christopher... Godspeed!' And the horse takes off like a rocket, I am not kidding, and all of a sudden there are planets and galaxies going past us like fireworks..." he pauses and sobs... "...and it is so beautiful it is almost overwhelming... we pass close by to some other worlds, so close that we can see trees and animals and maybe people, I'm not sure, but everything, everyone is bowing to us and hailing us... I am not even sure these are all physical beings, it's so crazy, and everything is happening and going by so fast... so then all of a sudden we are back in Heaven, or wherever we took off from, and all the people are there, smiling at us as if we never left, and Jesus turns around and He looks me in the eye, and He says... He says..." now he is sobbing, and having trouble speaking.

"Leonard," I say, "relax. You just need to relax."

"Okay," he says, and Catherine rinses his face again, and he sniffles. "So He looks at me and he says, with a sort of serious look, 'So Leonard,' and I say, 'Yes, Lord?' and He says, 'So Leonard, are you bored yet?' And I know that my mouth dropped open... I can't explain it, you just don't know what it's like, my mouth dropped open and I began to laugh... you know how I can laugh, but for some reason it was a good laugh, it was a perfect laugh, an appropriate laugh, and the Lord started to laugh, and all the multitudes and the angels, everyone began to laugh, and it was the best laughter I ever heard, the funniest thing I ever heard in all creation, and nobody is laughing *at* me, like they did when I was a kid, they are all laughing *with* me, including the Lord, because it is the most un-boring, incredibly perfect place anyone can comprehend..." He lowers his head and puts his hands over his eyes. "...There is not even any point in trying to describe it. I just want to go back... I want all of you to be there with me, I want the world to be saved, I... I am incapable of communicating anything more than this, right now." He lowers his head again, sobbing.

We all sit in awe for a moment. Then the Padre speaks.

"These messages," says the Padre, "are a such an incredible inspiration for all of us..."

And then, very suddenly, the Sarge enters the room.

"Messages?" repeats the Sarge to the Padre. "So, you can talk after all?"

The Padre turns to stare at the far wall and says, "I have a nothing to say to *you*."

The Sarge simply says, "Likewise," then he turns to Leonard and says, "So, the reports of your death were incorrect, I see?"

"Father," Alex says then, "Leonard *did* die, and he went to Heaven. He saw my grandfather, and the Padre's mother..."

"The Padre's Jewish mother? In Heaven? He has a brain tumor, he's deluded," says the Sarge with amazing quickness. Then he turns to Brother Ritchie. "Don't call me down here again until you have something important to tell me."

I notice that Leonard has been watching the Sarge intently the whole time. Then he says, "Fr. Harrison?"

The Sarge walks toward the door, glaring at the nuns as he passes them. "I'm leaving now," he says, ignoring Leonard's question, "I have work to do."

"Fr. Harrison? This is important," says Leonard, but the Sarge continues to ignore him as he passes through the door.

"Sarge!" yells Leonard all of a sudden.

The Sarge stops dead, turns halfway around, and says, "Don't...you...ever...use that..."

"Sarge," says Leonard, "*Look at me!*"

The Sarge is seething, and he turns toward Leonard.

"*Corporal Zimmerman...*" says Leonard then, as he stares at the Sarge with a commanding air that I never saw before.

The Sarge's expression changes completely. Like he hit a brickwall, or something. He almost stops breathing, and, with the strangest look on his face says "What? What did you say?"

"Corporal Zimmerman has a message for you."

The Sarge is dumbfounded. "Who... how did you... who told you..."

he says as he stares at Leonard in utter astonishment.

"*He* did," says Leonard, "I met him."

"You... you met... " He pauses. Then, "That's impossible..."

"Red hair," says Leonard, "Blue eyes. Nice looking fellow. About my age, maybe a little older." Leonard stares right at the Sarge and continues, "He says, 'Regards to the Sarge.'"

Now, for the first time since I met him, the Sarge's eyes are getting moist, and his voice shakes. "He said... he said that?"

"Yes," says Leonard.

"I cannot believe..." says the Sarge, "...It's impossible..."

"And he said something else," says Leonard. "He said, 'Everything's fine. You didn't need the water after all.'"

Now the Sarge, this stalwart man of iron whose demeanor always suggested that he never shed a tear in his life, almost stumbles over to Leonard's bed and grabs the back of it for support.

Alex quickly gives him his chair, and he sinks into it, and he buries his head in his hands, and sobs quietly.

Catherine, who is sitting close by, says "Here," and hands him a clean towel, which he accepts. "It's okay, it's okay..." she says over and over, as she pats him on the back. Then, still sobbing, he slowly reaches for her hand and wraps his fingers around it, and he holds it for a long time.

"And if you hold any-
thing against anyone,
forgive them, so that
your father in heaven
may forgive you
your sins."

Matthew 11:25

CHAPTER FORTY-THREE

Mea Culpa

I t is dinner time, and we have just finished first grace. Right after we have all taken our seats, I become aware of a silence in the room. Like ninety-eight percent of our meals, it is not Deo Gratias, it is a silent meal to begin with, so no one would be talking anyway. And even though the lector hasn't started reading yet, all the clanking dishes and silverware seem to go silent.

I look up to see the Sarge walking down the middle aisle, from the Fathers' table, straight toward me. He seems to be walking more slowly than usual, almost in a dreamlike fashion. Or maybe it's just my perception, since my pulse is racing and I am barely managing to think about what this could possibly mean. He is walking toward me, looking at me. What is he up to? What is going on?

He continues to walk until he is right up next to my table, then turns to face the community and kneels down on the floor, just feet from me.

"Reverend Fathers and beloved brethren," he begins, slowly, clearly, loudly, like a trained orator. I gaze around the refectory at a hundred open mouths as he continues, "I accuse myself... of a profound lack of compassion and sensitivity in carrying out my priestly duties as acting

409

superior of this house, and this province..." I am having trouble hearing him, or at least understanding him, because this is something that has never happened before, and may never happen again. I try to listen, "...for which fault Holy Obedience has imposed upon me the slight penance of kissing the feet of some of the members of the community."

I cannot explain the surreal aura that envelops me as I feel the slight pressure of this man's lips against my shoes as he kisses my feet. I know that my eyes are tearing up as he stands, and I catch a glimpse of eye contact with him before he bends over me and whispers, "I apologize."

***

The next morning I visit Leonard again, and return to him *"The Laws of Gravity"* diary that he gave me. He told me yesterday that he wanted to add some things to it, and now I watch him as he opens it to a blank page and writes at the top: "The Future."

I do not stay long, since I have some work to do, and I let him continue alone.

***

The following morning Alex and I visit Leonard again, and he is not good. He has had a relapse. Catherine is there, vigilant as always.

"Wally," says Leonard weakly, "I'm done with this now." He hands me *"The Laws of Gravity."* "It's yours to keep now; do with it as you wish."

I take the book and sit down by his bedside.

As he drifts in and out of consciousness, he manages to say, "Tell

Brother Larry that Fr. McKittrick wants to see him."

"Okay, Leonard," I say to him, "but Fr. McKittrick is in Rome right now."

"He'll be back tomorrow," says Leonard.

I want to ask him how he knows that, but I just say, "Okay, I'll give him the message." I can see that he is fading fast, and I ask him, "Leonard, could you do us a favor? You seem to have an inside handle on things now, a little persuasive influence with the Head Honcho, perhaps? So, could you just say a little prayer for us? And of course, we'll reciprocate." His lips begin to form into a smile. Then his color becomes more ashen, his breathing more labored. Catherine appears concerned, and calls Brother Ritchie on the intercom, and Sister Bernadette as well.

Soon we are assembled around Leonard's bedside, waiting for the end. Catherine seems to know when the time is near. She checks his pulse, then invites Brother Ritchie to do the same.

"It's getting very weak," says Brother Ritchie, almost in a whisper.

Now the Sarge enters the room, carrying some holy oils. He looks at Sister Catherine and asks, "Could you please hold these for me?" She takes them as he begins to anoint Leonard one last time.

After a few more moments, Catherine moves closer to Leonard. "Farewell, priestling," she says, and she leans forward and kisses Leonard's forehead. "Save me a spot..."

And now Leonard's breathing ceases. He is gone, this time for good. But his smile remains.

"The lucky dog," says Alex half to himself.

Leonard told me something else in his little return to our world. He said that he was praying fervently to God to let him return to Heaven as soon as possible. He said that after a little while, he somehow knew his request would be granted. He also "knew" that he was going to take another one of the brethren with him. I wondered what that meant? One of us? Even though I know that Heaven is an incredible place, I still don't feel ready to go just yet.

Then after meditating on all this, I suddenly realized who it would be, whose passing would be the most likely, the least upsetting.

Soon afterwards, Leonard is taken away by the undertaker. That evening, we go to the Infirmary to visit the Padre, only to learn that he has had a stroke, a real one this time. And a severe one.

The following day, quite quickly, the Padre passes away, and preparations are begun for a double funeral.

The morning after the Padre's death, I go to the Infirmary to ask Brother Ritchie if he needs any assistance. Catherine is there, being very helpful as usual.

"Hello, Sister Catherine," I say when I see her, resisting the very real urge to hug her.

"Hello Brother Wally," she says with a bright smile. "How are you this morning?"

"I guess I'm okay, considering all that's happened."

"We have a little surprise for you," she says, still smiling.

Brother Ritchie appears, and says, "Wally, we have something to show you," and he and the beaming Catherine lead me down the hall. "When was the last time you were in the Padre's room?" he asks as we approach the Padre's door.

"Two days ago."

He opens the door, and there in a row beneath the long window are the Padre's eight rose bushes, all in full bloom!

"When... when did this happen?" I ask.

"I don't know," says Brother Ritchie, "but we were in here yesterday, and the plants were bare, and I was thinking at the time of throwing them out."

"Now," says Catherine, "we won't need to buy flowers for the funeral!"

***

After lunch, I am leaving the refectory when I see the Sarge standing outside the chapel. "Come on," he says, and he holds out his arm and puts it around my shoulders. "We have to talk." And then we exit the building and go for a walk along the Rosary Path, and he begins to speak.

"First off," he says, "I was not being honest when I told you that you did not influence my decision about Leonard. Your 'admonishment' in my office was, in fact, the main reason I invited him back.

"Secondly, regarding Fr. Morris' sexual impropriety, his only 'victim' was an undercover vice squad officer. He did something obscene in a public rest room, and we came to an agreement with the authorities. That's why I gave him another chance.

"And regarding the Padre, I managed to make amends with him before his stroke. I even asked him to hear my confession, and he graciously accepted."

I have the strangest feeling as I am listening to him, almost like I am his superior, or counselor or something. He is almost like a different person, now.

And then he tells me about the war.

"Corporal Zimmermann was in my company on Iwo Jima. He was my buddy. I knew he was Jewish, and he knew I was Catholic. When the battle kept escalating he said, 'You think I'll go to hell because I'm a Jew?' And I said, 'If you go to hell, I'll go in after you and get you out. Wait. Don't look now, but I think we're already there.' The combat got horrendous, and eventually we were surrounded by Japanese troops. He was hit by machine-gun fire, and I managed to get over to him. I wanted to drag him out of there, but I could pretty well see that he wasn't going to make it... his stomach was torn open and he was bleeding profusely. I cradled his head in my arms..."

He hesitates for a moment, and I can see that this is not easy for him to talk about. "It was terrible. Bullets were flying everywhere, grenades going off within yards of us. Nasty. I wanted to baptize him. My canteen was empty, so I called out for some water, and someone threw me a canteen. I was going to try to unscrew the cap with my teeth. The bullets were whistling past so close that I could feel them parting the air near my face.

Then, before I could get the top off the canteen, before I could even begin, the canteen was blown from my hand," he lifts his scarred right hand and holds it out, "and Corporal Zimmerman... Corporal Zimmerman..." he pauses and looks at the hills, "Corporal Zimmerman's head was blown apart..."

I see real pain in his eyes.

"I never told anyone here about any of this. I did visit his parents, and I told them a version that was more acceptable, cleaned-up, as it were.

"Then I went through some mental difficulties... shell shock. Post traumatic stress disorder. I had episodes for years. Sometimes bad dreams, sometimes panic attacks. I saw shrinks, I went through a process of rehabilitation. Then it started to go away."

"When did you enter the order?"

"I entered after the worst of it was over. About three years after the end of the war... nineteen-forty-eight."

We are approaching the sewage treatment pond.

"But later on," says the Sarge, "it all started to come back again. Eventually I resigned myself to the fact that this may be a life-long battle." He stops for a moment, as we gaze over the pond.

"When Leonard said what he said..." his voice is thick with emotion as he pauses again, shaking his head.

"My faith," he continues, "has been far from perfect. Part of the reason I'm here is because I didn't know where else I could fit in. The war took something out of me, like it did to so many others.

"Whenever he saw me..." he says, "whenever Zimm saw me... we called him Zimm... he would say, 'Regards, Sarge.' And I keep wondering how could Leonard have known...? I never told anyone. No one could have told Leonard. To think that Zimm is actually somewhere, in a better place, somehow whole and complete, and happy... is almost too good to be true..." He looks away, and I don't want to embarrass him, so I pretend not to notice his uneven breathing.

Then we continue to walk along past the duck pond, discussing things, rationally and intelligently, like two adult men.

***

The morning of the funeral, the undertaker brings in the two caskets for the visitation in the Porter's Lodge. Alex and I are there to assist in setting things up; we are also going to be pallbearers. The undertaker, named Ned, appears a little concerned when he first enters, and he walks up to the Sarge and says, "Father, we have a little problem. I think we're going to have to leave the caskets closed for the visitation."

"How so?" asks the Sarge.

"Well, I tried everything I could," he says as he begins to unlatch the casket. "You know, we have special ways to change the shape of the mouth, to make it look right, but... well, for some reason our techniques failed this time."

"And so?" says the Sarge.

416

"Take a look," says Ned as he opens the top of the casket to reveal Leonard, serene in death, but with a broad smile on his lips.

The Sarge looks at him for just a moment, then turns to the Undertaker. "What about the Padre?"

"Same problem," says Ned as he lifts the door of the other casket, and sure enough, the Padre's smile is as big as Leonard's.

The Sarge gives Ned an authoritative stare and says, "I don't see a problem. Leave them open."

"Yes, Father, thank you, Father," says Ned.

* * *

So Leonard and the Padre had a great funeral, and there were a lot of guests, including Leonard's grandmother, Andy and Christina and their daughter, and the Rabbi from the synagogue Andy and I visited, along with some Protestant Ministers, Including the Reverend Huston from the TV show, and some priests and Indians from South Dakota, including Lone Eagle, and the Holy Man. And Fr. McKittrick, back from Rome just as Leonard had said. And Sister Margaret and Sister Bernadette and Catherine, along with some other nuns. And the nuns, especially Catherine, sang like angels, and it just reinforced what Sister Margaret had once told Catherine, that men are somehow allowed to become priests, bishops, cardinals and popes, while women get to be nuns.

And after I meditated on that for awhile, I realized that none of those churchy honors or titles get us men to Heaven; we still have to conquer our ornery, childish male egos, along with all of our other flaws. And

God puts good women, especially nuns, here to teach us men how to be good and honorable and holy. Our Lady, after all, was put here to bear, and raise, and teach God's Only Begotten Son.

CHAPTER FORTY-FOUR

The Challenge

I am walking out into the fields, and I am headed toward the old windmill tower. But I am wearing my cassock this time, and it is not made for walking through the tall grass. I know that in bygone times, the missionaries wore their cassocks all day long, everywhere they went throughout the foreign lands they traversed, riding horses or donkeys or sailing ships or paddling canoes, preaching the word of God. I have also heard that up until fifteen years ago or so, novices and juniors even had to wear them when they played active rec games, like baseball, tennis, or whatever. But I am wearing my cassock right now for one reason and one reason only, and that is because Andy once said that it had to be part of the ultimate challenge of windmill tower climbing.

I approach the old rusty tower now, and grab the first rung. The cassock may indeed make it more of a challenge, because the wind is gusting and billowy, and if it blows in the wrong direction, it can wrap the cassock around your feet and practically hog-tie you as you try to place your feet properly during your climb. On the plus side, though, our cassocks do not have buttons all the way down, like some designs. Ours are open from the collar down, like a bathrobe, with just a small clasp over the collar bone and a cincture around the middle, and so if there is a headwind, it simply blows the whole robe behind you, from the waist down, out of your way. You only have to deal with the flapping fabric in the air behind you, and your legs and feet are relatively free. I begin to climb, and now, due to the favorable wind direction, I manage to get the cassock billowing behind me, and it makes for an easier climb. Soon I am approaching the top, and I reach up to feel the unsteady wooden platform. It is indeed rickety, but on the plus side, I can see the entire House sprawling out below, and the lake and surrounding hills beyond, the whole countryside!

I climb the last steps until I am astride the shaky platform, as Andy was before me, just two years ago, but a long time ago in terms of life experience, and now I begin to seesaw on the platform with my feet, all the while holding onto the top of the tower, which is only about four feet or so higher than the platform. I am in a sort of squatting position, knees bent and leaning forward at the waist, like someone in the process of getting up on waterskis. It is definitely scary, because I keep thinking the platform could break, and even if it doesn't, I could slip and fall, and this thing is approximately forty feet high, but it seems more like a hundred feet when you look down...

I steady my feet on the platform now, and slowly begin to rise up, straightening my legs a little more. Then I reach into my cassock pocket and take out a little vial. The vial contains the ashes from the envelope I set fire to a few minutes ago, before I came out here. The envelope contained the letter to Fr. McKittrick, the one where I asked to be released from my vows and leave the Order. I uncork the small vial with my teeth as I hang onto the tower with my free hand, and I release the ashes into the wind. Now I put the vial back into my pocket and then slowly, very carefully loosen my grip and let go of the top of the tower and spread my arms out, and yes, this posture does help me to balance a bit. I briefly wonder if anyone in the house is looking out a window, because they would definitely see me if they glanced in this direction. The wind continues to gust, my cassock flaps in the wind behind me, and I have to adjust for its drag as I balance, and that of course is part of what Andy was thinking when he concocted this crazy idea.

Just one thing more now, I remember as I get the balancing down, and the seesawing with my feet; I have to look straight up. And I manage to do it, if only for a second or two. I manage to look straight up into the blue sky and the passing, changing, dizzying, billowy clouds, defying, as much as I can, the forces, and the fears, and the very laws of gravity.

And my brief thought is, you can never hope to overcome gravity until you acknowledge its power.

Oh yeah, and of course you can never do it alone. Deo Gratias.

If I find in myself a
Desire which no
Experience in this
World can satisfy,
The most probable
Explanation is that
I was made for
Another World.

C.S. Lewis

EPILOGUE

Brother Larry walks through the doors to the front offices. He knows his way around the house so well and can walk around the place with such facility, thanks in part to his keen sense of hearing, that he can appear, to the uninformed, not to be blind.

He moves down the hallway to the office reserved for the Provincial whenever he visits, and knocks on the already opened door.

"Larry, it's so good to see you, come in and have a seat!" Fr. McKittrick booms from his place behind the desk. Larry enters and closes the door behind him, and Fr. McKittrick quickly gets up and takes Larry's arm to guide him toward a chair. Larry sits down and faces the desk, and Fr. McKittrick sits down behind it.

"I have some news from Rome," says Fr. McKittrick then.

Larry appears concerned. "News? What kind of news?"

"I'll be short and to the point," says Fr. McKittrick, "Our Holy Father says that you may begin studying for the priesthood."

Brother Larry sits still, doesn't move at all for a moment. Then he finally speaks. "Now," he says quietly, "I think I know what it feels like."

"What?" asks Fr. McKittrick.

"What it feels like to see a rainbow," says Brother Larry.

"Feed the hungry and
visit a sick person,
and free the captive,
if he be unjustly confined.
Assist any person
oppressed whether
Muslim or non-Muslim."

The Prophet Muhammad

Selections from Leonard's Diary,

Entitled: The Laws of Gravity

In The Padre's Words:

▸Love is a decision.

▸ One of Man's greatest tasks in life: Figuring out the difference between what he wants and what he needs. If we were not fallen, our wants and needs would coincide.

▸Another great task: Discern the difference between love and desire.

▸Belief is not just a feeling. It, like Love, can be a decision, an act of the will.

Concerning bad priests:

▸There was a Judas among the first twelve. Why should things be any different now?

Concerning the souls in hell:

▸They burn forever. And they are unbending. And they

would not change anything.

▶Not even for eternal joy? And happiness?

▶No. Because of their choices, even what little they had, whatever joy and love they had, has been taken away. Whatever virtues they had are taken away. The *memory* of joy has been taken away. *All they know is loss. Not love, not God. Only empty, eternal loss. Forever. Love and Joy have no attractiveness to them. They are so warped and twisted that love and joy are as revolting to them as raw sewage is to you and me. It has been said that if the condemned man asked for salvation, he would receive it. But he will never ask... he is incapable of repentance.*

The Center of Gravity:

▶   When we went canoeing, Harshley told us that standing up in a canoe is very risky, and so you have to kneel, or at least sit, to get your center of gravity as close to the bottom of the canoe as possible, to make the canoe more stable. When he said *center of gravity*, Dubchek asked, "Where is my center of gravity?"

"Right around your pelvic area," Harsh replied.

"My center of gravity," said Alex, looking down. "Of course."

▶Jesus-substitutes in our secular mythology: Superman, Peter Pan, Captain Marvel, etc.

***

▶ "Padre, if there was only one thing you could tell people about how to live, what would it be?"

"Love one another."

"What if you could tell them two things, what would the second one be?"

"On the day before you die, repent!"

***

▶ "Pagans who practice the works of mercy may have baptism of desire."

"How do you know?"

"Because Jesus said, 'Come, you who are blessed by my Father; take your inheritance, the kingdom prepared for you since the creation of the world. For I was hungry and you gave me something to eat, I was thirsty and you gave me something to drink, I was a stranger and you invited me in, I needed clothes and you clothed me, I was sick and you looked after me, I was in prison and you came to visit me..." (Matthew 25: 31-46)

***

▶ "Who is"ecclesiam?"

"All Christians."

"You mean, all the baptized?"

"Yes. But remember, in the broadest sense, there is baptism of water, baptism of blood (martyrdom), and baptism of desire. Including the implicit kind. Christians are all those who practice the Beatitudes, and the works of mercy. And sexual morality."

"In other words, people who love one another?"

"People who *truly* love one another."

***

"One of the greatest Christians of the 20th century was Gandhi."

"I thought he was a Hindu."

"He was. But he practiced the Beatitudes, and the works of mercy, and nonviolence, better than most Christians, and so I believe he was definitely a member of 'Ecclesiam.' A Christian Hindu, if you will."

Words of Wisdom From
Various Faith Backgrounds:

"Hate the sin, love the sinner."

Mahatma Gandhi

"The unexamined life is not worth living."

Socrates

"In the attitude of silence the soul finds the path in a clearer light..."

Mahatma Gandhi

"Holding onto anger is like grasping a hot coal with the intent of throwing it at someone else; you are the one getting burned."

Gautama Buddha

"An eye for an eye makes the whole world blind."

Mahatma Gandhi

"What actions are most excellent? To gladden the heart of a human being, to feed the hungry, to help the afflicted, to lighten the sorrow of the sorrowful, and to remove the wrongs of the injured."

The Prophet Mohammed

"Man has an almost infinite capacity for change."

Fr. McKittrick

"Love your enemies. Pray for them."

Jesus Christ

More Thoughts From The Padre

There is a tug of war between the two Spirits, and you are in the middle. The closer you get to the Holy Spirit, the more the Enemy tries to pull you the other way, toward perdition!"

We are in Exile!

What is more important in a marriage? Sex, or prayer?

Sex is for procreation, not recreation.

Never underestimate the power of prayer.

Prayer can override the laws of nature!

You could journey across the universe looking for God, and never find Him. And yet, He is closer than a hair's breadth away; His Kingdom is within you.

Jesus did not come into our world to wave a magic wand and say, "Hey, I'm here now, so from now on you will have no problems; you will have Heaven on Earth!"

He came into our world to tell us that this life in exile must be lived through until death. Original Sin caused all this, but there is a light at the end of the tunnel, and we can get back to the garden. And it will be very, very worth it. Only catch is, we have to *ask* for it. Then we have to live through life's peaks and valleys, *repent* for our sins, and *die.*

"You see," the Padre says, "there are many flaws in our church, many flaws. But our most tragic flaw, in the eyes of the world, is that we are too forgiving... the Church is always willing to give the worst sinner another chance... But the world, in turn, would rather cry out for vengeance, retaliation, retribution, punishment!"

Concerning sex, drugs, alcohol, fame, fortune, and every other addiction: The greater the pleasure, the more painful the withdrawal.

Love and forgiveness come from the Holy Spirit; revenge and retaliation come from the Enemy.

Realize that the Enemy never shows up with horns or bat-wings. Rather, he shows up as a very attractive person or ideology or circumstance that appears to be a very convenient answer to your problems. The person who he might use to tempt you often does not even know that he or she is being used by the Enemy!

And also realize, a day seldom goes by without the Enemy tempting you at least once, maybe several times, in one form or another. This is why discernment is difficult. This is also why discernment is so important!

***

"Can anyone of you tell me," asked the Padre one night, "How Rome was finally converted to Christianity?"

"Didn't Constantine have a vision?" asked Andy.

"Yes. Can you describe it?"

"He saw a great cross in the sky, and the words, 'In hoc signo vinces,' 'In this sign conquer.'"

"Very good. But what do you think it meant?"

"Well, to him it meant that if he went into battle with this sign on his men's shields, he would be victorious."

"Could the sign have any other meaning?" asked the Padre then.

"Well... that's a good question," said Alex.

"Think about it. What does the cross signify to you?"

"Good conquering evil?" said Andy.

But then I said, "How about love?"

"Very good, Leonard," said the Padre. "So if you look at it as a sign of love, could it not be a symbol of love and peace, rather than violent war?"

"So," said Andy, "we don't have to conquer with violence... we can conquer with love. But does anyone ever do that? Do we Christians practice what we preach?"

"Well, in many small ways, yes. But in world politics? Not always."

"It seems that when war breaks out, people quickly forget about loving their enemies," said Andy.

***

"We are all weavers, you see. Each of us is spending our lifetime weaving the garment of his soul. It must be strong, to endure the fierce intensity of the fire of Heaven, the fire of the Holy Spirit, which is God's infinite, eternal love. As God said to Moses, 'No man shall look upon My Face and live.' If you spend your life ignoring your weaving task, neglecting your garment, you will wind up without one, and the fierce fire of the Holy Spirit becomes the tormenting fire of hell for your naked, unprepared soul. You will be like a man without skin jumping into the salty sea; the pain will be beyond description."

"How do you best weave your soul garment?" asked Alex.

"Good deeds, good deeds, good deeds," repeated the Padre. "Even the atheist may achieve eternal life, if he does enough good deeds."

"What about those who are not physically able to perform good deeds? What about those who are disabled? What can they do?"

"They can pray. Every time you say a prayer for someone, you are doing a good deed," he answered.

Who is a member of Ecclesiam? Whoever wishes to spend the rest of eternity with God, and loves his fellow man.

Excerpts from The Future

Written by Leonard shortly before his death.

The greatest false god of the future will be: The Self

Do you know someone who thinks there is no devil, no evil spirit in our modern world? Who thinks that he is not tempted by an evil one? Let me challenge you on something. I am going to describe a chain of thought to you, and I would like you to tell me if it sounds familiar. Have you ever had a thought like, "This age, this generation of mine, is finally going to change things... this generation of mine is finally going to show the world how outdated the church is, and how antiquated the older generations are... This generation, my generation, is going to finally break through and destroy all the archaic, outdated concepts of sin and guilt and repentance; this generation, my generation, is going to get rid of the outmoded ideologies of Heaven and hell and guilt and sin and all that prehistoric drivel, and start Living For Today? Have you ever had thoughts like that?

If so, understand that they are temptations. They are lies, and they come from The Enemy. We are not allowed to rewrite God's commandments to suit our own warped whims and desires. Instead, we are supposed to *reconform our distorted, fallen selves, change back* our hearts and souls to the way God meant them to be, and *overcome* our temptations in order to live moral lives within the structure of God's laws.

With every sin, the Enemy gains more power in the world, and with every prayer, he loses power. But in the near future, the sins will swell and grow and eventually outnumber the prayers many times over. With every one of these sins—and there will be billions committed every day —the world will become heavier with the baggage of iniquitous transgressions and sink deeper into the maelstrom of the Enemy's gravitational singularity, closer and closer to the "event horizon" of his Black Hole of hell, and he will gain more power over the world, every day.

Illicit sexual unions will become more commonplace than marriages. Young people will cohabit in sexual trysts for pure pleasure, with no thought given to marriage or procreation. These acts of fornication will become socially acceptable, and oftentimes the parents and families of the fornicators, not knowing how else to handle it, will not even voice their objections. "Times have changed," they will tell one another, "everybody's doing it. Maybe premarital sex isn't so sinful after all." *The global zeitgeist of shame and guilt that once helped to curb mankind's desire to sin will dry up, blow away, almost vanish.*

Abortion will become legal, and millions of young people will grow up assuming that because abortion is legal, it must be right. They will have no idea of what a terrible error this is.

The divorce rate will increase dramatically, and most cohabiting couples will never even bother to get married.

With the Enemy's increasing power, more tragedies will occur. Natural disasters such as fires, droughts, floods and earthquakes will increase. Man-made tragedies and cataclysms such as crime, increased drug abuse, hijacked airliners, terrorists blowing up buildings full of people, suicide bombings in crowded streets, and even genocide will occur. Some will even be tempted by the Enemy into shooting strangers at random, indiscriminately, as many as possible, before turning their guns on themselves. Some of these terrible acts will even be committed in the name of religion! Such is the Enemy's power at twisting the truth and persuading fools to believe it!

The ignorant atheists of the world will wonder what is going on, how could this possibly be happening, what can we do about it. They will stubbornly dig in their heels and refuse to believe in the devil of hell and his horrid power over the world that, because of its rejection of God's Laws, has handed itself over to his ways.

Eventually, the Ten Commandments will be looked upon as outdated and antiquated. None of them will be taken seriously by most of the populace. Political groups will even try to eradicate them from existence.

While these things are occurring, Our Lady will return to teach us and guide us, in the Place Between the Mountains.

She will tell us that there is a way out of this dilemma: Pray. Pray the daily rosary, if possible. Pray for at least an hour every day, no matter what your faith. Pray for the people of the world, pray for God's mercy. And fast on Fridays by eating bread and water. And on Wednesdays too, if possible. But many people will not heed her call; they will not believe, and will ignore the signs until it is too late.

If lack of faith makes prayer too difficult, do good works: feed the hungry, give drink to the thirsty, clothe the needy, visit the imprisoned. If even half the people did this, we could change the world radically, quickly. But will enough people actually seek this solution?

Finally, just as He did in the time of Noah, and later, in the time of Sodom and Gomorrah, and then in the time of Moses, and of course in the times of Jesus, God will intervene...

Isaiah says, "The Glory of the Lord shall be revealed, and all men shall see it together."

Never forget, *"With God, all things are possible..."*
Matt. 19:26; Mark 10:27; Luke 18:27.

Made in the USA
Lexington, KY
28 September 2019